The Angate (

Guardians of Re)

By

Joan Lightning

The Lord of Light created the universe and filled it with light, but where we have light, we also find shadows.

First Printing: 2017

ISBN < 9781549597510 >

Published by P.J. Lightning
Bedfordshire, United Kingdom.

Contact- rykatu@hotmail.co.uk

Cover art by PJ Lightning, includes images from stock websites – Depositphotos, Unsplash, & Pixabay.

Contents

Contents....iii
Part 1: Preparations....1
An Angry Rykatu....1
Tests....10
The King's dream....12
Rapprochement....25
Bonding Ceremony....36
A furious Rykatu....42
Understanding....47
On top of a mountain....52
Apology....58
Part 2: Zindon....67
Attack....67
A close call....78
Healing....81
Farmstead....92
Zindon....105
A promise....111
Reconnecting....116
Part 3: The Kingdom of Perrest....137
Angate....137
An Unexpected Reception....142
The model....154
Erian....173
Firstmeal....181
Soldiers....195
An unpopular command....201
A question almost asked....219
A surprise for Erian....224
Part 4: The Mountain....247
Challenge....247
After the challenge....265
A Zindon strikes....273
Aftermath....282
A pleasant morning....294
The shock at the feast....305
The wrath of a Rykatu....328
Explanations....341

A new gleaning 350
Tam's technique 357
Epilogue: Tenjian's gleaning 413
Maps 421
Acknowledgements 425
About the author 426

Part 1: Preparations

"While most Sorcerers already know with whom they wish to bond, we advise that you should interview many candidates before making your final decision. Your Ponfour will be your best friend, your advisor, your protector. Closer to you than parents, siblings, friends, or spouse.

He or she will swear an Oath of service to you and that service is to their death. You will be linked to that person for all of their lives so you must choose carefully. We will teach you how to recognise what you need in your future companion." Introduction to 'The Ponfour Bond syllabus for apprentice Sorcerers.

An Angry Rykatu

"Tarek! You are, without doubt, the most stubborn, mule-brained, pig-skulled, unmitigated, total idiot, with whom it has ever been my misfortune to be forced to share a room!

The voice bounced off the walls of the palace library. Despite his best intentions, King Tarek found himself leaning away from the powerful and irate Sorcerer who had leant over the desk and jabbed a finger at his face.

He remembered with irony the advice he had once given young Andar on the wisdom of angering Sorcerers who were considerably more powerful than he was; Tarek was stronger than Andar, but the Sorcerer glaring at him now was the most powerful in the known world!

"Now Jareth, I'm quite sure that not even you are supposed to address our king in that fashion. Remember his rank," Aren said from her chair by the window. Tarek gave her a grateful look which she returned with a cold stare.

Jareth straightened and nodded at his Ponfour/wife.

"Of course, my dear; you are right, as always."

He turned back to Tarek.

"I apologise, my King, I should have said you are the most stubborn, mule-brained, pig-skulled, unmitigated, total *royal* idiot! Is that better, Aren?"

"Well, those aren't precisely the words I would have chosen, but they will do for now," she replied, smiling at him. When she looked back at the king, her expression was once again icy.

Jareth walked away from the desk, ran his hand over his face, and then came back. When he spoke again, he was clearly trying hard to adopt a tone of pure persuasive reason.

"Tarek, my son has told me that the infestation of snow-ants…" He paused and turned to speak to Aren.

"I wish we had a better name for them, one that did not sound like something mildly unpleasant but easily dealt with."

He shook his head and returned to his point.

"This infestation of snow-ants is so large that we will require at least several hundred transmutation-able Tyreans plus…" he paused, and jabbed his finger towards Tarek again for emphasis, "*plus,* a Rykatu, to deal with it without flooding an entire inhabited district."

Tarek opened his mouth to speak, although he had no idea what he might say. In the event, he didn't have the opportunity because Jareth continued relentlessly, "At this moment, Aren and I are trying to organise the mobilisation of possibly fifteen thousand men and women. We have to work out how to get them from here," his finger stabbed towards the ground, "to an unknown destination," he waved a hand in the rough direction of the Cleansing Cave, "that could be up to three thousand miles away at worst, along with horses, weapons, tents, and food, as quickly as possible when we DO learn where they have to go. Even if we use every living translocator, including children, we cannot translocate so many along with their weapons, mounts, and baggage, so they will have to either walk or ride, and walking will be too slow, so we have to find horses for *all* of them, and they will have to camp each night, which means finding ground enough for so many, *and* for their mounts, plus *feeding and watering* them and their mounts, and providing washing facilities, and solving all the other little problems caused by the fact that food goes in and then comes out."

He paused. Tarek wondered if Jareth had become as lost in that sentence as he had, as the Sorcerer continued,

"Perhaps you think that, in the middle of the largest mobilisation in our entire history, Aren and I can just leave Tyreen, to spend a couple of weeks in Angate to deal with the problem there?"

Tarek shook his head.

"No, I don't think that," he managed to say.

Jareth slapped his hand on the desk.

"Then perhaps you have another Rykatu hidden away somewhere we could use?"

He looked around the room as though looking for a likely hiding place, then turned his scathing gaze back onto Tarek who made himself speak firmly.

"No, of course I don't, Jareth! There are only two Rykatuii, as you know well."

"Exactly!" Jareth jabbed his finger at Tarek once again. The king half expected to see sparks fly from it.

"They need Crystu in Angate, yet you continue to insist that she cannot leave Tyreen until Tam passes your tests."

"Tests, furthermore," Aren picked up his point and continued it, "which many of the Sorcerers and Ponfourii currently travelling through the Protectorates, would be unable to pass!"

"There are some who are beginning to wonder if you would still be so protective of Crystu were she not your daughter," Jareth continued as Aren paused for breath.

"And others who are wondering why you persist in insulting a Ponfour many look to as a role model," Aren inserted.

"She can go, but Tam stays here until he passes the tests."

Tarek finally managed to squeeze his sentence into a gap.

Aren stared at him.

"Go? Leave Tyreen? Without her Ponfour?"

The first word was whispered, but the last was almost a roar of indignation.

"Have a care, Tarek!" she continued. "The spells and oaths that bind Ponfour to Sorcerer are binding and far-reaching. They bind not only each individual Ponfour to her Sorcerer, but are also connected in a way that binds the Ponfourii, as a whole, to all the people of Tyreen. This symbol," she pointed at the circlet on her brow, "does not only represent the sun, or the light of the one God. The mixed metals in the centre represent the joining of two individuals to form a unity greater than the sum of its parts. They also represent the dedication of the Ponfourii to the people of Tyreen and to the Guardianship of Light. The rays emanating from the centre show that all the bonds are linked in the Light. If the king was to send *any* Sorcerer into the Protectorates alone, because he mistrusts her Ponfour's strength, the resonance of that mistrust would reverberate across those links and would damage the bonds of every Ponfour and Sorcerer alive. It could even destroy them completely, and the spells that accomplish the bonding would forever cease to function. There would be no more Ponfourii, ever!"

By the end of her speech, Aren was speaking so quietly that Tarek wondered how he could hear her. He stared at her as she finished, and then turned to Jareth who nodded confirmation of Aren's words.

Tarek was stunned; he had had no idea that his suggestion could be that dangerous. He had merely expected them to object on principle to the idea.

"Is that true?" he asked. "Why has no one ever told me of this?"

Jareth sank wearily into the chair beside his wife.

"My King, everyone who is bonded knows it without being told. It is simply a fact, like the colour of the sky, or the wetness of water. Would you think to tell someone about those things? You assume that they know, if you even think about it at all."

Tarek shook his head.

“I had no idea, but I will not change my decision. Tam passes the tests or he stays in Tyreen.”

Jareth jumped to his feet and roared, “TAREK! Have you listened to a single word we have spoken? Crystu is needed in Perrest!”

"She is nowhere near her full power yet and that mountain is huge!" Tarek argued, suddenly angry. He knew he was apparently being unreasonable, but he had his reasons and he *was* the king.

"She has not quite reached full maturity of power, but she is close now. It will not be many more months," Aren replied before Jareth could.

Tarek concealed his satisfaction at hearing her say that.

"I will not let her leave until I am sure that she is properly protected!"

"Silence!"

The queen's voice, cutting across a room in which she was not noticeably present, startled all three into quiet.

"Much better!" Elish stated as they all turned to look at her.

She stood in the connecting doorway to the king's inner chamber, Calline behind her, and glared at her husband.

"Tarek, stop casting shadows over your people, they need to know what you're up to!"

"What I'm up to?" Tarek asked, pretending he didn't understand.

She couldn’t possibly know. He had told no one of his scheme because he wanted to be sure that everyone would act naturally so that Crystu would not guess what he was doing.

"Yes, Tarek. What – you – are – up – to."

Elish enunciated the last five words clearly as she and Calline fully entered the room. Then she sighed in affectionate exasperation.

"Jareth is right: you really are a royal idiot sometimes. They need to know, Tarek, or else they will waste valuable time making plans that will allow Jareth to go to Angate. If Jathte has asked for a Rykatu, he needs one – he would not exaggerate. You know you intend to relent at the last possible moment and send Crystu with Tam, so just tell them that so they can get on with organising our army." She stared at his drinks shelf and grinned. "Besides, you already have one Rykatu practising her transmutation on your belongings, let's not have both of them doing it."

Tarek span round to look at his shelf and immediately saw what she had. He groaned.

"Not my best Ladecian whisky! Not again!"

The flask still held a yellow liquid, but the colour was no longer the rich amber of its former contents, but rather a more organic colour suggesting that, if unsealed, the liquid would emit an pungent odour more usually encountered at ground level in areas frequented by tomcats. Tarek transmuted the flask, contents and all, into rock, and threw it on the large plant in the corner.

Elish raised an eyebrow. "You didn't have to destroy the decanter too. I liked it."

"There is no way I would ever have used it again," growled Tarek and sat down.

Jareth and Aren were staring at him thoughtfully.

"So what are you up to, Tarek?" asked Aren conversationally. "You always were devious."

Jareth stabbed a finger at him again.

"Crystu *has* become stronger in the last few weeks; her gifts are sharper, more powerful, and also more focussed. Helping Tam strengthen his dreamwalking has helped strengthen her too. Is that what all this was about? To force them both to improve their abilities?"

Tarek sighed and sent a reproachful glance at his wife. He didn't often succeed in keeping plans hidden from Jareth and Aren, and he had been enjoying the novelty.

"Not at first," he admitted. "That Zindon came too close to repeating their previous success. I admit I was shaken and angry and I focused my anger at Tam. Unfairly, I know, but he *was* the vehicle through which a Zindon almost gained entry into Tyreen. So I decided that never again would I allow a Warrior who cannot dreamwalk to become a Ponfour, and I attempted to persuade Tam and Crystu to agree to break their bond."

He paused, and poured himself some water, wryly checking first to be sure that the liquid *was* still water. Then he continued.

"I should have known how she would react." He shook his head at his own foolishness. "But then, within hours of waking, she found the strength to go to the farm and found out that Tam now had the Gift of dreamwalking. I realised then that if I pushed her hard enough, she would not only help him learn to use it but might also strengthen her own gifts in the process. So that is what I did: pushed her hard and made her angry enough to prove me wrong."

He looked over at Aren.

"I don't actually expect Tam to pass my tests, but from the reports I have received, he is already as strong as most who have trained the Gift since childhood. Both of them have strengthened much faster than they would without the threat of being confined to Tyreen. When I do officially relent and send them out they will be as strong as they can become in such a short time. I need Crystu at her full mature strength, especially with this threat from the Shadowbringer. I want you to continue this subterfuge for at least a few more days, while you assemble the people you plan to send to Jathte."

He stared at first Jareth and then Aren until each nodded agreement. Then he grinned.

"I can tolerate losing a few bottles of whisky if the end result is a Rykatu in her full strength, or near to it. She'll forgive me eventually."

His wife snorted.

"Eventually!" she agreed.

"Tam will talk her round, once he understands," Calline said. "He will understand and be grateful, once he learns the reason for your actions."

Aren nodded agreement.

"You acted to make him better able to protect Crystu when they leave Tyreen. He will not only understand; he will approve."

She and Jareth stood up.

"Elish was correct," Jareth said. "We needed to know this, Tarek. We can now make the appropriate arrangements for the destruction of the snow-ants in Angate."

He bowed.

"Light be with you my King, my Queen, Lady Calline."

Aren echoed her husband's farewell and they left.

"Well?" Jathte asked as his parents entered their private room at the palace.

Aren glanced at Jareth, she could feel that he was considering telling Jathte what they had just learned, but he looked sideways at her and shook his head fractionally. She agreed: Jathte would have Crystu's assistance, but he did not need to know it yet.

"You'll have a Rykatu in Angate," Jareth told his son, "even if it has to be me."

Jathte looked surprised.

"The king still won't reconsider? Can you leave here now? Surely you are needed to organise everything."

"One way or another, we'll arrange it," Aren replied. "For now, there are a few recently bonded Sorcerers who can translocate with you tomorrow when you return to Angate."

She smiled at his grimace, guessing the reason for it.

"Sorry Jathte, I know you would rather have experienced people, but we have none to spare from other duties. It will take you some time to map the infested area and we will send you as many as we can when they become available. We had hoped that you would find nothing there and be able to assist Seldar and Trerin, but I doubt that you will have finished in time."

She saw Jathte's concerned look and anticipated his next question.

"There are wild reports of an invasion of Zindons in Bein. I hope that this is as spurious as most of the other reports we have sent people to investigate."

Jathte's eyes went wide.

"They are going to investigate that? Just the two of them? Suppose it's true?"

Jareth sighed.

"Invading in large numbers would be an unprecedented Zindon strategy, Jath; they prefer subterfuge. I seriously doubt there is anything to the stories, but I *would* have liked to send more people to check it if I could. Unfortunately, we are over-run with reports of strange happenings in the Protectorates, all of which must be looked at."

Aren could feel how heavily the responsibility of that decision was weighing on Jareth and she used their bond to give him her support. He had had no other choice, and Seldar was experienced and powerful while Trerin, though young, was resourceful. The two had only been bonded a few months, but they had been the only choice to send other than untried youngsters. Jareth smiled thanks at her for sharing her strength.

Aren realised with shock how much older he had grown in the last few weeks – his face was far more lined than it had been just that spring. Of course, he was four years older than her, at seventy-eight years old and, although Tyreans enjoyed a longer and healthier lifespan than non-magical humans, he was no longer in his prime. She knew he had interpreted the drift of her thoughts by the way that his smile turned wry and he shook a finger at her reprovingly.

The twinkle that suddenly appeared in his eye suggested that he intended to prove to her just how much strength he still had. She grinned at him; once Jathte had left...

"Jath, it's late, and you should rest after your translocation," she said brightly.

He glanced out of the window and the darkening sky and looked puzzled.

"It's not that late, Mother, I thought I might join Tam and Crystu at The Golden Moon for a little while, and..."

"That's fine, dear," Aren cut in – Light he could be dense! "Off you go, then!"

"We'll see you before you leave tomorrow," Jareth told him as he opened the door, and together they ushered their son out of their room. They waited until his footsteps had faded from hearing, then she turned to her husband.

"Well? I believe there is something you want to prove to me," she said.

Tests

Aren's eyes flew open at the sudden sound. She lay still a moment listening to it and then, moving as little as possible to try to fool her body that she was still asleep, she stretched one arm to the curtain and twitched it to one side. The sky was dark and dotted with stars. The archer constellation was edging into sight from behind the distant mountains, which told her that the night was no more than halfway through. She let the curtain fall back and then rolled over to stare accusingly at her chortling husband.

She tried hard to maintain a severe face, but Jareth's hilarity was vibrating through their bond as well as assaulting her ears. Such a double onslaught was too much and, despite her best efforts, she found herself irresistibly caught by his mirth. Even though she still did not know the cause, she rocked with laughter until tears streamed down her face.

Light! It felt good to laugh after the stresses of the last few weeks. Slowly the compulsion eased and they both lay back, gasping for breath.

"That was wonderful, Jareth, I haven't laughed like that in too long, but would you please tell me what we were laughing at?"

He grinned at her, eyes shining, as he told her, "Tarek is going to have a very big surprise!"

Aren frowned in puzzlement.

"About what?" she asked.

Her husband grinned again and she could feel that he was deliberately trying to tantalise her, so she leant forward and tickled him.

Jareth, the elder Rykatu, leader of the Tyrean forces, most powerful Sorcerer in the known world, was also extremely ticklish. He writhed and batted her hand away.

"Stop it, woman, I'll tell you!" he half growled, half laughed. "I decided to see just how much Tam has learned about dreamwalk defence so I entered his dream intending to wrest it from his control and test him."

He paused and shook his head ruefully. Aren gaped in surprise.

"Are you saying that you failed?" she asked in amazement.

"More than that," he replied, "he not only detected my presence immediately, he threw me out! Not easily, but he overcame my best efforts to remain in his mind. He's passed the first of Tarek's tests and if he can expel me, he can probably pass the other one too."

Aren clapped her hands together, delighted at the news.

"I truly didn't think he had much chance of doing that. I'm glad to be wrong," she told him.

Jareth nodded, grinning.

"I, too, thought he would be unlikely to pass them in such a short time, if ever. I wish I could be present when he tries Tarek's dreams. He may even do it tonight."

He yawned, pushing himself off the bed to walk naked across the room and pour a glass of water. He winced as he lifted the jug. Aren gasped and uncovered a glowstone to be sure that she had seen correctly.

"Jareth! Your back!"

Jareth looked at her with a questioning glance and then stepped in front of the mirror, using a little transmutation to illuminate his torso. He twisted around until he could see his back.

They both stared in amazement for a second and then started laughing again.

An area of Jareth's back was now covered in small bruises, as though something had repeatedly been rapped hard against his rib cage. The bruises were not randomly placed, but instead formed a pattern: a central circle with many lines stretching from it, the purple and yellow colouration perfectly placed to make a replica of the Ponfour symbol.

The King's dream

Tam felt immensely pleased with himself for succeeding in winning that battle. Jareth was far more powerful than he and, more important, far more experienced.

Tam had realised that in a dream you were as powerful as you could imagine you were. Dreams were not reality – they could reflect it, but they could also include things that were impossible in real life. Because of this, the fact that Jareth was a Rykatu was almost irrelevant while he was walking in Tam's dreams. All Tam had to do was retain control of his own dream, which he had done, although it had not been easy. Jareth had tried hard to wrest control from him, nearly succeeding several times, before Tam had managed to change the dream to exclude him.

As the water of his earlier dream reformed around him, Tam had a decision to make. When interrupted by Lord Jareth's unexpected appearance, he had been about to embark on the most challenging dreamwalk he had yet attempted. He had intended to attempt the king's dreams. Over the last few nights, since Crystu had dragged them both from the king's presence after yet another argument between her and her father, she had been trying Tam's defences and they had both been surprised by his strength in the dreamwalk. Crystu had insisted that he was already far stronger than most who had years of experience, so Tam had decided to act. Then, as he began to form his dream, Jareth had appeared.

Should he continue as planned, or wait for another night? He decided to continue. His success evicting Jareth from his mind gave him confidence, even though defending one's own dream was an easier task than was resisting eviction from another's.

Tarek would have the advantage when Tam was within his dream, but Tam wondered how much practice the king could have had in repelling intruders – few people would ever dare to risk offending their king by walking uninvited into his dreams.

Tam floated in the dream waters of his replica mountain lake and focused on the metaphor he had chosen for finding the minds in which he wished to walk. When the image was clear in his mind, he pulled it into the dream about him. The rocky mountains moved back further and further as the lake in which he swam enlarged. The floor dropped away beneath him too, until he was floating, submerged in an enormous ocean-sized body of water. Tam had never yet seen the sea, except in pictures, so did not know how that much water would move naturally, but that did not matter. This was a metaphor, not reality, and as long as he understood what each component represented, the image was effective.

He felt currents tug at his body as he hung submerged a few feet below the moving surface. He allowed the strongest current to tug him through the water. As he moved, he looked upwards at the images reflected from the boundary with the air.

Had this been real, he would have expected to see his own reflection staring back down at him, with the lake bottom reflected murkily behind it. Instead, many different images, some blurred and indistinct, others sharp and detailed, rocked and swayed with the irregular movements of the water's surface.

He did not try to focus on any of them, but let them flow past him as he moved through the water. Eventually, the current eased and he hung stationary once more.

Now he focussed on the images above him, but without concentrating on any particular one. He let them pass before his dream eyes and used them to feel the mind of the sleeping person. A pattern of colour, sound, scent, and other sensations that had no waking analogy, built up in his mind. Each sense merged seamlessly with the next and with the images above him, until he found a pattern which coalesced into an identifiable, unique, and familiar whole. He had found Crystu's dream.

He drifted closer and merged the images from her dream with his own dream lake, until the lake became insubstantial, barely sensed, behind his Sorceress' dream. She was walking in the palace gardens and appeared downcast. Tam knew that, although she had tried to hide it from him, the rift between her and her father had hurt her deeply; they had previously been close. Tam hated the fact that he was the cause of their dispute, and this further evidence of her sorrow made him even more determined to pass the second test. First, though...

Crystu looked up, sensing Tam's presence through their bond, but he had merged his consciousness into the solidity of the garden wall so that she would not locate him easily. He knew he would have only seconds before she *did* find him, so he made a slight change to her dream. The sudden blossoming of every flower in the garden distracted her and she twirled around staring at the blooms and laughing in delight.

He had chosen as many scented flowers as he could think of and he had added all their scents to her dream at the same time. Before she resumed searching for him, he eased out of her mind and back into the calm area in his lake.

Feeling happy about his night's work so far, he began to drift around the boundaries of Crystu's dream, looking for currents pulling from it towards other minds. Some pulled weakly, but others tugged at him more insistently and these would connect with her friends and family. Those connections were what he sought.

At each one Tam paused and let his awareness follow it to the mind toward which it flowed. Each of those distant minds glowed faintly, giving a hint of its own unique aura. He found the one he sought – a bright glow, the colour indescribable, but recognisably that of King Tarek. He paused, while he fought down the sudden nervous desire to leave this for another time.

Invading the king's mind was no slight matter, even if the king had ordered him to do it. It felt like breaking into the royal bedchamber while its occupants were inside it; even if you had been ordered to do so to test security, as they did not know when you would try, the possibility existed of coming upon them at a delicate moment, which would be embarrassing for all.

The same was true when you walked into another's dream – you might see images they could wish you had not. Nevertheless, he must attempt it, so he took a deep dream breath and let himself float along this current towards the mind of his sleeping king.

When he reached the calm area that was the king's mind, he focused on the images above him to see what Tarek was dreaming. He saw a large field full of children, all participating in a sporting contest.

Many activities were taking place around him, but the king was watching the opening round of an archery competition closely. A young girl stood with drawn bow and let her arrow fly. It flew straight to the centre of her target, and she turned to grin with great satisfaction at the king.

Tam recognised the young Crystu and this tournament; he remembered competing in it. His younger self was in the group of children waiting their turn in the opening round. Their faces were blurred and indistinct, as was the background of the dream. Those would be details that the king either could not remember or thought unimportant, but Tam could recognise his friends and himself.

He smiled inwardly; being already present in the dream would make his task much easier. He allowed the images to wrap around him and merged with the representation of his fourteen-year-old self. He must be careful to allow the dream to carry him with it until he was ready to make the small change that would shout his presence to the king. Even the slightest resistance to the dream flow would alert the king to an intruder.

Tam remembered this contest well for it marked the day that he had first spoken to Crystu. The contest progressed as he remembered: each round eliminating some of the contestants until only a handful, including Crystu and Tam, were still in the competition.

Just three rounds remained and Crystu stepped up to the mark and pulled her bowstring to her ear sighting along the arrow to the target. The string snapped as it reached full tension and the arrow flipped from her hands to land at her feet. She looked dismayed. The contest had a strict no-magic rule and a strict time limit for each contestant's turn. She had time to restring, but when she felt in her pocket for a spare, she had none. She looked to her father who spread his hands wide to show that he had no string for her either. The girl's eyes glistened with unshed tears as she stepped back, knowing that this had cost her any chance of placing in the competition. The young Tam had been impressed with the Princess's determination not to cry and to accept her loss, and he had stepped forward, his own spare string in his hand.

"Wait, Princess! I have a spare string!"

Crystu had stared at him uncomprehendingly for a fraction of a second and then her face had transformed with joy and gratitude. She took his gift, quickly restrung her bow, and then in one fluid motion loosed her arrow into the target with just seconds to spare.

Her aim was fractionally off-centre, but she was still in the competition.

The contest continued, the targets were moved further away, then replaced with smaller, then replaced with more complex shapes that were hard to sight on, until only Crystu and Tam were left, Crystu just one point behind Tam.

She shot first. The target was a twisted shape of wood and metal, with the spot to be hit positioned behind distractingly coloured projections. Only a perfect shot would pass those obstructions; if her aim was even a few millimetres off true, the arrow would bounce away.

Crystu's shot was, as it had been in reality, perfect. Tam stepped to the mark and took aim. In the real event, his aim too had been flawless, and so he had won the competition by one point. The Princess had been a little disappointed to come second, but her father had been proud she had done so well in her first tournament when her opponents were much older than she.

As the dream reached the moment that Tam had shot his arrow, he seized control of it. The arrow flew to the target, but clipped one of the obstructions and bounced away.

Tarek stiffened.

"That is not what happened," he said, and the dream froze as Crystu span round, eyes shining in triumph to make sure her father had seen. Tam relinquished his control at that moment and, allowing his younger self to freeze along with everything else, waited to see what the king would do in response.

Tarek walked up to the stationary Crystu, and looked down at her and smiled. Then he walked up to Tam, who felt the dream sharpen around him as the king brought into focus the face of the boy who had won the contest in reality.

Tarek sighed.

"So! It *was* you. I have wondered whether it might have been. And it's you now, in truth, isn't it, Tam?"

Tam took control of his image and aged himself to his true present age.

"Yes, I was the boy who gave her his bowstring."

Tarek looked at him and nodded.

"Does she know?" he asked.

"I do not believe so, although I have never asked," Tam replied. "She has spoken of coming second in her first tournament, but that is all."

Tarek nodded again.

"How long have you been here?" he asked.

"Since the opening round of the contest. I arrived as Crystu took aim for her first shot."

The king's eyes widened.

"That long? I did not sense you at all."

Tam was careful not to allow his dream image to show any trace of the satisfaction he felt at that success.

Tarek looked at him and then shrugged.

"You have surprised me by accomplishing this much, Tam, but I will have to eject you now."

"Of course, my King," Tam said courteously and then, unable to resist the urge, added, "but only if you can!" He braced himself.

He saw the king's eyes widen at his temerity and then narrow in concentration. The dream was replaced by a howling sandstorm.

The sand flashed and crackled with static electricity as it whirled around him, the sparks were multi-coloured and jaggedly clear. Tam knew that this was intended to disorient him until he lost his hold on the king's mind and fell back into his own dream. It would have worked against a large proportion of Sorcerers, but it failed against Tam.

Many Tyreans, especially the most powerful, made the mistake when defending their dreams, of using their own magical strength against the foe. Even though taught otherwise, they instinctively fell back on the strength and Light of their Gifts. Against Zindons this was usually effective, because they too relied on their magic to overcome their opponents, and generally lacked the imagination to try a different approach.

Tam had trained hard to become a Ponfour, and he had learned early on that the best defence was to turn an opponent's strength against them, and he had done this instinctively the first time Crystu had invaded his mind and invited him to eject her. He did it now, using the king's own power and turning it into both shield and anchor. He remained fixed and solid, as the king attempted to shake him loose.

Eventually, the attack abated and then the royal family room formed around him. King Tarek was standing in front of the fireplace, staring at him with an unexpectedly rueful expression.

"So I am shot with my own arrow," he said, shaking his head.

"I concede that you have passed this test, Tam. I did not expect that."

He walked over to thc drinks shelf and picked up a decanter. Tam noticed that he looked at it carefully and smelled it before pouring, and wondered why. Tarek saw his puzzled look and smiled wryly.

"I wouldn't put it beyond her reach even in my own dream."

Tam remained puzzled.

"You know that yesterday she transmuted my whisky into... well, let's say something that a cat uses to mark territory."

Tam was shocked.

"Crystu did that? No, I didn't know!"

Tarek looked surprised.

"She didn't share the joke with you? I imagined you both having a fine laugh over in the Moon."

Tam stared at him not knowing what to say. He was appalled and shocked that the king would think he would condone such a joke. Tarek sighed and sat down.

"Have I misjudged you that badly?" he asked.

Tam hesitated before replying but decided that honesty would be the best response.

"If you think I would have condoned or found funny such an act, then yes you have," he replied. "Had I known what she was doing I would have stopped her."

Tarek's eyebrows rose.

"Have you so much influence then?" he asked, sounding doubtful.

"In some matters, yes! This would have been one of those. She *must* exercise more control of her temper!" Tam replied resolutely, momentarily forgetting that this was her father.

He would have to have a talk with Crystu about this later!

The king snorted.

"Light aid you in that! I've been trying without success for over twenty years!"

With a start, Tam recollected where he was. His king stared sat him for a long moment and then seemed to make a decision.

"Come, sit down. I will know if Aren and Calline were correct." The last sentence was spoken more to himself.

He looked up at Tam and pointed at the chair opposite.

"I said, sit down! I have no intention of stretching my neck to look up at you, even if this is just a dream."

Tam obediently sat, making sure that the soft-looking chair was firm enough that he could sit without sinking into its depths, and waited for Tarek to continue.

"I admit that I was furious, *with you,*" Tarek said, stressing the last two words. Tam winced – that was not something one wanted to hear from one's king. Tarek snorted at his reaction but continued with barely a pause, "when a Zindon tried to use you as a way in to Tyreen, exactly as happened last time. The only difference was that Crystu was more observant than that previous Sorcerer and noticed that you were controlled."

Tam felt himself sink in the chair as his control slipped due to his shock at hearing that a Zindon had done this before. He regained control with difficulty but soon sat firmly again. Tarek had noticed his slip and raised an eyebrow.

"You didn't know? I expected Crystu, at least, would have told you once she had learned of it from Jareth."

Tam shook his head.

"It happened before?" he asked.

Tarek nodded.

"Oh yes! That's how I came to the throne: my father was assassinated by a controlled Ponfour."

Tam stared in shock and felt himself again sinking down into the chair, but ignored it.

Tarek continued, "That's why I opposed Crystu's choice of you as her Ponfour, I did not want her put at risk by partnering with someone who was also vulnerable to that same attack. She was furious with my attempted interference, of course, but at the time she didn't know the reason for it."

Tam could only stare at the king – he had also not known that the king had opposed the bonding.

Tarek sighed.

"She didn't tell you that either, did she? I'm sorry, I assumed you knew." He paused, then said, "That's the third assumption that I've been wrong about, I think. I wonder how many other of the things I believe are truly only mistaken assumptions?"

He shook his head and took another swallow of his drink and smiled sadly.

"It never quite tastes the same in a dream," he said and drained the glass.

"As I said, I was furious, but eventually I calmed down and I realised that I could not imprison a Rykatu in Tyreen, so then I tried to arrange to have your bond broken."

He snorted.

"You were the only person who didn't argue with me over that. Jareth simply refused to do it, and told me that he would personally make sure I couldn't sit comfortably on anything but cushions for the rest of my life if I persisted in trying to persuade him. Even Elish called me an idiot, and said that Crystu would never forgive me." He broke off and then said, "Then she said something strange. She laughed and said that even if your Ponfour bond was removed, the other would remain. She said that in the first week it might have been possible, but that you are now irreversibly double-bonded. Do you know what she meant?"

Tam frowned. He had never heard the term before that moment. Then the meaning became as clear as mountain water – she was referring to the deeper bond he and Crystu shared. Tarek recognised his moment of comprehension.

"You know what she means then? I wondered if she was referring to the fact that you and Crystu have that extra benefit that a few receive from the bonding spell."

Tam nodded, hoping that his king would not pursue this topic further.

"What causes it, do you know? Why do a few receive that little bit extra? Why would Elish call it a double-bond?"

Tam hesitated, wondering if he could avoid answering.

Tarek frowned at his silence.

"Tell me!"

Tam took a deep breath; he *must* answer a direct order.

"Name those you know are among that group, my King."

Tarek frowned again at being answered with an order, but then he began to list the few he knew.

"Jareth and Aren, Jathte and Trerisia, Kaleo and Caryn, Frey and Loel, Dansje and…" he paused, then gasped.

"Oh! Oh no!"

He stared at Tam, and then placed his head in his hands and groaned. The edges of the room wavered and flickered.

Tam felt a strong urge to run. He quelled it and, thinking that he would rather be facing twenty Zindons than sitting in the king's dream right now, forced himself to continue,

"With only a few exceptions, they are all married, or engaged, or if not, have probably not been bonded for long."

Tarek straightened in his chair and looked at him steadily.

"Does Crystu know about this?" he asked.

Tam considered for a moment before replying, "I do not believe so."

The king nodded.

"My sympathies when she learns of it. I suspect she may well react badly if she thinks that she has been magically coerced in some way," he said.

Tam agreed. So long as Crystu thought that their relationship deepening was her choice, all would be well. If she ever learned that her feelings were magically predestined, she would feel belittled and outraged.

Until she understood that no compulsion was involved, and that they could still choose, her temper would flare and Tam would bear the brunt of it.

His thoughts were interrupted when Tarek spoke again.

"How do you feel about this..." he paused, trying to find the right word, then shrugged, "implied predestination?"

Tam thought about it, and then replied honestly, "My King, I truly do not know."

Tarek's eyebrows rose.

"You could always try running, there are plenty of caves in the mountains," he said.

Tam knew that he *must* have imagined the fleeting look of amusement.

"I think it's a little bit late for that, my King," he replied, wryly. "She can locate me as easily as I can find her."

"Perhaps that is why the Elders do not make this widely known," the king mused. "The hills would be full of hidden Warriors and Sorcerers all terrified of bonding."

Despite himself, Tam smiled at the image.

"Is that why you agreed to break the bond? To escape this fate?" Tarek's voice was suddenly sharp.

Tam's answer was immediate, instinctive and heartfelt.

"No! Never!"

The king's face softened and Tam felt that he had just passed a second test.

"I'm glad to hear it," Tarek said, and leaned back, gazing at Tam with a thoughtful expression.

"Tonight has been a revelation for both of us, I think, so I will finish quickly and we can both *sleep*," he stressed the word, "on what we have learned. As I have said, I realised that I could not keep Crystu in Tyreen, so I decided that I would add more pressure on both of you to spur you, Tam, to develop your new Gift as rapidly as possible. I also hoped that Crystu's strength would mature further as she aided you. In both of these plans, I was successful. Now that you have passed one of the tests I can tell you that I always intended to relent and send you both out, but a king cannot appear to be indecisive, so it will have to be at the last possible moment."

Tam smiled, relieved to be on safer ground.

"My King, you may relent tomorrow with no fear of appearing indecisive. Lord Jareth tested my defences this night before I tested yours. I have passed both of your tests."

Tarek stared at him and then unexpectedly grinned.

"Had I learned this yesterday, I might have accused Jareth of holding back! As it is..." he shook his head ruefully.

"My scheme has worked better than I dared hope. Well done. I will make the announcement tomorrow morning that you have passed the tests and may once more travel."

He paused, and then continued, sounding curious.

"Tell me, Aren and Calline said that you would approve my actions once you learned of the true reason. Do you?"

Tam looked at him and spoke honestly.

"For my part, my King, I do. I can better fulfil my duty now that I have mastered my new Gift." He stopped, unsure whether he should continue.

"I heard a 'but' at the end of that," Tarek said, frowning slightly. "What sentence should follow it?"

Tam looked him in the eye.

"Crystu has been extremely upset by this rift between you. I cannot approve of that even though I understand your reasons."

Despite his best efforts, he knew that his tone was censorious, and he waited for the king's reaction.

Tarek looked shocked, but only for a moment, and then he chuckled ruefully.

"I *did* ask, and I deserved that criticism, I suppose. You're right, but I could not tell Crystu or it would have negated the plan. Perhaps I could have handled it better."

Tarek sighed.

"She is not the only one upset by this, I have missed her too. I hope she will forgive me when she understands."

The colours in the room greyed and its corners blurred. Tam noticed that ornaments on a shelf merged and changed and split apart. He understood then that the king had been as upset by the arguments as had Crystu, but he had chosen the course, and held to it despite the cost, because the benefit to Tyreen was more important.

"My King, I will explain it to her," he promised.

"Thank you, Tam, I appreciate that," Tarek said, and then added, "I was wrong to try to interfere between a Sorcerer and her Ponfour, the Lord of Light knew what he was doing when he brought you into Crystu's life."

Tam knew that was all the apology he would receive, and in truth, even that was far more than he had expected or felt that he was owed.

The king sighed and sat back in the chair.

"You may leave now, Tam, I would like to spend at least some of this night in true sleep, and you will be tired tomorrow and may have a lot to do. Lord Jareth will explain if Jathte has not already."

"Of course, my King."

Tam rose from the chair, bowed and drifted backwards out of the king's dream and into his lake. Then he relinquished all control over his dreams and sank into normal sleep. His last thought was that the king had reacted surprisingly calmly to the news that Tam would probably marry Crystu.

Rapprochement

Tam woke slowly into a stifling heat.

The tent about him was in total darkness, which surprised him because he had, as usual, set the walls to half-light before he went to sleep. Crystu must have reset them to full dark.

The heat sapped his strength and ability to think. He reached out through the bond to locate Crystu. She was wide-awake. Distance and the direction suggested that she was in the meal tent.

He moved his right arm to touch the tent wall and concentrated. He gathered a small quantity of transmutation energy into his hand and releasing it into the tent to set its walls back to half-light.

The walls now appeared to be partly transparent, showing the activity taking place outside. They were not in fact truly transparent, because the partition between his area and Crystu's did not reveal hers, but instead the view from the outer tent wall. The same would be true from within her room: she would not see into Tam's area.

He breathed a sigh of relief; the day was not as advanced as he had feared, although the sun *was* now shining directly on their tent, which explained the heat. Taking a deep breath, he forced himself to move despite the smothering air. Stuffing some clean clothes into a bag and fumbling with the door ties in his haste, he left the tent and raced for the shower area.

After Crystu's most recent fight with her father, she had refused to spend another night in the palace. Tam had suggested that they join the force that was gathering to meet the Shadowbringer's attack so they were now camping in the Valley of Treos. Here, Lord Jareth was assembling the largest army in history. Not just Warriors and Soldiers, not only Sorcerers and Ponfourii, but also reservists were being called to prepare to fight.

Tam had pointed out that, assuming he passed the tests, Crystu and he would fight on the front line, aiding those with fewer powers, and so it would be a good idea to get to know more of those people with whom they would fight.

Crystu had agreed, and so they had set up their paired-tent within a meadow already containing many of the large tents that housed up to fifteen people each.

They had spent their days since then joining group exercises and learning who had which ability and how skilful they were with it. Many of these exercises involved Crystu playing the part of a Zindon and attacking small groups with her illusions and transmutation, while Tam watched with concern and had to force himself to stay back when the group retaliated.

The exercises could be dangerous because they tried to make them as realistic as possible. Crystu held back her power, but the less experienced Reservists generally had poorer control over their gifts when fighting.

Although everyone spent some time each year training for battle, it is a different thing to know that a real battle may now be imminent and the stress was affecting some people's ability to concentrate.

Tam had had to heal Crystu's arm two days earlier when a man, who usually spent his days making shoes, panicked and let loose a blast of flame when Crystu threw an illusion over him.

The fireball had set alight her armoured sleeve, which should not have been possible. Tam had scolded her for neglecting the transmutation spells that protected her armour, making her promise to check everything every night.

Washed and feeling a little more alert, Tam jogged in the early morning sunshine, across several fields, to the nearest food tent. Crystu was still there, waiting for him, and he grinned in anticipation of her reaction when she learned his news.

The large tent had two sides rolled up to allow air to circulate inside. The place was crowded, though not as much as it would have been an hour earlier. Tam made his way to the small table where Crystu waited, smiling. A cold drink, with a bowl of mixed cereal grains with fruit and nuts, was ready for him on the table. The sight of the food reminded him how hungry he was, so with a smiled thanks, he sat to eat.

"Tam, the flowers last night were lovely, thank you," Crystu said, then she peered at him closely. He could feel her probe through the bond and grinned at her.

"You're so happy!" she exclaimed. "You haven't felt like this since we were travelling. What is it? What has you so excited?"

His mood was affecting hers and her eyes sparkled with reflected delight, as she waited for him to swallow and answer her.

"Tam! Congratulations!"

Jathte's shout cut across the conversation in the tent, and several people looked up to see who had spoken. Jathte came across the tent and pulled a chair from the next table to sit with Tam and Crystu.

"I have to return to Angate, but I couldn't leave without seeing you. Da told me what you did, and showed me the bruise you gave him."

Crystu gasped.

"You ejected Lord Jareth from a dream? And bruised him doing it? Tam! That's wonderful."

Tam coughed on the drink in his mouth – he'd left a bruise? But before he could say anything, Jathte laughed and continued, "Not just any bruise, Crystu, a near perfect replica of the Sun symbol, picked out on Da's ribcage in purple and yellow."

Crystu put her hands over her mouth, eyes wide with awe and stared at Tam.

The food tent went quiet.

Tam stared at Jathte.

"I bruised him? I had no idea! Light, Jathte! I would never do a thing like that to your father on purpose! I don't even know how it happened!"

He looked at Crystu, as he tried to understand how he could have done such a thing without knowing.

"I have been trying to work out how your mother did it to me, but," he looked back at Jathte. "I didn't know I marked him. Is he angry?"

Jathte chuckled and slapped Tam's shoulder.

"Not a bit of it. Da's very proud of that bruise, and you should be too. He said that he intends to let it fade naturally as a reminder never to underestimate a Ponfour. Don't worry, though, I will tell him it was an accident if you insist."

Tam nodded gratefully. "Please do."

He should feel ashamed of himself, he knew, for his lack of control, but despite the shock of learning about the bruise, he still felt elated when he thought about last night.

Crystu looked intently at Tam and her eyes widened.

“There's more isn't there, Tam. You’re too pleased with yourself and not even taking liberties with Jareth’s hide has dented it!

He nodded, and she gasped as she guessed the rest.

"I passed both of the king's tests last night, my Lady," he told her, conscious of the listening ears. "He has lifted all restrictions on my travelling, and said he will announce it this morning."

He would have said more, except the entire tent was suddenly full of clapping and cheering people, making further conversation impossible. Crystu didn't try to speak, but he could feel her overwhelming joy and relief that they would once again be able to travel – her feelings were a match for his own.

Tam would not have admitted it to himself before, but the prospect of being confined to Tyreen for the rest of his life had been oppressive. The endless years of palace duties would have bored him and the guilt that he would have felt at being the reason that Crystu likewise was confined would have been unbearable.

Crystu's eyes clouded as she caught the change of his emotions, and he knew that she could probably guess the cause. In the continuing celebration around them, she could not speak, but she smiled at him, shaking her finger reprovingly.

Tam sensed a wave of mischief flow across the bond but had only a second to wonder what she planned before she threw her arms around his neck and kissed him firmly.

Surprised, Tam pushed back against the table. The back legs of his chair caught on the uneven floor, and the chair tipped over, spilling them both onto the floor. The cheers around them changed to good-natured laughter and several hands helped them back to their feet and set right the chair.

Jathte had developed a sudden fit of coughing and Tam looked at him suspiciously as he sat down again. Crystu was laughing uncontrollably until she noticed that his breakfast had also spilled over.

"You're still hungry, I'll fetch some more food."

With a wave, she transmuted away the mess, and taking the crockery, went across the tent towards the food.

The others in the tent returned to their meals with only occasional glances towards their table.

Tam watched Crystu walk across the tent, feeling confused.

"You could always try running. It won't work, but you *can* try."

Tam looked round to meet Jathte's wry understanding look.

"The king said something similar last night," he said with a sigh.

Jathte looked surprised.

"The king knows about," he glanced around at the neighbouring tables and lowered his voice, "our type of bond?"

Tam replied equally quietly, "The Queen had said something about our being double-bonded, and King Tarek asked me what she meant."

Jathte's eyes widened with respect.

"And you told him? You're even braver than I thought!"

Tam forced a chuckle.

"He made it an order, and so I didn't have a choice."

"What did you say?" Jathte asked curiously.

"I told him to list all those he knows who fall into this category. It didn't take him long to spot the connection."

"How did he react?"

"He groaned."

Jathte winced sympathetically and then noticed Crystu coming back with a loaded tray. He stood up.

"I have to go, Zia will eat me if I'm away too long. I expect you'll both be joining us there soon, so I'll see you then. Congratulations again, Tam."

"Light bide with you, Jathte, and thanks," Tam replied.

Crystu put down the tray and kissed Jathte on the cheek.

"We'll be there as soon as we can, Jathte, Light shine on your path."

Jathte left with a wave.

Tam pulled the plate of cold meat and bread closer and began to cat. Crystu sat down and sighed and Tam looked at her, puzzled at her sudden low spirits.

"What's wrong, Crystu?" he asked around a mouthful of ham.

"I'm wondering if my Father will really let us leave, or if he will find another idiotic reason to keep us here."

Tam sighed, and placed his fork down on the plate; he had made a promise to the king and now seemed the time. He concentrated and, mixing transmutation and illusion, made a privacy shield around their table. They could see out of the shimmering wall that surrounded them, and hear some sounds, but anyone looking in would see only distortion and hear nothing.

Crystu looked at the wall in surprise.

"Why did you do that Tam?"

"Because, my Lady," he began, his formality gaining her full attention, "this conversation needs to be private. I promised the king I would explain something to you, and I think I must do so now."

Crystu frowned.

"What does he want now? For you to fly too?"

Tam shook his head.

"My Lady, you have misunderstood. Your father never intended to keep us in Tyreen indefinitely."

Crystu snorted in disbelief and would have spoken her disagreement but Tam spoke first.

"He said that only as a spur to make us work as hard as we could, and become as strong as we could, in the shortest possible time."

Crystu stared at him.

"Are you trying to persuade me that he did it for our own good?"

"Not just our good, my Lady, but for the good of Tyreen."

Tam could feel her intransigent refusal to believe his words. Light! She could be stubborn! He had to make her hear him.

"My Lady, listen to me! The threat of being restricted to Tyreen for the rest of our lives certainly made me willing to do whatever was necessary to master my Gift. That was the point. And it worked. I am now stronger than many dreamwalkers who have practiced since infancy, and you are much closer to your full mature strength. You know it! And I know that anger drove much of your practice, just as I know at whom you pretended you were aiming your powers."

Crystu flushed at that, confirming that she had indeed used her father as an imaginary target.

Tam pressed on.

"Your father knew well that you would be furious, and that he would bear the brunt of your fury, but he did it anyway for the good of Tyreen."

He paused, but she was still refusing to accept that her father's act had been necessary, so he continued.

"Just as you did when you arranged to inflict me with those nightmares."

Crystu gasped.

"You said you understood," she began.

Tam interrupted her.

"I did. I do. But that doesn't alter the fact that they were unpleasant. You used your deep knowledge of me to find the things that you knew would have me wake sweating and shaking with fear, and it worked. You feared I would be angry when I learned the truth, but you did it anyway."

"It was necessary – the best chance for you to learn to control your dreams."

Tam could feel that she was beginning to understand.

"Exactly, my Lady. You did it for my good, as your father did this for Tyreen's good and also for ours."

He smiled.

"You and he are very alike."

"He really never meant to keep us here?" She stared at him, and a tear slid down one cheek.

"My Lady, he has been as affected as you by this rift. When he spoke of it, his dream lost all colour and sharpness. He was prepared to forever lose your affection if that was the price required for Tyreen's youngest Rykatu to reach full strength and for her Ponfour to learn his new Gift in the shortest possible time. I think it too high a price, what do you think, my Lady?"

A second tear joined the first and rolled off her cheek to land on the table. Crystu wiped her face and straightened.

"I think that I have a very wise and forgiving Ponfour," she looked down at his plate and laughed suddenly, "who still hasn't had much firstmeal."

Tam smiled at her. Her emotions were jumbled but he could tell that she was no longer angry with her father.

"Then, while I eat, why don't you go and talk to your father? He has been sitting at the next table for several minutes." He nodded to one side.

Crystu span round and saw that her father was indeed sitting nearby. The rest of the tent was now empty of people. Tam allowed the privacy shield to dissipate, and Crystu ran over to throw her arms around her father's neck.

Tam began to eat quickly because he suspected that he would have little chance after Crystu and her father had finished. He doubted that the king had come out to the tent just to find out if his daughter would speak to him.

"Da, I'm sorry, please forgive me," Crystu whispered as she hugged her father.

"There's nothing to forgive, Chryssie," Tarek told her as he wrapped his arms around her and pulled her closer. "I should be apologising to you. Tam was right: I handled this badly."

She pulled back, surprised, though she kept her arms around his neck.

"Tam said that?"

Her father laughed.

"Well, not in so many words, but the meaning was clear."

Tam gave up on his food.

"I hope I was not quite that blunt, my King," he said.

King Tarek laughed again.

"Very nearly," he replied, "but as I said last night, I deserved it. I hope you will always give such honest answers to my questions."

Crystu stared at her father, astounded by his complete change in attitude towards her Ponfour.

"Da, you're being nice to Tam – are you ill?" She made a show of putting a hand on his brow.

"No, Chryssie, but even a king should admit when he was wrong. I should have listened to your mother, and to Jareth and Aren. You chose well, and I should have supported you."

Crystu's momentary stare of disbelief melted into happiness and she planted a kiss on his forehead.

"I forgive you, Da."

"Thank you, Chryssie, and thank you too for not tipping over my chair when you kissed me."

He said it with a side glance at Tam, making clear that he had heard what had happened before he arrived.

Tam was alarmed until he saw that the king was smiling.

Crystu giggled and waved to Tam to pull his chair over to this table. As he did so, without a glance at his unfinished firstmeal, she asked, "So Da, why are you here? To tell us officially that we can travel again?"

"Partly, yes," he replied. "I thought I should do it in person. But also to pass on a request from Jareth: there's a Bonding Service in a week's time and, as he is busy for the foreseeable future, he wants you to take the Rykatu's place."

Tam's eyes widened, and Crystu gasped in astonishment, jerking so much in surprise that she slid off her father's lap onto the floor.

"He wants ME to begin the bonding?" she squeaked as Tam helped her back to her feet.

Her father smiled at her sudden panic.

"You *are* a Rykatu and quite capable of initiating the process. Jareth says, and I agree that you must start sometime, and he really needs to be elsewhere on that day. So..."

Crystu gulped and looked at Tam for encouragement. Her emotions were a bewildering mixture of terror and elation.

The Rykatu's place in the Bonding Ceremony was largely ceremonial, but she would be required to initiate the spell by transmuting the first circlet, the rest of the complex process was completed by a mixed team of transmuters and healers who were experienced and practiced in the delicate physical adjustments made to those who were bonding.

"You are perfectly capable of this, my Lady," Tam told her, "but if you are worried, we can find out who is leading the team of transmuters, and..."

"That will be Lady Aren," the king interrupted.

"Thank you, my King. Then it is simple, my Lady. You have to hand the first circlet to her when you are done. You can ask her beforehand to check that you have done it correctly before she and the others do the rest. She will think it no more than a sensible precaution for your first time."

Crystu's feelings calmed as she realised that he was correct. She smiled her thanks and sat in the nearest chair. Some nervousness still shivered across the bond, but she took a deep breath and turned to her father.

"Please tell Lord Jareth that I am honoured to be asked, and I will do my best."

"Of course you will, Chryssie, and you will be fine," he replied.

"How many are bonding, my King?" Tam asked.

"It will be about seventy-four pairs I believe," Tarek replied.

Tam's eyebrows lifted at the number.

"So many at the same time?" Crystu asked in surprise.

"We have accelerated the graduation process," Her father explained. "We thought it best to bond those Sorcerers who were suitable now, and they can finish their education afterwards if there is time. This way they will have a little time to adjust to the bond before they are sent out. Besides, the Warriors who will become their Ponfourii are all older and did, of course, finish their education several years ago. All of them have some experience outside Tyreen, having fought as support for Sorcerers over the last few years."

Tam nodded, he had left Tyreen several times when he was a Warrior.

"There will be several similarly large groups bonding over the course of the next few weeks, but you won't officiate for them. Another large group bonded today. It will take a week or so for the new Ponfourii to adjust to the bond, but, once they have, that group and you will translocate to Angate to tackle the snow-ant infestation there."

Tam realised that Crystu was looking at him with a strange look, half sympathetic and half mischievous, on her face, which matched her feelings closely.

"That's going to be a long service for you, Tam," she said. "Do you have a suit of ceremonial armour?"

For a moment, her meaning eluded him but then he understood. Only the king's presence kept him from groaning aloud.

Bonding Ceremony

Tam stood motionless at the rear of the platform used for outdoor ceremonies. He, and other Ponfourii whose Sorcerers were members of the bonding team but who had no active involvement themselves, played a traditional role – they must stand, looking impressive in full ceremonial untransmuted steel armour, at the rear of the platform, for the entire service.

The service traditionally took place outside, in the full light and, what was more important to Tam at that moment, the heat of the sun.

Tam had attended many Bonding Services and had always been impressed by the motionless Ponfourii encased in shining steel from floor to head. The thing that impressed him the most at this time of year, was always the rivulets of sweat that ran across their faces, dripped onto their breastplates, and eventually formed expanding puddles at their feet.

Because of the large number who would bond, the ceremony was taking place in the large amphitheatre to the north of the city.

At some time in the distant past, the top of a hill had been removed, and then the new surface hollowed down, to form a gigantic bowl, surrounded on all sides by rank upon rank of seating, and with an enormous circular paved floor at its base.

The platform had been placed on one side of the floor, and the surrounding seats were filled with thousands of spectators all drawn to watch the largest Bonding Ceremony in recent history.

From where Tam stood, he could barely see the assembled spectators, but a shimmer that rippled across in front of them revealed the magnification spells that would allow those watching to see and hear everything taking place on the floor and the platform.

Crystu, Revered Father Teiron, and the team of transmuter/healers, sat on ornate chairs on the stage, in front of their motionless armoured Ponfourii. Crystu was resplendent in a flowing crimson silk robe, a present from Narah for Crystu's first ceremony as the presiding Rykatu.

She looked beautiful in the silken folds which shimmered as they caught the sun. Tam had been speechless when she appeared in it and was finding it a little difficult to stop his eyes straying to her figure as she sat in front of him. Mixed in with the nervousness that he could feel emanating from her, was an occasional mischievous satisfaction which he knew was due to his difficulty in remaining focussed on his task.

The service had already lasted for over an hour, as the young Sorcerers and their chosen warriors first assembled in neat rows in the centre of the amphitheatre, standing to attention, and then came forward in groups of ten, to stand in front of the platform and make their Oaths.

The Oaths were given to the Lord of Light and heard by the Revered Father and the assembled witnesses.

They swore to defend the Light, fight all shadow minions, and to give their lives if necessary to this end. The Warriors further swore to support, advise, and defend their chosen partners, and to be prepared to die protecting them.

Then followed a speech from the Revered Father, about the long tradition of bonding, and the honour and responsibility of all the Guardians of Reyth, but especially of those called to go out into the Protectorates and search for those who sought to throw shade over the world.

Tam was having difficulty remaining motionless because of the tickle caused by the sweat that ran down his back, chest, arms and legs, but so far, none of the other Ponfourii on the platform had shifted by so much as an inch.

The slightest movement of anyone wearing ceremonial armour would be betrayed by a loud clatter as the gleaming metal plates shifted together. Tam had no intention of being the first to disturb the hush, as the Reverend Father ended his speech with a prayer to the Lord of Light to shine brightly on those about to bond, so he endured the itching and hoped that the service would not be too prolonged.

The stewards arrived, carrying a large circular table which they placed on the platform near the front. The Warriors formed an orderly line and marched up the steps in the right-hand corner, over to the table where each one placed his or her new circlet, and then down the steps in the other corner and back to their starting positions. The first circlet went in the centre, and the others were positioned around it so that they formed a shape similar to the Ponfour symbol. With so many, the shape was a much better emulation of the symbol than was usual. Tam wondered what this group's competition had been, to decide who would have the honour of the central place and the Rykatu's touch.

Once all the Warriors had returned to their ranks, half of the transmuter/healers rose and formed a circle around the table. Lady

Aren picked up the central circlet and carried it to Crystu who, apart from Revered Father Teiron, was the only person who had remained seated. Crystu rose as Aren approached, and took the circlet from the older woman.

Tam knew that she was nervous, but she showed no outward sign of this as she concentrated her will and focussed on the circlet.

It began to glow as she made the delicate adjustments to the metal. When the glow had subsided, she handed the circlet back to Aren, who replaced it in its original position. The transmuter/healer team began to concentrate and all the circlets were soon glowing as they too were altered slightly.

The gold and silver merged and changed into artellium. They were now ready to act as amplifiers for the next stage of the bonding process.

To the eye they looked unaltered, but they were now so solid that even diamond would never scratch their surfaces. They were also impervious to any form of magic that might attempt to further alter their structure in any way.

Finished, the team sat back down, and the Warriors once more marched up the steps and retrieved their circlets. When they returned to their original ranks, each one handed the circlet to his or her Sorcerer and knelt. Then each Sorcerer tied the circlet into place around his or her chosen protector's head.

The Warriors stood, and they all, Sorcerers and Warriors together, marched to take up positions within a large circle drawn on the ground. The Warrior wearing the circlet that Crystu had transmuted, stood beside his Sorcerer in the centre and the others formed concentric circles around them.

As they all found their places, the other half of the transmuter/healer team positioned themselves around the outer edge of the circle. The service had been timed so that they were all in position as the sun reached the highest point in the sky so that it would throw the maximum possible light over those assembled.

At the sound of a gong, the Sorcerers all knelt and the Warriors placed their hands on their shoulders. All in the circle closed their eyes.

Tam could feel the tingling as the assembled healers began their work. Crystu was adding to the build-up of energy, although she would only assist, not having yet been trained in this delicate work.

At first, nothing visible happened, but then the circlets again began to glow. Rainbow colours flowed from each circlet and into the warrior wearing it, beginning the physical changes that made Ponfourii faster, stronger, and hardier than others. Then the glow spread down their arms and into the Sorcerer, forging the bond between them.

Tam could remember that moment well. It had been the thing he had thought he would find the hardest to adjust to, and he had been nervous. Despite growing up within a large extended family, or perhaps because of it, he had always been a private person. He had worried about how he would cope with the loss of privacy.

At the moment the bond formed, and Crystu's emotions touched and merged with his, he had been relieved and amazed at how natural it felt. Their minds had fitted together so perfectly, that her knowing his emotions was no different to him knowing them.

Slowly, the light brightened and merged, the colours flowing together and joining into one giant glowing globe that enclosed everyone on the floor. For a moment the light blazed, brilliant but not dazzling, then it sank into the ground, spreading outwards and fading until it had disappeared from sight.

The service ended with a blessing for the newly bonded pairs, and then they marched out of the amphitheatre, to whatever individual celebrations they had planned.

Tam and the other armoured Ponfourii turned and marched off the platform with an impressive clatter of steel on steel, and went down the stairs behind it, into the underground rooms to remove their armour.

As Tam thankfully stripped off his helmet and breastplate, an older Ponfour, who earlier had introduced herself as Avielle, handed him a bottle of water, which he drained with relief. His hair was plastered to his skull, and the padded clothing he wore was soaked with sweat. The odour was powerful.

He noticed that Avielle had an amused small smile on her face. He realised that she, and most of the others, were far less sweaty than he was. The only other Ponfour who looked as bedraggled was another youngish man, Darst, also here for the first time.

Tam looked at the woman and raised an eyebrow questioningly, already beginning to guess the answer to his unspoken question. She laughed and peeled back her padded top to reveal an underlayer of a fabric Tam did not recognise, while another Ponfour reached into his helmet and pulled out a dripping piece of something that looked like a sponge. Yet another pulled something similar from behind her leggings.

"I assume those are some sort of cooling equipment," Tam said in a resigned fashion.

"Oh yes!" Avielle nodded.

"The cloth is transmuted to remain at a comfortable temperature, while the drippers in helmet and leggings slowly melt, to give the impression of sweat running down the face and pooling at the feet. I believe you're a transmuter?" Tam nodded. "So I'll show you how to make them."

Darst had come over to look.

"Why didn't you tell us about these before?"

"Because," another grizzled veteran explained, "you youngsters too often think it's somehow noble to suffer, and that it is disrespectful to the Bonding Ceremony if we take steps to mitigate the heat. So we let you experience it unaided for your first time on the platform, so you know what it's like without them. Of course, this was an unusually long service, so you got an extra taste of the sun."

A couple of them were eyeing Tam as the man spoke. Tam realised that they thought that he might be one of those who would insist on suffering nobly for duty's sake. A few years earlier they might even have been correct to think that, but in the time since he had bonded he knew that he had relaxed slightly.

He chuckled and glanced sideways at Darst, who still looked indignant.

"I can't speak for him, but I will be glad to learn the technique. I don't suppose this will be Crystu's last time officiating."

Avielle nodded, and after they had all showered and changed, she spent half an hour showing Tam and Darst how to make the cloth and drippers.

Suddenly, Tam stiffened as Crystu's emotions suddenly flared and surged through his mind. Incredulity, disbelief, shock, embarrassment, and finally a raging fury, flowed through the link.

Without a word or even thought, he snatched up his armour bag and raced out of the room, up the stairs and onto the floor of the amphitheatre. Crystu stood with a small group of people near one of the gates. She was staring at Lady Aren and, as he drew closer, he could see that the tension in her body reflected the agitation in her mind.

"My Lady, what is wrong?" he asked as he stopped beside her.

She whirled around to face him, eyes narrowed with anger.

"Did you know about this?" she hissed.

"About what, my Lady?" he asked carefully, beginning to suspect what it might be.

A furious Rykatu

After the newly bonded pairs had left the floor, the audience began to shuffle out of their seats and leave. Crystu decided to join the members of the transmuter/healer team who had gathered around several large baskets containing drinks and snacks.

Crystu sat on the ground, sipping a fruit juice, while half listening to the chatter of several young people who were of similar age to her. They were discussing the ceremony and making appreciative and speculative comments about some of those who had bonded.

Crystu was in an excellent mood – not only had her first bonding officiation passed without problem, but Tam's reaction to her dress had been exactly as she had hoped.

One sentence suddenly floated free from the general background and caught her immediate attention.

"You'd be wasting your time trying for her, Erron, didn't you sense it when they bonded? Smooth and complete! They're double-bonded for sure. She'll never look at anyone else."

The remark came from a self-assured looking woman. Crystu frowned, wondering what they meant, and then her eyes widened as she began to suspect.

"Really? Is that what it feels like? I never encountered it before," a young man replied.

"Yes," said another woman, grinning. "Five years at the most and they'll be married."

"Ha!" The first woman snorted. "Didn't you see how they were looking at each other, already? I say no more than a year."

"Ha back!" the other retorted. "That's what you said about the Rykatu, and it's been almost two years now!"

Erron could see Crystu behind them and tried to shush the speakers, but the first woman replied without noticing.

"From what I've heard, it won't be long now."

Crystu stiffened and jumped to her feet fuming.

Lady Aren stepped in front of Crystu, blocking her view of the others.

"Enough! I've told you before about this, Sharla; it is *not* a topic for open conversation," the senior Ponfour said firmly. "You may all leave now, but I want to see you in my office this afternoon. I have some duty changes for all of you, I think."

The women, turning to face Aren, saw the angry Rykatu behind her and both paled. They nodded compliance and then hurried away as quickly as they could.

Aren turned round to meet Crystu's angry eyes.

"Double? Bonded?" Crystu made each word a question.

Aren sighed and glanced around before answering. The few people still present all began to move away hurriedly as she turned back to the young Rykatu.

"It's a technical term, my Lady, not widely used. It refers to the type of Ponfour bond that both you and I have. A bonding that is much more complete than normal."

She spoke in a brisk, emotionless, practical tone. Crystu waited for more.

Aren sighed and continued, "A normal bond joins mind to mind so that we can feel each other's feelings and more. A double-bond appears to join mind and heart in an even more complete union."

"They were gossiping about how long it would be before that pair married! They were even speculating about me!" Crystu forced the words out between clenched teeth.

Aren looked her in the eyes for a moment then stated calmly,

"Marriage is frequently the result of a double-bond, my Lady."

Crystu stared at her.

"How many people know about this?"

Aren shrugged.

"All those who become Bonders learn of it. I suspect that most bonded pairs also work it out although, of course, we do not ask about it."

Crystu looked around at the people nearby. Had they all been speculating on whether she would marry Tam? Gossiping about her? Laughing when she behaved as predicted.

She remembered the laughter when she had tipped over his chair the previous week, and felt her face heat at the memory. How many had nodded knowingly at that?

The wave of humiliation and anger that washed over her was intense. Did Tam know about this? Was he also waiting with eager anticipation for their nuptials? A part of her knew that she was being ridiculous, that Tam would never make any such assumption, but she was too angry to be reasonable.

"My Lady, what is wrong?"

Startled, she turned to face Tam as he stopped beside her. She had been so absorbed in her anger that she had not felt his rapid approach.

"Did you know about this?" she hissed.

"About what, my Lady?" he replied carefully.

She could feel his concern for her, but also a hint of something else, something resembling dread. Sun burn him! *Had* he known?

She spoke very distinctly.

"Apparently, people are assuming that we are going to marry. Apparently," she spat out the word, "we are double-bonded and it is inevitable."

She felt the plummet in his emotions at her words and she knew that he was choosing his answer carefully. She didn't wait to hear what he would say.

"You knew!" she accused.

"I knew," he agreed.

Beside her, Lady Aren stirred as if she wanted to speak, but this was between Sorceress and Ponfour; Crystu knew that she would not interfere.

"Why didn't you tell me?" she demanded to know.

His eyebrows lifted slightly, and she felt his wry amusement.

"Because, my Lady, I knew that you would react the way that you are. I *know* you, Crystu." He stressed the word 'know' and smiled slightly.

Light blister him! He was laughing at her like everyone else!

"And have you also been assuming that we will wed? Laughing with your brother that you will become a prince when we marry?"

Her accusation sent a cold wave of shock rocketing across the Ponfour Bond. The angry Sorceress could feel how deeply her accusation had hurt him and part of her was childishly pleased that he was upset; she was hurt so fairness demanded that he should be too!

"My Lady, you know that is not true. No matter what others may speculate, I have never made such an assumption."

She *did* know that he spoke the truth, burn him; she wished that she did not. She knew that she was being unreasonable, but she *wanted* him to become angry with her so that they could have the sort of screaming match she had had so often with her father recently. That was what she wanted to do at this moment – scream her fury!

"My Lady Crystu!" Lady Aren's voice was cold with anger. "You are being absurd and acting like a child."

"She is neither, and she has a right to be upset about this."

For the first time, Tam sounded angry but his anger was aimed at Lady Aren."

Suddenly, Crystu felt something she had never imagined was possible: she felt smothered by the bond. She stared at Tam and understood, in a way that she had not before, that she would feel his mind in hers for as long as they lived, and that he would always know exactly what she was feeling too.

No escape existed, for either of them, short of death. She had known all her life that this would be the case and had understood and thought that she accepted it, but now it didn't seem fair.

He had had a choice, he could have stayed a Warrior, and never linked his mind to another's, but she was a Sorceress and a Rykatu; there had been no choice for her.

A Rykatu had to travel and had to be bonded to a Ponfour. No alternative existed. Suddenly Crystu found that she resented that – she hadn't had a choice, but he had.

"Stop defending me when I'm being absurd!" she shouted, knowing as she did so that she sounded ridiculous.

Tam blinked, and then said simply, "I can't do that, Crystu."

His grey eyes were fixed on hers, and she could feel his understanding of her unexpected feeling that the bond was a trap that had caught her and held her tight.

She didn't *want* his sympathy at that moment. She wanted him to shout back at her so that she could justify her anger with his, but he understood that too and smiled sadly.

"I can't do that either, Crystu," he said, showing how deeply he had understood her.

Her rage peaked.

"Then, understand this!" she hissed and concentrated.

Tam inhaled sharply, as the translocation nimbus formed around him, but only had time for a reproachful look before he was gone.

Crystu stared at the empty space where he had been; her anger had evaporated almost immediately to be replaced by a deep horror at her action.

"Crystu! You go too far!"

She had forgotten Lady Aren's presence and turned, as if in a dream, to face the lady's ire. Around her, she could see shocked faces staring while the sound of bird song, drifting across from somewhere out of sight, accentuated the sudden profound silence in the amphitheatre.

She realised that everyone still within the theatre must have heard at least some of that argument. The theatre was designed to carry sound out to the seats and, for at least some of the time, she had been shouting loudly.

"Where did you send him, Crystu?"

Aren's voice was icy. Crystu just stared back at her. She felt cold and her thoughts sounded as though they were coming from a great distance, so hard was it to hear her own mindvoice.

The enormity of what she had just done crashed over her.

Turning from Aren's accusing face, she translocated herself back to her bedroom in the palace and collapsed weeping onto her bed.

Crystu woke a few hours later feeling heavy and miserable. For a second she puzzled at the unaccustomed emotion and then memory returned. She sat up, gasping in horror as her actions replayed themselves inexorably in her mind, to find her mother sitting beside the bed gazing at her with an unsympathetic frown.

"Well, young lady, do you want to explain yourself?" her mother asked, sounding as angry as she looked.

Crystu stared back at her, knowing that she had behaved abominably, and wondering how to explain an emotion that she could barely understand herself now that she had calmed down.

"Mei-mei, I..." her voice failed her, and she took a deep breath and tried again.

"I don't know! They were laughing at me and I was suddenly so angry, and then…"

She paused, remembering the terrible feeling of being stifled, trapped, and tried to explain.

"I suddenly felt as if I was penned in, smothered, trapped by the bond. I don't understand it, but I suddenly wanted to be free of it, and couldn't. It didn't feel fair that Tam had had a choice and I didn't, and suddenly I just wanted to scream at him, and when he just kept understanding and forgiving me, it made it worse somehow."

Her mother's face had softened.

"Oh, I see. I should have guessed."

"Guessed?" Crystu was confused.

Her mother nodded.

"Yes. Most Sorcerers have a moment early in the bond, when they suddenly understand that it is for life. They usually aren't quite so, err, dramatic about it though."

"But I knew that it's for life," Crystu protested.

Her mother shook her head.

"You knew it, yes, but you didn't understand it. No one really does until afterward."

She thought a moment, and then asked, "Where did you put him? Can you bring him back?"

Crystu felt for the bond. She could feel Tam, far in the distance – he felt sad, determined, and hungry. He was not where she had left him, but had begun to travel back towards her.

She looked at her mother and shook her head.

"He isn't where I put him. He's moved closer. I know roughly where he is, but not clearly enough to translocate him back here."

"Well then, you will have to go out and find him, but not until we have had a talk. He's well able to look after himself for a few hours. We'll go to the kitchen and find something to eat and we'll talk about this."

A short while later, the two of them sat in their family room with several plates of savoury snacks.

Crystu had been surprised at how hungry she was and wondered how much of that was Tam's hunger instead of her own.

The thought made her feel guilty to be sitting comfortably in a warm room, eating, when he was going hungry as a result of her actions.

"Now," Elish began, "do you understand the distinction I was trying to make earlier?"

"I think so," Crystu replied. "I was taught about the bond, and I knew that it is permanent, but I didn't truly understand what that meant until today."

Her mother nodded.

"Yes. And you thought it unfair that you never had a choice about it, and you're right – it is unfair. But that is the price we Sorcerers pay for our power: we must use our magic to defend the Protectorates, but to do that effectively we must bond with a Ponfour."

She looked at Crystu.

"Have you never wondered about the apparent absurdity that our protectors are weaker in the Gifts than we are?"

Crystu thought about that.

"I was taught that it is because we train different things."

Her mother nodded for her to continue.

"We train our Gifts for power and strength, whereas they train physical strength and fighting strategies more than their Gifts."

"Exactly!" her mother agreed. "Our training complements theirs to form a strong and equal, but different, partnership."

"But, if it is an equal partnership, why is our rank not equal?" Crystu frowned, trying to understand.

"Because we *are* the more powerful, and because of the extra vow they take that we do not," her mother replied. "They vow to serve us, protect us, and even to die for us. They swear it under the Light, in the Light, and by the Light. It is that Second Oath that really creates the bond, the spell just completes it." Elish stopped to sip at her drink, and then continued, "And that Oath is also the reason why you can never make Tam angry enough to fight with you, the way you and your father fight, no matter what you may say to try and provoke him."

Crystu frowned. "I don't understand."

Her mother smiled.

"I have already mentioned that the price we pay for being what we are is the loss of choice. We are Sorcerers, and we must bond. Ponfourii have the choice that we do not, and gain physical benefits that we do not, but they too must pay a price. Part of that price is that they can never become truly angry with their Sorcerer."

Crystu gasped. "Never?"

Elish nodded.

"But I've seen Ponfourii get cross with their Partners!" Crystu protested.

"Cross, yes. Exasperated, yes. Furious, no," her mother replied.

"Think Crystu, what is it that you want most to do when you are *that* angry with someone."

Crystu answered honestly, "If I am that angry, then I want to hurt the person I'm angry with."

Then she understood.

“But they can’t hurt us. They are sworn to defend us from harm, so the Oath itself stops them ever becoming that angry.” She was amazed and awed. "I had no idea it is *that* powerful."

Her mother nodded.

"Now you begin to understand. I know how frustrating it can be when you really want a shouting match, and the other person just remains calm – you didn't get all your temper from your father, you know – but when you feel rage coming over you, when you want to needle him into shouting back, try to remember this: he's not refusing to retaliate – he *can't* retaliate."

"Do they know about this? Before they bond?" Crystu asked.

Elish nodded.

"Oh yes, but few are bothered by it. Certainly not Tam. All Ponfourii know what they will lose, and what they will gain. Those that bond, do so by choice, knowing the price."

She snorted.

"As far as I know there's only been one recorded instance of Tam losing his temper, and that was when he broke Jathte's nose when they were both children."

Crystu gaped in astonishment.

"Tam broke Jathte's nose? I've never heard about that before. How did it happen?"

Her mother shook her head.

"It doesn't matter. The point I was making is that Tam would not have thought it at all important that he can’t lose his temper with you. The only price we pay is that we can’t choose to remain alone. We gain far more than they do: their strength, dedication, experience, support, friendship, love..." She paused, then asked, "Do I need to list it all? Next time the bond feels oppressive to you, think of all that you gained."

Crystu nodded.

"I'll try," she said, but then looked up at her mother to ask, "But what about the other thing? I knew I had to bond, but I always expected to have a choice about who I married."

"You still *do* have a choice. Of *course* you have a choice," Elish replied sharply.

Crystu frowned.

"But the women I overheard, said..."

"They are not yet the experts they think they are," her mother interrupted. "All a double-bond means is that you chose a man who would make an ideal marriage partner, as well as an ideal Ponfour. Your minds and hearts are perfectly suited to each other, but you *can* still choose another, as can he."

Crystu gasped at her mother's final three words, and Elish smiled and shook her head, and continued softly, "But I don't think that you will."

"Now!" Elish continued in a brisker tone. "Go and apologise to your Ponfour and bring him home."

"Yes, Mei-mei," Crystu replied obediently and opened the window to leave. Then a thought struck her and she turned back.

"Mei-mei?"

Elish raised an eyebrow. "Yes?"

"You said it is part of the price they pay – what is the rest of it?"

Elish smiled sadly and looked Crystu in the eye.

"Child, it is what they must suffer if they fail to protect us – if they live and we die. That is the rest of it and you know what a terrible price it is. Remember that too, the next time that you feel smothered. Thank the Light that only a few pay it. Now go."

Elish made shooing motions with her hands, and Crystu obediently shapeshifted into an eagle and flew into the afternoon sky.

She could have translocated to the spot where she had left Tam and then flown from there, but she had a lot to think about, and also an apology to rehearse, so she decided to fly all the way.

On top of a mountain

As the translocation nimbus cleared, Tam's sandaled feet sank a few inches into intense cold and he began to shiver. He looked around at his new location and thought wryly that it could have been a lot worse.

Crystu had been so angry that he had half expected to reappear in the hidden doorless cavern where they had killed the Zindon. He was grateful that she had 'only' sent him to the top of Mount Bangruaig. He recognised it, having been here twice during his apprentice years.

He stood on a thick layer of snow which was frozen nearly solid and shivered. Bangruaig was so high, that it remained permanently snow-capped, even in the middle of summer.

Crystu had deposited him on the summit, and the view was magnificent, and much preferable to the walls of a sealed cavern, but he decided that he was not going to stay and wait for her to bring him back. Ponfourii had thicker skins than ordinary Tyreans, but even he would not survive in this temperature for long if he did nothing.

He looked at his feet; boots were the first priority. Luckily snow was one of the easier things to use to make snugly-fitting clothes; however, the process was be uncomfortable.

With a sigh, he pulled out his pocket knife and began to loosen the ice crusted snow, then, when he had enough, he unfastened his sandals and stepped his bare feet onto the snow

They were now so numb that he could barely feel any difference as he piled the loosened snow over them and packed it down. Then he transmuted the snow into a perfectly-fitting pair of leather boots.

Before long he had made leather trousers and a jacket by the same method. They were rough but would keep him warm once he was moving.

He looked at his bag of armour but decided that it would be too much of an encumbrance while he climbed down.

Bangruaig was used frequently for survival training, and for physical fitness assessments. Tam knew that in descending he would have to scramble down steep rocky faces, which would be impossible while clutching the awkward bag. He would have to leave it behind and hope that Crystu could be persuaded to retrieve it when she had calmed down.

By now, Tam was now so cold that he knew he was in danger of hypothermia, but he did not dare raise the temperature of the air around him because that would cause the snow beneath him to melt. The icy layer had accumulated over centuries and was deep.

During Tam's first visit to this mountain, one lad had made that mistake. He had warmed the air around himself, and before he had realised his danger, was trapped at the bottom of a deep waterfilled hole.

Tam knew that he would warm up once he began to move so, without further hesitation, he began to walk in the direction he remembered as being the easiest way down. He knew that it would take several hours to descend. Even then, he would still be in a remote and sparsely inhabited region.

It took him nearly an hour to travel below the snow line, but once he was no longer in danger of slipping on icy rocks he could move faster. He was sweating now from the exertion but kept the trousers and jacket on for protection against sharp edges when climbing down cliff faces.

By the time he felt Crystu awaken, he was perhaps halfway down the mountain and had reached a forested area. The trail he had been following was clearer now, and less steep, so he could travel more rapidly. He stopped briefly in a coppice to make himself a short spear and spear-thrower so that he could hunt later when he reached a valley that he remembered from his previous visits.

Now that he did not have to concentrate so much on each step, Tam found himself replaying the earlier scene in his mind, trying to decide if he could have said or done something to calm Crystu down.

He had been correct that she would be upset when she learned about the implications of their bond, but he had not expected to be banished from her presence in so public a fashion.

He also had not anticipated that learning about it would trigger the moment that prospective Ponfourii were warned could happen, when a Sorcerer suddenly found the bond restrictive and wanted to escape the inescapable.

Tam had sensed how the bond had felt to her at that moment, and understood that the sense of claustrophobia had overwhelmed her, causing a need to lash out in an attempt to be free. In some ways, she had reacted to his presence in her mind as he had when he learned that the Zindon was in his: with terror and an unachievable need for freedom.

The idea that she had viewed him like that was painful, but he knew that the feeling was temporary. Indeed, he could feel that she now felt ashamed, shocked, and guilty. He wondered what she was doing as her mind tone changed slowly to be puzzled, surprised, and eventually thoughtful. Then her mind altered its colour and feel, taking on the aspects that he associated with her having changed form.

He sensed that she was moving and he realised that she was flying towards him. She was still a long way off, though, and would take several hours to reach him.

The trail abruptly emerged from the forest to reveal the valley he had been expecting. He stopped, seeing several deer grazing on the slope ahead. Moving slowly, he fitted the end of the spear into the thrower and took aim at the nearest animal.

The spear flew true, and the rest of the herd scattered as Tam ran to the fallen creature and quickly killed it. He threw the carcass over his shoulders and headed downhill towards the stream that ran through the centre of the valley. He followed the water to where it ran along the foot of a large rocky cliff with a deceptively small cave opening.

Inside, the cave was large and ran back into the mountain. The result of frequent transmutation, it had smooth walls, side rooms, and even raised flat projections that were a perfect height for either seating or sleeping. One side room contained a large pile of dry wood and an axe as well as other tools. Another had hooks embedded high in the wall and here Tam hung up the deer.

The valley was used for training students in survival skills and had, over centuries, been altered and adjusted by generations of tutors and students. Tam thought that a more natural environment would provide a better training experience, but the many resources located within this valley were going to be useful to him now.

He picked up a mattock and, leaving the cave, looked across the stream to the opposite hillside. Although the cliff behind him was granite, the quarry dug into the opposite hill revealed a limestone cliff-face vertically banded with layers of different density of limestone. One layer was soft and contained many rounded nodules of various types of rock while to the right was a thick band of marble – something that Tam was sure was not possible naturally.

Just visible further to the north, another quarry, close to the stream, dipped down into a bed of clay. Tam crossed the stream and headed for the clay pit. The clay, visible through the sparse vegetation struggling to grow within the pit, was a coarse bright orange colour at one end, changing to blue-grey smoother clay at the other end.

Tam walked carefully across the slippery surface to the smooth grey clay and swung the mattock into it. He soon had a large, heavy armful, which he carried back to the cave. He had been unable to carry the mattock as well as the clay, but, remembering with a grin the admonitions of teachers about tidiness, he went back to the quarry to collect it.

As he strode past the limestone quarry on his way back, something glittering in the sunlight caught his eye, and he stopped to pick it up.

The broken rock was about the size of his fist. Hemispherical and hollow, its inner side was lined with hundreds of pointed purple crystals. Tam recognised it as an amethyst geode.

Once the broken edge was smoothed and polished it would be beautiful. Tenji would be able to make use of it, but more important, Tam realised that he was looking at a possible solution to the problem of how to destroy the largest snow ant infestation ever recorded.

Back at the cave, Tam split a large piece from the clay and put it to one side for later. Then, using a well-positioned flat-topped rock as a table, he pulled lumps off the larger remnant and, shaping them into coils, he expertly joined and smoothed them to make a clay pot complete with lid. He transmuted the clay into solid iron and the resultant cooking pot was well made and solid.

He cleaned old ashes from the external cooking area, and built a fire around and under the short flat-topped rock pillars which stood upright within the fire pit. He filled the pot with water from the stream and placed it on a pillar just above the flames. He used his belt knife to skin and gut the deer, wrapping the entrails in the skin and carrying them to the nearby wood where he left them for whatever might eat them. Returning to the cave, he sliced off chunks of flesh from the carcase and dropped them into the water, which was now beginning to steam. The valley contained an unusually wide variety of edible plants to help youngsters learn to identify them in the wild, so Tam could add chopped roots and other vegetables to the pot.

He went back inside the cave and, using the rest of the clay, soon had three bowls and spoons. One of the spoons had a large bowl and a long handle to stir and serve the stew.

He took the larger bowl to the nearby fruit trees and as he had hoped, found some early greenfruit just beginning to swell. Using his healing Gift, it took just a few minutes to encourage a few of them to grow to full size and ripeness. He filled the bowl with enough to stave off hunger while he waited for Crystu.

Finally, all preparations finished apart from an occasional stir of the stew, he took a greenfruit to eat and sat on the grass to wait for his Sorceress.

The shadows had lengthened and deepened into early evening by the time she arrived. Tam had seen her when she was just a speck in the distance and had pushed a few fresh logs onto the fire to revive it and bring the stew back to the boil. Now, he watched as she approached, the speck slowly enlarging until the silhouette of the eagle was clearly visible.

Being connected by an empathic magical bond was a useful thing he decided; there could be no misunderstandings, or miscommunications, and no possibility of lying. He knew, without doubt or confusion, that Crystu was completely sorry about what she had said and done, just as she knew that he understood and had forgiven her immediately.

Both also knew that the other was feeling a little nervous about this first meeting after Crystu had learned about the double-bond and what it might mean for their future together.

Apology

The eagle swooped down and her body stretched and lengthened until Crystu stood in front of him in her usual form. Tam began to speak, but she held up her hand, forestalling him.

"Tam, I know that you know that I'm sorry," she began, grimacing a little at the awkward sentence, "but, at the least, I owe you a proper verbal apology."

Tam nodded, understanding that her sense of honour demanded this.

She looked him firmly in the eye.

"Tam, I behaved appallingly towards you. I said things that were unfair and I punished you for something that is in no way your fault. I lost my temper and took it out on you, and I am truly, deeply, sorry. Please forgive me."

"My Lady, I forgive you," Tam replied and, although he noticed and regretted her slight flinch at his formality, he continued, "It is better that you spent your anger on me than on one of those who triggered your rage." He smiled. "My skin is thicker than theirs."

She smiled back tentatively and then looked past him towards the stew pot, its contents now bubbling and emitting a delicious smell. Tam knew that she had flown without stopping for rest or food, and was almost as hungry as was he.

"You're right," she said, then the smile left her face as she realised what the result would probably have been had she deposited one or both of those young women on top of that ice-covered mountain – neither had been full Sorcerers.

She stared at Tam in shock.

"They could have died," she whispered, aghast at how close she had come to a deed that would have plunged her into irredeemable darkness.

Her sudden horror pulled Tam forward to envelope her in a tight hug.

"It didn't happen, thank the Light."

Then he pulled back and held her at arm's length, one hand on each shoulder and said sternly, "But now do you understand why you must control your temper? My Lady, you are one of the two most powerful Sorcerers in the world, you could kill by accident without realising what you were doing until far too late."

She nodded.

"Yes Tam, I knew it, but now I understand it."

She smiled again ruefully.

"That's a distinction I have been learning about just recently. I *will* try, I promise."

She looked at him, took a deep breath and then said, "Under the Light, in the Light, and by the Light, I swear it."

Tam's eyes widened – that Oath was binding, as he well knew.

"I will assist you as much as I can, my Lady."

Then he grinned as he added, "Use me as your target whenever you feel the need to strike out."

Crystu grinned back at him.

"Oh, so that is why Ponfourii are gifted with thick skin? To protect you from bad tempered Sorcerers?"

She punched him in the stomach and then blew on her sore knuckles.

"Of course, my Lady, why else? I hope that you haven't bruised yourself badly on my thick skin?"

Tam deliberately spoke in an earnest manner. Crystu shook her head, laughing, and then threw her arms around his neck.

"Thank you, Tam. I really don't deserve to have you as my Ponfour."

The pause which followed was broken by a hissing and spitting noise; stew had suddenly bubbled up out of the pot. Crystu let go and they ran over to the pot where Tam pulled away some of the logs from the fire to lower the heat.

"Will you have some venison stew, my Lady?" he asked, picking up a bowl and, without waiting for her answer, ladled some stew into it and placed it on a flat rock on the ground.

She dropped down and took the spoon he offered her. She dipped the spoon in and, after blowing on it, took a sip.

"Tam, it's delicious! If you cook like this every time I translocate you onto a mountaintop I should do it more often."

Tam filled his own bowl, and sat, before replying, "My Lady, if you start banishing me to mountaintops just to get venison stew, you will be amazed at how quickly I can forget how to make it."

He used a little transmutation to cool the stew slightly, but the wave of sadness that he felt overwhelm Crystu stopped him before he could dip his spoon into the soup.

He looked at her; she was staring into her bowl, her spoon motionless within it.

"Tam, we're alone. I thought we had got past the 'my Ladies' when in private."

Tam stared at her. It took a second to understand what she meant but, as he replayed their conversation in his memory, he realised the truth; he hadn't noticed that he was doing it, but she was correct: he had addressed her only as 'my Lady' since she arrived.

Tam realised that he was unwilling to use her name. He put his bowl down to consider the matter but instead found his thoughts straying to speculation about whether missed meals and hunger would be a permanent feature of his life or just a temporary one. He recognised the thought as an attempt to evade a difficult subject and brought his mind firmly back to the question.

Why was he suddenly unwilling to use Crystu's name?

He had not found it difficult before. He had even called her by name once or twice during his Ponfour interview, so why did he suddenly shy away from it now.

Then he understood, and was appalled at himself – the emotion that prevented him using her name was fear!

Crystu had accused him of reaching for high status, something she knew he did not want, and now he feared that further familiarity could support that accusation.

He opened his mouth to try to explain his feelings but discovered that he could not speak; his jaw muscles locked and prevented him making a sound.

If he explained the reason for his formality, she would be reminded of her conduct, and be hurt by the reminder. He could not do it – the bond itself prevented him.

Speech-lock!

Tam had heard of it but never experienced the phenomenon before today.

"Tam?" Crystu prompted. He could only stare at her, helpless to answer.

"I think I understand," she said. "You have never sought high rank; you are uncomfortable when addressed as my Lord. Yet, even knowing that, I accused you of something that you would never do, and although you have forgiven me for it, the accusation still hurts. So you pull back to a more formal address to prevent me suggesting such a thing again. And you cannot explain because you think the reminder of my own behaviour would hurt me, and you cannot do something that will hurt me. Am I correct?"

Tam managed a nod, though even that small movement was difficult.

Crystu shook her head.

"You're wrong: the truth will not hurt me," she told him. "It's not being reminded of my own stupidity that hurts, it is knowing that I have damaged our friendship that is painful to me. I am hurt when my friends pull back from me and set me at a distance. You know that I dislike it when friends call me 'my Lady', yet you are closer than friend, brother, parents. If you push me back and hold me behind my title, I do not know how I will stand the pain. Please don't do that to me, Tam. I want you to only use my title when formality demands it."

Crystu's words broke the lock, and Tam realised what she had just done. Just as the bond had prevented him from speaking a moment before, it should now prevent him using her title in any but formal situations. He had sensed her complete sincerity as she spoke, he knew without doubt that she would be hurt if he continued to call her 'my Lady' in private, and so the bond would prevent it. He also knew that she had known exactly what she was doing, and had consciously used the bond to get her own way.

His lips twitched, and then he threw back his head and laughed uncontrollably, pointing a finger at her, which she batted away before she too collapsed into laughter.

The cleansing laughter removed the last awkwardness that had fallen between them.

"Cleverly done, Crystu," Tam said when he had regained control of himself. He didn't even attempt a 'my Lady' – he knew he would be unable to say it. "Now, perhaps I could eat something?"

Crystu blushed, remembering that she was the reason why he had gone without food all day. She waved at his bowl, picking her own up again.

They finished their stew in companionable silence and then Tam offered her a greenfruit from those he had picked earlier.

When they had finished, he put the bowls into the pot and then looked at Crystu.

"While I return these to the clay pit, would you please retrieve my armour? It's still up there." He nodded towards the mountain that dominated the landscape to the north.

"Of course I will, Tam, and then I suppose we had best return to Tyre."

She sighed, looking around at the valley.

"It would be nice to stay here a little longer, but we do need to finish packing if we are going to Angate tomorrow."

Tam put down the pot and braced himself for an argument.

"We are not going to Angate tomorrow," he stated.

"We're not?" asked Crystu, surprised. "I distinctly remember both Lord Jareth and my father giving us orders to go."

"They did, my Lady."

Tam replied, with a small smile for her evident surprise that he had been able to circumvent the compulsion to avoid her title.

She frowned.

"How did you do that, Tam?" she asked. "And why do you say that we are not going?"

"I am speaking as your Ponfour, my Lady, and so the formality is appropriate."

Crystu nodded, accepting the distinction, and gestured for him to continue.

"My Lady, there will be at least one hundred and fifty people translocating to Andar, along with their bags and horses. I know that some of them can translocate, and will join their Gifts with yours to move so many, but your power will carry the largest part of that weight. Without you, the others combined could move only one third of the amount. I will not permit you to attempt it until you have gone a full day without utilising your Gifts. Especially not when the task waiting in Angate is also likely to require a great deal of your strength. Had you done nothing today, beyond what was needed for the bonding ceremony, we could have gone tomorrow as planned, but in addition to that, you have translocated me, shapeshifted yourself, and must still take both of us back to Tyre. So tomorrow you will rest and the day after that we will go."

Tam could feel her searching for counter arguments, and as soon as she opened her mouth, he interrupted with a response to the most likely objection.

"Lord Jareth can send someone ahead to tell Jathte that we are delayed, but we are not going until I," he stressed the word, "am satisfied that you are fully rested."

He held her eye until he sensed her capitulation.

"Yes, Tam," Crystu replied meekly. Then Tam felt the streak of mischievousness that faced through her emotions, as she grinned suddenly. "I'll let you explain to Lord Jareth and my father why we are ignoring their orders."

Then her grin vanished and Tam felt the sudden trepidation that had wiped it away. He could guess the cause: The king and Lord Jareth would probably want her to explain her behaviour today.

"You will not face them alone," he told her. "What happened was between us and is over, WE will tell them that if they comment on it."

"Thank you, Tam," she began, but he interrupted.

"Besides, I think that today was intended to happen just as it did."

Crystu frowned, puzzled.

"What do you mean?" she asked.

"It is written in the Book of Light, that everything that happens within the Light, even a Rykatu's anger, is intended to be, and works towards the will of God," Tam quoted in a deliberately pompous tone.

Crystu looked at him quizzically, then murmured, "There were one or two words in that quote that I don't recall being in there."

Tam grinned.

"It's possible I may have misquoted slightly," he admitted.

Crystu's eyes went wide with delight.

"You? Misquote the Book? Have I corrupted you that far?"

Tam laughed a little ruefully.

"It would seem so, Crystu, but I have digressed. My point was that I found this today."

He handed her the geode that he had found in the quarry.

"I think it may be the answer to the snow-ants."

Crystu glanced at him, and then looked back at the stone. Tam felt the moment that she understood his idea as she gasped in astonishment.

"Tam, that's brilliant."

"You will have to be quick," he told her, "but if everyone there transfers energy to me through the dreamwalk and I slide it downstream to you, you can do it."

"Can I keep this?" she asked. "I would like it as a reminder of today."

"Of course you may have it. I'll ask Tenji to polish it if you like."

Tam picked up the stew pot from the ground.

"Thank you. I'll ask him to take a small slice and make a pendant. Whenever I feel my temper rising, I will look at it and remember what I did today."

She smiled a little ruefully. "I don't suppose that *you* are likely to need any reminders of today."

Tam shook his head.

"No, Crystu. I think that I will remember today for as long as I live, and certainly every time I say your name."

Crystu chuckled and gave him a push towards the clay pit.

"Go and replace your pot while I fetch your armour, and then we can go home."

Part 2: Zindon

"We know little about Zindons. They look human but don't have any seta so aren't alive as we understand life. They appear, usually in twos or threes. They have Gifts like ours. They kill or create trouble. They can alter a person's mind so that he or she becomes a servant of shadow. They can control someone through dreamwalking. They serve the Shadowbringer single-mindedly with courage. We do not know where they come from." Princess Rykatu Crystu's notes taken during a lecture in her thirteenth year.

Attack

Azxet wheeled in a large arc, scanning the ground below. Seething with anger, although he kept his attention fixed on the earth below, another part of his mind was plotting revenge. To keep his fury fresh, he once again replayed his memory of the events of the day after he had killed the old priest:

He awoke to find Xareht gone and the bed where she had lain was cold. A quick search revealed that the ward, which he had 'forgotten' to return, had gone too. He laughed, amused at her audacity. He would punish her for this, but not too severely; he would have done the same in her place. She was intelligent, and would make an excellent partner, once she understood that he was the stronger. He left his room to search for her, but was stopped by a Xiantu who had been waiting for him.

"Xianton Azxet. Xiantona Kajzte orders that you attend him in the control room at midday. He will send an escort. Until then you are to remain in your room."

Furious, Azxet prepared to translocate the man into the sea. As he reached for the power, the Xiantu opened his hand to reveal a symbol etched into the palm – a double spiral along which moved pulses of darkness. They sucked the light around his palm into them and drew it down into the centre of the spiral.

Azxet abandoned his intention. The Xiantu was one of the Xiantona's Voices, and as such, his words were the words of the Xiantona.

The Voices were the result of failed attempts to copy the Ponfour bond, which the Xiantu knew gave increased speed and strength to those bonded. Unable to replicate the spell, they had managed to create a lesser bond, and the Voices were the result.

Each Xiantona chose several Xiantu to bond. Being chosen was an honour that no-one wanted, but refusal was not an option. Once bonded, they lost all initiative and ambition, becoming totally dedicated and unswervingly obedient to the Xiantona.

They spoke his words and carried out his orders without question or thought. Azxet could kill this one, but the Xiantona would know immediately through the link; the punishment would be severe.

He ground his teeth, nodded, and returned to his room to await the escort. As he closed his door, he saw the Voice taking up a position in front of it as a guard.

He had no food in his room, but he knew better than to open the door to ask for some to be sent to him; a knife in the belly would be the most likely reply. Clearly he had incurred the Xiantona's displeasure.

Shortly before midday, the Voice escorted him to a waiting boat. He was taken ashore to the office warehouse which the Xiantona had chosen for his offices.

"How dare you consume the old Guardian's Seta instead of subduing him and bringing him to the ship for questioning," Kajzte began.

He did not raise his voice, but the ice of the northern waste was audible within it.

"He was too old to be worth converting, but we could have used him in the Gifting ceremony when next Lord Xian honours and raises a Xiantu or Xianton."

Azxet was sure this was an excuse and that Kajzte had wanted the strong Tyrean energy for his own feeding.

"We received no such orders, and my energy reserves were depleted," he replied, trying to sound confident.

"You just wanted the status that comes with killing a Tyrean," Kajzte accused.

"As do you," Azxet retorted, his anger overcoming his caution.

"I have the right! You do not! You overstepped your authority Azxet, and you will regret it!" Kajzte told him.

Azxet tried to hide his dismay. He might be able to bluff his way out if he remained confident. He started to speak, but Kajzte spoke over his words firmly.

"Not only that, but you let the innkeeper and his family escape, knowing they had been released from our domination. He has already begun telling people that Bein is invaded by their ancient foe. Sooner or later, despite the distractions that we have prepared across all of this land,, Guardians will hear those tales and come to investigate, and we are not yet ready for them."

"I sent you word that he was leaving!" Azxet protested. "You could have sent someone to intercept him. I did not have enough men to send some after him and capture a fifth level Tyrean. Besides which, we need the Guardians to become aware of our presence here eventually or else the plan will fail; the innkeeper's burblings will serve that purpose."

"The timing for that is my decision, not yours," Kajzte replied coldly. "Just one second-level Xianton would have been sufficient to kill a couple of light-chasers and their spawn. You had enough in your command to detach one and that is what you should have done."

"It makes no difference!" Azxet replied hotly. "With all the rumours, we have started, this will just seem like one more unlikely tale amongst all the others. We were almost due to release a few light-chasers to spread some tales about this town and you know it! That anthill we prepared will keep the Guardians too busy to take notice of any other tales immediately. They won't be arriving in strength tomorrow as you seem to fear, but we do need them to come here eventually!"

He had gone too far but he was too angry to be cautious.

Kajzte smiled coldly.

"If they arrive too early, all is for nothing. I have sent messages to speed the arrival of the rest of the fleet, but we need to know in advance if any of Guardians decide to come here earlier than we want them. *You* will watch for their approach."

Kajzte smile broadened at Azxet's sharp intake of breath. The humiliation was intense! The reprimand and re-assignment would be made public, and the position of watcher was one only given to those who had failed badly.

"You will accompany another shapeshifter and begin flying sweeps over the countryside to watch for approaching Tyreans. If you find any, send Erxe back with the information about numbers and location, while you harry the Tyreans to slow their approach. We will set an appropriate trap for them when we know how many to expect and when. You will leave immediately and not return until they arrive at our gates."

"Oh, and I will return this to the store," Kajzte held up the ward that Azxet had stolen.

Azxet's eyes widened with fury and his arm twitched as though he would snatch it from the Xiantona.

Kajzte smiled coldly.

"You can have it back if you are prepared to challenge me for it. Are you?"

Azxet took a deep breath and curbed his anger. Kajzte was a fearsome fighter, Gifted with transmutation and illusion as well as the dreamhold and, unusually for someone of high rank, healing. Azxet knew he would lose an open confrontation and therefore had no choice but to accept his demotion and loss.

So now he flew in the sunlight, several days' journey from Bein, across peaceful rolling hills covered with ripening crops and grazing cattle, wearing the form of a derstral to avoid detection from the ground.

Beside him flew Erxe, another shapeshifter, also shaped as a derstral. From below, their camouflage made them almost invisible, from above they would be almost as hard to spot, but they could see each other because derstrals' eyes saw heat as well as colour.

The fields below were dotted with industrious, hardworking, light-chasers who would make excellent, hardworking, slaves if they survived.

Movement on the road a few miles ahead caught Azxet's eye. He drifted across the sky for a better angle.

At that point, the road ran at the edge of a huge forest. Long branches overhung the track, making anyone on it hard to see from the air, but Azxet caught sight of two mounted men, leading a packhorse.

One of the men was fat, which suggested that he was wealthy. The other was tall, had unusual yellow hair, and was lean and muscular, with an alert, watchful manner.

A rich lord with his bodyguard perhaps.

The bodyguard looked up at the sky, eyes narrowed, and the sunlight flashed off the sun symbol on his brow.

Not a lord and bodyguard, but a Sorcerer and Ponfour!

Azxet flew higher and looked for Erxe, but he was already flying hard in a straight line towards Bein to report.

Azxet scanned the terrain. While they were screened by trees he could not easily harass the riders, but a mile ahead the road moved away from the forest to cross the fields of a hamlet. There he could attack. If he could inflict enough damage to one or both men, it should slow them down a little.

He felt safe – the camouflage of a derstral was effective; they would not be able to see what was attacking them, so would be hard pressed to defend themselves. He circled around and made his plan and watched as the two men progressed towards the open.

Trerin tensed – he had glimpsed movement at the corner of his eye. He turned and saw a shadow flit across the side of the hill on the other side of the fields to their left, and then dance across the leaves of a field of corn. He looked up in the sky, but could see nothing to account for that shadow.

He felt the slight tingle that usually accompanied a warning gleaning.

He scanned the countryside, using the edges of his eyes, and again caught a glimpse of a moving shadow before it vanished behind some shrubbery. He could see nothing obvious that could be throwing that shadow.

Seldar felt his Ponfour's heightened alertness.

"What is it?" he asked.

"Maybe nothing," Trerin replied, scanning the countryside around them. "I saw a shadow thrown by something flying, but I can't see anything in the sky, and my gleaning is nudging me. I'd like to try that illusion we discussed."

Seldar nodded.

"The horses are tired, I'll give them a little energy, my Lord." Trerin spoke at a more normal volume and nudged his horse close to Seldar's.

He leaned across and placed his hand on its flank. He felt the whisper of power as Seldar began his illusion, building it slowly to keep the tell-tale emanations to a bare minimum.

The precaution was probably unnecessary, but if there were any magic users watching, Trerin's stated intention to refresh the horses, should account for the magic use they would sense.

He slowed his horse, his vision darkened and then he was looking at the back of his own head as a duplicate of himself pulled ahead of him. As his double moved forward and separated from him, Trerin was left with the peculiar sight of his real body, apparently riding a truncated horse. He could only see a few inches of it wherever he was in contact with its skin – the rest of him was invisible.

Anyone watching would have seen nothing out of the ordinary, just the two mounted men continuing up the road, but the visible men and pack horse were illusions.

Trerin could not see the real Seldar, or his horse, but he could sense his location, immediately to his left. Seldar, of course, as the author of the illusion, could see Trerin without difficulty.

Trerin pulled his armour out of his bag by touch. Donning it rapidly, he jumped off his horse and ducked behind some bushes. After changing into a fox as slowly as he could manage, he dashed into the forest and after the illusory riders. He ran past them for a short distance and then changed form into a large eagle. He once again changed form as slowly as possible to minimise the magical emanation. He did not know if such precautions were necessary, but he would rather not find out too late that they were.

As the illusory riders drew level with him, he rose into the air as if startled by them and, gaining height as quickly as he could, looked for anything that could account for the shadow he had seen. There! From his new vantage point, he could see a vague area that moved between him and the ground. It changed colour as it moved, but against such varied foliage, its colour changes were not quite fast enough. The young Ponfour had never seen anything like it, but he knew of just one natural creature which had the ability to change colour like that; it had to be a derstral. Those savage flying lizards were supposedly extinct but obviously that belief was wrong.

Satisfied that the creature was scanning the ground, Trerin changed the colour of his feathers to adopt his usual camouflage, and he began to stalk the hunter.

He wondered what it was after, as his own eagle eyes could see no trace of the small animals that would usually form the prey of a large predator of this kind.

The illusory riders emerged from the cover of the tree canopy and the Dersral immediately swooped to attack Seldar. The young Ponfour was already in motion when the creature screeched in surprise as it passed straight through Seldar's illusion. Trerin plummeted onto its back and plunged his beak into its neck. They landed rolling on the ground.

He was surprised by how strong the creature's scales were. His beak, its strength and sharpness enhanced by his shapechanged weapons, should have slashed with ease into the creature, but instead, although it penetrated, it did nothing like the damage that it should.

The derstral shrieked at his attack and twisted to rake its claws along his belly. His enhanced feathers deflected most of the attack but some of the claws penetrated his skin.

Trerin struck again aiming at the join between two scales near the neck and again did far less damage than he had expected. He could sense something odd about this creature. He had researched what little they knew about derstrals in the hope of learning to shape change into one. This one was a lot larger than usual but everything he had read had suggested that even an unenhanced eagle's beak should be able to penetrate its scales.

As well as that oddity, although he knew that a derstral was a natural creature, a predator, but not a creature of shadow, he could sense a deep darkness within this animal that was far from natural.

The creature shrieked as he attacked again, and then did something no derstral should be able to do – it translocated. One minute Trerin's claws were fixed on its tail while he slashed at its back, and the next it vanished.

Lord of Light!

He could think of only one possibility – a Zindon, shapechanged as Trerin was, its armour making its scales stronger in the same way that Trerin's did for his feathers.

Trerin leapt into the sky, wings beating furiously, clawing for height. His eyes scanned the sky for the Zindon, knowing that it must be above him somewhere, but its camouflage was too effective; he couldn't see it. His gleaning warned him just in time to evade the strike as the Zindon hurtled past him, missing his wingtip by a whisker. It vanished again.

Trerin continued to gain height as quickly as he could, and concentrated on keeping his camouflage adapted to the ground below. He searched the sky for any sign of the Zindon, but he knew that a derstral was nearly impossible to see from below; he needed to fly above it.

His gleaning screamed at him again, but this time he was a fraction too slow and the Zindon's dive clipped the edge of his right wing and the impact broke the bones at the tip.

Trerin twisted and managed to catch the Zindon's tail as it went past, and once more began to strike at it with his beak.

The Zindon in turn twisted and aimed its claws up and under his feathers. Trerin felt a stab of agony as its claws sank into his stomach and tore a deep gash. He felt his strength begin to wane as he bled freely.

The Zindon bared its teeth at him in a parody of a grin, and then translocated them both.

Trerin realised they were now very high up and wondered why the Zindon had brought him here. He soon learned its intent as it fastened teeth and claws firmly onto him, but instead of the slashing attack he expected, he felt its mind ram into his and pierce straight to his Seta.

With shock, he realised that it was attempting to suck out his life energy. They fell through the air – the Zindon not bothering to slow their descent, and Trerin too distracted by the attack on his Seta to notice.

He fought back, his mind slashing and pushing at the Zindon's, but he was weakening. Each time that he knocked it away from his Seta, it returned. Each time it returned, it took him longer to knock it away, and until he did so it fed on his energy and he weakened further.

Its presence in his mind was vile: a pulsating, sucking, dark, and hungry void, surrounded by a never-healing, psychic wound caused, though Trerin did not know it then, by the Shadowbringer, when he ripped out the human Seta to replace it with his own energy, on the day that the JarXian became a Xiantu.

That terrible nauseating blackness, and the pain as the creature consumed his Seta, overwhelmed Trerin's courage, and he panicked, frantically struggling to escape the creature's clutch.

With a sound that was unmistakably mocking, the Zindon released him and vanished.

Trerin realised then that he was falling, the ground rushing towards him. He barely had the necessary strength to open his wings and slow his descent, but slowly he came to halt and hovered. Scanning the skies about him, he wondered where the Zindon/derstral was.

He noticed movement below and, looking down, saw the Zindon flying below him. It was making no effort to camouflage itself from him now, and it turned its head to look towards him, again making that sound that was so obviously a mocking laugh.

Then it turned its head away and began to scan the ground, flying in large sweeping arcs. Trerin understood; it was searching for Seldar, attempting to locate him by the residual energy he emitted as he held the illusion that kept him hidden. Trerin understood, too, that it no longer considered *him* a threat.

He was badly injured, losing blood, and the damage to his Seta had weakened him considerably. Plus, it knew that he had been panic-stricken and must think that he would not dare another attack.

The creature was correct about his injuries being severe, but wrong about the rest. Trerin was furious and ashamed with himself for panicking but Tyrean training included preparation for terror.

The innocuously-titled Self-knowledge course was intended to help each Tyrean learn his or her strengths and weaknesses. This included learning that every man and woman, no matter how brave or strong, could and would panic given the right stimulus.

The instructors taught it, and then proceeded to demonstrate it. Each student was invited into a prepared room, the first time many went in confidently, others, wiser, went in with trepidation. Everyone left that room shaking, with their clothes sweat-plastered to their bodies. All Tyreans, from the humblest baker up to the king, were given that demonstration at least once a year.

Within that room they learned first-hand what could bring them to such a level of fear that they would panic.

The purpose was partly so that no one could feel contemptuous towards another fighter if he or she panicked, because all knew that they too were capable of it.

The second purpose was more important: to enable each person to understand and learn from their terror, so that if it happened to them in battle, they would more quickly recover their courage and return to the fray.

Trerin had been in that room many times in his life, and each time he had been terrified out of his senses. He used the anger and shame to fight down the fear he felt at the idea of resuming the battle. He looked at the creature below which was ignoring him. It undoubtedly thought that it could kill him at its leisure because he was too badly wounded to escape. Trerin knew that it was correct.

He could sense Seldar's worry and hoped that his partner would remain hidden; Sorcerers often felt compelled to risk themselves for their Ponfourii even though they should not.

Seldar was trying to urge him to come down for healing, Trerin thought, attempting to interpret the emotions he could feel through the bond. If he did as his partner wanted, the Zindon would find them both with ease.

He had only one possible course of action. The Zindon was certain that Trerin was cowed and would not attack. If he did attack, it would kill him – draining his Seta to complete the kill. Better Ponfourii than he had died at Zindon hands, but Trerin decided that if this was to be his fate, he would have his beak at the shadow creature's throat and his talons in its belly when it happened.

He knew if he waited until Seldar was in immediate danger, that the bond would erase fear, but he could not wait for that – he would not! Trerin folded his wings and fell, gathering speed as he plummeted towards the unaware Zindon.

He crashed sideways on into its back, the impact shattering his left shoulder, wing and several ribs, but he shrieked defiance and wrapping his remaining talons around one of its forelimbs, again tore at its throat with his beak.

The Zindon growled its annoyance, then translocated them both back high into the sky, and resumed its attack on his Seta. Trerin knew that this time it would not let go until it had killed him.

Once again, he felt the terrible consuming blackness with the raw wound that surrounded it, as the Zindon smashed through his defence and fastened onto his life force.

A nudge from his gleaning suggested a course of action. It was insane, but Trerin could think of nothing else to try.

He abandoned his futile attempts to detach the Zindon from his Seta and instead threw all his remaining strength into a healing flow aimed at that psychic wound with its seething oily shadow.

For a second, nothing happened, but then the Zindon screamed as that wound began to close, cutting off its access to the dark energy Gifted by its god, and beginning to return it to its former human state.

Now the Zindon was the one struggling and fighting to break free, as Trerin clung on with all his waning strength and continued to heal the wound deep within the creature.

They fell through the air, tumbling and rolling, until Trerin's strength gave out at last and the Zindon broke free. They smashed into the top of a tree, falling in different directions as they bounced off branches. The Zindon hit a branch and rebounded, falling into the river.

Trerin bounced onto a sloping roof, rolled down it and off its edge, coming to rest in the yard of a water mill.

A close call

Trerin couldn't move. He lay, barely conscious, able to hear but unable to understand what he heard. Their speech was peculiar and the strangely-pronounced words rolled into his ears, ebbing and flowing like waves washing on the seashore.

"Wha es et?"

"Thass u neagle!"

"Thass never u neagle, thass bleuw!"

"Not all on ets bleuw, thass green on top."
"Thass alrite then! I'er seen looads er green un bleuw eagles!"
"Hev yew? Wher'er yew seen 'em then? I hent never seen any!"
"Dun't be stoopud!"
A wave of agony swept across Trerin as someone touched him, even though he could sense that they were trying to be gentle.
"Thass hurt!"
"What'er we gonna dew with et? We carn't leave et."
"We cahn't leave et hare nor we cahn't jes move et. Thass in aagony, por theng."
"Gie us the shuhvel, Jonti, I'll do et."
Something about the last few words sounded very wrong. Trerin opened his eyes to see a man standing over him holding a shovel, its blade poised above his neck. Two other men stood nearby watching.
His gleaning was screaming a warning at him, and he fought to clear his mind to understand what the danger was.
The man with the shovel suddenly flew backwards across the yard, an astonished look on his face. He landed heavily against a wall and the shovel continued across the floor to come to rest in the stream of the millrace that powered the mill. The other men watched this occurrence with wide eyes and gasps of consternation
"NO!"
That was Seldar bellowing over the sound of galloping hooves.
"Step away from him."
Seldar sounded half furious, half terrified, and his emotions felt through their link matched his voice. Trerin wondered why, but he was too tired to chase the thought.
"Es tha yoor eagle, Lourdshup?" a voice asked.
"In a manner of speaking," Seldar replied as he crouched beside Trerin's crumpled form.

Trerin felt a healing probe travel through his body, poking into wounds and broken bones, then examining the damage to his Seta.

"Lad, you're badly hurt, but you have to change back. I can't heal you like this! I'm useless with birds!"

Trerin felt a tingle in his skull, and then he was once again fully aware of his surroundings, and his injuries.

And the pain!

He now understood what had almost happened a moment before. Death at the hands of a well-meaning farmer would have been ironic after surviving a battle with a Zindon, Thank the Lord of Light that Seldar had arrived in time.

He also understood what Seldar had said. Trerin must shapeshift back to his usual form in order for Seldar to heal his injuries. Seldar's understanding of bird anatomy was not yet good enough to attempt to heal him in this form.

Shapeshifting while injured was going to hurt.

A lot.

If only he could change shape into a healthy unbroken body, but he couldn't – it didn't work like that. His body was broken and would remain broken in whatever form he adopted.

As he changed shape, his bones and muscles would change size and position, dragging the broken edges into new places and probably tearing new injuries. The armour that would appear around his limbs would further complicate the process by forcing bent, twisted, limbs to move to fit within it. Seldar could dampen the pain when he was human again, but not before. Trerin needed to feel his body fully to be able to change form.

He gathered his will, concentrated on his human appearance and released his Gift into the image. He screamed as his body lengthened, stretched and warped, broken eagle bones enlarging and becoming broken human bones, their positions twisted and warped by the pull of muscles which became stronger and moved to their human positions, pulling the bones with them.

The pain was excruciating, but he had no choice other than to bear it.

The watching farmers jumped back with exclamations of fear, except for the man Seldar had thrown across the yard, who was retrieving the shovel from the stream.

"Tha int no eagle!"

"Darken me! Thass a person!"

"The're Teerens! Thassa Ponfer! Kerji, yew narely chopped the hed offa Ponfer!"

"I nehver!"

"Yew did, bor. Yer muhther'l loike this'n when we tell 'er."

"I dint kno! I dint kno, Lourdship!"

"I know, or I would have been considerably less gentle," Seldar replied.

Trerin finished his shapeshift and gasped, "It's done."

Immediately he felt numbness wash over his body as Seldar applied a pain block. He could still feel *something* as Seldar began to work, but the pain was distant, more like a memory than an active thing.

"You – put the shovel down, and help me. The breastplate unbuckles either side; that plate folds open to reveal the clips. You – fetch clean water and lots of it."

Seldar gave instructions briskly and soon they had lifted off Trerin's breastplate to reveal the very deep gashes underneath – that was the most serious injury, stretching from Trerin's collarbone down across his stomach.

Blood loss was beginning to remove the alertness that Seldar had given him to enable him to shapeshift, and Trerin's mind began to drift.

Healing

Seldar had not seen much of the fight at first, hidden as he was beneath overhanging branches, but he felt Trerin's initial surprise, and had been shocked when Trerin's location had abruptly changed to be high in the sky.

He suspected then what the lad faced – no derstral could translocate, and Trerin did not possess that Gift.

Leaving Trerin's horse and the packhorse tethered to a gate, Seldar wrapped his invisibility illusion tightly around himself and his horse, and sent his mount galloping along the track.

He could see the distant falling speck, he felt Trerin's injury and caught an echo of the lightless void that attacked the lad's Seta. He felt the moment of understandable panic, and the self-fury that followed it. He felt, too, the moment of decision, and saw the distant bird fold its wings and dive, although he could not see its target.

He knew that Trerin was badly injured, weakened, and that the lad expected to die.

Seldar had felt one Ponfour die and did not want to repeat the experience. His inability to join the fight frustrated and infuriated him, but with no visible target he could do nothing except gallop furiously towards the distant battle.

Trerin's location was suddenly high in the sky again, and Seldar could feel the resumed attack on the lad's Seta. Then, unexpectedly, the situation reversed; Trerin was winning the battle – Seldar could feel the lad's concentration and his growing triumph.

As he galloped onwards, the falling speck, which had appeared to be such a long way up, was now rushing towards the ground. Seldar saw the eagle plunge into trees beside a mill a short distance ahead.

He expanded his sense through the bond, Trerin was badly injured, broken, and would soon die without healing.

He urged his horse onwards, cursing himself for his weight that slowed it down, and using healing to keep its tired muscles working. He could see, ahead of him, the group of men who had gathered to stare at something in the yard, and realised with horror what was intended when one picked up a shovel and handed it to another who positioned it for a downward thrust.

Seldar created a moving, expanding block of solid air in front of that man, sending him and the shovel flying backward.

The Sorcerer jumped down from his horse, throwing himself to his knees painfully on the cobbled yard surface. He barely noticed what was said to him, and he answered automatically, as he sent a healing probe into his Ponfour.

The lad was barely conscious, his entire body broken, and though the damage to his Seta was not a great as Seldar had feared, his power was badly depleted. Seldar had only recently begun to study bird anatomy and knew that he could not repair Trerin in this form. The lad would have to shift back first.

"Lad, you're badly hurt, but you have to change back. I can't heal you like this; I'm useless with birds."

He sent healing energy into the lad's mind and brought him back to consciousness. A moment later the eagle began to stretch and grow. The bird shrieked in pain, which turned into a human scream, as his body writhed and twisted with the shift to its normal form. The larger human muscles pulled on unanchored broken bones and dragged them into new positions.

As soon as Trerin finished the shift, Seldar applied a pain block to the lad's body and decided what to tackle first as he told one of the watching farmers to help him remove the chest armour.

He unfastened the central clips of the damaged chain mail and pushed it off Trerin's torso. He quickly sliced through the torn padded leather undershirt, revealing the damage below it. Murmurs of sympathy followed the revealing of the wounds.

Seldar felt Trerin begin to drift back towards unconsciousness and knew that he would have to work quickly.

"Where's that water?" he demanded, as the man came running up with a jug and a mug. Seldar grabbed the jug, and transmuted a hollow, invisible tube, through which he pushed the water.

Trerin had lost too much blood, and he must replace it before he did anything else. Seldar sent the tube down Trerin's throat and into his stomach and pushed the water along it. He handed back the jug with a muttered "more please," and then speeded up selected areas in Trerin's metabolism, so that the water was quickly absorbed. Blood began to flow more easily, oozing out of some lesser wounds, pumping rapidly out of others.

Other watchers had gathered around, both men and women. One of the women watched for a minute and then organised others to fetch more jugs of water.

Seldar worked quickly, looking at the ragged deep slash across chest and stomach first. The shattered left ribs were clearly visible; however, by some miracle the lungs were not punctured, so the belly wound was the most serious.

Seldar sank his Gift and his hands into the wound. He pushed organs and tissues back into their approximate places and then speeded up the healing process so that they joined back together as he watched. The watchers gasped in amazement as tissues flowed back together and became whole, though Seldar heard some muttering about dirt.

He felt Trerin's return to consciousness with relief.

"Welcome back, lad." He smiled as the eyes opened again. "I was beginning to think you planned to sleep right through. You won't be able to talk until I finish this next bit. I'm feeding oxygen directly into your blood, and keeping your lungs still so I can work on the ribs."

He turned back to the chest, and began piecing together bones and rejoining them until the ribcage was rebuilt. Then he concentrated and the connective tissues regrew. Finally, he covered the scar with a fresh growth of skin.

Then he released his hold on Trerin's lungs, monitoring them for a while, as Trerin began to breathe on his own again, to be sure that the repair would hold. It did. Seldar realised that he had been holding his own breath, and took a few deep breaths of his own before turning his attention to the other injuries.

He quickly removed the half plate from arms and legs, and cut away the leather padding.

The injuries there were not as bad as he had feared at first. Multiple compound fractures of both legs, left arm and shoulder likewise, and several fingers of the right hand were also cracked, but the other bones were intact. Trerin's leg bones would be the hardest to straighten so Seldar would begin there.

"Lad, I know you're one of those who doesn't take well to the sensation, but I must disconnect you for a few minutes while we straighten these legs. Your muscles will fight if I don't, and it'll take much longer to get the bones re-aligned, and likely cause more damage as we do it."

He felt Trerin's resignation as the lad replied faintly, "If you must, but don't stop for a drink midway through."

Seldar laughed. "I'll try not to do that."

He sank his mind into Trerin's nervous system. He deepened the pain block to total loss of feeling below the neck, with the sole exception of a single channel of sensation from his lungs, which would allow Trerin to feel himself breath. This was necessary to stop the lad's muscles resisting the attempt to extend them as the bones were realigned back into their original positions.

Seldar knew that Trerin was one of those who found the lack of feeling unbearably unpleasant to the point of panic. All healers learnt the technique by first experiencing it. Some found the lack of sensation pleasantly soothing, but shapeshifters were often badly affected by it, finding the inability to feel their own bodies distressing in the extreme.

Seldar looked up at the watching faces.

"You, shovel-man, get down here and take hold just below his knee. Firmly now."

He looked at another man while Kerji obediently grasped Trerin's knee.

"You, come next to me and be ready to take his foot when I tell you."

The man crouched beside him his hands ready.

Seldar took a firm grip of Trerin's foot and began to pull, firmly but carefully straightening the leg, until the protruding bones slid back inside the torn flesh.

"Hold it, just here, no movement."

He waited until the man had the foot solidly held, and then let go of his own grip. Once again, he pushed his fingers into the wound and adjusted the bones before fusing them together.

"I'm not doing a full fuse now, Trerin, just enough to keep them in place while I get you completely, err straightened out, so to speak," he told his Ponfour.

Seldar worked as rapidly as he could, but he could see that the lad's breathing had quickened, and feel the effort that Trerin was making to remain calm while he endured the disconnection from his own body.

"What was it that you fought, lad?"

He asked, suspecting the answer but hoping that the distraction of conversation would help Trerin retain his composure in front of these farmers. He felt the effort with which Trerin focussed his mind enough to answer, and sent support through the bond to help him.

"I thought at first it was a derstral."

Trerin's voice was faint, but firm. There were some gasps from the farmers as he mentioned the legendary predator.

"It looked like one, but then it translocated and that's not a derstral power. And when I got close I could feel the wrongness within it – a black hungry void."

He took a deep, steadying, breath and then continued, "It was a Zindon, Seldar, and it was hunting us."

There were more gasps from the farmers, and some looked around at the ground and hurriedly stepped into sunlight if they found that they stood in a shadow of any kind. Others picked up shovels and scythes and began looking around as if they expected immediate attack.

Seldar continued working. One of the men assisting had begun to stand at the mention of the Zindon, but a look from Seldar sent him scurrying back to his position.

"Are you sure it was hunting us, lad?" Seldar asked, as he worked on Trerin's other leg.

"It attacked the illusion you made, and later, when it thought I was beaten, it started a clear search pattern, trying to trace you by the residual energy from your invisibility illusion."

Trerin's certainty coloured the bond, and Seldar had to agree that it sounded as though it had indeed been hunting for them.

"Did you kill it?" he asked, as he began work on Trerin's arm.

"No."

Seldar looked up at the puzzlement that suddenly coloured the lad's mind.

"But I'm not sure that it's still a Zindon," Trerin finished.

"What do you mean, lad?" Seldar asked, pausing to drink some of the water before continuing. Despite his promise he could not keep up this pace without a short break.

Trerin was silent, letting the memory run through his mind, before he said,

"There was a terrible, old, unhealed wound within it, where its Seta should have been. It was killing me, and nothing I did was affecting it. My gleaning pointed at that wound, so I tried to heal it."

"You healed a Zindon!" Seldar interjected, as startled as he had ever been.

Similar murmurs of astonishment spread through the watching farmers.

Trerin smiled weakly.

"I suspect no one ever tried it before, but it worked. As soon as I began, the Zindon screamed as though I was inflicting the most intense pain imaginable. The black energy inside it writhed away from the healing, and began to shrink as the healed area spread. The Zindon had been consuming my Seta and channelling it into that darkness, but as I healed it, my Seta began to fill the new area instead of vanishing into the void. By the time it broke free from my grip it felt almost human again – the dark energy had gone. I don't know if it can survive, or if it's trapped as a derstral permanently, or if the dark energy can return."

Seldar suddenly realised that he had paused in his work.

"There's just your shoulder to do now, lad, but I'll have to roll you over," he said as he returned to his task, gesturing to his helpers to roll Trerin onto his side and support him there.

He had to transmute part of the chain mail to pull it away from the shoulder, and once again transmuted the immediately underlying leather jerkin to air.

"Did you see what became of it, after it broke free?" he asked as he pulled out his belt knife.

The shoulder was broken into several pieces and Seldar needed to peel back the flesh to be able to get his fingers in the required places. Some of the villagers, who had been watching with fascination, suddenly ran out of sight, though not out of earshot, as Seldar plunged his blade into the skin around the joint. He could hear them retching somewhere nearby, much to the amusement of stronger-stomached farmers.

Seldar smoothed the flesh back over the rebuilt shoulder, and rolled Trerin back. He checked that he had dealt with everything necessary, and then reconnected Trerin's mind to his body.

Trerin took a deep shuddering breath as a single convulsion went down his body at the resumption of sensation, then he began flexing his fingers and limbs to be sure that they worked. He looked up at Seldar and grinned, a shadow of his normal brightness, but an improvement on his earlier appearance.

"Nice work, Seldar, thank you, and to answer your question: no, I didn't see where it went."

"Sumthen splashed inter thu river, same time yew splashed in thu yahd – I cuunt see what thet wus tho." One of the women spoke up excitedly. "Dew yew reckon thet wus thu Zindon?"

"Maybe," Seldar replied, watching Trerin carefully.

"No you don't, lad," he said quickly, at the moment that Trerin started to press his weight onto his hands to stand up.

"I told you, I've only fused the bones lightly so you can't stand on them yet. If you recrack them through impatience I may just leave them to heal naturally next time."

Trerin sank back onto the ground, the pain that had shot through his left arm and shoulder giving emphasis to Seldar's words.

"You'll need to rest and sleep now, to replenish your Seta, and also to allow your body to recognise that it's already partly healed. I'll finish your healing tomorrow. Don't attempt to rise again until I say so. That's an order, Trerin, so no Ponfourii stubbornness!"

Trerin nodded. A wave of weariness had washed over him when he had tried to stand, so Seldar was sure that he would not try again.

Seldar looked up at the watching locals.

"Is there somewhere I can set up a camp, while he recuperates?" he asked the group.

The young man, who had so nearly decapitated Trerin, spoke to the older woman who had organised the water fetching.

"The lad shunt ha' tuh camp, Ma, he cun ha' my bed. Oi'll goo in tha bahn."

Seldar felt Trerin glare at him, and grinned an apology. He had been trying hard in recent days to remember not to call Trerin 'lad' in front of villagers, but it had completely slipped his mind in this crisis.

The woman had also seen Trerin's look and correctly interpreted it. She clipped Kerji around the ear.

"He's a Ponfer, end he's jus bait a Zindon. He int no lad! He's a Lourdship and dun't yew ferget et!"

Seldar was probably the only person who heard Trerin's "Thank you, Lady."

The lad was more than halfway asleep now.

"He call em 'lad' the whoel toime he work on em," protested Kerji, pointing at Seldar.

His mother drew herself up and clipped his ear again.

"The Lourdshup cun cahl hes Ponfer 'Petal' if he wahnt tew, but thet doon't main thet yew cen doew the same!"

Seldar grinned broadly, as Trerin's eyes flew open and he twisted his head to stare at the woman in disbelief, then he turned to fix a very determined gaze on Seldar.

"The 'Lordship' can *not* call me any such thing!" he said firmly, if with less volume than he had probably intended. "I mean it, Seldar, not even once!"

Seldar laughed, and concentrated on projecting a feeling of sincerity and innocence. "Would I do such a thing?"

Trerin gave him a look of deep suspicion, and then sank his head back onto the ground. Seldar sensed the tiredness that had claimed him again after his brief alertness, and quickly sent a healing probe through him; the depletion of his Seta from the fight, coupled with the stress to his system of the healing forcing quick bone and tissue regrowth, were the cause.

"Lad, the best thing for you now is sleep, so sleep."

Seldar used his Gift to trigger deep dreamless sleep. Trerin resisted at first, but then succumbed.

"Thare I goo, sayn thu wrong theng. I'm as bahd as Kerji!" the woman had walked closer.

"Howsumever," she continued, "he hev tha rite iydare. The young Lourdshup shun't havta cahmp after he sayved us all from uh Zindon so yew'll buoth stay in owr hoome fer as lohng as yew naed."

She looked over at her son.

"Kerji! Doo yew get tha grayn sacks offa tha caht an inter tha mill. The young Lourdshup cahn lie on thet an we'll draive 'im hum"

"That's very kind of you, lady, I accept, thank you," Seldar replied, once he had translated her offer.

She smiled, smoothed her apron, and replied,

"Thass polite uh yew, Loourdshup, but thass just Gal, thass not 'Lady'. Oi'm Gal Alsy, Tha thare's tha Bor Kerji, moy ehldest," she said, pointing with her chin at her son, who was rapidly removing sacks from a cart.

"An tha thare's the Bor Alcor, moy Husman." She indicated a man of similar age to herself, who nodded at the introduction.

"Gal and Bor, are these titles?" asked Seldar. A ripple of laughter followed his question, which Gal Alsy waved down.

"Wull, ina mahnner uh' spayking thay are, I spooz. Thass just how wa're called, all on us."

Seldar nodded.

"I'm Seldar, and this is my Ponfour, Trerin. Perhaps someone can lift him onto the cart for me, please? He's a little long for me. Don't worry about waking him, he won't awaken now for many hours. I've placed him in a deep sleep to continue healing."

Two men carefully lifted Trerin and placed him gently onto the cart. Seldar gathered up the pieces of armour and leather from the floor and pushed them beside Trerin. He looked at the pools of blood in the yard and the stains on his hands and clothes, and transmuted them away.

Alcor and Alsy climbed onto the front of the cart, and Seldar mounted his horse to ride beside them. Then he remembered something, and called down to the folk remaining in the yard.

"Oh! I tethered two horses a mile or two up the track. I'll fetch them once I've seen Trerin settled. No one can fetch them for me, I'm afraid, because they don't react well to strangers. It will be best if no one tries to touch them."

Alcor flicked the reins and his cart began to move, he kept the pace slow, to avoid jolting Trerin.

A short time later, they arrived at a cluster of buildings, surrounded by fields. A well-built, large, two-storey building with two large wings, was the family's residence, and proclaimed them successful and moderately wealthy.

The main residence was built completely of shaped stone, while the two wings were half-timbered. A small number of pigs, a flock of hens, the kitchen, and a dairy, occupied the ground floor rooms. The family lived in the upper storey, which was reached by a flight of steps running up the side of one wing.

"Just yew wait hare, Lourdshup, while wey goo and clare owr rums for yew. Thet wun't tek long."

Gal Alsy jumped off the cart and trotted up the steps, followed by her laconic husband.

Seldar dismounted and tethered his horse next to the water trough. Then he checked Trerin, and sent another healing probe into the lad's Seta to reassure himself that the damage was not life threatening and it would replenish with rest.

It felt very strange for the lad's mind to be so deeply sunk in sleep. Ponfourii usually slept like nervous cats when out of Tyreen, with part of them always alert and ready for action. Now, though, Trerin's mind was almost silent with just the faintest trace in Seldar's consciousness.

Light! The lad looked like a sick child lying there so still, for all he was so tall. The relaxation that accompanied deep sleep, smoothed the few lines from his face, and removed about ten years from his age.

Farmstead

Seldar sent a heartfelt prayer of thanks to the God of Light, for not calling the lad back to him just yet.

The Sorcerer knew that it had been a very near thing. If Trerin hadn't thought to try healing the Zindon, or if the tree and mill roof had not broken his fall, or if Seldar had arrived a minute later, Trerin would be dead.

He knew how it felt when the bond snapped at the sudden death of a Ponfour. Not only all the usual grief that accompanied the death of a close friend, but also the pain of amputation, as though part of his brain had been ripped from his skull.

Afterwards, when the first pain had receded, it left behind a lonely emptiness where before there had been a constant presence.

Seldar was not sure he would survive the feeling a second time. Only the call of duty had enabled him to move past Arella's death and eventually choose a new Ponfour.

Not for the first time, Seldar wondered what in the Light had induced him to pick such a young Warrior for his Ponfour. He had not intended to choose a youngster when he had been deciding which of the available and interested Warriors to interview earlier that year. He had deliberately only interviewed Warriors close to his own age, except for Trerin. He had included Trerin purely because of the practical joke that the lad had played a few years earlier on Midsummer Day. Seldar had been impressed with both the scale of the joke, and the audacious nature of it, targeting, as it had, the Cathedral in Tyre.

He'd only wanted to meet the person responsible and yet, somehow, ended up choosing the lad. In many ways, Trerin reminded him of a younger version of himself. Seldar's own best Midsummer Day joke, so many years before, had been equally audacious, targeting the then very young king Tarek.

Seldar's mind returned to the present, he had been correct that their relationship would be different from the usual Sorcerer/Ponfour partnership. The lad was, after all, almost half his age, and Seldar often felt more like an uncle or even grandfather towards him.

"And I am *not* that old!"

"But sumtimes yew feel ut, doon't yew. Thass how et es with yungsters: won minnut yew feel hahf yor age, an then thay mek yew feel tired loike yor three times older'n what yew are!"

Seldar looked up, startled, to see the Gal Alsy looking at him over the other side of the cart. He chuckled wearily in response to her sentence.

"You're right: that's exactly how it is. And right now, I feel so tired, I feel more like four times my age."

She nodded, an understanding look on her face.

"Yew thort he wuz gorn back to God, din't yew. Fust a Zindon, an then my Bor Kerji with 'is shuhvel."

Seldar shuddered.

"Oh yes! That certainly gave me a shock: knowing Trerin was alive, but seeing someone about to drop a shovel on his neck."

"I spooz thet did! Thass a gifting from the Light thet yew were thare in toime."

She shook her head fondly.

"He've a good harht my bor. He wun't leave an animal te suhffer, an' if he cahn't help ut, he'll kill ut fahst, but thes time he were a bit too fahst."

"I hope I didn't hurt him too much when I knocked him away. Normally I would approve his intention, but not when the animal in question is my shapeshifted Ponfour!"

"A foow bruises wun't huht 'um, he've had wuhrs'en thet from the old boar thare." She nodded toward a large boar, with impressive tusks, grazing in the nearby field. "Anyway, he'd'uh never f'given hisself ifn he'd killed a Ponfer by mistake."

She straightened, as three figures came around a corner and entered the yard.

"Hare cum Alcor now, an' thass Jarrol an' Colm, my other two bors. Thay'll carry the Ponfer up to Kerji's rum. Thoo Oi dun't kno how he'll fit on thu bed, he's taller'n Kerji by abowt three heads!"

"We'll manage," replied Seldar. "He can lie on his side, curled up if need be."

Alcor climbed up onto the cart and got a good grip under Trerin's shoulders, while the two younger men grasped a leg each. They lifted him off the cart, and managed to carry him up the stairs. The process was not a dignified one, and was not aided by the continuing fragmentation of what was left of Trerin's padded leather clothing. Seldar picked up the pieces that fell off, as he followed them up the stairs.

He could have translocated Trerin up into the room, but he had used a great deal of energy in the healing and as the locals were willing, he saw no reason not to accept their help.

A couple of young women were peering around the dairy door, and watching the procession with interest and many giggles.

Seldar sighed – the lad could flirt even when unconscious! He picked up another large piece of Trerin's trousers, which had fallen off to the accompaniment of loud giggling.

Gal Alsy hurried across the yard and ushered the girls inside. They were unmistakably more of her offspring – both resembling her closely.

Inside the house, they carried Trerin through a large family gathering room, along a corridor, and into a good-sized bedroom. As the eldest son, Kerji occupied the second-best bedroom alone.

A large brick fireplace, empty now in the heat of early summer, was built into one wall, opposite which stood a well-made, solid bed. The mattress and bolster were stuffed with scented herbs and straw, filling the room with a pleasant fragrance. The rest of the room contained a chair, table, and several chests, plus two large cupboards, built into the wall either side of the fireplace.

They placed Trerin on the bed, but even with his head up against the headboard, his feet dangled off the bottom end.

Seldar rolled him onto his side and tucked his legs up.

"There! He'll be fine on his side. Leave him to me; I'll settle him. Thank you for your help."

Seldar politely, but firmly, ushered the men out of the room and closed the door.

He quickly removed what little of Trerin's clothing remained attached, and piled it on a chest with the pieces that he had picked up earlier.

He would have to repair it later, but Trerin's horse and the packhorse had been left tethered untended for some time now and he wanted to fetch them as soon as possible before he slept to begin replenishing his Seta lost to the healing.

He pulled the hand knitted blanket over Trerin and then left the room.

He found Alsy waiting for him in the gathering room.

"Will thet do Lourdshup?" she asked anxiously.

"Yes, the room is fine. Thank you," he replied, "but I must go and fetch the other horses."

He frowned over his shoulder in the direction of Trerin's room. He did not like leaving the lad alone, when he was unconscious and a Zindon was somewhere in the area, but he had no choice. No one else could fetch the horses – Trerin's stallion, Darren, was very bad tempered towards strangers who tried to touch him.

"Thuh sooner yew gohw, thuh sooner yew get back," said Alsy.

Seldar nodded and forced himself to move. He stepped briskly downstairs to his horse, and set off at a canter.

An hour later, he returned, leading Darren and the packhorse. He saw all three horses stabled and fed, and then followed his nose to the kitchen, where he was delighted to find that the evening meal was almost ready to serve. He was ravenous, and not only did the food smell delicious, there appeared to be plenty of it.

Alsy left the final preparations with her daughters, and took Seldar to the eating room, stopping on the way to show him the bedroom that would be his, and the private wash and comfort room that led off it.

He left his and Trerin's baggage in the bedroom, and returned to the eating room to eat his meal which tasted as good as it smelled. Then he excused himself and went to bed for the sleep he could feel trying to claim him.

Next morning, Seldar was woken by the sounds of activity in the yard. Opening the shutter a crack, he saw that the sun was just above the horizon, and the family were beginning work for the day. His Seta felt almost fully replenished. Trerin's injuries had been severe, but uncomplicated, and the healing had taken less than an hour. The good night's sleep had brought Seldar's Seta back almost to normal levels.

He dressed and went to check on Trerin, who had not moved from the position in which they had left him the previous day.

Seldar sent a healing probe into him and checked his Seta. The damage was starting to heal and his energy had partially replenished, but Seldar decided that he would need another day of complete rest.

Seldar then checked the areas that he had healed the previous day, and also the lad's general health. As he had expected, the lad's physical reserves were completely depleted and he would need to eat a large meal before the healing could continue.

Seldar decided to leave him sleeping until food was ready. He would be ravenous when he awoke.

Seldar made his way down to the kitchen, where he found Alsy just starting the fire in the range, while one of her daughters was beginning to assemble a selection of foods ready to prepare for their firstmeal.

"Sunrise on yew, Lourdshup. Did yew sleep restfuhl?"

"Light shine on you, yes, thank you. I hope that you did also? And your sons?" Seldar replied.

Alsy and Alcor had taken the room usually occupied by their younger sons, who had slept in the barn with their older brother.

"Way all slept cumf'table, Lourdshup, thass gud ev yew to ahsk. How's the young Lourdshup?"

"He's improving, thank you, Gal Alsy, but he'll need to eat a very substantial meal before I can continue the healing. At what time you usually eat your morning meal?" Seldar asked.

Alsy looked a little anxious.

"Thet wun't be for anuhther hour or two yet, Lourdship, we're oonly just lit the ohven! Jes an' the bors hev gone teh milk thuh cows, and collect thuh eggs, but thet'll be more'n a foow minuts befor thare done."

"There's no immediate rush," Seldar hurried to reassure her. "I'll leave him asleep for now, but he'll be ravenous when he wakes up, because of the healing."

She looked puzzled so Seldar explained,

"The magic speeds up the body's natural healing processes, but the new flesh and bone come from the body's available resources – it isn't created magically. Trerin didn't have a great deal of fat on him, but right now he has none at all, and I had to borrow protein and other elements from uninjured or less injured areas, to fuse his bones and seal the wounds. At the moment, his body resembles that of someone who has gone a full week without food. He will need to eat a very large amount of flesh and fat, before I can finish his healing, or he could die of starvation as I worked."

Her eyes widened as she listened, then she laughed.

"Well, thass a gud theng this es a fahrm, lourdshup. We're got loodsa those. Alcor killed a buhlluck lass noight, and thare's plenty a cheese an craym, an' wey'll soon hev loodsa fresh milk. Yew say he'll need loods? Loods he'll hev." She nodded to emphasise her words.

"That's very kind of you, thank you," Seldar said.

Alsy shrugged off his thanks.

"Thass owr dooty, Lourdshup. Whare'd wey be without yew Guardians? None 'er us could'er fought a Zindon up in thuh air. Thass oonly roight we luk ahfter thoose who cahn."

She jabbed a ladle in the air to emphasise her words, before giving a stir to the contents of the porridge pot, congealed after sitting overnight on the range top.

"Now, Lourdshup, do yew sit down, end oi'll pore yew some kehris. Thass made from some herbs we grow speshull, see what yew think."

She poured a steaming stream of hot brown liquid from a large pot into a mug.

"There's honey thare, if yew wahnt et, sum loike the drink sweet."

Seldar took a sip, and then added a spoon of honey. The flavour was mild and pleasantly refreshing.

"Oi never thort about how healing wouhd work," Alsy mused. "Oi spooz oi always jus thort, thass magic, I never thort that et would need oordinary thengs loike food an water. I thought magic jus made what was needed from nothing."

"Oh no!" Seldar told her. "Magic has its rules like other things. You can't make something from nothing; there has to be something to begin with. And you can't create living flesh from something non-living."

He drained his cup and she poured more for him. Her daughter, Jes, entered carrying two buckets of fresh foaming milk. Some of this she poured into a large jug, and the rest went into a large metal urn. She sealed the lid carefully and then carried the urn across to a door in the corner, which opened onto stairs leading down under the building. She disappeared down the stairs.

"I could transmute something into an object that appeared to be alive, but it would be an illusion of life only, with no ability to move without my manipulation, and no mind."

Seldar remembered the mist monster that Tam had created while controlled by the Zindon – it had appeared very alive at the time. He remembered how tired Tam had been afterwards, from such an expenditure of energy.

"So yew coon't jus make noo blud 'n boons yew had to tell hes body to make 'em fahster 'n what it woold normally? And thet used up all what he'd aten and had stored thare, soo now he hev t' eat twice as much to get back to whare he were?"

Alsy nodded her understanding.

"Doon't yew wohrry Lourdshup, we'll soon hev him filled up again. And yew too, cahn't feed him 'n not yew."

Seldar laughed.

"I appreciate that! Healing is hungry work!"

He put down his mug.

"That was a very refreshing drink, thank you, Gal Alsy. I'll stay out of your way, until you tell me you're ready."

As he got up to leave, Jes returned to the kitchen from below, and picking up the empty buckets, left the kitchen to fetch more milk. Seldar went out into the yard and looked across the fields towards the distant river.

Somewhere out there was the Zindon, and Seldar knew that whatever happened, he and Trerin could not leave this region until they knew what had become of it.

He wandered idly around the yard, watching the activity with curiosity; he had grown up within Tyre, in a craft family, and knew little of farming. He watched Jes milking cows for a short time, and backed quickly out of the pig stall that Kerji was cleaning – the smell was almost overpowering!

After a while he went back to Trerin's room and examined the remnants of the lad's leather clothes. He would have to repair both them and his mail eventually, but he had used a lot of power yesterday, and still had more work to do on Trerin's healing.

"Come in," he replied, in response to a knock at the door.

The door opened and Alsy entered, followed by her youngest daughter, who looked to be about fifteen years old, both carried trays which were piled high with food.

The aroma of cooked meat made Seldar remember how hungry he was, and he knew that Trerin would feel ravenous.

They deposited their burdens onto a chest and Alsy slid two clean plates from underneath a bowl that was filled with what looked like chops, and pulled forks, knives, and spoons, from her apron pocket.

"Thare yew go," she said, as she removed bowls from the trays and distributed them around the chest top.

"Thare's steaks, chops, blood puhdding, ehggs, cheese, onions, bread, buhtter, honey, milk, and some porrij too. End thare's some more kehris too."

She nodded at one of the jugs, "There's more as well if yew need it."

Seldar stared at the feast, and quickly judged the amount.

"That will be plenty for now, thank you, but he will need a little more in about an hour. I'm sorry that we are putting you to so much trouble,"

Alsy smoothed down her apron, and picked up the empty trays.

"Thass noo truhble, Lourdshup, cuhm on Sash."

She took a step, and looked back at her daughter, who was staring in fascination at the exotic yellow-haired stranger asleep in her brother's bed.

“Sash!" Alsy called sharply, and the girl jumped and followed her out of the room.

Seldar snorted, and shook his head, and then filled the two empty plates with food.

He put one hand on Trerin's head and carefully removed the sleep compulsion that he had applied the previous day.

Trerin's eyes flew open immediately and he straightened, knocking his head on the headboard, and sending his feet flopping over the end of the bed. He didn't appear to notice the blow to his skull, and Seldar reminded himself that Ponfourii bones were dense so maybe he really had hardly felt it.

"Where are we?" Trerin asked, his eyes flicking around the room, taking in the layout and furnishings.

"We are staying in the home of the woman you may remember from yesterday: the mother of the man who nearly beheaded you with a shovel. Her name is Gal Alsy."

Trerin nodded, and then pushed himself up the bed until he was leaning against the headboard and his feet were back under the bedcover.

"Careful, lad, your left arm bones still aren't very strong," Seldar reminded him, and held out a plate of food.

Trerin's eyes widened as his hunger surged, and he seized the plate, and began to stuff his mouth. Seldar too started to eat.

When Trerin had emptied his plate, the Sorcerer handed him a mug. The Ponfour took a deep gulp and gagged.

"Seldar! This is milk!" he protested in disgust. "I haven't drunk milk since I was five!"

Trerin's family came from a region of Tyreen where milk was drunk only by young children.

"It contains calcium, which you need, so you'll drink it, and eat the cheese I've put on here." Seldar indicated the plate.

"The cheese is one thing Seldar, but milk? It tastes revolting, and I can smell the cow!" Trerin grumbled.

"Drink. That's an order, Trerin. Your body needs something to work with if I'm to finish healing those long lanky bones of yours."

Trerin opened his mouth to continue, but Seldar waggled a finger at him.

"I *said*," he stressed the word, "that's an order."

He pointed at the mug, and sent a determined pulse along the bond to emphasise his command. Trerin's mouth closed with a snap on whatever he had been about to say. Seldar did not often give orders, but the Ponfour Oath included a vow of service and obedience.

"Yes, my Lord," he replied, reluctantly.

Trerin drained the mug as quickly as he could, pulling a face at the taste. Seldar removed the empty mug, and handed over the well-filled plate.

"Good lad. Now eat up everything on this plate so that I can finish your healing."

A short time later Seldar removed the emptied plate and placed it on the chest with the other, mostly empty, dishes. He poured another mug of milk and handed it to Trerin, who drank it with a shudder, but without resuming his earlier protest. Seldar refilled the mug again, this time with water, which Trerin drank with more enthusiasm.

"This will be uncomfortable for you, but I must speed your digestion, to release the nutrients to finish your healing."

Trerin chuckled.

"I suspect it will be uncomfortable for you too. You had better open all the windows first. You know what happens!"

Seldar grimaced, but the lad was correct so he opened all the windows as wide as they would go, and returned to the bed.

"Make yourself as comfortable as you can," he said, before putting one hand on Trerin's head, and another on his stomach. He concentrated and released his healing Gift into the lad's body.

Trerin's breathing speed and heart rate increased, and his temperature began to climb, as Seldar speeded up his bodily functions to rapidly digest and release the nutrients of his recent meal. At the same time he speeded the natural healing process and Trerin's bones began to increase in density more quickly than they would have naturally.

Within seconds, sweat was pouring down Trerin's face and torso, soaking the bed. The usual by-products of digestion made the atmosphere unpleasant, but Seldar could not spare the energy to eradicate the gas, so had to endure it.

Suddenly, something else took over the healing. Seldar had been expecting this, and began to withdraw his own power, leaving only a connection that allowed him to observe what was happening. He had observed it before, when he had healed Arella, his first Ponfour.

As the healed flesh and bone reached normal human density, energy suddenly suffused Trerin's body. Bones and flesh altered and became the denser bone and flesh of a Ponfour. This always happened when Ponfourii had been healed, and was caused by the bond itself. No one knew where the energy originated. Some thought it the direct intervention of God, others said that as the bonds were all linked in a slight fashion with all of Tyreen, the energy must come from every living Tyrean.

As suddenly as it had appeared, the energy vanished, and Trerin was physically completely healed, although the tone of his mind, which Seldar could feel through their bond, showed that he felt as exhausted as if he had spent three days in constant battle.

Seldar ran a healing probe through his body, from toes to crown, to check all was complete. Trerin was tired, his Seta was still slightly depleted, and he was once again very hungry, but other than that he was as healthy as normal.

Someone knocked on the door.

"Lourdshup? Oi broughht mor food, like yew ahsked."

"One moment, please," Seldar replied, as he quickly cleansed the air and dried the sweat from the bed. "Enter."

Alsy entered carrying another tray of food.

"Yew said he'd need more en an hour, Lourdshup, so hare et es."

She looked at Trerin, who was sitting up in the bed and eyeing the tray hungrily.

"Well, yew look better then yew did arlier, Lourdshup," she commented, but she saw where his eyes were and, to his surprise, placed the tray directly on his lap, and placed a knife and fork into his hand.

Seldar laughed.

"Trerin, meet our hostess, the Gal Alsy, who cooked the meal we enjoyed earlier. You were half asleep, but you may remember her from yesterday."

He deliberately ran the 'petal' comment through his mind, so that his amusement and a sparkle of anticipation for its future teasing possibilities, would ripple down the bond.

Trerin's eyes flicked towards the Sorcerer, before turning back to Alsy. Seldar felt exaggerated tolerant patience flicker across their link, as the lad spoke.

"I am in your debt, Lady. If I had been forced to rely on what Seldar could hunt or forage, I fear our morning meal would have been sparse indeed and consisted mainly of leaves and roots."

Seldar shrugged.

"It's true, I'm not built for stealthy hunting. All that creeping around trying not to make a noise is not for me."

"Being unable to see where you are putting your feet must make silent stalking quite hard." Trerin nodded in an understanding way. "And finding trees wide enough to hide behind, while you study your prey, must also be a challenge, I expect?" he continued in a tone of innocent enquiry as he pushed his fork into a sausage.

Gal Alsy suddenly developed a very nasty cough, as she tidied the empty dishes from the earlier meal onto the trays, and discreetly left the room, closing the door behind her.

"At least I can cook the things you catch, Trerin," Seldar replied, grinning. "I don't know why you find it so hard to tell when things have cooked long enough, it's really very easy."

"There's nothing wrong with my cooking," Trerin began.

"That another half an hour in the pan, and some seasoning, wouldn't fix," Seldar interrupted automatically, but then he realised that Trerin was eyeing his sausage longingly, and at the same time struggling to stay awake.

"I'm sorry, lad, eat your meal. We can continue this discussion another time. I'll make you sleep again when you're finished, but that will be the last time and only for a few hours. I'll wake you for the midday meal; you should be fully recovered by then."

Trerin nodded, too tired to argue, which was a good thing, thought Seldar, because he was still a little tired himself from yesterday's healing session, and glad that he would not have to waste strength arguing with a stubborn Ponfour.

Zindon

When Trerin was asleep, Seldar took the remaining plate downstairs to the kitchen and, to the surprise of the Gal Alsy, washed it.

"Trerin will have completely recovered when I wake him at midday," he told her.

"I'm afraid we must stay at least until tomorrow. He has exercises that he must do to realign his abilities to his healed body, and I must repair his armour and clothing. Before we leave, though, you and I must discuss some payment for your food and time."

Alsy drew herself up, eyes flashing.

"Payment! Dew Oi look loike a trayder? Guahrdians are welcum hare for as lohng as they need, without talk er payment! We'er got plenty, and to spare."

"I meant no offence, Gal Alsy, but I don't like to take without return, and Trerin was right about my hunting skills. His healing would have taken a great deal longer if we had had to rely for food on what I could catch. There must be some service we can do in thanks."

Seldar prepared himself for the inevitable argument, but then the sound of hooves on the yard cobbles, was followed by hurried, heavy footsteps and Kerji ran into the room panting.

"Lourdshup, Lourdshup, Bor Tahrvin hev cort the Zindon! Do yew cuhm quick an kill et."

Seldar's eyes widened.

"The Zindon? Are you sure?"

Kerji nodded.

"He tell me he check hes trahps this morning and thare thet was, cort in one. He din't kno what thet was, but he say thass loike a lizzuhd but size loike a sheep, an ets bleuw an brown an green, and has huge claws, and loods of teeth, and he coont go nare et without thet trying to bite. He say if he din't kno better, he'd think thet was a big ol' derstral, so I tell him what happen at the mill, an he cahll me a liar, but then Bor Merl tell him thass all trew, and he say he's not gorn nare thet again, and Oi say Oi'll get yew to kill et."

He took a deep gasping breath in.

"So yew'll cum, wun't yew?"

"Yew kill thet Zindon, an' thass payment enough for everything we'er got," Alsy said with a decided nod.

Seldar smiled; a wolf baring its teeth would have looked less fierce.

"That will be a pleasure," he told her.

Then he turned back to Kerji.

"Wait here while I fetch my armour and saddle my horse, then take me to this Zindon."

He was very glad that Trerin was asleep. He knew that the lad would have insisted on killing the creature himself, but Seldar wanted to be the one who destroyed it. This Zindon had almost killed his Ponfour – Seldar intended to make it wish that it had never entered this kingdom.

Within a few minutes, Seldar was armoured, armed, and mounted. He followed Bor Kerji along tracks through a forest until they reached a small clearing containing a several rough wooden huts. A pungent stench emanated from the tanning pits in a fenced area, and there were several people busy scraping fat from skins stretched out on frames. All stopped work to stare at Seldar and Kerji.

One man came up to them, eyes wide.

"Lourdshup, this es Bor Tahrvin," Bor Kerji introduced the man.

"Bor, the Lourdshup'll kill the Zindon for yew. Do yew show him whare thet es."

"He's rarely a Tyreen? Are yew sure? He dun't look like I thort."

Tervin's eyes addressed Kerji while staring at Seldar. Seldar snorted.

"Show me where the creature is, Bor Tahrvin," he said over the top of Kerji's reassurances. "Quickly, before it escapes."

"Thet wun't escape one er my trahps, Lourdshup," Tahrvin told him proudly. "Cum on then, thass this way, yew'll hav tew lave the horse thoo."

He pointed into the wood. Seldar sighed and dismounted. Strapping his sword to his side, he strode after Tahrvin. They jogged along narrow paths in a dense part of the forest. Seldar had to duck underneath the low branches, and sent God a quick prayer of thanks that he was not as tall as Trerin, plus a request for lrenewed strength to deal with the Zindon.

Despite the rapid pace set by the trapper, Seldar had no difficulty keeping up with him. The man stopped and pointed towards a grassy stream bank.

"He's oover thare, Lourdshup, on th'other end er thet chain," he whispered. "I dazen't go narer then this."

Seldar stepped past him and saw a chain lying on the ground. One end was fastened around a tree, undergrowth and bushes obscured the other.

"How long is the chain?" he asked using a normal voice because the creature must already that they were there.

"Thass about two man lengths, Lourdshup," Tahrvin replied, speaking even more quietly than the first time.

Seldar nodded.

"Then you are safe here," he said judging the distance to the tethered end. "My Ponfour has destroyed its ability to use magic."

He hoped that he was correct, but he made himself sound certain, for Tahrvin's benefit.

He focused on the air surrounding the chain, and began a complex transmutation. The air solidified, rippled, and flowed, gripping the chain and pulling powerfully on it. The Zindon was jerked out of the bushes by its front leg. It fell into the track, landing gracelessly on its back, before a twisting leap brought it back onto its feet.

Seldar released the air around the chain and deliberately began walking towards it, sword ready. The Zindon watched him, its intelligent eyes glaring hatred, and its teeth bared.

When he was close enough, it leapt at him as he had expected it would. He grinned. The Zindon froze mid-leap as he solidified the air around it. He could see the muscles in its shoulders moving as it tried to beat its wings, or move its legs, but he held it trapped. It could breathe, and move its eyes, but no other movement was possible.

Seldar stepped up to it and studied the trap that held its right leg in a solid grip of steel.

Nasty!

A spring-fired pair of steel jaws, with long curved and barbed teeth, had snapped closed over paw and lower arm. Dried blood covered the trap, and fresh blood was flowing down the chain as he held the creature suspended.

Seldar did not approve of such traps, but in this instance, he found himself grinning.

"That must hurt a lot," he said conversationally, as he walked around the creature, examining it.

He noted other injuries; its throat and belly were crossed by several deep slashes, all encrusted with dried blood. One laceration was deep and showed signs of starting an infection. These must be the wounds inflicted by Trerin in their battle.

He walked around to its head. The snarl made clear what it would do if he released it, but the shadow-servant was not trying to use magic against him. Seldar could feel no emanations from it at all.

Was Trerin right? Had his healing changed it so that it was no longer a Zindon? He knew only one way to be sure.

Seldar placed his hand on the creature's head. He ignored its futile twitching as it attempted to move, and sank his mind into its body with a healing probe. Inside it, he found a recently healed area. The small quantity of Seta within it had a familiar feel; it was clearly that stolen from Trerin. The Sorcerer could feel no trace of the dark pulsating force of which he had experienced an echo, through the bond, while Trerin fought with this creature.

Trerin was correct, this was no longer a Zindon – this was a human trapped in a derstral body.

Seldar reluctantly sent his mind into the Zindon's. Hatred, violence, a complete disregard for any life but its own, darkness, enjoyment of killing, and worse, flooded into his mind. Seldar broke the connection with revulsion, struggling to keep from vomiting.

He stepped away, mouth twisted in disgust at what he had felt.

"I had thought of leaving you like this," he told it, "trapped forever in the form of an animal. It would be a fitting punishment, I thought, but I can't do that. I know that now. If you were in some other form perhaps, but a derstral is a powerful predator, and you may no longer have any magical powers, but you are still a servant of shadows. You would kill and maim as many as you could."

The creature's eyes almost blazed with its furious effort to break free.

"The problem with killing you is that I will enjoy it. You nearly killed my Ponfour, and I would dearly love to remove your skin one scale at a time, slowly, while you screamed in agony. I would enjoy that immensely, but I don't want to enjoy killing something that is helpless, even you, so I'll do it quickly. It is mercy that you don't deserve, but I do it for me, not for you."

With no further procrastination, Seldar modified the air trap so that the head stretched forwards, extending the neck. He released the air immediately around the neck, which began to twitch more freely, but as head and body remained firmly held, it still could not move far.

He lifted his sword over his head and brought it down on the exposed neck. The Zindon shrieked – a strangely muted sound due to the limited movement of chest and jaw. Seldar's sword had gone no more than half way through because the magically enhanced scales had deflected much of the force.

The Sorcerer could see the twitching that swept across its body and knew that the creature was in agony. He was tempted to pause and let it suffer, but he swung his sword up again, and again let it fall, aiming for the same spot. This time the sword went all the way through, separating the head from the body.

He waited until he was sure that all trace of life had gone before releasing the air that held the Zindon's corpse suspended. Head and body fell to the ground and lay still. Strangely, although the wounds inflicted by Trerin and the trap had all bled freely, the severed ends of the neck bled little.

Seldar pulled a cloth from a pocket and wiped the blade before sheathing it. He looked down at the head and nodded with satisfaction.

"Es thet dead, Lourdshup?"

Seldar had forgotten the presence of Bor Tahrvin until he spoke. The trapper had emerged from behind a tree and was edging nervously closer. Seldar waved him over.

"Yes, it is," he replied. "Do you want the corpse? The skin is very strong, it will make long lasting leather once tanned."

"Es et safe?"

The man stared at the body, then put a hand on it to feel the skin. He jerked it off quickly.

"Thass still warm!"

Seldar laughed.

"Yes, it's safe. It's nothing more than a large dead animal now."

Tahrvin nodded then decisively pulled a knife from a belt sheath. He hesitated just a moment before kneeling to skin the creature. He had trouble making the incisions in belly and legs but, once through the tough scaly skin, he soon detached it from the corpse and rolled it up to carry. They left the head and skinless body to the scavengers and walked back along the track to the huts.

A promise

Seldar and Kerji returned to the farm, Seldar now had several hides strapped to his saddle – a present from the grateful Tahrvin. They would be useful to repair Trerin's clothes destroyed during the healing.

Bor Alcor was in the yard, sharpening an axe, when they arrived. Two small piles of tools lay on the ground beside him. He looked up as they dismounted.

“Es et dead?” he asked, surprising Seldar. Those were the first words that he had heard from Alcor.

“He killed et, Da,” Kerji said, his eyes shining with enthusiasm. “Chopped ets head off, so Bor Tahrvin say.”

Alcor ignored his son and looked at Seldar.

“Es et dead?” he repeated.

“It’s dead,” Seldar confirmed.

“Good,” Alcor grunted, nodding. Then he bent his head back to the axe and grindstone, and resumed his task, seemingly oblivious to anything else.

Seldar raised his eyebrows, shrugged, and led his horse into the stable to unsaddle him.

When he came out, he started to walk past Alcor to get to the steps up to the living floor of the house. Alcor looked up.

“What’s ours is yours, Lourdshup, whatever yew need. If we’er got et, thass yours,” he said, emphasising each ‘yours’ with a nod.

“Zindons hare,” he shuddered. “Thet int right!”

“No, it’s not right,” agreed Seldar, “and thank you.” He waited to see if the farmer would speak again, but with a final nod, Alcor returned to his sharpening.

Seldar continued up the stairs, and glanced at the sun which was now past the midday point. He had been gone longer than he realised. He entered Trerin’s room and checked him; the lad’s Seta was almost fully replenished.

Seldar once again removed the sleep compulsion, but this time, Trerin did not awaken immediately, as he had before. Concerned, Seldar sank his mind into his Ponfour’s but the sleep was natural.

If Trerin remained asleep it must be because he chose to do so, which in turn suggested that someone was walking in his dreams and that he remained asleep to talk with them.

Seldar could detect no magical residue, so he knew that Trerin had not initiated the dreamwalk. It must be Lord Jareth.

Seldar sighed, he considered joining the dream, but he had used a great deal of energy in the last two days, and dreamwalking from an induced trance used more power than doing it from a true sleep. He decided to wait for Trerin to wake and tell him what Jareth had said.

Looking around for something to occupy him while he waited, his eye fell on the ragged remnants of Trerin's leather jerkin and trousers; he could start repairing them.

He transmuted the top of the table, to make it impervious to his blade, and unrolled the skins that the trapper Tahrvin had given him. He selected one and laid it on the chest then, using the original clothing as a template, began to cut pieces from it.

Trerin had very strong beliefs about using magic to make clothing without need, and would disapprove if Seldar did it the easy way. In addition to that, Seldar had used a great deal of magic in the last two days and he knew that he should have a rest from it while he had the chance.

Trerin woke up, and rolled off the bed leaving behind the bedcover. He stretched – a long cat-like stretch that ran in a wave up his body, beginning with his feet and ending at his fingertips. He had to stretch his head and arms forwards to avoid the ceiling. Seldar laughed and, scooping up one of Trerin's bags, threw it towards his stomach. Trerin caught it easily before it hit him and raised an eyebrow at Seldar.

"Lad, there are teenaged girls in this household. Cover all that decently before their mother walks in and decides that you are a threat to their well-being, or worse – suitable marriage material!"

Trerin grinned and, pulling his second favourite trousers and a shirt from the bag, quickly dressed. He glanced up at the very low ceiling and sat on the bed.

"I had a visit from Lord Jareth while I was sleeping," he told Seldar, who put down the leather he was sewing.

"And what did our esteemed commander say? Will we shortly be joined by more Sorcerers as we travel to Bein?" Seldar asked, speaking more lightly than he felt.

The amount of trouble given them by just one Zindon, made him sincerely hope that they would be joined before they reached a town that was rumoured to contain many.

Trerin grimaced.

"No. Lord Jareth said that there's a substantial problem in Perrest, which will require all the Sorcerers, Warriors, and Soldiers, that he can free from other duties. Everyone else is dealing with other problems. There are large numbers of grinnets, derstrals, dragons, and worse, being reported all across the Protectorates. He said that the only people he could send us would be reservists and, if there really are Zindons in Bein, we will have a better chance of avoiding detection by them on our own."

He shrugged.

"He also said that, so far, except for the problem in Perrest, almost every rumour investigated has turned out to be false. He's sure that Bein is equally likely to be just a wild story."

Seldar's eyebrows rose.

"I hope you told him about the very real Zindon you just fought, and about that equally real grinnet in Tarvinstoft."

"I did. He was surprised that we had found two shadow creatures, especially a Zindon, but we're not the only ones to meet something real. A few other Sorcerers *have* encountered grinnets, also clay-worms, a water-grell, and there has been one fledgling dragon caught and safely relocated. Only eleven out of hundreds of rumours have been substantiated. The others are all misunderstandings, misidentifications, or practical jokes."

He shrugged again.

"Lord Jareth says that when we have investigated Bein, assuming that it is another empty story, we are to carry on westwards to Samvar and look into a rumour of another water-grell. However, we must make sure that our Zindon is dead before we leave here."

"Already done. I killed the creature an hour or so ago."

"You went after the Zindon? Alone? Seldar! You should have woken me!"

"There was no time. The creature had been caught in a trapper's snare, and I couldn't risk it escaping. I was quite safe. Your healing was effective and it was unable to use any magic. I examined it very carefully, and there was no longer any trace of the dark energy within it."

Seldar spoke rapidly, hoping to soothe the lad.

"Also, it had injured you, nearly killed you, and when I learned that it was caught, I wanted very much to be the person who killed it. If I had woken you, you would have insisted on fighting it again, and I wanted to kill it myself preferably causing it as much agony as possible."

Trerin gasped sharply.

"Seldar? Tell me you didn't!"

Seldar smiled reassuringly.

"No, I came to my senses, and killed it quickly."

Trerin let out his breath, relieved.

“The choice was a hard one." Seldar shook his head. "I did not know I could feel so angry."

"I understand, my Lord," Trerin’s voice was soft, "but still I want your word, never again to tackle a shadow creature alone. We work together, and I take the risks first, not you. Do you think I would thank you, if I had woken to find that it had killed you while I was safe? You know what would happen to me if you died while I lived! Your word in Light, Seldar, I insist on it."

Seldar looked out of the window towards the distant forest, remembering the hatred that had suffused him for a short time when he faced the Zindon.

He wondered if rebonding had been a mistake. If he lost a second Ponfour, the pain might drive him to actions that he would later regret. Despite this, He knew that Trerin was correct: the Ponfour's task was to protect his Sorcerer, including dying if necessary. Seldar knew that he must accept that, but he was not sure he could. The lad was so young.

His previous experience with Arella had taught Seldar ways to keep secret some of his emotions, and he did his best to conceal his uncertainty and worry. He knew, however, that he could not prevent his Ponfour sensing at least some of it. He could feel Trerin's determination changing to puzzlement at his silence and the dark aura colouring his thoughts. If he further delayed answering, Trerin might guess some of what was going through his mind, and he would be outraged and insulted.

Seldar reminded himself again, that Trerin was not a lad, that he was a man grown, an experienced Soldier and Warrior, and

Seldar's sworn bonded Ponfour. He must, and would, try harder to remember those things.

He took a deep breath and then nodded, and looked back at Trerin.

"I suppose I shouldn't argue with someone whose main purpose is to keep me alive," he said.

"No, you shouldn't," Trerin agreed. The young Ponfour folded his arms and waited.

"Very well, I will not embark on any more solo monster hunts..." Seldar paused, wondering if he could get away with just that, but he felt Trerin send a reproving tug along the bond.

"In the Light I swear it," he finished reluctantly.

Trerin grinned, and Seldar felt approval colour his Ponfour's feelings, eradicating the puzzlement.

"Good. Now why don't we find the source of that wonderful smell? I'm hungry!"

Reconnecting

Trerin sat on a large, low, branch in a corner of a small orchard near the farmhouse. To his left stood apple, pear, and plum trees, all bearing half grown fruit. To his right, the orchard gave way to a herb garden, containing a wide variety of aromatic plants and shrubs.

The oak tree, from which the branch projected, was ancient and large. Several centuries older than the fruit trees near it, it had perhaps been left unfelled out of respect for its age.

The branch was wide, and Trerin sat comfortably on it, leaning against the trunk with one leg bent and the other stretched out along the wide upper surface of the branch.

He had changed clothes, and was now wearing just shorts and circlet. The basic reconnection exercises he had come outside to do were more easily done without the distracting sensation of clothes on his skin. At home, he would have stripped completely, but out here in the Protectorates that would be inappropriate.

He closed his eyes and sank his awareness within his body, expanding his senses to become aware of every sensation. He felt the roughness of the bark below his left sole, and against his right heel, calf, and thigh, and against the skin on his back. He felt the movement of air across his skin, gusting across right arm, then chest, then left arm.

He relaxed further. He felt the slight change in position of the hair on his arms and legs as the sun went behind a cloud and the temperature lowered.

He smelled flowers, and herbs, and ripening fruit, and freshly turned soil, and the faint but unpleasant odour that spoke of some small creature dead in the nearby field. He heard birdsong, and wind rustling the leaves in the trees nearby, and the quiet scratching sounds of insects moving on plants nearby. He also heard the quiet breathing of someone nearby, working in the herb garden, but trying very hard to be quiet.

After one quick glance when she entered the garden, Trerin had ignored the girl, the youngest daughter here. She clearly had tasks to perform, and was just as clearly not in any rush to perform them while she had something more interesting to look at.

Trerin was used to attracting female attention. Even before he had grown to be possibly the tallest living Tyrean, his thick sungold hair had turned heads.

Trerin had no objections to that, especially not if the turned heads belonged to pretty girls near his own age. This one, however, was far too young even to flirt with.

He put her from his mind to concentrate on the necessary reconnection exercises. He must finish them, even if someone was watching. The exercises took several hours to complete, and there would be nothing to see for some time so maybe she would become bored and leave.

When he was sure that he was aware of every external sensation, he sank his mind deeper. While keeping hold of the external, he added the internal sensations. He felt the blood moving through his arteries and veins, and the strong pulsating beat of his heart. He felt air sliding through his nose, across the back of his throat, down into his lungs, and then reversing direction. He felt the muscles expanding in his torso, and pulling down his diaphragm to suck in the air. He felt the many tiny movements of muscles across his entire body as his body adjusted automatically to hold balance on the branch. He felt the small movements of stomach, (pleasantly full of roast beef,) and the organs around it as his body proceeded with the process of digestion.

He went deeper still, becoming aware of individual cells throughout his entire body. He could feel the microscopic movements as cells subdivided and adjusted position to take the place of others that had died and detached.

He sat on the branch, apparently still, and knew that the stillness was an illusion; every cell in his body was in motion.

He sought out the recently healed areas, noting the slight differences between what was now, and what had been before: nerves in new positions, slight variations in elasticity of the new muscles, and the minor changes to bone shape.

He found the reference points at each joint, and each tendon attachment, and rebuilt his body image to allow for the alterations caused by such a widespread healing.

Now he could begin the second exercise.

Slowly, he began to make changes to the structure, beginning with the smallest alteration, the first learned by any shapeshifter: he changed the colour of his eyes. He smiled at a fleeting memory of Seldar shaking a finger and saying, "Forgot your eye colour, indeed!"

Next, Trerin lightened his skin almost to pink, then darkened it to a jet black, then changed through less natural colours before returning to his normal dark brown. A small gasp had accompanied the initial lightening, followed by a quiet giggle as he transformed through yellow, green, and blue.

Another easy change – he sprouted fur across his body. Short at first, he lengthened it and then changed it to a mass of tight dark curls. Feathers replaced the fur, causing his watcher to laugh with delight, forgetting that she was trying to be quiet.

He dismissed the feathers, and resumed his normal appearance.

His eyes remained closed, and he continued to be aware of every sensation. A second set of footsteps entered the garden; presumably someone had come to look for the girl. The steps sounded heavier, the stride longer. One of her brothers, he decided. Low whispering ensued and then ended. Now he had two watchers.

Everything had behaved as it should, so Trerin moved without pause to the third exercise. Up till now, the changes had been cosmetic – his form had remained unchanged with merely the external appearance had altered.

Now he began to make more substantial changes, beginning with his hands. He opened his eyes and held up his right hand. Slowly, he lengthened the bones until fingers and palm were elongated to almost twice their natural size. He next lengthened his arm until it was as long as his leg. He restored arm and hand to their normal size, and repeated the exercise, with first his other hand, and then both legs.

He continued with similar changes across his entire body – lengthening, widening, shrinking – until every bone had been changed and restored.

Up till now, he had merely been making alterations to what already existed, but now he would begin creating appendages that he did not naturally own, beginning with a tail.

This would be a little awkward wearing shorts, but they were loose enough for it to grow.

"What er yew doin?" a male voice, sounding very curious, was immediately followed by a hissed, high-pitched, "Kerji!"

Trerin looked across at his audience. Kerji was squatting beside his sister, on the path between the herb beds. She was glaring at her brother who, mistaking the cause of her annoyance, hurriedly corrected himself.

"Uh, what er yew doin, Lourdshup?"

Sash rolled her eyes and Trerin suppressed a grin.

"I'm reconnecting," he answered, as his tail emerged from the leg of his shorts, lengthened, and grew long bushy golden fur. Sash squeaked in surprise, as the tail flicked from side to side before shrinking and disappearing under his clothing.

Kerji just stared in amazement. Sash elbowed him and tilted her head toward Trerin, her eyes conveying a message that, this time, he interpreted correctly.

"Wha do thet mean?" Kerji asked for her, with an amused smile for her sudden shyness. "Uh, Lourdshup," he added.

"You don't have to call me that every time, my name's Trerin," Trerin said absently as he was concentrating on his next task.

A horn grew up from the top of his head. Long and thin, it twisted as it lengthened and split into fine branches. He had to alter his skull at the same time, thickening the bone to take the additional weight. He wished that he had a mirror to view the result, but the expressions on Kerji and Sash's faces suggested that his appearance was impressive.

He resumed his normal shape again.

"We coon't cahll yew by yer name!" Kerji sounded scandalised, and Sash's eyes were wide and shocked.

"Ma'd do her nut!"

Trerin had to think about the last bit for a moment before deciding that Kerji must mean that his mother would be angry.

"I won't tell her if you use my name," he assured them with an internal sigh, certain that they would not.

"To answer your question," he continued, "a shapeshifter needs to have a complete knowledge of his own body to change it into another shape. A major healing, such as I just had, leaves slight alterations. Reconnecting involves a series of exercises that enable me to learn those differences. I can't change shape fully until I've completed them."

As he spoke, he watched a sixth finger appear on each hand, and then made retractable claws on all twelve digits. He reshaped his hands back to normal, and began to concentrate on a harder task: a second pair of arms. This required a major restructuring of spine and back for a second pair of shoulder blades to hold the new limbs.

"Did yew rarely fight a Zindon?" Sasha blurted.

Trerin gasped. The unexpected question triggered a memory flashback of the fight which broke his concentration for a second. Pain flared in his back as he struggled to regain control of the shapeshift, and finish the restructuring of his torso.

"I'm sorry!" the girl squeaked, eyes wide and frightened.

Trerin couldn't answer while he fought to refocus, but he eventually succeeded and straightened the bones that had slipped out of his control. He continued the exercise, drawing the new limbs out and attaching muscles so that they were useable. He was sweating by the time he had finished them, and paused to regain his breath.

Trerin looked at Sash, she had bitten her finger hard enough to draw blood, and tears were running down her cheek. Kerji had stood up and taken a step towards Trerin, but had stopped uncertainly, obviously unsure what he could do.

"It's not your fault," Trerin told the child gently. "I should have better control than that."

He banished the extra arms, and smoothed his back into its usual shape.

"And yes, I did really fight a Zindon."

He slid his legs off the side of the branch, dropped to the ground and walked over to the girl. Squatting beside her, he took her hand from her mouth and healed the bitten finger. The girl twisted her hand around to examine it and to show it to her brother, who stared at the skin with eyes as wide as his sister's.

"Thanku fer that."

She smiled, her previous upset forgotten.

"Were yew scared tew fight the Zindon?" she asked.

"Sash!"

Her brother sounded shocked that she would ask such a question. Trerin remembered the moment that he had panicked.

"Yes," he replied honestly, "but I still had to fight it, just the same."

"And yew won!" she said, her eyes shining.

Trerin grinned. "Yes, I won, but only just!"

"End then ahlmust got killed by an idiot with a shuhvel," muttered Kerji under his breath.

Trerin laughed.

"That's true! You nearly succeeded where a Zindon failed. In future, I'll be far more wary of farmers with shovels!"

Kerji smiled uncertainly. He shook his head and rolled his eyes as Sash blurted another question.

"Can you change into anything you want?" she asked rapidly. Trerin looked at her and smiled. She was so young!

"Not yet," he told her. "Some shapes take more years of practice than I've lived. The more different a shape, the harder it is to change into it. A horse, or a dog, or even a mouse, has much the same structure as a man so it's relatively easy to adjust to them. It's merely a matter of lengthening and reshaping. Birds are harder because of their hollow bones and the different function of the front limbs. Insects, and other creatures which have their hard parts on the outside and lots of legs, are the hardest because they are so completely different from a man that everything must be changed. I can't yet manage all of those."

The girl had frowned in puzzlement partway through his answer, and she opened her mouth for another question, but Kerji spoke first.

"Mowse? But a mowse is tiny! Sew ar insects! How, Oi mean..." he paused, uncertain how to ask, and Sash took her chance.

"Wha happens tew the rest of yew, if yew becum so small? End your clohthes, what happens tew them? End did yew hev tew learn how tew fly like birds dew? End can yew becum a fish? End ..."

Trerin held up his hands.

"Stop, and I'll answer," he said, chuckling at her babble of questions, and wondering if he had ever been that young.

Kerji was staring at his sister in astonishment at the flow of words issuing from her mouth.

"In order: if I change into a mouse, all of me becomes the mouse. I know a mouse is small, and I don't know how it works, but I know that every little bit of me is in the mouse. My clothes have been altered magically so that I can shape them with me: they usually become part of my fur, scales or feathers. And before you ask, if I was wearing ordinary clothes they wouldn't change, I would have to remove them first. Yes, I had to learn how to fly, and how to swim as a fish swims."

She started to ask another question, but Trerin stopped her.

"I really must finish the exercises now. You can carry on watching if you wish; I don't mind. I have to shift into several different animal forms and then I must become an eagle and make sure that my wings still work."

He made the last part a joke, but becoming an eagle was more important than he made it sound. He had been attacked, and almost killed, in eagle form when in flight, and he must return to the skies as soon as he was able. If he did not, the residual fear from the experience could grow until it affected his Gift.

The longer he left it untried, the harder it might become to fly again, and it could even become impossible to shift to eagle form. Trerin had no intention of allowing that to happen to him.

He stepped away from the young people, and began the next part of the reconnection.

In quick succession, he shapeshifted into a horse, a cow, a dog, a mouse, and finally his usual large cat. Trerin did not resume his natural shape in between, but instead just flowed from one form to the next, pausing only to check that each transformation was complete.

Kerji and Sash stepped back hurriedly from the very large, shaggy, curly-haired cat that suddenly stood before them.

Trerin lowered his eyelids slightly in a cat smile, and then ran past them towards the gate of the garden. He jumped over it and, as he did so, shapeshifted into an eagle. The timing had to be perfect; he had to finish his shift at the top of his leap to allow time for a strong down beat of his wings to keep him in the air. A second too slow and he would land beak first on the ground in a huddle of feathers.

He did it perfectly and soared.

As he rose higher into the sky, he found himself feeling exposed, as though hostile eyes were watching his every move. The feeling was unpleasant, and he considered changing colour to his usual camouflage. He wore no armour and could be shot down by a single well-aimed arrow.

Caution would be sensible, but he knew that if he changed colour now, it would be because he felt nervous, and not because he was being sensible. Trerin refused to do something out of fear; he would remain as he was until he was sure that fear played no part in his eventual decision to change.

He reminded himself that the Zindon was dead, and in the unlikely event that another shapechanged Zindon appeared, he now knew how to defeat it. Healing as a weapon! He wondered what the Healers' Council would say about that.

He circled higher and kept alert, scanning the countryside below.

There! A group of rabbits chewing grass were blissfully unaware of the predator above them. He folded his wings and stooped, at the last second changing angle to miss the rabbit below him and just frighten it instead.

Had he been able, in this shape, he would have laughed at the look on the creature's face as it narrowly missed death. He flew back up into the sky, feeling much more like himself after the joke.

The wind blew through his feathers as he glided high in the sky. He banished thoughts of Zindons and armour and just allowed the sensation of flight to fill his senses. The view was magnificent; the ground lay below him, spread out in wrinkles and folds, some bright with sun, some deep in shadow.

In the far distance, he could see sunlight glinting off the sea. He could also see a strange black cloud that hugged one point on the distant horizon. Even his sharp eagle's eyes could not see what caused it, but he had an uncomfortable feeling that it lay in the direction that they were travelling.

He wondered why he had not noticed it before, but he rarely flew as high as he had today; Usually when he changed into an eagle, he was hunting and stayed a little closer to the ground where his prey was.

Now, He flew higher still, hoping for a clearer look, but the cloud remained indistinct.

This reminder of their mission took his thoughts to Seldar. He had had the strangest feeling that his Sorcerer was hiding something from him during their conversation earlier. He wondered what it could be or if he had imagined it.

The girl's face, eagerly asking questions, intruded into his thoughts. She was so young, and yet, he knew that she could be no more than eight years his junior.

Lord of Light! Could that be it? He was more than twenty years younger than Seldar. Could the Sorcerer possibly see him as that young? Think him a child to be protected instead of an adult?

For a moment, Trerin considered the idea, but then rejected it. Seldar was an experienced Sorcerer; he knew what a Ponfour was, and no one could mistake one for a child, especially one as tall as Trerin.

Trerin decided that he must still need a little more sleep: first he had been distracted mid-shift by a child's questions and now he was entertaining the ridiculous thought that Seldar might think he had to protect his own Ponfour. Perhaps he should ask Seldar to check his skull again because maybe something was still loose in there!

He flew across the countryside until all thought of Zindons, Bein, and even Seldar had left his thoughts, and he was left simply with the pure enjoyment of flight.

Trerin returned to thought when he felt a tug across the bond, and he circled until he could see the farm. Seldar was standing in the yard waving for him to come down.

Movement in a meadow caught his eye. Several small deer were crossing it towards the river. Without thinking, acting purely on instinct, Trerin stooped on them, and rose with one hanging limp in his talons. He dropped it in the yard just before he landed, and then changed back to human. Seldar looked at the deer for a second and then asked curiously, "Why did you do that?"

Trerin shrugged.

"Instinct. I'd caught it before I noticed what I was doing. I suppose the family will be happy to eat it," he replied, looking at the things Seldar was holding.

"Are those my clothes and mail?"

Seldar pulled his attention back from the carcase.

"Yes, all mended. Put them on so that I can make any adjustments and then key them to your Gift."

Trerin dressed rapidly.

"You repaired them very quickly," he commented, wondering if Seldar had used transmutation. "They fit perfectly."

"So they should, lad, I was helping my father make clothes even before my Gifts appeared. That's well over forty years of practice." Seldar spoke absently as he pulled and tugged to check the leather lay correctly.

"You know what to do, so let's get these keyed to your Gift, and then I think we should move on. We've still got a few days travel to reach Bein, and there are several hours left to the day."

Trerin nodded and, filling his mind with the image of his cat, began to shapeshift as slowly as he could.

He knew that Seldar was combining his healing and his transmutation Gifts, to enable him to follow the change and transmute the clothing, melding it into Trerin's magical aura. Trerin felt the items become a part of him, and melted them into the shapeshift. He continued to shift slowly so that Seldar could monitor the change to be sure that he had overlooked nothing.

He changed form several times and then returned to his human shape.

"It all works," he said,

"Good! Here's the rest of your armour, put it on and let's be sure it all works together."

Seldar nudged the bag at his feet with his toe. Trerin quickly donned the rest, including his helmet, and then changed shape again. A moment later, a large shaggy cat stood in the yard and looked expectantly at Seldar.

Seldar sighed.

"Very well, I suppose I must," he said, and, to the considerable surprise of Alsy and her daughters who were watching from the dairy windows, kicked the cat in the ribs as hard as he could.

Trerin changed back to human form and watched Seldar hop across the yard to lean against the wall, face screwed up in pain.

Laughter warred with concern, and laughter won. Trerin doubled up, laughing uncontrollably, as Seldar glared at him and shook his foot as if he could shake away the pain.

"Seldar," Trerin gasped eventually, "you're supposed to use something considerably more solid than your foot for that test! What were you thinking?"

He walked across and squatted beside the injured foot. Pulling off his gauntlet, he applied a pain block and then began to unlace Seldar's boot.

"Your sympathy is touching," Seldar growled. "Would you mind healing it for me please?"

Trerin grinned, and removed the boot and sock to look at the foot. He sank a healing probe into it, and then pulled out his belt knife.

"You've broken several bones in there; I'll have to open it to get at them. You'd better sit down."

As Seldar slid down the wall onto the ground, Trerin glanced across at the faces watching, eyes wide, from the dairy window. Then he shrugged, and began to work. A few minutes later he put the knife away and Seldar replaced his healed foot into his boot.

Trerin stood up and, walking across the yard to a pile of handles not yet attached to tools, picked up a solid one and returned. He handed it to Seldar.

"This time, use this. The armour becomes my fur, remember? You kicked my breast plate!"

"I'll remember that in future, lad, and thank you," Seldar replied, with a wry grin for his idiocy. "If you will change again, I'll do it properly. In fact, your laughter may make my arm stronger."

Trerin grinned and changed back to the cat form. Seldar shrugged and swung the handle at Trerin's ribs as hard as he could.

Trerin staggered under the force of the blow, but stood still as Seldar landed more blows on his legs, back, and head.

After a few minutes, Seldar stepped back, and Trerin rose to his hind legs, changing as he stood. He had several tender areas, but no serious injuries or cracked bones; the shapeshifted armour had done its job.

He removed his helmet and grinned, pretending not to notice the impressed faces peering from the window.

"It all works. Thank you."

"Glad to hear it," Seldar replied. Trerin knew that he must be aware of the bruising, but he made no other comment. He did, however, allow a distinct feeling of amused tolerance to colour his mind aura. Seldar knew that Trerin would never admit to the slightest injury in front of admiring females, whatever their ages.

"Saddle up our horses, Trerin, while I fetch our bags. We'll make our farewells and see how far we can get before sunrise. Oh, and you'd better put that deer into the cold-room below the kitchen," Seldar said briskly, already moving towards the stairs to the upper floor.

Trerin nodded and, hefting the deer, disappeared into the kitchen. When he had deposited the carcase in the icy cold-room, he returned to the yard and saddled his and Seldar's horses. He led first them, and then the packhorse, out of the stables and found Seldar talking to the Gal Alsy.

"I doon't think yew shud be gorn til tehmorrow, but if yew insist yew'll take these with yew, an no ahrguement!" Alsy was pressing a bag into Seldar's hands. "Thass just sum bread, and dried meat, and sum fruit pies becoz yew'll want somethin for tonight. Espeshlly thuh way thuh young Lourdshup ates."

Trerin bit back his urge to point out that Seldar also had a large appetite. Seldar threw him an amused glance that suggested that he had interpreted the thought in his Ponfour's mind.

"That's very kind of you, Gal Alsy," Seldar replied to her, as he accepted the bag.

Trerin stripped off his armour, except for the mail, packed it, and then began attaching their saddlebags onto the horses. He took the bag from Seldar to add to the packhorse's burden.

"Are yew shur yew wun't stay tonight? Thass no bohther if thass what yew think. The young Lourdshup oonly got up this morning!"

She threw an anxious glance at Trerin who smiled reassuringly.

"I'm fully recovered now, thank you," he told her as he mounted.

"You have been extremely kind, Gal Alsy, Trerin recovered much faster thanks to your hospitality, but we still have a long way to go." Seldar also mounted as he spoke.

"If yew're sure, then, Light shoine on yew Lourdshups, Alcor end the Bors wud want tew say et too, but thare gorn tew the mill tew collect the flowr," she said trotting beside as the horses walked out of the yard.

Cries of "Light shoine" also came from the dairy door, as Alsy stopped at the gate and watched as the Tyreans rode away.

“That was an amazing accent,” Trerin commented once they were far enough away that no-one would hear him. “There were several times when I had to guess what they meant. I haven’t heard such a strong dialect before, are there many others like that across the Protectorates?”

Seldar smiled.

“A few, though not as many as supposedly once existed. I heard a legend many years ago about it. They said that people in different lands used to have completely different words for things, until one day God became tired of being called by different names. He decided to act, and in one night, he chose one word out of each of the differences, and when everyone awoke, those were the only words left. For a while after that, everyone spoke the same, across the entire world, but over time people in isolated areas, like here, began to say words differently again. Some say that one day, those variations will grow so great that, once again, people from different areas will not understand each other. When that happens, they believe, the Shadowbringer will use the confusion to spread shadows across the world. Because they believe this, there are scholars who spend their lives writing every word they learn, along with its pronunciation and meaning, into books to try to keep back the day of confusion."

Trerin was astonished.

"Is that true, or one of your tales?" he asked suspiciously.

He could feel sincerity radiating strongly from Seldar, but he had been fooled before. He knew that Sorcerers often developed ways to try and hide feelings from their Ponfourii. Seldar had been bonded for many years to another; he knew all the tricks.

Seldar laughed.

"That one? No, it's true, or at least it's true that it's a legend that I once heard. The word collectors do exist, and a strange group they are."

He shook his head, smiling at a memory, then he looked up, and Trerin suddenly caught an impression of mischief dancing through their tie. His eyes narrowed as he waited to find out what Seldar intended.

"You understood the Gal Alsy well enough in the mill yard, I think. That was an interesting suggestion that she made, don't you think?... Petal."

Seldar spoke in a light, teasing manner, and Trerin's felt his eyes widen in outraged indignation and knew that he was behaving exactly as Seldar had hoped, but still he could not control his reaction.

However, he had been expecting something of this nature and had prepared a response.

"Seldar, I've been thinking, your poor horse is strong and does his best, but don't you think that, for his sake, it's time that you considered a diet to lessen his burden? You could have arrived at the mill yard much quicker, I'm sure, had he been less tired."

The reaction from Seldar was everything for which he had hoped. He felt the abrupt shock that caused the Sorcerer to rein in his horse and stare at him with horror.

"Diet? Trerin, that's a terrible thing to say to a man. I'm shocked at you."

Trerin just looked at him and then raised one eyebrow encouragingly.

Seldar stared back, and Trerin sensed a grudging capitulation from him, followed by amused respect. Seldar sniffed and looked away.

"Oh, very well, I will never call you 'Petal' again, if you will forget the word 'diet'.

Trerin grinned.

"I can live with that," he replied.

They began to move again, and continued in companionable silence for a few minutes, and then Seldar spoke.

"So you thought 'Petal' was worse than 'lad', did you Trerin?" he asked, colouring his thoughts with polite enquiry.

Trerin looked at him suspiciously.

"Of course it's worse."

"You find 'lad' preferable to 'Petal' then," Seldar persisted.

"Yes, of course it's prefe..." Trerin's voice trailed off as he recognised the trap into which he had just walked. He stared at Seldar, who was grinning broadly.

"Glad to hear it, lad, so let's have no more complaints about it."

Seldar slapped him on the shoulder, before trotting ahead, humming gaily. Trerin shook his head in disgust.

"Oh, very clever!"

He could tell from the extreme, and almost certainly enhanced, smugness that he could sense, that the Sorcerer agreed.

That evening they camped in a cave by a stream. Trerin had caught another deer, and they sat beside the campfire watching the meat roast.

The smoke rising from the fire reminded Trerin of the cloud he had seen earlier that day. He had meant to mention it earlier, but had forgotten.

Seldar looked up. "What is it, lad?"

"I just remembered that there's something I intended to tell you," Trerin said.

"You saw something, when you were flying earlier?" Seldar asked.

Trerin looked at him.

"I noticed then that something had caught your attention," Seldar explained. "It was just before you started to enjoy yourself. So what was it?"

Trerin wondered if he would ever be able to interpret what he could sense from his partner, through the bond, as easily as Seldar did. Seldar's mouth quirked up on one side, in a half smile.

"You'll get there, lad, it just takes practice. Now tell me what you saw."

Trerin blinked, then nodded and began.

"I went higher than I do usually, high enough that I could see the sea on the horizon. I saw a dark cloud shrouding the coastline in one spot. As far as I could tell, it is in the right place to be right on top of Bein. It looked ...wrong."

"Wrong?" Seldar asked. "In what way? Was it a gleaning?"

Trerin thought back to his flight and tried to work out what specifically had been un-natural about the cloud.

"Nooo… not a gleaning, at least I don't think so. You know that my Gift rarely works that way. But something was ..."

He paused, staring at the clouds as they moved across the sky. They were travelling from ahead of him, passing above, and disappearing behind. Something about them nagged at him. Seldar remained silent, allowing him to chase down and catch the elusive thought that skittered just out of reach.

"That's it!" he whispered. "The wind is blowing straight across from beyond Bein to here. I could see the cloud stretch out to sea, blown towards Bein from across the water, but it doesn't come inland. It stops at the coast. Something holds it on top of the town."

He looked at Seldar, who nodded.

"That would take magic," the Sorcerer agreed. "So now we have two conundrums."

"Two?" queried Trerin.

Seldar nodded again.

"Yes, lad: your stationary cloud, plus the puzzle of why that Zindon attacked us the way he did. What could he possibly have expected to accomplish?"

Trerin stared at Seldar. He knew that Sorcerers' training focussed more on magical skills and strength than on tactics and fighting, but he had assumed that Seldar would have understood the only possible explanation for the Zindon's attack on them.

Seldar raised his eyebrows as he caught Trerin's surprise.

"You know what he intended?" he asked.

Trerin took a deep breath and replied, "Seldar, if I had not noticed that shadow and fought the Zindon, if we had emerged from that shaded track to be attacked by a derstral, which then disappeared behind the hill, what would we have done? What would we have *had* to do?"

Seldar considered for a moment.

"We would have hunted for the derstral, and we would have had to stay here until we either killed it or could be sure that it had left the area. Oh!" He inhaled sharply as he understood. "It could have kept us occupied here for days, or weeks, if it chose. An attack here, a sighting there, we could not have left this place with a derstral loose."

Trerin nodded.

"I think he meant to delay us, I can think of no other reason for him to draw attention to his presence."

Seldar looked along the track towards Bein.

"That implies that something is being prepared ahead of us. That someone knows we are here and wanted to buy themselves time."

Trerin grinned.

"But they failed in their plan; we were delayed one day, but no longer than that. The Light shines on us! *They* have less time to get ready and *we* have discovered a new weapon."

Seldar looked at him soberly.

"You think that there are Zindons in Bein, just as we heard? I hope that you're wrong! Your new weapon can only be used if we are much closer to one than I prefer; we can't heal without contact."

Trerin smiled grimly.

"There is certainly something somewhere ahead of us, and that cloud defies the winds to sit above Bein. Yes, I think that we'll find at least one Zindon in Bein, and probably several. That *is* why we're going there, after all, to learn if the innkeeper's stories held substance. If we do find several, you must translocate back to Tyreen and tell Lord Jareth."

Seldar frowned and poked a stick into the campfire, unnecessarily.

"Without you? I hope that it doesn't come to that."

Trerin shook his head against the strong flood of reluctance, worry, and remembered grief, that surged across the bond. He smiled gently.

"You can't translocate both of us however much you may wish it otherwise. I, too, hope that it doesn't come to that, but we'll do what we must. If there is need to return quickly to Tyreen, you'll go, and I'll teach any Zindon I can find that a Ponfour is dangerous to get close to."

By the end of his sentence his smile had changed to a grimace of determination and he realised that Seldar was staring at him with incredulity.

"Just one Zindon almost killed you; are you really so eager to face several? The idea scares me juiceless."

Trerin shook his head.

"Eager? No, of course not. The thought of another Zindon sucking at my Seta is revolting!" He shuddered, "But if I must face that, I will; it's my duty. You know that, Seldar. I won't flinch from it just because I'm afraid. And neither will you."

Seldar nodded, and stared into the fire.

"Yes, we'll do what we must. Do you ever wish that you had been born with just one gift and could live your entire life without meeting a creature of shadow?"

"I? No! Never! I would hate to be confined in Tyreen my whole life. If I knew that I would die in Bein next week, I still wouldn't regret the circumstances and choices that led me there, neither would I change them even if I could."

He peered at Seldar across the flames, puzzled by the sombre nature of the Sorcerer's emotions.

"Why? Would you?"

Seldar straightened.

"No, lad, I would not! You're right: we are what we are, and that is the best thing to be."

"Besides," Trerin continued as a sudden thought struck him, "this may be my best chance of a place in the Hall of Statues."

Seldar looked at him, both eyebrows raised in astonishment.

"The Hall of Statues? The statues of those killed facing terrible odds? *That* Hall of Statues?" he asked.

"They didn't ALL die facing terrible odds," Trerin protested. "Some survived."

Seldar nodded.

"That's true. Technically, Tamat did survive his battle, of course he *did* die a few days later, never regaining consciousness."

Trerin grinned at his dry tone.

"There are a few others – people who lived, and died in old age in their beds."

Seldar shook his head.

"Not many! Trerin, I devoutly hope that neither of us is ever a candidate for that Hall."

He poked the deer with his knife, and deliberately changed the subject.

"This is cooked. Shall we eat?"

Trerin nodded agreement and applied himself with enthusiasm to his meal.

Later, when they had finished, he felt how tired Seldar was.

"I'll take the first watch," he said, standing up and walking towards his bag of armour. He put everything on, including helmet, before changing to the cat, and then he set off to prowl around the campsite.

Part 3: The Kingdom of Perrest

"They're coming here! I can't believe it, but it's true. Tara just told me. In a few hours there will be real live Tyreans staying in the palace. Maybe now I can find out the truth: are they the noble heroes of legend or the failed and fallen hypocrites that Kalis describes. Are Ponfourii really enslaved or not? I have a chance to find out, so I will. Uncle Ran says I can stay at the palace and meet them." Diary of Erian Tolene.

Angate

The translocation nimbus cleared and Tam released a breath he hadn't realised he was holding. Beside him, Crystu also sighed as she shared his relief that they were finally once more out of Tyreen.

"I didn't really believe that Da would let us leave," she murmured. "I was sure that he would find some new reason to keep us in Tyre, just like he did when we first bonded."

Tam chuckled.

"I, too, thought he might find a reason for further delay."

Crystu looked sideways at him.

"You're the one who insisted on this last delay, Tam," she reminded him.

"With good reason, Crystu, and I was right to do so. Even a Rykatu needs to be at full power to translocate this many people, along with their horses and baggage." He waved around at the mass of men and women who had appeared with them in this large field on the outskirts of Angate.

Crystu nodded, admitting to herself that he was right; She would be glad when she could sit and rest after the strain of this translocation. Sitting on a horse, as she was now, did not count as rest; a nice soft chair would be much better.

"True. Even merged with the other translocators here, this was a heavy load for me. I *am* glad that I had that extra day to rest."

Tam and Crystu were at the centre of the large group. Flanking them were the neat rows of five full Septs: three of Warriors, two of Soldiers. Each Sept comprised seven Septines, and each Septine was seven Warriors or Soldiers. Two hundred and forty-five men and women, all mounted, in full armour, filled a large area of the field.

Beyond them, were almost all of those who had bonded recently. While the Ponfourii were as well presented as the Soldiers and Warriors, the Sorcerers were more variably dressed: some in robes, some in trousers, some wearing armour. In all, not quite four hundred men and women, plus their horses, weapons, armour and bags, had translocated into this field.

The sun was just above the horizon, and the dew clung to the ground plants, outlining leaves, flowers, and spiders' webs into sharp detail until disturbed by the shifting hooves of the horses.

The new Sorcerers were all staring around at the countryside; for all of *them*, this was their first time outside Tyreen. Their more experienced Ponfourii also looked around, alertly assessing their surroundings for threats.

"Crystu!" Jathte's voice called.

Tam and Crystu urged their horses through the crowd to where their friend, also mounted, waited beside the gate to the field.

"I am very glad to see you, Crystu, and so many with you. Maybe now we can get something accomplished. The few of us here until now have been hard pressed just to keep the ants from starting new colonies closer to the town; we have had little time for anything else and it's getting larger."

"Is it really so big?" Crystu asked.

For answer Jathte simply pointed. They turned to look where he indicated, and Tam gasped as he realised that the snowy mountain, which they could see above the ridge, was not a mountain at all. Crystu stared, eyes wide.

"That? Light above!" she looked back at Jathte, who nodded confirmation.

"I hope you're feeling strong, Crystu."

She took a deep breath.

"Not just me, it will take all of us to deal with that, but that's why we brought so many."

Jathte nodded.

"The duke is providing quarters and stables for all. He has a spacious palace and even all these will leave some spaces in it. Once we get everyone to their quarters, I'll show you what we have done so far. I should warn you that, tonight, all Sorcerers and Ponfourii are invited to a dinner that the duke is throwing in our honour. It was meant to take place yesterday, but then we received the message that you were delayed..." He paused and looked at Crystu.

Tam felt the rush of embarrassment that she felt and he scowled at Jathte. A voice drifted through the crowd of Sorcerers at that moment, as if in response to Jathte's words, though probably not intended to be heard.

"When a Rykatu throws a temper tantrum, lesser mortals have to wait while she grows up!"

Tam twisted round in his saddle, eyes searching for the origin of the offensive remark, but Crystu placed a restraining hand on his arm.

"Leave it, Tam, it's no more than truth after all," she told him ruefully.

She turned back to Jathte.

"I must apologise to the duke for the inconvenience."

"I insisted on the extra day, Crystu," Tam interrupted.

Crystu smiled sadly.

"With good reason, remember?"

"We can decide who takes the blame later, Crystu. We should get everyone moving before those rain clouds reach us," Tam said decisively. "Which way, Jathte?"

Jathte looked a little surprised at Tam's authoritative tone, but pointed along the track towards a group of mounted local soldiers who were waiting.

"They'll ride ahead to show the way, and clear the road if it needs it," he said. Tam nodded and walked his horse across to a solid looking veteran Warrior waiting patiently nearby.

"Captain Amil, quarters have been arranged. Those local soldiers will be showing the way. Get the Septs moving, the Sorcerers will follow behind."

The Warrior nodded and turned to begin barking orders as Tam used illusion to project his words to the Sorcerers and Ponfourii. Speaking at a normal voice, while creating an illusion that the sound was audible across the entire field, he instructed the Sorcerers and Ponfourii to follow the Septs into Angate. Then he rejoined Crystu and Jathte.

Jathte nodded.

"So Da has put the two of you in command? I thought he would. Don't worry, Crystu, I am happy to relinquish the responsibility to you, though I must warn you that one or two of the Sorcerers already here may be less than cooperative. They have made it clear that they think that I am too young to be in charge."

Crystu's eyes narrowed.

"We will see about that!"

Tam laughed.

"You can always threaten to drop them onto a mountain, if they are annoying. The fact that there is only that one," he nodded to the ant-hill, "in the immediate vicinity should help them to behave."

She grinned reluctantly.

"It didn't work with you," she pointed out. Tam grinned back. Jathte looked on with interest.

"I assume that is a reference to the other day? I know it's none of my business but I would like to hear the full story about it one day," he told them.

"Where's Trerisia?" Crystu asked, deliberately changing the subject.

"She's been scouting around, but she's getting nearer; she'll join us in a few minutes," Jathte replied.

As the last line of the Septs went past, they followed behind, and the new Sorcerers followed behind them. A short way along the track, Trerisia rode up to join them.

"Anything?" Jathte asked her.

She frowned.

"Only a group of those idiots, skulking over in that wood." She gestured across to a copse. "They tried again to recruit me!"

Jathte frowned.

"You didn't...?"

"I was more polite than they deserved when I refused their invitation, Jath, and I didn't even draw my sword," she assured him.

He still looked doubtful and she smiled at his worry.

"None need a healer, though some may limp for a few days. I was very restrained."

Jathte closed his eyes and shook his head. Then he glanced at the ice mountain as if considering Tam's suggestion of a moment earlier.

Crystu asked, "Who are the idiots? Why would they try to recruit Trerisia, and for what?"

Jathte chuckled.

"Oh, you'll find out soon enough! There's been a group of them permanently outside the duke's gates almost since we arrived there. They are very dedicated, and only want to help. Even this early they are there."

He chuckled again and looked sideways at Trerisia who was scowling.

"It is not funny, Jath; they are insulting!" she growled.

Tam and Crystu exchanged perplexed glances.

"You'll see," Jathte repeated. "You really need to see it for yourself; I doubt that you would believe me if I told you. No Zia, let them learn, as we did, what those people think. I really am looking forward to seeing your faces when you understand," he said to Crystu and Tam. "Zia's was hilarious."

He laughed again as his Ponfour's scowl deepened.

"I think that they are more dangerous than you believe, my Lord. I will continue to watch them and keep them as far away from you as I can."

Tam was surprised by the bite in Trerisia's tone. He decided that, if *she* saw a threat, he too would keep a close watch.

An Unexpected Reception

As Tam and Crystu rode away, a Ponfour nearby let out a sigh of relief. He shot a look of pure exasperation at the short red-haired young woman riding beside him.

"Astley, if you truly want to see me beaten to a pulp, I'll challenge Tam tonight and you can watch."

She grinned impishly, the red tints that glinted even in her eyes sparkling with her mischief.

"You're almost as big and muscular as he is, Karan, and the bond gives you the same speed and endurance; maybe you would win!"

Her Ponfour rolled his eyes.

"Firstly, I don't want to win; Tam is a friend of mine, and I have no desire to know who is better. Secondly, I believe he is a little faster than I am. The bond doesn't make us all identical."

"It doesn't?" she queried, as the people in front of them finally started to move. They were near the back of the long line of Sorcerers and Ponfourii as they began the slow walk along the track towards Angate.

"No, it doesn't," he confirmed, his eyes flicking around the surrounding fields.

"Some are a little faster than others, not a lot, but enough to make a difference in a challenge. Tam is one. I'm fairly sure that I am not."

"How do you know that you're not," she asked curiously.

Karan smiled.

"Because, as you know, many of us spent part of our extra day yesterday in sports competitions, and there were two who clearly were just a little bit faster and stronger than the rest of us."

He said it without envy. Karan was happy with his new speed and strength, and proud of the gleaming Ponfour symbol on his brow. He smiled down at his younger cousin, more like a younger sister really, but now his bonded Sorceress.

Four years older than Astley at twenty-seven, he had watched over her since she first began to demonstrate her uncanny talent for getting into trouble. It had been a natural progression to go from protective older relative to Ponfour.

"Anyway, what I said was no more than the truth," she pointed out, stubbornly returning to her previous topic. "She *did* throw a tantrum and delay our escape from Tyreen by a full day."

Karan sighed.

"That is between Sorcerer and Ponfour, Ast. It's none of our business."

Astley continued as though she had not heard him. "And besides, if he is a friend of yours, why hasn't he spoken to you?"

Karan shook his head.

"Probably because he doesn't know that I'm here. We were in the same Septine before he bonded, but I haven't seen him since then until the other day and he was a little busy then; I had no chance to talk to him."

She snorted.

"Busy? Busy coping with a Sorceress who can't control her temper."

Several faces cast disapproving looks at Astley because her voice had once again carried further than she had intended.

Karan sighed again.

"And I'm busy coping with a Sorceress who can't control her tongue! You're older than she is and should know better," he said pointedly.

She huffed.

"Aren't you supposed to call me 'my Lady' now?" she asked.

Karan laughed.

"I'll use the formal address in a formal situation, but unless you have an invitation to dine with the royal family that you've forgotten to mention...?" He raised an eyebrow enquiringly, and she shook her head and grinned.

"Then I see no reason to change."

"You did swear to serve me," she said teasingly. "Suppose I order it?"

He smiled.

"If you order me to use formal address, my Lady, I will obey, but I think that you will soon tire of the novelty. Do you so order?"

Astley cocked her head as if considering it, but then shook her head.

"No, you're right, that would just feel too strange. This," she waved at her head, "feels strange enough without you suddenly being polite to me."

She rode in silence for a few minutes, and he could feel her concentration as she thought about something.

She was right: he had known her all her life and had become skilled at guessing her emotions, but being able to sense Ast's feelings inside his own head was disorientating.

He knew that, with practice, he would have no trouble knowing which feelings were hers and which his, but at the moment he was sometimes confused.

She suddenly shook her head.

"You're right: I should know better. What is between Ponfour and Sorceress is between them alone. I would probably become angry too if I overheard people gossiping about me, though I hope that I wouldn't take it out on you."

She looked sideways at him, and he smiled, relieved that her usual good sense had prevailed.

"I hope so too, Ast, but I'm tough; I'll cope if you do and forgive you afterward."

Their conversation was interrupted by a sudden noise ahead. They were riding through an affluent residential area, with large mansions to their right, and a long high wall to the left. They could hear a smattering of laughter, but also some angry sounds, and then Tam's voice loudly cutting across.

"Keep moving, you can read these letters inside, don't stop here to do it; keep moving through the gates." He sounded angry.

As they got closer to the noise, they could see that the last of the Soldiers were riding between a pair of large ornate gates.

Beside the gates a small number of local people were waving signs attached to long poles. Some were chanting something, although Karan could not make out exactly what they were saying. A group of local soldiers stood nearby watching them warily.

The Sorcerers and Ponfourii riding past stared at the signs. Some held pieces of paper, which they stared at with a variety of expressions. Karan noticed that most of the Sorcerers found the sheets amusing, but the Ponfourii almost all looked furious.

Tam, Rykatu Crystu, the younger Lord Jareth, and his Ponfour, had their horses between the group of locals and the moving Tyreans. Karan saw that the Rykatu was nearly doubled up with laughter, and Lord Jareth was grinning broadly, but both Ponfourii looked angry.

Karan felt blank incomprehension sweep across Astley and glanced at her. Then he looked to see what she was staring at. One of the signs had turned enough that he could now read the words on it.

"Tyreans abandon Slavery," he read aloud. "What does that mean?" he asked his partner in confusion.

A child ran up to him, clutching a sheaf of papers, and held one out. Karan took it and smiled at the boy, who smiled back and then, inexplicably, scowled at Astley before dashing to offer paper to the next Ponfour.

"What is it, Karan?" Astley asked as he unfolded the large sheet and began to read. His eyes had skimmed a full third of the page before the meaning of the words hit him. He gasped in astonishment and anger.

"They insult us, Ast! This..." He waved the paper at her, at a loss for a suitable word to describe what was on it. "This insults both Sorcerers and Ponfourii!"

He turned to glare at the people by the gate as he handed the sheet to her.

"We need to get to the front," Jathte stated, as the procession approached the outskirts of the town. "There may be trouble when people see what is beside the gates."

He began to ride around the flank of the Soldiers ahead, Trerisia followed him. After exchanging a perplexed glance, Tam and Crystu also urged their horses to the side and caught up with them. Soon they were at the front of the column, just behind the local soldiers who were leading the way.

"You need to see it first, to have time to understand before the others see it. Come on, we know the way."

Jathte cantered past the soldiers, Trerisia close behind, and again, Tam and Crystu followed.

The early morning streets were largely empty in this affluent, residential area of the town. The only people about, besides the Tyreans, were busy making early morning deliveries to the large houses hidden behind impressive walls.

A baker's cart laden with wrapped bundles on trays, stood beside an open gate. Another cart carrying large canisters had a long queue of people, all holding jugs or bottles, waiting beside it for their turn to fill the containers with milk. Most turned to watch as the group of armoured men and women cantered by, followed shortly afterward by the procession. One or two even cheered and waved.

They reached a long street that ran alongside a high wall which clearly enclosed a large estate.

"That wall boarders Duke Rannis's estate." Jathte waved a hand towards the high wall. "The east gate is a little further along here; you can already see our 'honour guard'." He stressed the last two words.

He pointed ahead, to where they could see a small group of people sitting beside the wall. They appeared to be well-dressed, and had brought folding chairs and a small table. As they approached, Tam could see the ornate gated entrance to the palace a little way beyond the group. Twenty local soldiers were standing between the reclining group and the gate.

One in the group, seeing the approaching Tyreans, jumped to her feet with a shout, the others copied her, picking up large signs on poles as they rose. These they proceeded to wave vigorously, as they shouted something that sounded strangely like, "Return to the Light."

Tam stared at the signs trying to make out the words on them. One by one, they became legible as he approached.

"Tyrean slavers repent," he read out loud, and he and Crystu exchanged bewildered looks.

"Tyrean shame," was written on the next sign.

The words on a larger sign now became intelligible, but although he could read them, the only sense that he could grasp from them made no sense at all.

He read the sign aloud, in a tone of utter disbelief. Beside him, he knew that Crystu was equally confused. Her mind aura was a swirl of yellows and cinnamon as she stared at the same placard.

"Free the enslaved Ponfours!"

Tam stared at it for a moment, wondering if he could have misread it somehow, but the words remained, even when he was only a few yards from the sign.

The people holding those signs were now urging him to take a sheet of paper and read it, but he ignored them, and turned to Jathte.

"Who or what are the enslaved Ponfours?" he asked, guessing what the answer must be, but unable to make any sense of it.

Jathte snorted.

"You are, Tam, and Zia, and everyone who has one of those sun circlets on his head. Apparently we, sadly shadowed, Sorcerers use our magic to force all of you to serve us and die for us."

He reached down and grabbed some of the sheets from the table.

"Here, read these. You too, Crystu."

He handed them a selection.

Trerisia positioned herself between Jathte and the group of campaigners, and scowled at them. The nearest ones edged away from her glare. None of them addressed her, but several began calling out to Tam, telling him that slavery was forbidden in Perrest and that they would aid him if he took his chance to escape.

He stared at them; they were mostly women, some accompanied by children. They all looked educated, intelligent, and affluent.

Tam looked at the sheets in his hand. The first one told how Tyreans had drifted from the Light and the more powerful used their Gifts to bind the less powerful to them in servitude. That once bound, the lesser Tyrean was forced to use his or her Gifts in defence of the stronger, and could be forced to die in their defence.

It urged all Ponfours (as it called them) to flee and seek refuge in the safety of Perrest. It also urged Sorcerers to acknowledge their fault, repent and return to the service of the God of Light.

Crystu eyebrows rose as she read the same leaflet.

"Whoever wrote this has a future as a playwright!" she said brightly. "It is the most imaginative thing I have ever seen."

"Ha! Read the other one – it's even better," Jathte urged.

Tam opened the other sheet and began to read. The misconceptions in this one were even worse! How could anyone think that this was how Sorcerers bonded Ponfourii?

He was so distracted by the missive that he did not at first notice that the procession of Tyreans had caught up and were filing through the now open gates, into the estate.

Crystu found the sheet hilarious; after an initial flood of astonishment, her emotions were now overpowered by laughter. She had doubled up, shaking her head and howling with mirth.

"Oh, Jathte, this sounds like fun! We should try it."

Tam stared at her, wondering how she could be amused by such an insulting piece of libel, but his disapproval made her laugh harder. He looked at the sheet again, wondering if he was missing something. It purported to describe the method by which Sorcerers chose and bound their Ponfours. His mind spun off at a tangent for a moment, puzzled by the incorrect plural in what was otherwise a well-written and correctly spelled, if totally inaccurate, piece of literature.

According to the sheet, Tyreans who had successfully completed their tests of power to become Sorcerers, would set off disguised, across Tyreen, in search of a strong and attractive protector. They would roam in groups or singly, through the towns and villages, using illusion to hide themselves from their prey. When they found someone, they thought sufficiently skilled in fighting, they wove enchantments around their luckless victim robbing him of willpower and independent thought, and binding him to them as a helpless slave. (Him? Did they think only men could be Ponfourii? Tam wondered what they had thought when they saw Trerisia.)

Thereafter, the Ponfour was totally dedicated to the safety of his Sorcerer and would die without hesitation to defend them.

He heard a rumble of noise begin behind him and looked up to see that Sorcerers and Ponfourii were passing by, most holding sheets, and their reactions were similar to his and Crystu's. Most Sorcerers found the sheets amusing, while their Ponfourii scowled and looked insulted.

He thought it unlikely that any would take action against the smiling campaigners who were urging Ponfourii to take advantage of the laws of Perrest, but one or two looked angry enough to cause concern.

"Keep moving! You can read these letters inside. Don't stop here to do it. Keep moving through the gates!"

He waited a moment to be sure that they were complying with the order, and then walked his horse back to the main group of women beside the table.

"Will you free yourself, brother?" asked one of them. "Our laws will protect you."

She scowled at Crystu.

Tam stared at her in disbelief.

"The only sentence that is correct, on *any* of these sheets is that I would die to protect her," he told her, making himself speak calmly. "The rest is an insult, to me, to my Sorceress, and to all of Tyreen. How can you possibly believe such lies?"

She smiled in a bright and understanding manner.

"It's alright. I understand that you cannot speak freely in front of her, just remember that this is your chance."

He stared in astonishment.

"Do you not understand? This," he waved the sheets in his hand, "is wrong. Ponfourii are not bound in this manner."

She continued to smile at him, her face making clear that she thought that he was forced to speak as he did.

"You're wasting your words. I have explained this many times, but they are certain that if the Sorcerer is close by, we are controlled by them completely," Trerisia told Tam.

Her glance at the woman was coldly furious, but still the woman smiled at them. Tam shook his head, wondering how such a belief had come about.

"Look at them, Lady," he said, pointing at the Sorcerers and Ponfourii passing by. "Every Ponfour is as offended by this as I am, can you not see that? Your belief is false!"

A woman at the back of the group did as he suggested, and a slight frown appeared, but the woman to whom he spoke, just shook her head sadly.

"They are too tightly held to see the ropes. If they could be parted from the Sorcerers, they would see that we are trying to help them."

She looked back at him, then stared pointedly at Crystu, who was still laughing at the sheet.

"As would you, if she were elsewhere."

Her certitude was unshakeable! Tam could understand now why Trerisia had spoken of these people as she had. They were irritating and Crystu's amusement did not help his mood.

As the end of the procession went by, a familiar voice suddenly rose above the others.

"This insults both Sorcerers and Ponfourii!"

Glad of the distraction, Tam wheeled his mount to stare at the last few going past in search of the owner of the voice……. there!

"Karan!"

Hearing his name, the other Ponfour looked up, anger still showing on his face until he saw who had called him.

Tam urged his horse over and reached across to clasp arms with his old friend.

"So you finally joined the Ponfourii! And is this Lady the cousin you spoke of so often?"

He looked at the Sorceress riding beside Karan. She smiled back, a little tentatively, he thought.

"Yes, my Lord, this is my Lady Astley," Karan replied proudly.

Tam flicked a sideways glance at his friend but, he thought sadly, he was in command of this group so the formal title was correct in public. He turned his attention back to the Lady.

"My congratulations on your ascension to Sorceress, Lady Astley."

He smiled, trying to put her at ease. She glanced at Karan and sucked in her lower lip, before replying, "Thank you, Lord Tam."

She spoke in a surprisingly low voice. Tam knew that he had heard that voice recently and suddenly understood her evident nervousness; this was the same voice that had made the earlier remark about Crystu's temper. He frowned and glanced at Karan, who looked as if he was holding his breath.

"I apologise, my Lord, for my earlier remark. Karan has already scolded me for it. I spoke without right, about something which is none of my concern."

The woman spoke quickly, and Tam sighed.

"Indeed you did, Lady, but..."

"But," Crystu's voice interrupted, "you said no more than everyone else thought."

She had joined the group so quietly that even Tam had not noticed her. He glanced around and realised that the four of them were the only Tyreans still in the street. The group of 'idiots' was watching them with obvious interest.

"Jathte and Trerisia have gone within to organise everyone into their accommodations," Crystu told him, before turning her attention back to Astley.

"I behaved in an appalling fashion, and did so publicly. I cannot in fairness take offence if people talk about it."

The two women looked at each other and then, suddenly, both smiled.

"This is Karan, a friend from my old Septine, and this is Lady Astley," Tam told Crystu.

Crystu smiled at both.

"Congratulations on your bonding, Lady Astley, Lord Karan. I hope that you will sit with us for a meal while we are here in Angate."

"Thank you, my Lady, you are most gracious." Astley meant more than the invitation.

Tam looked sideways at Karan. He grinned at the look on his friend's face.

"Did you think I would challenge you over this, Karan?" he asked.

"It crossed my mind, Tam, and I have no wish to defeat you in a public challenge fight." Karan grinned back. For a minute, Tam felt as though they were back in the Septine barracks.

"You? Beat me?" Tam chuckled. "I don't recall *that* ever happening in the past; it certainly couldn't now."

Karan shook his head.

"Well, they do say that the memory is the first thing to go as you age, Tam, so perhaps you've forgotten."

Tam snorted. "You're older than I am!" he pointed out.

"And neither of you is ancient."

The two women spoke in unison, and then glanced at each other.

Crystu laughed.

"We seem to think alike, Lady Astley. I hope that we can be friends."

Astley smiled shyly. "As do I, my Lady."

"Tam, what is this about?" Karan waved the sheets. "Is *this* what all the people of this land believe about us?" He sounded appalled at the thought.

"Light! I hope not!" Tam replied, startled; that this belief might be widespread had not occurred to him. "I think Jathte would have said so if it were; I think that it must be just a small group. I hope so anyway. They are completely fixed in their beliefs. I told them they are wrong, and they just smiled and offered me refuge if I fled my captivity."

He glanced at the women; their smiles were beginning to irritate him.

"We should go within. Trerisia and Jathte are doing my work, and I tire of being stared at in that fashion," he said.

"Yes, my Lord. Come, my Lady."

Karan bowed his head, and he and Astley rode ahead to the gates.

"Crystu?"

She was staring at the distant ice peak that loomed over the chalk ridge above the town.

"I think I will fly over for a closer look," she announced, and shapeshifted into her favourite eagle form.

Tam timed his move perfectly, so that as she spread her wings and leapt skywards, his hand shot out to grasp her leg. He pulled her back to her saddle, holding firmly. He could feel her surprise and annoyance at his action, but kept his hold until she changed back and stared at him. Her mind radiated jagged ochre hues of irritation across the bond.

"Why did you stop me?" she asked.

"My Lady, I do not believe that mountain could have grown so large so quickly without assistance," he told her. "Assistance, which may still linger in the vicinity."

Crystu inhaled sharply as she understood his meaning.

"I know that I cannot go with you when you shapeshift, but I will not agree to any solo ventures by you. You must wait until there are other shapeshifters, including Ponfourii, available to go with you."

Tam held Crystu's eyes until he felt her annoyance melt into acquiescence.

"Thank you, my Lady." He smiled. "Shall we go within?"

"Of course, my Lord," she said teasingly, copying Karan's bow of the head before riding ahead through the gate.

As Tam rode through after her, his sharp ears overheard something that made him think that some at least of the idiots might still be capable of reason. A woman's voice spoke quietly but intensely.

"Did you see that? Could a slave so order his mistress? Could Kaliss be wrong in what he says?"

Tam glanced back as he rode, through the gate, and saw the woman, who had earlier seemed puzzled when she saw how astonished and offended the Ponfourii were, leaning close to another and both were watching him as he went through the gate.

"Kaliss wrong? Impossible! You've heard him speak. How can you..." The reply was cut off by the closing of the gate behind him.

The model

Nearly an hour later, after Tam had made certain that everyone knew where they would sleep, he and Crystu joined Jathte and Trerisia in a large ground floor room in one wing of the duke's palace. The room ran the full width of the wing and both the side walls contained long windows, which extended from the floor to the ceiling.

The room usually functioned as a ballroom or dining room, one of many, but now it housed a long, central table, on which they could see a model of the landscape above the town. The rolling chalk downlands were dwarfed by the white mountain sitting upon them.

Some parts of the model were rendered in exquisite detail – the southernmost feet of the mountain, and the downs close to it were so sharp, that Tam knew he would be able to see individual leaves on the plants if he transmuted a magnifier – the rest was only roughly shaped, with no detail at all. Around the room, on other large tables, Tam could see paper maps showing the area around Angate at different scales.

"We have done what we could," Jathte began, walking over to the model, "but only nine Sorcerers and their Ponfourii could join us while we waited for you, and none of them are shapeshifters, so we could only do the areas that are visible from safe ground, and then only a small portion at a time."

He walked round the table to peer at the north side, and then shrugged.

"I split them into three groups: three pairs go out as far as they can for two days, to triangulate their combined view and build an illusion here, three pairs stay in here to transmute the model to match the illusion, and the other three pairs rest. Meanwhile, Trerisia and I have been riding out most days to destroy all the smaller sized anthills that have been appearing."

Tam looked up at that.

"Are they forming near the town," he asked.

Jathte shook his head.

"So far the closest was halfway down the ridge, but they are getting nearer all the time."

Crystu walked round the model, examining it closely.

"It must be complete before I can use it, or it won't work as a focus. The mountain is too large for me to transmute it without something smaller to focus on."

"I know that, Crystu," Jathte said patiently.

"Sorry, Jathte, I know you do."

He nodded, accepting her apology, then asked, "How many shapeshifters did you bring with you?"

She shrugged.

"All those available who can also dreamwalk: Twenty seven in total. Fourteen of those are bonded pairs who can both shapeshift, and of the rest, four are Ponfourii, two Sorcerers, six are Warriors, and there is one soldier." She walked back around the table, and then looked up. "Plus me, of course," she added.

"The king is holding to that restriction, my Lady?" Trerisia asked, "Won't that be difficult when the main army must march? Many of them cannot dreamwalk."

Crystu nodded.

"He is, although he has accepted that the army cannot be restricted in that way. They will be securely warded when they march, but wards are impractical in *this* sort of endeavour. Lord Jareth may need to contact us, so we cannot use shield wards against dreamwalkers, and we cannot ward against illusion, or we would not be able to build the model."

Jathte nodded.

"I have set up shield wards against transmutation and translocation around the palace, but of course if I were to set up blanket wards to block magic completely, that too would prevent us working on the model."

"Then we must be vigilant," Tam said. "I do not believe that this ant-hill formed by itself, and the shadow minions who assisted its formation may still be nearby."

"I agree with you on that, Tam," Jathte replied. "In fact, I am certain that at least one is. I've sensed a slight magical residue in the town a couple of times in the last week."

Crystu and Tam both looked up at that, and Tam nodded decisively.

"Then I will assign three Septines of Soldiers and two of Warriors to patrol the palace walls. We do not want anyone," he paused, "or anything, climbing or flying over the walls to get through the shield wards."

He looked up at Jathte.

"Will that cause any problem with the king's guards?" he asked.

Jathte shook his head.

"They've been ordered to accommodate themselves to whatever we want, and they'll probably be glad of the assistance."

"Good," said Tam, relieved, "because I intend to borrow as many local soldiers as I can to assist us."

Jathte raised his eyebrows and glanced at Crystu who waved his attention back to Tam.

"How do you plan to proceed, Tam?" he asked quietly. "I'd like to repeat that I'm glad to be relieved of the responsibility, so don't think that you're treading on my toes in any way."

"Or mine," Trerisia added, smiling.

Tam glanced at him and smiled.

"I am relieved you feel that way, Jathte. You and Trerisia have been out in the Protectorates far longer than have Crystu and I, and are more experienced. I was surprised that Lord Jareth put us in command here."

"No, Tam, he put *you* in command," Crystu interrupted, "and he was right to do so. I could give orders to Warriors and Sorcerers and they would obey, but they would not trust me. I am too young, and too volatile. You, they trust."

Trerisia nodded.

"Lady Crystu is correct, Lord Tam, you are respected and your orders will be trusted."

"Da knows what he is doing, Tam," Jathte agreed.

Tam took a deep breath. He knew that he had not completely regained his confidence in himself after what had happened with the Zindon, and he found the unexpected affirmation hard to believe.

He had to tell himself firmly that neither Jathte nor Trerisia would say that unless they believed it, and the bond relayed Crystu's certainty. It also relayed her support as she recognised his difficulty in accepting that other Tyreans respected him.

"Thank you for that," he said seriously. "I hope that you are correct, because some will not like what I will order."

"You still haven't told us," Jathte prompted.

Tam nodded. He looked at the model again.

"We will follow the usual two days' work, one day rest pattern. I have drawn up a rota so that, as far as is possible, we have equal numbers of shapeshifters, transmuters, and illusionists available on each day. Some of the shapeshifters: One Sorcerer, two of the Ponfourii, and five of the Soldiers, are not illusionists. They will act as lookouts while the others concentrate on projecting their views onto the model. That leaves twenty shapeshifters: fourteen of them bonded pairs, and the others, except for the soldier and Warrior, are bonded to a Sorcerer or Ponfour who can transmute but not shapeshift. With all of the bonded pairs, I intend to have one of them shapeshifted and flying over the mountain, while the other is in here transmuting the model."

Tam smiled wryly as Trerisia gasped and Jathte's eyes widened.

"Yes, I know that will be an unpopular order, especially with the Ponfourii who must stay here while their Sorcerer is over there." He jerked his head in the approximate direction of the ice mountain.

"I don't like it either, but it should make the work easier."

Jathte frowned.

"I don't understand,"

"I'll answer with a question," Tam replied. "How do the illusionists out there," he waved towards the window, "know when the transmuters have finished the area of the model that they are focussed on? How do they know when to move to another area?"

Jathte shrugged.

"That is a problem. I ended up setting an arbitrary time limit of exactly two hours an area, but we often have to go back the next day, because the transmuters hadn't always finished, and sometimes they finished more quickly and had to just wait out the time. Oh, I see!" He nodded. "If you split the partners, then they can use the bond to let the other know that they can move to the next area."

Tam nodded.

"And the shapeshifter will signal the others in his or her group to move on too. We can do the work more efficiently that way, so whether we like it or not, those bonded to a shapeshifter must work this way."

"You will do this too?" Trerisia asked.

"Of course," Tam replied, with a rueful smile. "I can hardly expect others to agree to it, if I don't do it myself." He looked at Crystu. "You will be careful, won't you Crystu."

She nodded.

"I can look after myself if I have to, Tam…" she paused mischievously, then relented at his spike of concern, "but I will be careful. You have my promise."

Tam smiled back at her. The sunlight streaming through the window made her hair gleam beautifully.

"You were telling us the plan, Tam?" Jathte prompted a second time, a small smile on his face.

Tam pulled himself back to his task with an effort.

"Taking everything into consideration, there are thirteen or fourteen shapeshifters, who are also illusionists, available to fly each day, most of whom will have a partner who can transmute. I intend to send ten groups out each day, each based around one

Septine of Warriors. The Soldiers will be divided – three or four going with each group. Similarly, four or five Sorcerers and their Ponfourii, including at least one shapeshifter, will join each group. The remaining shapeshifters will go wherever there is a need for additional eyes – those who can add to the illusion doing so, the others keeping watch. In each group, no matter how many are illusionists, no more than half will merge their Gifts for the task, while the others will keep watch and defend as necessary. The illusionists should preferably be Sorcerers, Warriors, or Soldiers, leaving the Ponfourii to act as defenders."

Trerisia nodded agreement with that, and then asked, "You don't intend to split the bonded pairs on the ground?"

Tam shook his head.

"No, I consider that those on the ground are at far greater risk of attack, than are those in the air, so their Ponfourii should remain with them."

"Agreed," Jathte and Trerisia said together, and then grinned at each other before Jathte looked back at Tam.

"The illusionists and transmuters are going to be using a lot of magic for long periods, Tam. Even with one rest day every three, some may not have the strength."

Tam nodded.

"That is the other reason to only allow half to participate. There will be healers among those standing watch. As each area is finished, all the illusionists are to be checked by the healers in their group before they begin the next area. If any are too tired to continue safely, they will swap places with a defender."

"And the transmuters?" asked Jathte.

"There will be healers amongst those I assign to guard the walls. They will have to undertake the same duty here, except that the transmuters will have to just stop and rest if they cannot continue safely. I will not call on those who should be resting; they will need that rest."

Jathte nodded, and peered at the unformed model again.

“It sounds like a good plan, Tam, the only problem I can see will be getting the bonded shapeshifters to agree to split."

Tam nodded.

"I've arranged to meet with them all after the firstmeal today to explain what I want. I'm not intending to make it a request though, Jathte, they *will* do as I order."

He glanced at Crystu as he caught a combative element to her emotions.

"No, Crystu. I will meet them alone. If I have to threaten them with a Rykatu to make them obey, then I should not be in command, so you will stay away."

He held her eyes until she nodded, but he sensed that she was distracted by something.

"You have a question, Crystu?" he asked, she looked up and grinned.

"Not about your plan, Tam, I was just wondering about something." She looked at Jathte thoughtfully.

"You said that you timed two hours exactly, but how did you manage that? We all have excellent time sense while human, but when I change into a bird I scarcely notice time at all. I certainly would not know when two hours had gone by."

Jathte grinned and, walking over to a table cluttered with maps and several small objects that Tam did not recognise, he picked up something cylindrical, about the size of a plum, and handed it to Crystu. Tam stepped beside her to look at it.

She held a small metal object with a numbered dial on one side and several small projections on the other. Attached to the casing was a strip of looped leather. She and Tam glanced at each other, equally perplexed.

"What is it?" Crystu asked.

"Believe it, or not," Jathte replied, "it’s a cooking tool, called a telltime. They use it to time how long a roast or cake has been cooking, but it works just as well to time an illusion."

"How does it work?" Crystu asked.

Tam felt a slight tickle of magic and knew that she was probing the object.

"It's full of tiny round pieces of metal and a long coiled flat piece! How can metal judge time?" Crystu exclaimed.

Jathte took it from her.

"You turn this piece until it stops, then set the dial to the amount of time the roast needs in the oven, the outer numbers are minutes, the inner, hours, and when ready, you push in this part." He did so, and the object began to emit a ticking sound. "Then you wait. I've set this to one minute." He held it up by the strap.

"You can wear it around your neck. The illusionist sets it to two hours, begins the illusion and then at the end of the period..." He waited.

Tam and Crystu both jumped when the telltime suddenly began making a loud noise. Grinning, Jathte pushed a button and the sound stopped. Crystu stared at it, eyes wide in awe.

"That's amazing, and it used no magic at all! It's ingenious! They make these here? Entirely by hand?"

Jathte nodded.

"Yes. Incredible isn't it? They have other things too that are both inventive and useful. Here," he handed Tam a long, tapering leather covered tube which had glass at either end, "point the wide end out of the window towards that tree, hold the narrow end to your eye, and turn this part slowly."

After a puzzled glance at Crystu, Tam did as instructed. He gasped as the grey and red blur, which he saw at first, suddenly resolved into a small bird. Each feather was distinct and he could even see the sunlight glinting off its eye. He pulled the tube from his eye and looked at the tree with his eyes; he could still see the bird, but not even its colouring was clear at his distance.

"That is astonishing," he said still staring at the bird and remembering the amazing detail that he had seen.

"What is it?" Crystu asked as he probed it with his Gift.

"It's just glass!" he said in disbelief, "but it works as well as a transmuted air magnifier, how can glass do that?"

He handed the device to Crystu, who stepped through the open door-length window, and put it to her eyes. Tam could feel her amazement as she moved it around pointing at different things.

"The duke recently began an annual competition for the most interesting and useful new device. People all around Perrest work hard trying to find ways to do, with *made* things, what we do with magic," Jathte told them.

"There'a place in town where the best are made and sold. It's an interesting place to visit.

"This will be useful for those who are illusionists but are not transmuters," said Crystu as she re-entered the room, "they will be able to see details otherwise lost to them. We should have at least one of these for each group if possible."

"Yes," agreed Tam. "Can we get that many, Jathte?"

"Yes. The local soldiers already use them so they have a good supply. I'll ask Captain Pendin to supply you with ten," Jathte answered.

"Good. Then after everyone has eaten, I will inform the shapeshifters of my intentions and then we can begin to organise. The rotas for the Warriors and Soldiers are already drawn up, but I did not know for sure how many Sorcerers Lord Jareth would send with us, or who they would be, until yesterday, and I don't yet know their abilities. So, after I've spoken to the shapeshifters, Crystu and I will find out what Gifts the Sorcerers and Ponfourii have, and then we can assign them to the groups. We should be able to begin the survey this afternoon.

Jathte nodded, and then looked again at the model.

"It is going to take days to finish this," he said, and then he straightened as a thought struck him.

"What about the new ant-hills that will be appearing while we work on this, Tam."

Tam grinned.

"They are your job,– yours and the other Sorcerers who were already here when we arrived. You know the land better than we do, so I will leave that to all of you."

"Thank you," replied Jathte dryly as Trerisia smiled.

Tam frowned.

"Problem?"

Jathte sighed.

"Nothing serious, I just wish that Vellte would stop acting like I've only just learned to wipe my own nose."

"You exaggerate, Jath. She's not that bad," smiled Trerisia.

Jathte snorted.

"You're a Ponfour! She approves of Ponfourii, and assumes you're all sensible, intelligent adults. She thinks any Sorcerer under the age of forty needs to be watched constantly to stop them breaking something!"

Tam looked at Crystu.

"She may have a point," he said, grinning.

Crystu looked up guiltily, the leather strip which she had just removed from the magnifier falling to the ground.

"Crystu," Tam admonished, "if you want to take one to pieces, buy one; don't use one of the king's."

She stuck her tongue out at him, picked up the fallen piece, and placed it back into position. She put the tube to her eye and pointed it outside.

"It still works," she said, lowering it again, "I just wanted to see inside." Tam felt her probe along the bond and then she crowed, "I thought so! You're just as eager to take one apart, and that telltime, too!"

Tam shook his head ruefully, she was correct of course: he would love take both apart to learn how they worked.

"When I have my own I may do just that, Crystu, but not with the king's."

"Which reminds me," said Crystu, deliberately changing the subject. "You keep referring to the duke, Jathte. Do I assume that he does not want any mention of his other title?"

"Oh! Yes, thank you for bringing that up, Crystu." Jathte slapped his forehead.

"Few people in Angate know that their duke is also their king, and he wants it to stay that way if possible."

Tam nodded.

"Only Sorcerers and Ponfourii are likely to know about his dual title, so that should not be a problem. I'll make certain that everyone knows to refer to him as duke and not king."

At that moment, a knock at the door was followed closely by its opening to admit a middle-aged retainer. The man was slim with short grey hair and a neat, but surprisingly ginger, beard. He looked confident and competent and walked across to address Jathte.

"My Lord Jareth, Lord Rannis sends his respects and he hopes that you, Lady Trerisia, Lady Rykatu Crystu, and Lord Tam will join him, and his family, in his private rooms, for firstmeal."

"That's very kind of him, Bredge," Jathte replied. He turned to Tam. "Tam? It's your command now, so you're the one who must reply. This is House Bredge."

Tam had noted the flash of surprise in the man's eyes as Jathte deferred to him, but Bredge quickly schooled his expression and gave a short bow as he was introduced.

"'House' is a local title for a household organiser," Jathte continued. "He keeps the entire household running smoothly, including Duke Rannis. If you need anything, just ask Bredge and he will organise it."

Tam nodded.

"We will be glad to accept the duke's invitation, but first I must be sure that our people have all found the meal room."

Bredge inclined his head slightly.

"Of course, my Lord. Duke Rannis anticipated that any good commander would make certain that his men ate before he did, so I am to take you to the meal room first where you can assure yourself that they are being well looked after. At your convenience, of course."

"Thank you," Tam replied. "My Lady, if you're finished?"

Crystu laughed and placed the tube on the table.

"Of course, Tam. There's no need for you to miss *this* meal."

"Thank you, my Lady; I appreciate that," he replied, with a wry smile.

As she stepped past him towards the door, she paused and looked at him,

"You're being formal again, Tam," she said, teasingly, and he could feel her trying, unsuccessfully, to colour her mind touch with hurt feelings.

He raised an eyebrow at her, as he waved her back and then stepped through the door, glancing up and down the corridor before beckoning her through. Trerisia followed Crystu, with Jathte close behind, and finally Bredge.

Tam noticed that Bredge appeared surprised that Tam went through first, and wondered why, but then he remembered that Perrestian custom had women going through a door first, followed by any men with them. Tyrean custom was different: the Ponfour stepped through first, and then the Sorcerer.

Anything could be hiding on the far side of the door, out of sight in the corridor, and a Ponfour would never allow his sworn charge to step through into unseen danger.

"My Lady, an invitation to eat with the duke surely counts as a formal situation, and you are not in the least bit upset so please stop trying to pretend that you are," he told her as she stepped beside him.

Trerisia looked at him piercingly for a second, then at Crystu, and finally she grinned at Jathte, who suddenly developed a cough.

"Bond games, Crystu?" he said when he could talk again. "That's a slippery slope."

"And he should know!" Trerisia grinned as she took a graceful grip on his proffered arm.

"Ha! I had to do something to get you to use my name! All those 'my Lords' were getting in the way."

"I know the feeling!" Crystu muttered, with a sideways glance at Tam.

He deliberately cultivated a feeling of tolerant patience and projected it along the bond. He knew that only the presence of Bredge prevented her from sticking her tongue out again in response. Then he felt a mischievous sparkle, shimmer across her mind and into her eyes.

"You will talk to Trerisia, won't you Tam? I've been trying to persuade her to call me Crystu ever since she and Jathte bonded, but she is very stubborn. You know how upset I am by friends who keep me behind my title." She grinned at Trerisia.

Tam sighed.

"Of course, I will, Crystu. I'm sure I can persuade her to relent."

He looked at Trerisia, who stared back with eyes slightly narrowed. She suddenly smiled.

"I will do so on one condition, my Lord Tam."

Tam raised his eyebrows.

"And what is that condition, my Lady Trerisia?" he asked.

"I think that it is time that we put an end to the speculation, and finally learn which of us is the faster," she replied.

"Trerisia!" Jathte exclaimed, looking worried.

"You're challenging me?" Tam asked, surprised.

"No, Lord Tam. *You* are going to challenge *me*," she replied, staring him in the eye. Tam nodded slowly.

He understood: if she challenged him, then he would set the terms of the fight, but if he challenged *her*, then she decided the conditions.

"If you agree to this, I will do my best to be less formal in private as Lady Crystu wishes. I swear it in the Light," Trerisia promised.

Tam did not hesitate further.

"Then I challenge you to prove which of us is the better fighter, Lady Trerisia. On which terms will you accept this challenge?"

She smiled.

“A private match, just the two of us. Lord Huryn’s Game: best of five rounds, no weapons, no padding, and no one else will know the result, except of course Jath and Lady Crystu.”

“Just the two of you?” Crystu interrupted. “Can’t Jathte and I watch?”

“Absolutely, I want to be there,” Jathte agreed, though with less enthusiasm, “if only to heal your two idiotic skulls afterwards.

Trerisia nodded.

“Very well, the four of us, and no one else.”

Tam nodded.

“When?” he asked.

“The sooner the better,” she replied. “Make sure that your rest days coincide with mine, and we will do it on the first one.”

“Three days from today,” Tam told her.

“Challenge accepted,” Trerisia said firmly, and the two Ponfourii grinned at each other. Jathte rolled his eyes and shook his head, and Crystu was almost jumping with anticipation.

Tam found that he too was looking forward to the match, even though he was not at all sure that he would win. Trerisia might not be quite as strong as he was, but she was probably faster, and had a longer reach with both arms and legs. He reluctantly pushed thoughts about the fight to the back of his mind, to get on with today’s duties.

Bredge was discretely pretending complete deafness, as he walked a little way ahead. When they reached the meal room, in which the other Tyreans had already gathered, Tam could see that the Perrestians had provided plenty of food. Tables, along one side of the room, were laden with platters full with various cooked meats, eggs, bread, and preserved fruits. Perrestians believed that the first meal of the day should be substantial; Tyreans agreed with that idea.

"My Lords, my Ladies!"

Captain Amil had appeared beside them almost as though he had been waiting for them, and perhaps he had.

"Captain, is everything all right, does everyone have what they need?" Tam asked.

Amil nodded.

"Yes, my Lord, the quarters are eminently suitable, and the food is excellent."

"Good," Tam replied, glancing around the room. He saw Karan and Astley in one corner and nodded to them, then turned back to the Captain.

"Captain, I intend to meet with the shapeshifters later this morning, and after that I will issue the rotas. I intend that we start surveying the mountain this afternoon, as soon after the midday meal as possible. Before then, please make sure that all have checked that their armour spells are solid. Immediately after this meal, I need you to detach five Septines: three of Soldiers and two of Warriors, to begin patrolling the walls."

He turned to Bredge.

"With whom should we liaise about this, House Bredge? I would like to work with your own people, not annoy them."

"You should speak to Captain Pendin, my Lord," Bredge replied. "I will have a message sent to him immediately after I have escorted you to my Lord Duke's chamber. Who shall I tell him to contact?"

"Captain Amil." Tam indicated the officer, who nodded once to Bredge and then spoke to Tam.

"Lord Tam, if I may ask, how likely is it that someone may try to climb over the walls? It will affect my choice from the Soldiers. Some of them are on their first outside mission, and I need to know whether I should use them, or more experienced Soldiers."

Tam hesitated, conscious not only of Bredge's presence, but also that of various household staff around the room, who were busily serving his people. He did not want to mention Zindons when he did not know for sure if one was in the vicinity. Rumours would fly and people might panic. At the same time, Amil did need to know enough to make his choice.

"Use experienced people, Captain, and tell them to be wary," he replied.

Amil's eyes flickered across Bredge and the liveried servants and nodded. Tam knew that he had understood.

"Yes, my Lord," he answered.

Tam could feel Crystu's growing hunger, and he too found that the sight of everyone else eating was sharpening his own appetite.

"Thank you, Captain Amil, please return to your meal." he said and, after the Captain had walked away, he turned back to Bredge.

"Thank you for organising all this, House Bredge."

The man inclined his head.

"It is my job, my Lord," he replied simply, and then opened the door into the hall.

"If my Lords and Ladies are ready to proceed?" He made it both a question and a polite suggestion.

As she was closest to the door, Trerisia went through first, and then nodded for Jathte to follow. Tam stepped through next, and once again checked that the corridor was safe before beckoning Crystu through. Bredge followed, closing the door behind him, and once more walked ahead to show the way.

"I am so glad that I took the time to change while you were organising people into their rooms earlier," whispered Crystu, as they proceeded.

Tam looked down at her flowing green silk dress and thought that she looked beautiful and regal. He, Trerisia and Jathte, still wore their usual leather clothes, which, though well-made and well looked after, had worn patches in places where mail and armour plate rubbed. Crystu frowned at him and he felt a tingle of magic use, accompanied by slight movement over his body.

"There, that's better," Crystu said with satisfaction, as Tam stared down at himself.

"Crystu! Please ask before you do things like that! They were my favourite leathers!" Tam protested, trying to ignore another suspicious bout of coughing from behind.

"I haven't altered them much, just cleaned them, repaired the worn spots, and improved the colour. Now you look like a Rykatu's Ponfour."

They did still feel the same, he admitted to himself, but they were now a deep, rich green in colour and perfectly matched her dress. As they walked past a mirror, he glanced at his reflection and saw that they did make a striking pair.

"Ha! See? You like it, and it looks good on you, so no complaining."

A startled gasp behind them, made them spin round, to find Jathte staring accusingly at Trerisia, who looked as satisfied with herself as had Crystu a moment before. Both she and Jathte were now wearing matching leathers in a deep red colour.

"Not a word, Jath," she said, "We could not go to eat with the duke looking like we had just crawled out of a tent."

"Our clothing hasn't bothered you before today," he pointed out.

"Before today, is not today. Today it bothered me," she replied calmly with a slight smile, which disappeared with Jathte's next words.

"I suppose I can always change them back afterwards," he said, looking at his reflection in the mirror, "and so can Tam for that matter."

Tam's eyes widened, he wasn't sure whether that was the bravest, or the most foolish thing, that he had ever heard anyone say.

Jathte looked around at his Ponfour, presumably warned by something he had felt from her through their bond. Her eyes had narrowed, her face was cold, and she had let go of his arm.

"That was an extremely stupid thing that I just said, wasn't it, Zia? I'm sorry. The colour is very nice and I wouldn't want to change anything that you have made for me."

Jathte clearly meant it. Trerisia immediately smiled and took his arm again without a word.

Tam felt Crystu's eyes on him, and turned to look at her.

"I never even thought it," he told her honestly.

She smiled at him.

"I know you didn't, Tam. You have more sense."

"I'll have to keep these for best, and get more to use for everyday," Jathte said. "I couldn't mar these with oily mail and armour."

Tam realised that he was correct: these were now too fine to put mail and armour over. He, too, would have to make new leathers to wear under his armour, and it would take months before they were as comfortable as these. He looked accusingly at Crystu, who grinned back.

Bredge had gaped at them all in amazement, his usual unshakeable attitude of calm competence shaken by the unusual sight of clothes that changed colour by themselves, but he quickly recovered his poise, and indicated a large double-door ahead.

"Duke Rannis' chamber. I will announce you."

He knocked discretely, and then at a command from within, opened both doors wide, stepped through, and bowed.

"My Lord Duke, Duchess, Ladies and Lord: The Rykatu Lady Crystu, with Lord Ponfour Tam, and Sorcerer Lord Jareth, with Lady Ponfour Trerisia."

He stepped aside and, despite their custom, Crystu took hold of Tam's arm to step into the room beside him, followed by Jathte and Trerisia.

Inside the duke's meal chamber, a large table was set with places for ten adults and a child. Duke Rannis and his family were standing just inside the door to greet the Tyreans. Tam knew that the duke had two adult children and that his son was married and had a child of his own. The young man with his arm around a woman holding an infant must be the son and family, while the young woman beside Duke Rannis must be his daughter; the resemblance was marked. Another young woman stood beside the daughter and Tam was startled to recognise her face.

She had been one of those outside the gate, the one who had listened to what he said, and who had wondered aloud about whether someone called Kaliss might be wrong.

Erian

Lady Erian Tolene stood patiently in front of the long mirror, while her maid carefully fastened the many buttons at the back of her ornately stitched, floor-length dress. She surreptitiously watched the maid in the mirror and pondered the differences between service and servitude. Were those differences so great?

Gerine received pay, food and a place to live, for her work, but was expected to obey orders without question and had to spend every day performing menial tasks for another. Erian knew that she was no hard task master, but some members of the aristocracy treated their servants no different than slaves.

Theoretically, any servant could leave their job and go elsewhere, but in practice this rarely happened. They had no opportunity to seek other employment while they were working full time, and who would give up a wage not knowing if they could find another paid job?

If they failed to please their employer, they could be thrown out, and without a reference would have a hard time finding more work. Those who were without work, and had no other income, ended up relying on the charity of the Church of Light for food and clothing.

Slavery was outlawed in Perrest and had been for over two hundred years, so Erian had only written accounts by which to judge what it entailed. Before then, slavery had been a frequent punishment for theft, and sometimes people, without any other way to provide for themselves, had sold themselves into slavery simply for the chance to eat.

There had been laws governing the rights of slaves, giving them some protection from abuse, but Erian knew that there had been a time when a slave had no rights at all, could be maimed or killed at their owner's whim.

The idea that the Guardians of Reyth might be practicing some form of slavery was unbelievable, and yet, Kaliss was so persuasive when he spoke that she could not easily believe that he was wrong.

Then again, the anger in the large Ponfour's eyes as he read the sheets, his insistence that they were incorrect, the way all the Ponfourii had reacted, with incredulity and anger, plus the laughter of the Sorcerers, all suggested that Kaliss was, in truth, wrong in his belief that the Sorcerers used magic to enslave those whom they chose for their Ponfourii.

The large Ponfour had stopped the Rykatu flying off on her own; surely that did not fit with a man whose mind was under her complete domination.

Gerine had finished fastening her dress, and Erian sat automatically to allow the maid to comb and style her long, straight, black hair. She looked at her reflection in the mirror and thought back to the stream of Soldiers and Warriors, followed by Sorcerers and Ponfourii. The Tyreans were mostly darker skinned than the warm copper that characterised the inhabitants of Perrest, but that made sense because the Tyreen Mountains were in the south so the sun was much stronger over Tyreen.

Erian had expected most of them to be men, but Kaliss had definitely been wrong about that! There were almost as many women amongst the Ponfourii as there were amongst the Sorcerers, and many of the Soldiers and Warriors were also women.

Erian had been fascinated at the sight of so many women wearing trousers. The uniforms of the Soldiers and Warriors were the same for men and women and even most of the Sorceresses had been wearing leather trousers. A few, older, Sorceresses wore robes, but so did some of the Sorcerers. The majority, however, both male and female, had their legs individually clad in leather, which Erian supposed was sensible if they intended to wear armour.

Erian had been surprised when she had learned that the first Sorcerer to arrive in Angate had a female Ponfour, but the woman was huge, and clearly stronger than most men. Some of those Erian had seen today were little taller than Perrestian average, yet they too moved with that same flowing, dangerous grace, and had looked easily capable of violence, especially as they read the sheets handed to them.

She knew that she needed to learn more. She had heard Kaliss' view, so in fairness, she needed to hear the Tyreans' side too. How else could she decide whether to commit fully to the breakaway Group of Light?

She had attended the protest at the gate because if Kaliss was correct, then the Tyreans needed to be reminded of the way of Light, and if he was wrong, then at worst she made a fool of herself and she could stand that if she had to.

Lady Erian Tolene was a strong and self-confident young woman. Her mother had died in childbirth when Erian was two years old and the baby too had died.

Her father had raised her to be self-sufficient. Despite being of high birth, at need she could make her own clothes, cook, and even make pottery. She had had instruction in the basics of many crafts that were not considered suitable for a young lady, including metal-working, and glass blowing. She was even able to handle a sword with almost as much skill as a sewing needle.

She wondered if her father perhaps had had a premonition that she would need that sort of attitude to life. He had died of a fever when she was fifteen, leaving her with a large fortune and no close relatives. She lived in the large family home, not far from Angate, with a few older, less well-off, female relatives for company.

Several distant cousins had offered to help guide and protect the young heiress (and her fortune) but Duke Rannis had made her his ward, until she was old enough to have charge of her own life and money.

Erian had been friends with Rannis's daughter Taranel since early childhood, and had been a frequently-invited visitor to the ducal palace since her father's death.

Taranel thought her current involvement with the Group of Light was foolishness, and told her so clearly and succinctly, but had agreed to invite her friend to stay while the Tyreans were present, once Erian had explained that she wanted to ask them first-hand whether any of Kaliss' accusations were true.

Tammia, Kaliss' aide, had been incensed when Erian explained what she intended – she saw it as insulting to Kaliss – but Kaliss himself had said he thought it an excellent idea. He had told her that she must do whatever she felt was right, and seek her own answers from the Tyreans.

As often happened, just being in the same room with him had sent a pleasant tingle across her scalp. He had such a soothing pleasant voice, even though his features were nondescript.

Gerine finished brushing her hair, and Erian dismissed her with a smile of thanks for her work, then she pulled on her shoes and hurried along the corridor to the next room. A cheery 'Enter' replied to her knock, and she stepped into Tara's dressing room, ignoring the guard who stood beside the door.

"They're here, Ri, they arrived more than two hours ago, Dap told me a little while ago!" Tara said excitedly as she grabbed her friend's arm to pull her within the room. She was beautifully dressed in an elegant red silk gown and her hair was arranged in coils of neat braids around her head.

"I know, Tara, I was outside when they arrived. I've just finished changing my clothes for firstmeal."

She smiled at her friend's enthusiasm and wished that she could share it.

"You were outside? With the Group, I suppose." Tara's voice was disapproving. "You do know that the Guardians are here to help us, don't you? Suppose your 'friends' annoy them enough that they just leave? Have you thought of that?" Then she gasped, "Light, will they recognise you?"

Erian laughed.

"Yes, I was with the Group, and yes, I know they are here to help us, and no, I don't want them to leave without destroying the ice mountain, and I don't know, they may I suppose. I was not in disguise. Why do you ask?"

"Because..."

Tara paused for effect, but Erian just waited patiently until her friend pouted at her and finally continued, "Dap has invited their leaders to join us all for firstmeal. Sooo, we'll have *four* real Tyreans at the table with us: the two who came first and," she paused again, but only for a breath, "the Rykatu and her Ponfour."

Erian inhaled sharply, remembering the look in the Ponfour's eyes when he looked up from reading the sheet. He had looked directly at her several times and she was sure that he would know her again.

"Are you sure you want to join us? I could have something sent to your room instead," Tara offered, but Erian shook her head.

"I can hardly ask them questions if I hide from them, now can I? I would still like to join you, that is, if your father doesn't think I would be an embarrassment to him."

"Dap wouldn't think that, Ri; he said that he is happy for you to join us." Tara grinned. "He hopes that meeting them will cure you of your strange notions."

Erian smiled.

"I hope so, too, Tara, I really do. I would be very happy to find that Kaliss is mistaken in what he tells us. The idea that the Guardians of Reyth might have drifted so far into shadow is..." she paused, unable to find a suitable word.

"Is nonsense!" her friend said firmly, "as you will have plenty of time to learn for yourself. Enter!"

The last word was in response to a discrete knock on the door, which opened to admit a liveried woman who curtsied and announced that Duke Rannis was waiting for them in his meal chamber. She curtsied again and withdrew, closing the door behind her.

Erian and Taranel looked at each other, and both grinned with shared excitement.

"Just think, Ri – firstmeal with a Rykatu at the table! I'm almost glad that mountain appeared!"

"So am I," Erian admitted, and then grinned. "If nothing else, her Ponfour is cute."

Tara laughed.

"So that's it! You're really here just to get a better look at a handsome man! I knew that the real Ri must be lurking in the dedicated Group member somewhere. I *wondered* why you had suddenly started attending a group with so few men! Obviously, it was for the chance to get close to the Ponfourii when they arrived."

"Dedicated *prospective* group member," Erian corrected. "I haven't joined yet."

"So how cute is he?" asked Tara, her eyes mischievous. "As cute as Taro?"

"Oh, there's no comparison – Taro is just a boy!" Erian waved away the suggestion.

"Really? Cuter than Taro?"

Tara stared at her friend in astonishment; Taro had always been the standard that other males failed to reach, and now Ri brushed him aside as 'just a boy'?

"You can't mean he's as cute as..." she looked around to be sure no servants remained working unobtrusively within earshot, and then whispered, "Captain Pendin?"

Tara would die if anyone else ever found out that she liked him, but of course Ri knew it. She liked him too.

Ri considered for a moment.

"Captain Pendin is almost as cute, but not quite," she declared.

Tara's eyes widened.

"You're serious?" she gasped. "Then what are we waiting for?" and they linked arms and ran, giggling, from the room and along the corridor until they reached the meal room.

Outside the door, they stopped to compose themselves and then Tara nodded to the guard to open. Still arm in arm, they stepped through into the meal room, and were met by the delicious smells of hot food and fresh bread.

"Come in, girls, well timed! Our guests will be here in minutes." Duchess Thianel hurried across.

"You stand here beside me, Tara, you're next to her, Ri, and smile, child, they won't bite you."

She tugged them across and indicated the places where they were to stand.

Duke Rannis was watching with an expression of amused tolerance. He, and Tara's brother, who were dressed in the maze-embroidered robes required for a formal visit by high ranked guests, had clearly already been ushered to their appointed places by Thianel.

"Good morning, Father, Mother," Tara said as she allowed herself to be positioned. Erian waited until Thianel was satisfied with her arrangement and then curtsied.

"Good morning, my Lord, my Lady, thank you for inviting me."

Duke Rannis smiled at her.

"Such formality, Ri? What has happened to 'Uncle Ran?' and 'Aunt Nell?"

The Duke was not, in fact, her uncle, but he and her father had been close friends, and she had grown up calling Rannis and Nell by the more familial terms.

"I'm sorry, Uncle Ran; I'm a little nervous." She smiled back, tentatively. She hadn't been sure how he would behave towards her now that she was involved with a group of which he disapproved.

He snorted.

"I'm not surprised! You and your friends managed to annoy a large number of the Tyreans, including two of those who will be here shortly. I don't think I would like to be in the same room with two angry Ponfourii if I was the person who had angered them. If nothing else, they are rather tall!"

Erian took a deep breath against the thumping in her chest, as she glanced towards the door.

The Duke grinned sympathetically.

"At least you have the courage to face them to learn the truth for yourself. I'm sure they will respect that. I do."

She looked back at him, surprised at the compliment.

"Thank you, Uncle Ran. I appreciate that," she replied, and then heard a knock at the door.

Everyone silenced, and Rannis glanced at his wife quickly. She made one last check that everyone was in the right place, and then nodded.

"Enter," Duke Rannis called, and the doors opened as House Bredge entered the room.

"My Lord Duke, Lady Duchess, Lord and Ladies: the Rykatu Lady Crystu, with Lord Ponfour Tam, and Sorcerer Lord Jareth, with Lady Ponfour Trerisia."

He announced and then stepped to the side as the Tyreans entered.

Erian's first thought was how tall they all were. She had not really noticed it earlier, because it is hard to judge the height of someone who is seated on a large horse.

The Rykatu Crystu was the shortest yet she stood a full inch taller than Duke Rannis. Erian would stand no higher than her shoulder, and that only because she wore heeled shoes. Lady Crystu's boots were, she noticed, flat.

Her second thought was that they too had changed clothes since their arrival. Three of them now wore leather clothing of similar design to their earlier dress, but in richer colours and without the signs of regular use that she had noticed before. The

Rykatu was resplendent in a flowing green silk gown and her Ponfour's outfit was a darker shade of the same green.

Erian was surprised to note that both Ponfourii remained fully armed, despite the rule banning weapons in Duke Rannis' presence. Both had broadswords strapped to their backs and a smaller blade at their waists.

She supposed that they probably had other weapons concealed in their clothing, and besides that, the blades were hardly their only weapons when both were Tyreans and possessed magic Gifts. Also, as Tyreans, they stood above Perrestan laws.

Two pairs of Ponfourii eyes stared at her with recognition, and both looked unfriendly.

Erian took a deep breath and lifted her head. She had nothing to be ashamed or defensive about, she told herself, trying hard to make her pounding heart believe that.

Firstmeal

Duke Rannis stepped forward and bowed.

The Rykatu curtsied gracefully, while the other three all bowed in return. That surprised Erian because a Tyrean Sorcerer was above even a king in rank, and she knew that the Rykatu was also a Tyrean Princess, so they need not have returned the obeisance. Doing so was a compliment of the highest order.

"Welcome. Thank you for agreeing to join us for firstmeal. May I present my wife, Duchess Thianel, my son, Lord Thian and his wife, Lady Serrel, and this is my daughter Lady Taranel."

The Duchess also received a curtsy and bows in exchange for her own, and Erian was amused to see that she looked slightly flustered at the unexpected honour.

Thian, Serrel, and Tara received the more expected nods of acknowledgement for their bow and curtsies. Now it was her turn.

"And this young lady, who I suspect you already have seen once this morning," Rannis said dryly, "is the daughter of an old friend of mine, and also close friend to Taranel. Her name is Lady Erian Tolene."

Erian sank almost to the floor, in the deeper curtsy required by her lesser rank. She rose and looked up at the Rykatu's face to see amusement glittering in eyes little older than her own, as the woman inclined her head.

"I believe I may indeed have seen your face somewhere before, Lady Erian," she murmured. "Wherever could it have been?"

"Beside the gate, Lady Crystu, behind a table," Erian replied boldly. She pleased that she could hear no trace in her voice of her nervousness.

She saw the other Sorcerer, Lord Jareth, grin in appreciation of her boldness, so she continued, "I hope that you are not offended by my presence here, my Lady?" she asked. "I seek the truth, and my friendship with Tara gave me an opportunity few others have."

Lady Crystu smiled at her, with a warm, friendly smile that made her look even younger.

"Offended? Not I. Seeking truth is laudable. I wish you Light on your search. What do you say, Tam?"

She turned a teasingly affectionate look at her Ponfour whose grey eyes now appeared less unfriendly and more speculative.

"I say the same, my Lady, and I hope that Lady Erian not only finds it, but also recognises it."

"As do I, my Lord," Erian told him.

Behind them, she saw Duke Rannis breathe a sigh of relief before he said, "Lady Crystu, as Lord Jareth already knows, I prefer a certain informality at a family meal. Once the food has arrived," he indicated the side tables with their burden of well filled dishes, "the servants leave and we serve ourselves and sit where we like. And usually, as it is just family, we dispense with titles too, but if you prefer..."

For some reason, all the Tyreans seemed to find that funny, especially the Ponfourii, both of whom wore identical amused half smiles.

"Oh! But that is fine!" The young Rykatu smiled. "Please call me Crystu, and I will call you Rannis. I dislike titles."

"A great many Sorcerers share that dislike."

The quiet comment came from Ponfour Trerisia, who gave Lord Jareth an affectionate look. Erian recalled that Tara had told her that the two were engaged to be married.

"I told you she wouldn't object, Rannis," Lord Jareth told him. "Can we eat now? I for one am hungry."

The duke laughed.

"Of course, Jathte." He gestured towards the food. "Guests have first choice."

Erian noted how at ease Duke Rannis was with Lord Jareth, even to using what must be a short name. She knew him to be a good judge of character and he clearly liked the Sorcerer.

Erian had wondered if the Sorcerers would expect their Ponfourii to serve them, but the Rykatu picked up a plate and filled it with a good selection and then, to Erian's surprise handed it to her Ponfour before filling another for herself. He too acted surprised and murmured some comment, which made the Sorceress grin. Erian could not make out what she replied, except for something about missed meals and going hungry, but it made him snort in amusement.

The other two Tyreans served themselves, but Erian noticed that Lord Jareth's Ponfour insisted that he take several items that he would rather not have had, on the grounds that they were 'good for him'.

Erian found that she was finding it hard to reconcile Kaliss' tales of enforced bonding with the real affection visible between the Sorcerers and their Ponfourii. Could affection be enforced magically too?

"You're next, Ri. You're a guest too."

Thianel's voice interrupted her musing, and she quickly stepped up beside Lady Trerisia and began to fill a plate. She glanced up and met the Lady's eyes. The look in them made her remember that this woman had caused several group members to need the services of a healer to treat their broken bones and lacerations.

Erian took a step back despite her best efforts to stand her ground. She decided to ask the other Ponfour what she wanted to know; he looked more approachable.

She looked towards the large central table where the Rykatu and her Ponfour had already taken seats on one side. Erian noticed that the Ponfour had looped his broadsword strap over the long back of his chair. She had a sudden image of the chair toppling over under the weight of that enormous blade if he were to stand too quickly. The brief amusement gave her courage to walk over to them. The Ponfour looked up as she stopped by his right side.

"Do you mind if I sit beside you, my Lord?" she asked.

"I have no objection." He smiled. "And my name is Tam. Informal, remember? And you are Erian. Please sit, Erian."

"Tam dislikes titles even more than I do." Rykatu Crystu laughed, and Tam chuckled.

"That is true, although I have never gone to the lengths to avoid them that *you* have."

Erian was astonished to see the Rykatu, the most powerful woman alive, stick her tongue out in response to the Ponfour's comment. He ignored it, and turned back to Erian, as the other two Tyreans sat opposite their friends.

"Do you want to ask something, Erian? You may. I will answer if I can."

"Everyone calls her Ri, at least all her friends do."

Tara sank into the seat opposite as Erian gratefully took the chair beside Tam. Erian looked ruefully at her friend.

"He can hardly want to claim me as a friend, Tara, not under the circumstances, and yes, err, Tam, I have questions."

"Will you listen to the answers?"

Erian looked across the table to the other Ponfour, who had asked that question. The woman's stare was challenging and Erian felt herself answering the challenge in her eyes.

"I will listen. I do not promise to believe, but I will listen," she replied, giving stare for stare.

To her surprise, a slow smile crossed the woman's face, and she nodded at Erian.

"A good answer, girl. 'The beginning of wisdom is the decision to listen. The beginning of foolishness is to believe all you hear.'"

The quote was from the Book of Light, and Erian remembered how it continued.

She closed her eyes and recited the next line.

"Test your belief – it can be a light for your feet or a blindfold around your eyes. Remember always that your belief may be wrong."

She opened her eyes and looked at Tam.

"That is why I asked Tara to invite me here today: I wish to test what I have recently been told."

"A laudable intent, Ri, but it can wait until after we have all eaten."

Duke Rannis smiled to soften his words, and Erian realised that everyone was now seated, but no-one could begin eating until thanks had been given to the Lord of Light for the food.

She nodded.

"Of course, Uncle Ran."

They all stood while Duke Rannis gave thanks for the gift of food, and for the presence of the Guardians who had come to the assistance of the people of Angate.

They all sat and began to eat. The custom was for light conversation while eating, so Erian's questions would have to wait.

"Oh Light! My taret has gone cold," Tara complained a short time later, making a face and staring accusingly at her mug. She gasped as steam suddenly began to emerge from the surface of the liquid within.

"I could heat yours too, if you want," Lady Crystu said, looking at Erian, who was still shivering from the draft that had just wafted over her from somewhere. She looked around and saw that one of the windows was open; the cold air must have come from there.

"Hers never goes cold!" Tara said, sipping at her, now perfectly hot, drink. "It doesn't matter how it looks now, when she picks it up it will be hot."

Erian laughed.

"I'm just not as fussy as you are, Tara."

She picked up her mug and sipped; the temperature was just right. She inhaled the aroma in the steam rising from her cup and missed the startled looks exchanged by the Tyreans.

"Has your family lived long in this region?" Erian looked up at the unexpected question from Lord Jareth. His gaze was strangely intent.

"Yes, they have. For generations," she replied, and then laughed as she remembered something, "Although my father did once claim that we have a Tyrean ancestor."

"I would like to meet your father, and hear about that," Lady Crystu said, smiling, as she sipped at her own drink.

Erian shook her head sadly.

“I wish that you could, but he died four years ago. And my mother died when I was an infant.”

“I'm sorry,” Lady Crystu replied, her eyes sympathetic.

She leaned over and murmured something to Lord Tam, Erian didn't hear what she said because she was distracted by another shiver. She glanced up at the open window.

“Uncle Ran, do you mind if I pull that window closed? I'm feeling a draft,” she asked.

“Of course, Ri,” he answered, and she jumped up to close it. When she sat again, Thian was asking Lady Crystu to describe Tyreen. He wanted to know if their kingdom was as mountainous as legend said. Erian let the conversation wash over her, listening to the way that they spoke, more than the words.

She found something unexpected: she had expected to be awed, or even frightened, by these tall and powerful Sorcerers.

She had not expected to find that they were likable. She had expected cold inscrutability, not warm friendliness.

She heard Tara's voice break into a brief lull in the conversation.

"Can I ask a personal question, Tam?"

"Tara!" her father's voice was sharp, but the Ponfour looked at Tara with a slight smile.

"You can ask, but I may not reply. What do you want to know?"

Duke Rannis relaxed slightly, but Erian thought he still looked as though he was afraid what Tara might ask.

Tara paused, and then spoke rapidly as though she wanted to get the question out before he changed his mind.

"I watched as you all arrived this morning, and I noticed that all the Soldiers, Warriors, and all the other Ponfourii have short hair, even the women, but yours is long. I just wondered why, that's all."

"I've often wondered that myself, Tam." Lady Crystu looked at him. "Not that I mind, but why is your hair long?"

Lord Tam was silent for a long moment, and Erian wondered if he would answer but then he shrugged and said, "It's not really a secret, Crystu. You know that my mother died when I was born. When I was a child, my father often commented how much like hers my hair is. When I became an apprentice and the others began cutting their hair short as is usual, I cut mine too at first. Da never said anything but I knew that it had upset him, so I decided to let it grow back, and I never cut it short again. It's not actually a rule, after all."

"It is, though, a sensible precaution," Lady Trerisia interjected. "If a foe gets close enough, she could catch hold of it and you might find it hard to get loose. Short hair is better."

Lord Tam grinned at her.

"If a foe gets that close I hope that he or she," he stressed the 'she', "will have other things to worry about."

Lady Trerisia grinned back. Erian thought that grin looked predatory and wondered if something lay behind their words.

"We will soon know."

Lady Trerisia looked as if she was anticipating something enjoyable, and Erian thought that Lord Tam looked the same way. Lady Crystu, too, was grinning with anticipation, although Lord Jareth was less enthusiastic.

Lord Tam nodded to Lady Trerisia.

"We will."

Erian glanced at Duke Rannis. He had also noticed the exchange and looked thoughtful. She wondered how soon after firstmeal Bredge would be called in to report on whatever he might have observed when he escorted the Tyreans to the room.

The conversation moved on to other things as their plates emptied. When she was certain everyone had eaten their fill, Erian glanced at Duke Rannis enquiringly. He shrugged and nodded reluctantly.

At a lull in the flow of words, she cleared her throat, wondering how best to ask. Lord Tam glanced at her and smiled.

"You are ready to ask your questions now?"

Erian nodded nervously, and he turned in his chair to give her his full attention. To her discomfort, the entire room suddenly went quiet as everyone waited to hear what she would ask.

Erian took a deep breath and then placed one of the Group of Light's information sheets on the table in front of him.

"You said that almost everything on this is wrong. So how does a Sorcerer choose and bond a Ponfour?"

His eyes had narrowed with displeasure when he looked at the sheet in front of him, but when he looked back at her he had a speculative, measuring, look in his eye.

"Aren't you afraid that with Crystu beside me, I cannot tell you the truth? That I am 'too tightly held to see the ropes' as your friend said."

"I will not lie and pretend that I have not thought of that," she replied, "but I must start somewhere, and I am not likely to find you alone, so I will ask now, and listen, and decide later what I believe."

He nodded slowly.

"And besides that," she continued, "the sheet also says that Ponfourii obey their Sorcerer with 'mindless, unthinking, unswerving, obedience'."

She paused as Rykatu Crystu spluttered and began to laugh helplessly, and Lord Jareth developed a sudden severe coughing fit, while both Ponfourii looked sideways at their bond partners with similar looks of tolerant patience.

When the two Sorcerers had regained their composure, Erian continued, "From what I saw earlier, and see now, *that* at least cannot be correct."

Lord Tam smiled.

"Well, thank you for that at least."

"If Ponfourii were mindless, there would often be no one thinking at all," Lady Trerisia commented dryly, with a side glance at Lord Jareth, who stared at her in exaggerated outrage.

"The occasional 'mindless obedience' might make a nice change, now and again, Zia," he retorted.

Trerisia snorted.

"Then you should have bonded a dog, Jath."

Lord Jareth grinned back at her.

"I think I prefer you, Zia, I hate to be bored and I suspect that constant 'unthinking obedience' would quickly become boring."

Lady Trerisia patted his cheek.

"Then I will do my best to make sure that you are never bored."

Erian looked on in amusement as Lord Jareth opened his mouth and then closed it again, clearly unable to find words.

"I think she won that one, Jathte," Lady Crystu told him.

"I think you're right," he said, shaking his head ruefully. He looked at Erian and then at Lord Tam, and obviously decided to return the conversation to its starting point.

"Tam, you were going to explain to Erian how Sorcerers and Ponfourii choose their bond partners." He looked back at Erian. "I'm afraid that you will find it quite prosaic compared to the, er, *energetic* process described in there," he told her, tapping the sheet of paper with a snort of derision.

"Indeed," Lord Tam agreed, and looked at her. "When a Sorcerer is ready to bond a Ponfour, they write their name on a sheet of paper and then attach it to the Sorcerers' wall in the Warrior Barracks. Any Warrior who is eligible, and interested, writes his or her name on the sheet. After a week, the Sorcerer removes the sheet and chooses some or all of those names to interview. Some will be people they already know well, others may be strangers, but each will be invited to a meeting and they talk. The Sorcerer will then send Formal Invitation to his or her choice, who may accept or decline."

"Do any decline?" Erian asked.

"Some do, if they have another invitation from another Sorcerer, or if they are not sure that they are compatible."

She nodded.

"And the bonding itself? How is that done?" she asked.

He shrugged.

"A ceremony, something like a marriage service, except that several will bond in the same service. We all swear our oaths, and then a group of transmuters and healers combine Gifts and send a flow of magic that creates the bond between us."

"What is it like," Tara blurted, "to feel someone else inside your mind?"

Erian saw Lord Tam's eyes widen, and heard a quiet gasp from the seat beyond him, and she stared at her friend in astonishment that she would ask such an intimate question.

"Tara!" Duke Rannis said sharply. "Some things you do not ask."

"I'm sorry, I meant no offence." Tara sounded anxious and looked down with embarrassment.

"Curiosity is normal. We understand that and make allowance," Lord Jareth told her kindly, and the others nodded, but an awkward silence followed.

Erian searched for some way to distract attention from her friend.

"Couldn't there be some confusion? Suppose there are several Warriors or Sorcerers with the same name? The Sorcerer might find that the ones invited to talk were not the ones expected."

Lord Tam looked at her, and she had the feeling that he understood what she was doing.

Understood, and approved.

"We have other names," he told her, "but they are long and we rarely use them. For this we use just the first part of our name."

"Our personal name and our parents' names are usually enough," Lady Crystu added.

Erian nodded, and looked at Lord Tam.

"What is your full name? If you don't mind my asking."

She realised immediately that she had made an error of some kind. Lord Tam looked first startled and then amused.

"What do you say, Crystu? Should I answer her?"

He spoke without taking his eyes off Erian's.

"Don't you dare, Tam!" came the instant response, making Lord Jareth chuckle.

"You heard her answer, Erian, I may not tell you my full name," Lord Tam said.

Erian knew that she was being gently teased, although she did not understand the jest. Clearly the question had another meaning of which she was unaware and clearly that they did not intend to enlighten her.

She smiled a little ruefully and shrugged.

"Then I must live without knowing it," she said, meaning both his name and the unknown meaning of her question.

She glanced at Duke Rannis, he too looked amused and winked at her. She wondered if he knew or had guessed what other meaning her question might hold.

Probably.

She realised that he had been playing little part in the conversation so far. Of course, that was deliberate – he was allowing his family to ask their questions and taking the opportunity to watch his visitors without their realising it.

She suddenly understood that her invitation was a part of that; he knew that she wanted to ask questions that the Tyreans might find offensive, and it gave him a good opportunity to see how their leaders conducted themselves.

The meal was over, and everyone stood up as the Tyreans prepared to leave, the Ponfourii strapping their huge swords onto their backs. Lord Tam looked down at her.

"You will have opportunity, over the next week or so, to speak to Ponfourii without their Sorcerers. Those of us who are bonded to shapeshifters must stay beside the model, to transmute it, while our partners fly above the mountain itself. I will give instruction that if you ask a question you should receive an answer if possible."

"Thank you, Lord Tam," she replied, surprised. "That is very generous of you."

"Generous indeed," Duke Rannis said smiling. "Thank you, my Lords, Ladies, for honouring us with your company. I hope you will join us again while you are here."

As he escorted the Tyreans to the door, Tara tugged at Erian's arm and pulled her back a little.

"Thanks for coming to my rescue earlier, Ri," she whispered, "you were amazingly brave, asking those questions."

They watched as the Tyreans began to walk out through the large double doors.

"You were right too: Lord Tam IS cuter than Pendin."

Lord Tam hesitated a moment and threw an amused look back before following Lord Jareth out of the door with Crystu close behind him.

Erian and Tara looked at each other with horror and then back at the now closed door.

"Oh no!" exclaimed Tara. "Could he have heard that?"

Erian nodded.

"I think he did. The stories say that Ponfourii can hear a stalking cat as clearly as you or I can hear a barking dog."

"I am now going to lock myself in my room and not come out again until they leave," Tara announced, her face flushed with embarrassment. "I can never look him in the eye again."

"Oh, no you're not!" Erian told her firmly. "You'll be coming with me to look at that model, just as soon as they begin to work on it again."

"That's an excellent idea." Duke Rannis' voice made them jump guiltily, and he smiled at them both.

"You both did very well this morning. See what else you can learn about them. We know few facts about Tyreans, and I don't like having to rely on people I know so little about, even if they are the Guardians of Reyth."

Erian looked at him, eyes narrowed.

"I wondered why you were so quiet, Uncle Ran. You were using our questions as an opportunity to observe the Guardians without them realising."

He nodded.

"Well done, Ri. You are correct. I hoped that the two of you and Thian would hold their attention and give me a chance to see what kind of people they really are. I'm not sure that they were unaware though; both Ponfourii cast a few looks my way that suggested that they knew what I was up to, and that they had no objection."

He poured himself some fruit juice and sipped, and then he looked at Erian.

"As Lord Tam has said that he will give orders for your questions to be answered, I want you to ask as many questions as you can think of. Stay as close to them as you can and find out all than you can," he told her.

"And tell you what I learn?" she asked, troubled. "Uncle Ran, I don't like that order, it sounds..." she hesitated.

"Dishonourable?" Rannis finished for her. Erian nodded reluctantly.

"Not if you tell them beforehand, and you may do so," he replied. "I suspect you will find that they expect it."

She frowned, puzzled, and he laughed.

"It's not that I don't trust them, Ri. I do – implicitly." He sipped his drink. "But as I said a moment ago, this is an opportunity that comes no more than once in five hundred years, and I don't mean to let it slip by unused. Until the last few days, almost all we knew about Tyreans was from legend, and the snippets of information that the Church Clerics drop. Now we have several hundred of them living here in my palace. I intend to learn whatever I can. During the last week or so, I have found Lord Jareth and his Ponfour to be honourable and likeable. I am a little surprised that their king has placed a younger man in charge, but he treated you nicely, Ri, despite the poor first impression that you had made earlier." He smiled to soften his words.

"So tell me Ri, what did you think of them? Do you still believe that the Ponfourii are forced to serve?" He waited patiently while she gathered her thoughts.

"I found them surprisingly likeable," she told him. "I was expecting people who are more aware of their power and importance, but they were relaxed and friendly, and prepared to give me a chance even though, as you say, I had made a poor first impression. When they came in and recognised me, the Ponfourii both looked..." she took a deep breath at the memory, "very unfriendly, but they were willing to speak to me regardless."

Duke Rannis nodded.

"And?" he prompted.

"I can't believe that they are compelled, they seem too..." she tried to find an appropriate word, "contented, and they all, Sorcerers and Ponfourii alike, appeared to share a deep affection. I can't believe that that could be imposed. Kaliss *must* be wrong, and yet..."

She paused, remembering how persuasive and impassioned Kaliss sounded when he preached on the subject.

"I don't know, Uncle Ran, but I hope that I will find the truth."

He nodded.

"So do I, Ri, now run along, both of you! Bredge will be here shortly and I expect to find his report most interesting."

"Dap!" Tara protested. "Couldn't we stay to hear it too?"

Duke Rannis hesitated, then shook his head.

"No Tara, I want you to join Ri in asking any questions you can think of. Two young women fascinated by the exotic visitors, and asking questions. What could be more natural? I want your impressions today to be your own, not coloured by anything Bredge may have observed. We will talk tonight, but not now. Do you understand?"

She nodded reluctantly, then looked at Erian.

"We should begin immediately. Let's go and walk in the long garden. The wing that Dap gave the Sorcerers is on one side, and the barracks and yard where the Warriors will live is on the other. We're bound to see something interesting."

Erian nodded eagerly.

"That's an excellent idea, Tara. Thank you again, Uncle Ran."

She curtsied and then she and Tara linked arms and walked sedately from the room. As soon as the doors had closed behind them, they looked at each other, grinned simultaneously, and then began to run.

Soldiers

At the gate into the long garden, Tara paused.

"Are you sure that you want to do this now, Ri?" she asked. "I shouldn't think that Lord Tam has had time to issue the order to answer your questions so if we meet any Tyreans in there, they may not be friendly."

Erian nodded.

"I'm sure. If there has been insufficient time to give any orders, then I will know that I am getting an honest reaction from any we meet."

She opened the gate and stepped through, followed by Tara.

The garden was wide and long. To their right, lawns, flowerbeds and low shrubs were interwoven with meandering gravelled paths. Beyond, and over-looking the garden, was a higher paved terrace, with seats and tables. Behind this was the wing in which the Tyrean Sorcerers and Ponfourii were housed. Its large windows gave excellent views of the garden to the occupants of its rooms. To their left, more lawns and flowerbeds gave way to a dense wood that was smaller than it looked. Behind the wood, and completely obscured by it until you were almost up to the gate, was a large barracks and stables that housed the local branch of the Perrestian Army. Usually half empty, those buildings now housed the Tyrean Warriors and Soldiers.

Erian and Tara paused, looking first one way and then the other. The garden appeared empty but, through the large windows of the Palace wing, they could see a large gathering of Sorcerers and Ponfourii, all intently looking towards one end of the room in which they sat.

Not wanting to be seen peering through windows (which would be inexcusably rude), the two friends decided to walk through the wood and look into the barracks yard. If they saw any local soldiers whom they knew, it would give them an excuse to enter and have a closer look at whatever the visitors might be doing.

They hurried along the path until they reached the far side of the wood. There the path ran along the rear of one of the barracks buildings. The brick wall was high and featureless with no windows looking out from it onto the wood. Between that building and the next was a high wall broken by a low wooden gate, over which Tara and Erian had a clear view of the barracks yard and the training fields beyond. Yard and fields were a hive of activity, with men and women busy at a variety of tasks, only some of which the two friends could identify. Most of the people in view were Tyrean, although Erian could see a group of local soldiers practicing sword work in the far corner of the field.

She and Tara gazed around in fascination at the visitors. Some were examining their armour, though for what purpose Erian could not work out. It all looked perfectly shiny to her and no one was applying any sort of polish or cleaner, yet they looked over every inch with close attention.

A small number of people were sewing together pieces of leather, and Erian was astonished when one woman tied off her thread and then tried on the garment. They were mending their own clothes, by hand! She and Tara exchanged bemused looks, and then Erian laughed ruefully and shook her head. Of course! She should have realised!

All the stories stressed that magic was tiring and that using it for too long was dangerous. If she had ever thought about it, she should have realised that they would not use it for everyday things like repairing clothes.

She looked back into the yard and saw two Tyreans looking towards the gate. They were sitting together examining some armour and weapons. They looked about the same age as her and Tara.

Both had short brown hair but the woman's, neatly cut and shaped around her face, was slightly lighter in colour than most Tyreans. The man had tight curls, which, although short, somehow managed to give the impression of untidy length. The two Guardians smiled and beckoned her and Tara to enter.

Erian glanced at Tara, and then opened the gate and went in, followed by her friend. They went over to the pair. Close to, the man looked even younger than she had thought.

"Hello! Are you Perrestians?" he asked eagerly.

"Of course they are, Allyn. Who else could they be?" The woman beside him said. "Please excuse him. This is his first time out of Tyreen, and he's a little over-excited."

"Ha! Says the highly-experienced veteran who's been outside all of once before this trip," her companion retorted.

She ignored him.

"I'm Caffy, and my wide-eyed friend here is Allyn," she told them. "Are you members of the duke's household?"

"I'm Tara, and this is my friend Erian, and yes, Duke Rannis is my father."

To Erian's surprise, the two Soldiers scrambled to their feet and bowed. Allyn scattered pieces of his armour and several daggers in his haste, which incurred reproving looks from others around the yard for the noise.

Caffy rolled her eyes and squatted down to pick up the things that had landed on her feet.

"Light! Allyn, you'll be cutting yourself on your own sword next!"

Tara and Ri grinned at each other as Allyn hurriedly removed his hand from his mouth and tried to look as if blood was not welling from a fresh cut. Caffy rolled her eyes again, and grabbed his hand. As Tara and Erian watched the cut closed and the blood vanished. A chill made goosepimples appear on Erian's arms, although the sun was warm.

Several other Soldiers came across to help pick things up, some making jokes about Allyn's clumsiness, and everything was soon in a neat pile. Erian found herself surrounded by tall, smiling Soldiers and, suddenly, she felt threatened. She told herself she was being silly, that these were Guardians of Reyth here to help her people, but still she instinctively moved closer to Tara.

"Whatever's the matter, Ri?" Tara asked. "You look terrified."

Erian shook her head, unable to speak through her dry throat, and anyway, even if she had been able to speak she could not have answered. She didn't know why the close proximity of so many Tyreans was making her feel so trapped.

They were looking at her with puzzled concern, not hostility, but she knew that in a moment, if they didn't step away, she would be unable to control her panic.

"If your Sept has finished its assigned tasks, Septian Janno, I can always find more work for it."

A woman pushed through the group, glaring about her. The Soldiers all quickly melted back to their respective jobs, leaving behind just Caffy, Allyn, and another older man, presumably Septian Janno, all standing to attention.

"That's better," she commented, gazing around the yard at the energetic and industrious activity now filling it.

She looked at Caffy and Allyn, and a twitch of her head sent them back to whatever they had been doing with the armour.

"It was our fault, err Lady," Tara began. "We were asking questions."

"Of the whole Sept? At the same time?" The woman turned to Janno.

"Were their questions so difficult to answer that all were required, Janno?"

She spoke quietly but Erian shuddered at the bite hidden behind the words.

"No, Captain," he replied, smartly, eyes fixed somewhere above the woman's head.

Erian suddenly realised that the captain was only an inch or so taller than herself, but she somehow appeared to tower over the taller Septian.

The captain nodded slowly and looked around the yard again, then back at the Septian.

"If Captain Amil had not specified experienced people for the task, I would be putting your Sept onto permanent wall duty so that they may learn not to be so easily distracted. As it is..."

She gazed around the yard again as the noise level had dropped slightly at her words, it rose again immediately, and she looked back.

"As it is, that is not an option. Instead, you can prepare yourselves to join the first groups this afternoon. None of you will be taking part in the illusion or the transmutation because I can't trust you to concentrate for that long, but if you fail to pay attention while on watch for your groups, you can be sure that the Sorcerers, and particularly their Ponfourii, will have something to say to you about it. If I hear that there has been another such lapse..." She paused and stared around again.

"I feel sure that a town this size must have some nice full cess pits and septic tanks that require emptying, I'm sure that a day spent visualising their contents in sufficient detail for transmutation would have a wonderful impact on your attention spans. Do I make myself clear, Septian?"

Erian and Tara exchanged looks of revulsion at the image that had suddenly appeared in their minds.

"You do, Captain Tiarn!" the Septian replied crisply, but his face was grim.

"Then get back to your own task!" the captain ordered.

Septian Janno nodded once and walked swiftly to a nearby bench where he had been sharpening swords.

Captain Tiarn turned back to Tara and Erian.

"My Ladies, I appreciate that you are curious, but we are busy preparing for the work we must do. Might I suggest that a better time to ask questions would be after the evening meal? Most will have free time then and may speak with you as they choose."

Her words were courteous, but the dismissal in her voice was as clear as her previous orders to the Septian.

"Of course, Captain. I apologise for disturbing your people. Come on, Ri; we can wait till later." Tara took her friend's arm and guided her out of the gate.

"What happened, Ri? What scared you like that? They were all being friendly. More than friendly! Even a Tyrean Soldier outranks me and yet they bowed. That was generous of them and certainly not threatening, so why?" Tara asked as they walked slowly back through the wood.

Erian shook her head.

"I don't know, Tara, they were just all so tall that when they crowded round I couldn't breathe. I never felt like that before."

She laughed shakily.

"I'll have to make sure that I only ask questions when there's just a few of them around. It's a little hard to talk when you can't breathe!"

She glanced at Tara, and saw her concerned face.

"I'm alright now, but I think I'd like to forget all about Tyreans for a few hours and go somewhere."

"Then let's have a picnic!" Tara said, immediately. "We'll get some food, take horses, and go see if Jerri, Taro, and the others want to come. Then we'll go to the river meadow, and stay all day if you like."

Erian nodded gratefully.

"That's a good idea, thanks Tara."

Feeling much better, she smiled at Tara, and they hurried through the garden towards the kitchen.

An unpopular command

Tam glanced through the window as the ladies Tara and Erian walked through the garden towards the barracks – a problem to solve, but one for another time. He looked back at the faces staring at him with disbelief as they absorbed what he had just said.

The room was full of Sorcerers and Ponfourii, and a few Soldiers and Warriors standing at the back. A little over half of them were shapeshifters. The others were their bonded partners. One other person was present who Tam wished was not: Captain Pendin.

His title of Captain belied his true rank. He was Commander of Duke Rannis' garrison and also Knowledge Gatherer for the King of Perrest.

And the King of Perrest was also the Duke of Angate, which was undoubtedly why the man had invited himself to this meeting. He had simply walked in and taken up a position in the corner and stared confidently at Tam. Tam had considered asking him to leave. He had the authority to do that, but he did not want to antagonise Rannis.

Tam also did not want to add speculation and mystery to the bizarre stories being circulated by the Group of Light. He had a feeling that Pendin, and through him Rannis, was about to learn a great deal about Tyreans.

Tam shrugged mentally; perhaps that was a good thing. He just wished the man had not chosen to be here in this room now, when Tam's first major command was meeting its first big test.

Tam had just told the assembled group that when they began to work on the model, one of each bonded pair would remain in the model room while the other flew above the ice mountain; even where both partners could shapeshift, one would stay.

They were reacting exactly as he had expected!

The Ponfourii and some of the Sorcerers, immediately began to raise objections. Although Rykatu Jareth had put Tam in command of the operation, Sorcerers, and their Ponfourii, tended to be an independent-minded group and no Ponfour wanted to be separated from his or her Sorcerer in a kingdom threatened by creatures of shadow. They would obey if Tam ordered them outright because he did outrank them, but they would argue and resist every step of the way if he could not persuade them that his order was necessary.

A few days earlier, when all these Ponfourii had still been Warriors, they would have accepted and obeyed any order without question. Now they argued.

Tam almost smiled; what had the girl said? 'Mindless, unthinking, unswerving, obedience'?

Idiocy! An oath of service did not mean that a Ponfour had to obey without thought! Many a Sorcerer had been talked out of a foolish action by his or her Ponfour. An order was an order and must be obeyed, but never without thought.

Tam let them protest for a minute, without comment, waiting for them to quieten as they ran out of arguments. When he judged that the moment was right, he spoke quietly, not even using illusion to carry his voice further.

"What is the First Duty?"

The room quietened. Tam waited.

"Our First Duty is to God, the Lord of Light, who Gifted us for His Work. We shine His Light into the darkness."

Tam looked for the speaker and recognised Astley, sitting in the corner with Karen beside her.

He nodded at them.

"And the second?" he asked her.

"Our second duty is to the people of Light, to defend them against the Shadowbringer,"

Tam nodded again. Every child could recite the Duties, but sometimes their meaning could be forgotten with familiarity.

"And the First Oath?" he asked. "It should still be fresh in most of your minds. You, Torde."

He picked another familiar face from the group, a much older man who had at one time been one of Tam's illusion teachers, but now a Ponfour circlet shone brightly at his brow.

"Remind us all what we all promised when we bonded."

Torde stood and stiffened to attention.

"I swear service to The Lord of Light. I will use my Gifts to spread Light where there is darkness. I will place my body and my life between the People of Light and whatever may assail them. I will defend and protect the Church, the Congregation of Light, and the kingdoms in this land. I will do this whatever the cost to myself, and if darkness surrounds me, I will defy it to my last breath without surrender. I swear it, under the Light, in the Light, and by the Light."

He sat down. The silence in the room was almost deafening. Tam glimpsed a movement from the corner of his eye and glanced round – Captain Pendin was listening with great interest and his fingers were twitching as though he wished he could take notes.

Tam looked around at the intent faces. Some he knew, and some were strangers, but all were under his command. He could just order them to obey, but they would resent it; he had to persuade them.

He glanced at Pendin again, wishing again that the man was not present to hear Tam's next words, and again considering placing a shield around him so that he could hear nothing more. Once again he rejected the thought. Let the man hear and understand that more was occurring in the kingdoms than a large infestation of snow-ants. Tam took a deep breath and asked, "What is happening in the Treos Valley, at this moment?"

Ponfourii and Sorcerers exchanged looks, and a few glanced at Pendin and back at Tam, obviously wondering why he permitted the man to listen. After a moment, a Sorcerer near the front spoke up.

“Lord Jareth is mobilising an army, and they are camped in Treos Valley.”

Pendin sat up straighter when he heard that, inhaled deeply once with shocked comprehension, as he stared at Tam.

Tam stared back at him, with a slight smile. Pendin must be wondering why he had been permitted to hear that. Well, he was about to learn far more than he probably wanted to know.

"How would you describe this army, Molyn? Compared to previous mobilisations, I mean."

Molyn replied slowly, "It's the largest we have ever mustered."

Tam nodded.

"Exactly! And why is Lord Jareth assembling such an army so quickly? The details of the gleaning that were released confirm what we already knew, that the Shadowbringer is moving, but it gave no clear details. We know that he has promised to plunge this entire land into darkness by the new year."

Tam looked at Pendin as he said that and the Captain stared back in naked horror as he understood Tam's words. Tam continued, holding Pendin’s eyes as he spoke again.

"We do not know what, where, or how he will strike, and yet Lord Jareth seems intent on mobilising every Tyrean who can draw a sword. More than that, he is doing so as rapidly as possible."

"What are you implying, Tam?" Karan asked, sounding thoughtful, and Tam looked back at him.

"There was guidance hidden in that gleaning," Tam replied. "I know that because I was there when we began to interpret it, but I think that Jareth found more later. I think that he is building this army as quickly as he can because he knows that we will need it very soon."

"What has this to do with your insistence that we stay here while our Sorcerers fly alone over that mountain?" a voice asked.

Tam identified the questioner – Talitha, one of the older Ponfourii. Her tone was questioning, but not, he was relieved to note, confrontational.

Tam shrugged.

"I want us to deal with that mountain as quickly as possible so that we can return to Tyreen and be ready when we are needed. If you can think of a more efficient way to let the illusionists out there," he waved towards the window, "know when the transmuters here have completed one part of the model, so that they can move on to the next, then please tell me now."

He waited. The room was silent, and he could see a few people nodding, reluctantly perhaps, but agreeing with him.

"It's not like you can help me out there," a Sorcerer said to his Ponfour. "I'll be on my own above that mountain whether you follow me to its feet or not. You can't set foot on it, so you would be unable to help me even if we do encounter trouble."

"How likely is it that there may be trouble?" Karan asked.

Tam shook his head.

"I don't know, but Jathte and Trerisia have felt magical residue, so there is at least one magic user somewhere near. I think that the shapeshifters are far less likely to be attacked than are those on the ground, which is why the Sorcerers and Ponfourii on the ground will stay together." He paused for breath. "And before someone asks – yes, Crystu will be flying, and I will be in the map room."

"A well-aimed arrow could bring one down; toughened feathers are not as solid as armour," someone argued stubbornly.

Tam didn't, at first, see who made the comment, but he knew they were correct.

"I know that," he replied softly.

At the same time, someone else laughed and said, "Then I'll look where I'm flying, Galet. I'm not *totally* helpless without you."

Tam stifled a smile at the look the Ponfour gave his Sorcerer, at the same time other shapeshifter Sorcerers also began to insist that they were able to after themselves for a few hours.

He straightened.

"I don't like it any more than you do, but we *are* doing it this way, the First Duty and the First Oath require it."

He was relieved to see acceptance on all faces in the room, and nodded.

"I will put up the rotas before the midday meal. You have until then to rest and prepare. We begin this afternoon."

His tone told them that the meeting was over, and they began to leave, except for Captain Pendin who looked shaken by what he had heard.

When everyone had left, he stood up and walked to Tam.

"Why did you let me hear all this?" he asked.

"Because if the Shadowbringer strikes before we have finished here, we may have to leave immediately. The king should know this and I know that you will tell him."

Pendin looked horrified and glanced towards the ice mountain.

"You would leave us undefended against that?" he asked accusingly.

Tam nodded.

"If we must." He held the man's eyes. "Understand Pendin, that a direct strike by the Shadowbringer is a far greater threat than snow-ants, no matter in what numbers they have infested a region. We will return if we can, but the Shadowbringer's threat is real and his action, whatever it may be, is imminent."

Pendin nodded, reluctantly.

"I can see that, but I don't think many of our citizens would understand or forgive."

Tam shrugged.

"That is why I intend to do this as quickly as possible, but the king should prepare to evacuate this region, just in case."

Pendin nodded again.

"Such plans already exist. Duke Rannis," he stressed the name, "believes in preparing for all eventualities."

"I hope it will not be necessary, but I am glad that Duke Rannis," Tam matched the emphasis that Pendin had given the name, "is prepared for the worst, because even if the Shadowbringer does give us time to deal with this, evacuation may still be necessary."

Pendin frowned.

"Why?"

"Because that ice mountain is at least twenty times larger than the largest mentioned in any of our records. The usual method of dealing with a normal sized anthill would cause it to melt, and it would flood this way."

He walked to the window and peered at the top of the mountain just visible in the distance.

"That would be a large flood and we would have to evacuate not only this town, but also every settlement near the river, between here and the sea."

Pendin joined him looking out the window.

"That would be ...difficult!" he said. "I assume that you intend to try a different way to destroy it?" That was half question, half statement.

Tam nodded.

"Yes, it involves using a technique which we have never before used on such a large scale, but I believe it will work."

Pendin was silent for a moment.

"How sure are you?" he asked. "Both the king," a faint smile crossed his face, "*and* the duke, will want to know."

Tam looked at him, considering how much to tell him. If the technique was needed to counter whatever the Shadowbringer planned, the fewer outsiders who knew the details the better. Jathte suspected a Zindon was hiding in the vicinity and if that shadow minion could dreamwalk it could easily take information from Pendin's mind.

"I am sure that it will work, but I can tell you no details. If there is a Zindon nearby, and I suspect that there is, he could take the knowledge from your mind."

Pendin inhaled sharply at the thought.

"You're right, and if there is one in Angate, it would almost certainly want to know what the duke is doing. *I* would. It may already know all my Lord's secrets."

Tam nodded.

"Exactly!"

He knew that he did not need to say more. Pendin understood that the Zindon almost certainly knew about Duke Rannis' other title, which meant that the Shadowbringer knew it too.

"I must go and report to my Lord immediately, if you will excuse me, Lord Tam. I will need to review his security arrangements in light of this."

He was already backing towards the door as Tam nodded, but then Tam remembered something.

“Captain Pendin, before you leave, there is something else.”

Pendin paused in the act of opening the door to look at him enquiringly.

Tam returned the gaze firmly as he spoke.

“Your men, who followed Crystu and me to her chambers, are sleeping in the large cupboard near her door. They will awaken when someone speaks the king’s name to them.”

He walked across to where Pendin stood, and said softly, “I understand that your people are curious, and that providing information and protection for Duke Rannis is your task, but do not set anyone to follow us again. I will not tolerate it, and neither will any other Ponfour.”

Pendin stared back, eyes slightly narrowed, and then, with a wry half-smile, nodded.

"I did not believe that you would, my Lord. Lady Trerisia did not either, but as you say, it *is* my task to provide information for my Duke and my King. I had to try. There will be no further attempts to follow you or your Lady."

His gaze held no trace of apology, and Tam had not expected it to.

"I advise against following *any* of us, Pendin, especially any Sorcerers. Many here are newly bonded and their Ponfourii may be less inclined to gentleness than I."

Pendin's wry smile broadened fractionally, as Tam's words showed that he had spotted the deliberate omission from the man's previous statement.

"I will pass on your recommendation to the duke, my Lord, I feel sure that he will see the wisdom of following it. Now if I may leave?"

Tam nodded permission.

Pendin bowed and then he turned and hurried out of the room.

Tam leaned one hand against the window, careful not to rest too much of his weight against the fragile glass, and looked out at the visible tip of the ice mountain.

He had not expected to be placed in command, especially not when Jathte was already present in Angate, but he admitted to himself that he was enjoying the challenge. He was glad, not only to be out of Tyreen, but also to be feeling more like himself again. Over the last few months he had frequently felt that events were dragging him along by his hair, with little chance to find out where he was before he was somewhere else. Now he was once more in control of his life, or at least as much in control as was anyone.

The door opened and even *he* could barely hear the footsteps of the first person to step through. The person following was more audible, but still trod softly, while the third was the most easily heard.

Tam looked around. The Ponfour and Sorcerer who had entered were elderly, although both were in robust health. The Ponfour glanced around the room once, nodded to Tam, and then took up a position a little behind his diminutive, but formidable, Sorceress as she advanced fully into the room. The Perrestian lady accompanying them was also elderly, and she too gave an impression of vigour despite the stick on which she leant as she walked. Tam had the impression that the stick was more of an accessory than a necessity.

"Lady Vellte, Lord Gann." Tam nodded to the two whom he knew and looked enquiringly at the third.

"This is Lady Shorante," Vellte introduced. "She's Rannis' aunt."

"Lady Shorante." Tam bowed politely, as she curtsied and murmured "Lord Tam," in return.

"We've been listening to your meeting from the next room," Lady Vellte announced brusquely. "Because Jareth has seen fit to put an even younger man in charge than was already here, especially someone who has commanded no more than a few Septs before now, I wanted to learn how you conduct yourself."

Her face was stern. Tam could read neither her face, nor her Ponfour's. The Lady Shorante was looking him up and down appraisingly, and appeared to approve of what she saw.

Tam raised an eyebrow. They should have been present at the meeting, not listening from elsewhere, but he decided to let it pass.

"And?" he asked.

"You'll do, I suppose," Vellte replied as she walked up to him. She stared upwards towards his face and then smiled.

"Well get down here where I can reach you, boy, and let me give you a hug. You've grown, Tam."

Tam laughed.

"It's not been *that* long, Aunt Vellte! You were at my bonding, and I am certain that I have not got any taller since then," he replied as he obediently bent down so that she could reach around his neck and plant a kiss on his cheek.

"I wasn't referring to your height, boy," she said, as Lady Shorante exclaimed, "He's your nephew, Vellte? You didn't tell me that."

"Not as you use the term, Shorante. He's my grandmother's brother's great great grandson. I think you would say second cousin twice removed?" Vellte explained as she let go of Tam's neck.

"We're from the same Homestead, so our custom is to simplify it to aunt and nephew. Now, Tam," she turned back to him, "young Jareth says that we," she tilted her head at Gann, "are to accompany him to search the countryside for any new incursions, instead of helping build that model. It's nonsense, of course, we'll join one of the groups going to the mountain."

From the side of his eye, Tam could see Gann roll his eyes as Vellte made this statement. *I was just been thinking how much I enjoyed the challenge of command,* he thought ruefully, and now the challenge was even greater. He wondered how best to deal with her flouting of his authority, and decided that polite firm intransigence was best.

"No," he said, and waited for her reply.

She stared at him with incredulity.

"No?" she spluttered indignantly.

"No!" Tam repeated. "I know that you are not used to hearing the word, Lady Vellte, but I believe that you know what it means."

His use of 'Lady' instead of 'Aunt' was a deliberate reminder that his rank had changed and that he was no longer just Vellte's younger kinsman. Her mouth opened soundlessly; Tam had never before seen her lost for words.

"Tam!" she finally managed, "you used to be a good obedient boy, what happened?"

His eyebrows raised.

"I was put in command, Lady Vellte. That is what happened," he said firmly, "and I need those of you who are familiar with this land to keep it free of snow-ants while the rest of us prepare to deal with the mountain."

He held her eyes, and was surprised when Gann suddenly spoke.

"Enough Vellte, he's passed your test. Stop pretending to be a rebel."

He looked at Tam.

"I'm sorry, Tam, but she insisted that she had to know if you would give in to pressure from a relative. I told her that she was a fool if she thought that you would, but you know how stubborn women can be when they've got an idea fixed in their heads."

Two pairs of female eyes glared at Gann, and then swung around to point at Tam, who had a hard time suppressing the urge to smile, and instead pretended not to notice them.

"I believe I have noticed that on occasion," he told Gann gravely.

Vellte chuckled unexpectedly.

"I expect that you have, and now that we are on the subject, where is that volatile young Rykatu of yours?"

"She's sleeping," Tam replied.

"Asleep?" Vellte spluttered indignantly. "While the rest of us prepare to work? Does she think she is in her father's palace still, with servants to look after her? Spoiled and lazy, I always knew it!"

Tam gritted his teeth to stifle the anger that almost overwhelmed him. He noticed Gann cover his eyes and shake his head, while Lady Shorante developed a sudden intense interest in a painting on the wall.

"That was a large group to translocate, even for her, so I encouraged her to rest," he replied icily, "and even you may not insult Crystu in my hearing, Aunt. She is neither lazy nor spoiled, and you will apologise."

He was startled by her grin.

"Good! I heard something about what happened two days ago, and I wanted to be sure that it had not soured your bond. I once knew someone that happened to, and I would hate for it to happen to you too, Tam. Of course I apologise. No Rykatu could grow up lazy or spoiled! Their training is far too intensive for that."

Tam looked at her through narrowed eyes.

"Another test, Aunt? Are there any more or have you finished now?"

"I told you, Tam – stubborn!" Gann said shaking his head.

"No more tests, Tam. Forgive me?"

Suddenly the robust elderly person in front of him blurred and changed into someone with the same face but who looked frail and vulnerable. Tam couldn't help himself, he laughed, and dispelled the illusion that she had built.

"Of course I forgive you, Aunt Vellte, but please don't do that again, I don't like to get that angry."

Then he realised what she had said.

"Soured? A bond can sour?" he asked, astonished.

She nodded.

"Oh yes! And it's a horrifying thing when it happens. Two people who can no longer stand each other, yet whose minds are joined."

She shuddered, but said no more.

"Is it safe now, Vellte, or should I find another picture to study?" Lady Shorante asked dryly.

"I think she has finished, Shorante," Gann replied. "You have, haven't you?" he asked his Sorceress. She smiled fondly at him, and chuckled, casting a side glance at Tam.

"For now, Gann, for now."

Tam was astonished. That was the second time within a few minutes that she had laughed. He had known her as a distant authoritative figure who visited the Homestead rarely.

Occasionally, as he got older he had caught glimpses of a tantalising and fascinating person hidden behind the severe facade, but he had never known that she could laugh. He was fond of her as a respected senior family member, but did not truly know her as an individual and a fellow adult.

She chuckled again.

"Didn't know I could laugh, did you, boy? I never was very interested in children. I prefer to converse with adults who have some experience of life. You're an adult, and a Ponfour, now, and I hear that you have had some interesting experiences this year."

Tam caught his breath at the unexpected oblique reference to his time controlled by the Zindon, but the memory was far less troubling now than it had been. His aunt noticed, and smiled sympathetically, and then continued.

"So maybe now we can get to know each other. I've had a few encounters myself that were too close for comfort, but once the memory loses the sting, it can become a source of strength for the future."

She took a breath, and spoke again, changing the subject.

"Now, the other reason I came in here is to find out exactly how we are going to destroy that mountain, without flooding this entire town."

"I'd like to know that myself, as would my nephew," Lady Shorante said, emphatically, lifting her cane as though she intended to poke Tam with it before she remembered who he was.

Tam looked at her and grimaced. He could no more tell her than he could tell Pendin, and for the same reason.

"Lady Shorante," he began, "Lord Jathte believes that there may be a Zindon present in Angate. If he is correct, I cannot tell the details to anyone who cannot protect their dreams from a dreamwalker. I do not want any shadow minion to learn anything about this technique."

He expected her to argue, but to his surprise, she just nodded.

"Then I will have to live without knowing," she said with acceptance. "There are many things that I don’t know so one more is not going to bother me overmuch. I'll leave so that you can tell Vellte what you intend."

She turned to Vellte.

"You'll join me for the evening meal again?"

The Sorceress nodded.

"I will, thank you Shorante," Vellte replied.

Lady Shorante curtsied to Tam and left the room. When the sound of her cane had faded up the corridor, Vellte turned to Tam.

"Well?" she prompted, "I understand from young Jareth that we will not, as I had expected, have the transmuters merge their Gifts to tackle the ice. He said something about a new technique." She shrugged. "I stopped listening at that point; I'm too old to learn new techniques."

Gann snorted.

Tam looked at her for a moment, and then said solicitously, "We are going to combine two techniques for the task, one of which is new, but if you are too old to learn them there is little point in my describing them to you. Perhaps you should return to Tyreen and begin your retirement?"

Gann barked a laugh, as Vellte spluttered indignantly. Tam felt her trigger a Gift. He hastily transmuted an air shield around himself. He felt the impact on his shield of an air strike that would have bruised even his posterior had it landed, and raised an eyebrow at her in admonishment, as Gann once again covered his eyes while shaking his head.

"I repeated your own words, Vellte," Tam told her, "and I must remind you that I am in command here, and there are rules against assaulting a commander."

Her eyes widened in embarrassment and he realised that she had managed to forget that he was not just her young relative, but was now Ponfour to a Rykatu, and that she was actually currently under his command.

He waited a moment and then removed the air shield replacing it with a privacy shield so that they could talk freely.

"Now, will you listen to the techniques and agree to learn both? Or will you return to Tyreen. The choice is yours, Lady Vellte."

She glanced at Gann, who nodded once, and then she looked back at Tam.

"You will issue a punishment for that infraction, won't you, Tam?" The question was almost pleading.

Tam understood.

"Lady, the only possible excuse for your action would be if you truly *are* too old to still be travelling," he spoke severely, but then smiled. "I do not believe that, so you will listen to the new technique, and you and Gann will learn it, and I will decide on a suitable punishment."

She let out a relieved breath, and then nodded.

"Thank you, Tam, we will listen and learn, won't we, Gann?"

Her Ponfour laughed.

"Vellte, I have already learned the dreamwalk energy boost technique that Jathte told us about. I thought it might be useful and it will be." He looked at Tam, "But I have yet to learn the other one using the bond. I wanted to master the first before I tried the second."

Tam nodded.

"Did Jathte tell you that only a few can learn the second technique?"

Gann shook his head.

"No, he mentioned nothing like that."

"I think he may have left Tyreen before I discovered it," Tam told him, "but you should have no trouble at all."

Vellte looked up sharply.

"You mean because we're double-bonded? It's that which makes whatever it is possible? But those with the more usual bond cannot learn it?"

Tam nodded. Vellte stared at him thoughtfully.

"You discovered this technique first, didn't you, Tam?"

He nodded again, wondering what she would say next. Vellte opened her mouth, drew breath, and then hesitated and visibly changed her mind.

"You still have to tell us how we are going to destroy that mountain without flooding the entire plain," she said, reverting to her main question.

Tam wondered if she had caught the slight narrowing of his eyes, or a more tangible warning from Gann through their bond, either way he was relieved that she had not made any further comments about Crystu.

"It is very simple, Aunt, when the model is finished, except for a few who will stand guard, everyone who can will use the dreamwalk method to send energy to me while I use the other spell to flood all that power along the bond to Crystu. With the combined Setas of that many, she will have the raw power she needs to transmute the entire outer surface of the mountain in a way that holds enclosed any melt water, as she destroys the ants."

"I see!" she said. "That method will definitely supply more raw power than would a merge of all the transmuters, but what if it doesn't work?"

Tam shrugged.

"If Crystu decides that she can't make this work, then we will evacuate all of the thousands of people in Angate, and along the entire length of the river, attack the mountain the usual way, destroy as many of the ants as we can, and hope that the flood washes the rest out to sea. However, I believe that our method will work."

"You sound confident of that, but the technique is untried. Why are you so certain that it will work?" Gann asked.

"Because," Tam replied, "the mass gleaning earlier this year contained guidance that we will need to use this technique to combine our Setas to defeat the Shadowbringer's plans. The Lord of Light would not tell us to use a technique that does not work, therefore it will work."

Gann and Vellte both nodded acceptance of his reasoning.

"Then I will learn this technique, and," Vellte nodded decisively, "I will apologise to young Jareth for not listening to him earlier."

Gann smiled approvingly at her.

"I have one other question, Tam, if I may." Vellte looked up at him, her face serious.

"Have you considered the effect that the open presence of so many Tyreans is having on the population of this region?"

Tam was puzzled.

"What do you mean, Aunt? Have I overlooked something?"

Vellte nodded.

"I think perhaps you have, Tam. The Palace of Healers is already full and more arrive daily seeking help."

Tam's eyes widened as he understood her. The main reason that Tyreans rarely declared themselves openly was that they were likely to be swamped by sick people seeking healing. Tyrean healers were strong, but even they could not heal *everyone* who needed it. No Tyrean was that powerful, not even a Rykatu.

"You are correct," he told her. "I did overlook that. Thank you for telling me. How have you dealt with them so far?"

Vellte shrugged.

"As and when we can. We have been kept busy hunting new snow-ant infestations, but we have taken turns to spend some time each evening helping the Perrestian Carers tend the sick. A few of them actually have a small measure of Gifting."

Tam looked at her sharply, and she shrugged again.

"None of them knows that they have it; they just see those particular Carers as extremely good at their craft. I checked them all carefully without them knowing, and each one is using the Gift on a purely instinctive level while applying their customary treatments. I judge that none of them would be able to use it consciously even if we made them aware of their ability."

Tam nodded.

"I will accept your judgement on this, Aunt Vellte. You should know that we may have found one Perrestian who should come back to Tyreen for training, but I don't know that for certain at the moment."

Vellte and Gann both looked at him, surprised.

"There's someone here who may have a powerful enough Gift to merit taking them to Tyreen? Who?" Gann asked.

Tam shook his head.

"When I am certain, I will let you know."

He changed the subject abruptly.

"I had best be arranging the rotas for the work we must do. I will assign several people to help the carers at the Healing Palace. Is it nearby?"

"Yes," Vellte replied. "Rannis takes his ducal obligations seriously. He bought one of the estates opposite his own south gate, and set it up for the sick. As you would expect from something he has organised, it is clean, and well stocked with everything the Carers may need."

"Good! That will make things easier."

Tam took a deep breath, and then smiled.

"It's good to see you, Aunt Vellte, and you too, Gann, but I must have these rotas prepared by midday, so that we can continue the model after the midday meal."

"It's good to see you, too, Tam," Vellte replied. "You won't forget that punishment, will you? I acted badly! I deserve whatever you decide is fitting."

Tam laughed.

"I already have an idea about that. I will let you know soon."

And with that, he left the room to begin work.

A question almost asked

Tam pushed aside the sheet on which he had been writing, and stretched. He wished he knew an easier way to make copies of handwritten papers. When younger, he had once tried to use transmutation to copy writing from one sheet to another. He had found that the level of concentration required to keep the writing legible meant that it took twice as long as the other way and was much more tiring.

He glanced out of the window. The sun was high and that, plus the smell of cooking food, suggested that the midday meal would soon be served. The rotas were complete and he must awaken Crystu.

He quickly rolled the papers into a bundle before walking through the connecting door between his bedroom and Crystu's.

She was fast asleep, with a thin cover pulled neatly over her. Underneath that she was fully clothed; she had not known that she was going to sleep. Tam knew that she might be annoyed with him for what he had done but she had needed the rest.

He placed one hand on her head and woke her. Her eyes opened sleepily and she stretched.

"What was I saying?"

He felt her sudden burst of indignation as she looked past him and saw how far the sun had moved since she last glanced that way. She stared at him.

"Tam! You laid a sleep compulsion on me!" she accused.

"I did," he admitted. "You needed the rest."

He held her eyes.

"And now you need food. You can scold me after the midday meal, if you wish."

"I'll scold you now! Don't you ever send me to sleep again! I'm not a child to be put to bed when you decide I'm tired," she said but then smiled reluctantly. "I do feel refreshed, so I'll forgive you this time, but don't do it again! Promise me."

Tam folded his arms and stared back at her steadily, but he did not reply.

"Tam! Promise me that you will never do it again."

Tam continued his silence, concentrating on sending a feeling of unending patience along the bond. Crystu glowered at him, frustrated by his silence, but he could feel a tickle of amusement at the back of her emotions.

"You are not going to promise it, are you?"

"No, Crystu, I am not."

He waited patiently until she smiled.

"You take good care of me."

He smiled back at her, but continued to wait, arms folded. Crystu sighed.

"Very well, I withdraw the demand for your promise, but *please* don't do it again."

He smiled again.

"I'll do it if I think it necessary," he told her, ready for her likely response. As he had expected, she stuck out her tongue and immediately he solidified the air around it and held it firmly poking from her mouth.

Her eyes bulged in surprise and she squealed in protest, but then Tam felt an impish mischievousness colour her mind, and suddenly his hair braid was yanked upwards and held uncomfortably tightly. He was forced to stand up on his toes in a vain attempt to relieve the pressure.

They stared at each other for a moment, then released each other simultaneously as they both began to laugh.

"I'll promise not to grab your tongue again, if you'll promise not to pull my hair again," Tam told her while rubbing the back of his head. At that same moment Crystu growled, "Tam, if you *ever* yank my tongue again, it won't be your *braid* I retaliate on, but something more painful."

She was grinning as she spoke, but Tam could feel that she meant the threat to be taken seriously. He blinked.

"Then I will never do that again," he promised fervently, realising that he had lost that round.

"Good!" Crystu replied, with one more tug on his braid to emphasise the fact that she was making no promises.

"Now," she continued, "if we are going to eat, I need to change." She looked down at her clothes. "I'm all rumpled, because *somebody,"* she shot an accusing look towards Tam, "left me sleeping in my clothes."

He grinned.

"Would you rather I had removed them?" he asked. "I will remember that for next time."

He had spoken without thinking, giving the obvious response to her complaint, but the image that came unbidden into his mind required considerable discipline to force away.

Crystu's mouth opened and then closed again, as she struggled to find a suitable answer to his comment, but then she drew herself up and lifted her head high.

"On the day we marry, you may do that, Tam," she replied with great dignity, "but I *hope* that you won't have laid a sleep compulsion on me first!"

She tilted her head down slightly and looked at him through her lashes, an impish smile on her face.

"But as I don't yet know your full name, that day won't be soon, so I'll take care of my own disrobing and dressing, or else sleep fully clothed."

The smile left her face and she stared at him thoughtfully. She opened her mouth to speak again and, suddenly, Tam knew that she was going to tell him her name. He could feel her intent firmly through the bond and his breath caught in his throat at the thought. He knew he was not yet ready.

Crystu hesitated.

"Then I will wait until you are," she told him.

Tam managed to smile back at her somewhat shakily.

"Should I now demand that *you* stop understanding *me*?"

Crystu snorted, and then her manner abruptly changed.

"Out! So I can change,"

She pushed him towards the door to the corridor.

"Go on, and wait outside, I won't be long."

She opened the door and pushed him through into the corridor, shutting the door quickly behind him.

Tam leant back against the door and closed his eyes. He could feel the conflicting mix of emotions coming from the other side of the door: confusion, anticipation, relief, disappointment, excitement, and fear. All of which matched his own feelings completely.

He wondered what it would have been like to have a normal bond, without all the extra complications, but rejected the thought as futile. The bond was fixed and he knew that he would not change it for anything, even if he could.

He could sense that Crystu had gone into the next room to wash, and smiled to himself. 'Not long'? She clearly intended to take as long as required to allow both of them to regain their equilibrium.

Tam saw a chair opposite the door and he sat on it to wait. The seat was uncomfortably low, as were most of the chairs in the palace; the Perrestians were a short people and built their furniture to match. A long legged Tyrean Ponfour would just have to make do.

A gong sounded in the distance announcing that the meal was ready. A few moments later, Jathte and Trerisia emerged from a door further along the corridor.

"Tam, are you coming to eat?" Jathte asked as they reached him.

Tam gestured at Crystu's door.

"When she has changed her clothes," he said patiently.

Jathte chuckled.

"I never have understood how a woman can make the simple task of changing garments take so long. All you have to do is take one thing off and pull on another, but they insist on washing and checking that the colours match, and then brushing their hair, and..." His voice trailed off as he met Trerisia's narrowed-eyed gaze.

"Yes?" he said with exaggerated innocence, before he turned back to Tam.

Trerisia sniffed, but made no other comment.

"We'll make sure there is something left for you, Tam, however long she takes, and save you both seats," Jathte said.

As he and Trerisia continued along the corridor, Tam leaned back against the wall, stretched his legs out, and settled himself to wait patiently, ignoring his hunger. Crystu was hungry too, so he knew that she would not take too long.

A surprise for Erian

The next day, Erian and Tara walked up to the large double doors of what was now being called the model room and paused.

They looked at each other for encouragement and then Erian pushed open one door and they stepped through. Midmorning sunlight flooded through the large windows, throwing dark shadows from the people within.

The room contained a large number of Tyreans, many of whom stood around the large central table talking quietly. Others were clustered around the room, some looking at maps, some sipping at drinks, and a few sat with closed eyes apparently just resting. Tara glanced at Erian, presumably wondering if she would repeat her previous reaction to a large group of Tyreans, but Erian shrugged. She was unaffected so far.

Erian saw that Lord Tam was among the people beside the model. He looked up as they entered and nodded to them, then looked towards another group and said something that Erian could not hear. She looked where he had, and saw a man nod once, and then that man walked over to her and Tara. The sunlight flashed brilliantly off the Ponfour circlet on his brow. He was slightly shorter than Lord Tam and not quite as broad-shouldered, but moved with the same deadly grace.

"Hello! You are the ladies Tara and Erian." He nodded to each in turn. "I am Karan. Tam has asked me to answer any of your questions until my group must work again. Then someone else will take my place. Tam also said that he understands that you will tell Duke Rannis anything that you learn, and he is happy for you to do so."

"Thank you, Lord Karan," Tara replied.

"Yes, thank you, Lord Karan," Erian echoed, relieved she could obey Duke Rannis's orders, to report what they learned, without dishonour.

"I have a question that has puzzled me for several days."

She looked towards the table with the rough model on it. Lord Tam and several others were now all staring at the model. As she watched, she saw an image appear over the rough clay. She could see incredible detail in that image – so much that she thought she could almost see individual leaves on the trees. The Tyreans concentrated and the clay moved. The surface of the model began to match itself to the image, with shape and colour equally detailed.

Erian shivered as a draught blew over her, and then frowned in puzzlement: where had the draught come from? The windows were all closed, as were the doors. She realised that Lord Karan was staring at her intently, and she realised that he must be waiting for her question.

"Yes?" he prompted. She nodded and waved a hand towards the model.

"Why are you building that?" she asked. "What will you use it for and why does it have to be so detailed? Why do you need it? There is a real mountain that must be destroyed, yet you spend time building a model."

Lord Karan smiled.

"It's because of the way transmutation works," he began. "When we change one thing into another, the alteration happens most quickly if we can hold a clear image of the thing in our minds and then change that image into the thing we want. The greater the detail, the more easily the transmutation occurs. A small thing is easy to visualise in detail, but something as large as that mountain?" He shook his head. "Do you both know this Palace well?" he asked.

They both nodded.

"Then try and build a picture of it in your mind, every room, every window, every door, the carpet and the furniture too. Try now."

He waited.

The girls looked at each other, closed their eyes and each tried to build an image of the Palace in their imaginations. Erian found that although she could imagine a reasonably detailed picture of the front wall with its doors, windows, and even the crenellations at the top of the wall, she could not hold it complete in her mind when she started to add on the side walls and wings.

Karan gave them a few minutes and then asked, "Can you do it?"

They both opened their eyes and shook their heads.

"Now, look at these."

He handed both girls an orange.

"Study the orange carefully, then close your eyes and try to create an image of it in your mind. You should find it much easier."

Erian stared at the orange in her hand, turning it around until she had seen all of it, and then she closed her eyes and built a picture of it in her head. This was much easier than the palace, and she soon could see the orange in her mind's eye.

"Don't open your eyes," Karan told them, "but now try and alter the image slightly, perhaps its colour."

Erian concentrated, and after a moment, the orange in her mind had changed to purple.

"It was much easier to imagine the orange, wasn't it?" Karan said. "That's because it's so much smaller. You can open your eyes now."

Erian did so, and saw that Lord Karan was once again staring at her with a strange intentness.

Beside her, Tara gasped.

"Ri! Your orange!" Erian looked at her friend and then at the orange in her hand, and her eyes widened in shock – it was purple.

"Did you do that?" she asked Lord Karan. He shook his head.

"No, Lady. You did," he told her.

He stared at her appraisingly for a second.

"Tam was right: you didn't know."

"Know? Know what?" she stared at him.

"That you possess the Gift of transmutation," he replied, in a matter-of-fact tone.

Erian was speechless and shook her head, rejecting the idea.

"N-no! That's impossible! Only Tyreans possess Gifts!"

She glanced at Tara, who was staring at her in awe.

"Your father always claimed that you had a Tyrean ancestor," her friend reminded her. "Maybe you inherited magic from him?"

"It's possible," Lord Karan nodded, "but Tyreans are not the only people with Gifts. We are the strongest, and most commonly Gifted, but sometimes we find people like you out in the Protectorates. Most often they are not aware of it, and if their powers are weak, we don't interfere, but Tam said that he thought that you are strong enough to learn to control it. So we devised this test to find out if you can. If you had not asked the question that you did, I would have found another way to bring up the subject."

"But how did he know?" she stammered. Lord Karan smiled.

"Lady, yesterday when you ate with Lady Crystu, Lord Jareth, and their Ponfourii, they felt you heat your drink, although you seemed unaware of what you had done. Then you reacted noticeably when one of them used magic. You shivered and asked for the window to be closed. You also reacted just now, when they," he nodded to the group by the table, "began to transmute the model. I saw you shiver and look at the windows as though expecting one to be open."

"I felt a draught," Erian whispered.

"No. You felt magical residue emanating from the transmuters. The ability to sense magic use only exists in those who have Gifts strong enough that they can learn to control them. You are a transmuter, Lady, and you may also have other Gifts. I can find out for you if you will allow."

He lifted one hand as though to touch her head, and sudden alarm flared through her.

"No!" She stepped back, her heart racing in fear of his touch.

He frowned.

"I won't hurt you, and I can't read your thoughts or memories, but I can quickly find out what other Gifts you may have."

Erian shook her head and stepped back again, almost falling as the backs of her legs hit a chair. The idea of someone looking into her mind was unbearable.

"No," she whispered. Karan dropped his hand and stepped back.

"As you wish, Lady Erian, we may be able to learn if you have other Gifts another way, although it will take longer. But you *must* learn to control your transmutation consciously. Your Gift seems strong, and you could have an accident if you don't learn control. If you dreamt of fire, for example, you could wake to find your room burning in reality."

"Could that really happen?" Tara asked. Lord Karan nodded, but Lord Tam's voice answered, "Yes, it could."

Startled, Erian looked up at the tall, broad-shouldered Ponfour; she had not heard his approach.

"How do I learn to control it?" she asked nervously, wishing that she had room behind her to step back again. Light, they were all so tall!

Lord Karan suddenly straightened and appeared to focus on something within himself.

"Astley is ready to begin the illusion, Tam. My group must prepare."

Lord Tam nodded, and Lord Karan bowed to Erian and Tara.

"Excuse me ladies, I must work," he told them. He hurried back to the group with which she had first seen him and they gathered round the table.

Erian watched the Ponfour cross the room and then looked back up at Lord Tam. He gazed back at her thoughtfully for a second, and then gestured behind her, to the chair that she could feel pressing against the back of her legs.

"Please sit down, both of you."

Erian fell back onto the chair, sinking deeply into its soft padding. Tara sat on the similar chair beside her. As soon as they had sat down, Lord Tam pulled a third smaller chair from the wall, placed it in front of theirs, turned it around and straddled it with his arms crossed loosely on its back, facing them.

The chair was small even by Perrestian standards, and made him look like an adult sitting on a chair built for a toddler. He looked ludicrous with his knees sticking up like that, and despite herself, Erian's mouth quirked into a smile. The slight crinkle around his eyes told her that he knew exactly how he looked, and that he had done it on purpose to help her feel more at ease. It worked; she felt far less intimidated by a man with his knees sticking up near his ears, than one who towered above her head.

"Karan is correct: you must learn to control your Gift, and you should try and find out if you have others. To answer your question, you learn by having someone to teach you," he told her gravely.

"They wouldn't have to..." She gestured at her head, not knowing the correct term for whatever Lord Karan had intended.

Lord Tam shook his head.

"No. There is no need for any kind of probe. The lessons involve sharpening and focussing your imagination, nothing more."

He rested his chin on his clasped hands and gazed at her, and she forced herself to meet his grey eyes.

"Who will teach me?" she asked, more boldly than she felt.

Tam paused for a moment as if making a decision, then said gently, "You seem to find our height intimidating, Lady, but we are not all as tall as I am. Have you met Lady Vellte?"

Erian shook her head, at the same time that Tara exclaimed,

"Lady Vellte? Ri, she's *tiny*! She's shorter than I am! And she's old too, and so is her Ponfour. They and Great Aunt Shorante have become great friends!"

Erian looked at her friend, and back at Lord Tam.

"This is real, isn't it? I really did change that orange! I really can learn to use magic!"

A dawning wonder filled her mind at the thought. She told herself firmly that she was being silly to fear the Guardians. Why, she was almost one herself!

"Yes, it is real, Lady Erian," Lord Tam told her, "and if your Gift is as strong as I think that it may be, then you should return with us to Tyreen for full training if you want to be able to properly utilise it. "

She stared at him speechless as he continued, "In the meantime I will ask Lady Vellte to begin to teach you what you need to know to avoid setting your room on fire as you sleep. Now that you are aware of your Gift, the possibility of such an accident is greater."

"I could go to Tyreen?" she gasped.

Such an opportunity was extremely rare unless one entered the Church, and no less than the Ponfour of a Rykatu had invited her!

A stray corner of her mind laughed at the irony that she, of all people, had an invitation to enter Tyreen and receive training in a Gift. Another corner repeated the thought that she had best overcome this foolish fear of Guardians if she was to travel to a land full of them.

He smiled at her.

"Yes, you can. You could live there too, if you chose."

Tara squeaked at that, and Erian could understand why – an invitation to a non-cleric to visit Tyreen was rare, but an offer to stay there was granted to no one except in legend or story.

Every child in Perrest had at some time dreamed of such a thing, and she was granted it in reality.

She took a deep breath to gather her courage and gazed back at the Ponfour.

"Then I must learn to bear the tallness of your people, if that is to be possible," she said firmly. "I will learn what Lady Vellte will teach me, and I have the time that you are here to overcome this foolish, unreasoning fear."

She could see his approval in his eyes. He stood up and, using one hand, moved the chair to the side. He offered her his other hand and raised his eyebrows in a look of challenge. Erian, took another deep breath, gritted her teeth and, taking hold of his hand, found herself being pulled easily to her feet, to stand staring up at him.

"No fear is foolish, Lady," he told her. "We all fear something, but without fear there can be no courage."

Erian frowned, trying to understand his meaning.

"Courage lies in recognising and facing one's fears, in continuing with what must be done despite your fear," Tam explained.

Erian nodded slowly.

"I think I understand, but it is easy to say that when..." She paused, uncertain how to continue, but he finished her sentence for her,

"When you are a tall, strong Ponfour with magical Gifts and a large sword?"

He laughed as she nodded.

"Lady, don't tell anyone but," he bent down, and whispered in her ear, "I do not like spiders! I sometimes ask Crystu to remove them if they crawl near me."

Erian stared at him for a split second and then began to giggle, her shoulders shaking. She pressed both hands against her mouth to try to stifle the embarrassingly childish noise.

She didn't know if he had told her the truth, or just said that to make her feel better, but the thought of him jumping back in terror if a spider ran across the floor was just too funny.

"I won't tell," she promised.

"Thank you, Lady, I appreciate that!" He grinned, then held out his hand towards hers again as he became serious again.

"Karan did not finish his explanation of the model, Lady, if you will come for a closer look at it, I will finish what he began."

"Thank you, my Lord, you are most kind," Erian replied, and forced herself to walk beside him towards the crowd of Guardians clustered along one side of the model. Tara hastily scrambled to her feet and followed.

They walked to the side of the group and the two shorter women stepped up to the edge of the table. Erian stared in fascination at the construct in front of her. This close she could see that much of the model was nothing more than unformed clay shaped and coloured roughly to match the mountain, but with no detail.

The area in front of the group of Tyreans was different. There she could see the exact shape of the ice mountain and the land nearby in minute detail. She could see every plain, curve, and crack in the ice, the rocks that it sat on, and the few remaining plants near its foot.

The image was slightly transparent and she could see the clay behind it, but she realised that that clay was slowly fitting itself to the image that overlaid it. The movement was almost imperceptible – a slow flowing motion that was only visible at the corners of her eyes, but not if she looked directly at it.

She could feel the strange sensation, which she had previously ascribed to a draught, tickling across her arms and face, and looked carefully at the Tyreans. Each one concentrated on the model, with no outward sign of magic use. There were no glowing eyes or sparks or incantations as imagined by many storywriters.

She looked back at their work, and wondered if she might one day be capable of such an endeavour. As she watched, she noticed details that she had missed at first. The illusion was not uniformly detailed across its whole area. She realised that there were several distinct, overlapping areas to it. At the edges, the detail, though still intricate, was flatter somehow and the colour less vibrant, but in the overlapping areas the detail was exquisite. She was sure, that if she had a magnifier to hand, she would be able to see small stones and the tiniest imperfections in the ice.

She glanced around and found Lord Tam standing beside her. She pointed at the illusion.

"When the map of the new Royal Park was drawn, the mappers

first laid out a long line with markers at regular spaces, up the centre of the park. They called it their base-line. When they began measuring to the trees and to the displays, to mark them on the map, they took measurements from several different markers. They said that it gave a much more accurate position to do that. Is this something similar?" she asked him.

He nodded.

"Yes. There are ten groups, each with a shapeshifter in the air. Those on the ground spread out so that they have different views of the mountain, and the shapeshifter flies above it for a different view of the same land. They combine their views into an illusion and project it onto the relevant area here. That takes a great deal of skill, because they must be constantly aware not only of the view that they must make into an illusion, but also of this room, so that they project the illusion onto the correct spot on the map. In addition, they must also merge the overlap with the next group's illusion. The groups' views overlap as much as possible for greatest accuracy of detail. The relative heights of the hills would be far less accurate without this high level of overlap."

Erian nodded.

"What about scale? How do they know that they are all making their illusion the same size?" she asked.

Tam nodded.

"The same way your mappers do. Look closely at the hills around the feet of the mountain."

He pointed towards the model, and Erian looked closely, searching for something like the mappers baseline. She couldn't see it at first, but then, as her eyes shifted from one spot to another, a slightly different texture in one unformed area suddenly resolved into a linear strip winding around the feet of the mountain. She hadn't noticed it at first because at each point the colour quality of the strip matched that of the model around it, whether in an area that was still only roughly formed, or in one of the few places that were finished. She could see that, in the unformed areas at least, the surface of the strip had much smaller and more detailed undulations, and she realised that the ground surface within that strip was almost certainly accurately rendered, rather than the smoother approximated contours beside it.

Within the strip she could see tiny pegs positioned at regular intervals, and she could follow these into the finished area where they were the only visible remnant of that curving baseline. She considered what she could see, walking around the unoccupied side of the table to follow the strip around the model.

"It goes around the entire model. Is that your baseline?" She glanced at Lord Tam and saw his nod in reply. From the corner of her eye, she could see Tara's puzzled expression.

"And those pegs? They must have placed real ones in the land that match these?" she continued. The Tyrean nodded again, apparently waiting to see how far she could work it out.

"They must include several of the pegs in each illusion and adjust the illusion so that their illusory pegs overlay exactly the ones on the model," she said slowly, "That way, each illusion will be at the same scale. And where the illusions overlap, you have another check on the accuracy."

Lord Tam smiled.

"Exactly correct, Lady. Well-reasoned." He glanced at Tara. Seeing that she remained puzzled, he pointed towards the strip. For a second the strip glowed yellow becoming clearly visible; Erian realised that he had placed an illusion over it to make it easy to see. The yellow faded and the model resumed its previous colouring.

"Oh, yes, thank you, Lord Tam. I can see it now that I know where to look."

Tara walked around to join Erian, and then frowned in puzzlement again.

"How did they manage to measure the distance between the pegs so closely? It looks exact as far as I can estimate, but the ground undulates steeply which would make it hard to use a measuring strip like the mappers do for flat ground, and I have seen no sign of the sort of tools that they would use to do it on a slope."

Erian looked at Tara with surprise; she had not expected such a question from her friend. Tara wrinkled her nose at her in response to her astonished look, and then looked at Lord Tam as he spoke.

"We can judge distance more accurately than can most non-Tyreans, Lady Tara. We simply know when the distance is correct. We don't use magic or tools," he paused, "but I would be interested to see the tools your mappers use. Your people are very clever at making tools to do things for which we use magic."

He glanced towards a table on which she saw several distance magnifiers and a few timers. Erian was astonished to see an expression of eager interest on his face, an expression she had seen on Tara's face several times as she pulled something apart to learn how it worked. She exchanged a grin with her friend, who had also recognised the look.

"If you take one of the magnifiers apart you will find pieces of glass held on a wire frame. The timers are all wheels with teeth, and a spring that may suddenly jump from the case and fly under a chair," Tara said, grinning at his surprised look.

"I have a room full of things that I have taken to pieces," she explained. "Some even still worked when I put them back together again. You may look at some of them if you like, while you are here."

The Ponfour grinned.

"I would enjoy that, and so would Crystu. Thank you, Lady Tara," he replied, but then he visibly pulled his attention back to the model.

"You wanted to know its purpose," he said. "It is quite simple: the real mountain is far too big for anyone, even Crystu, to picture in sufficient detail for a rapid transmutation, which this will have to be."

He saw the questioning look on Erian's face.

"If the transmutation is too slow, the snow-ants will be able to fight back with their own transmutation ability and they may break free. Crystu must transmute the entire outer surface of the mountain into rock within a few seconds, and then push the transmutation inwards rapidly, crushing the ants before they can retaliate."

Erian nodded, and Tara suddenly exclaimed, "Oh! I see! She will use the model to help her visualise the real mountain. Because it is small enough to walk around, it is easier to visualise."

Lord Tam nodded.

"That is correct, Lady. She will do the transmutation from this room using the model to aid her focus."

Erian thought a moment and then asked, "Is she really that powerful that she can do the transmutation alone?"

Lord Tam did not reply immediately. She realised that he was trying to choose his words carefully, but Tara interrupted before he could speak.

"He can't tell us any details, Ri. Dap said he wouldn't even tell Pendin, in case any shadow minions are still in Angate. A Zindon could take the knowledge from our minds as we slept, and use it to plan an attack."

Erian gasped sharply.

"A Zindon? There could be a Zindon here in Angate?"

The idea was both terrifying and strangely exciting. She stared at Lord Tam, eyes wide, and he nodded reluctantly.

"I would not have mentioned it as we do not know it for certain, but as Lady Tara has said, that is a possibility, so I will not tell you, or any other Perrestian, exactly how we plan to do this."

"Then, as we now know the answer to Ri's question, I will change the subject and ask one of my own, though," and Tara grinned, "it is an impertinent question and you may refuse to answer it."

Lord Tam's eyebrows rose, but he grinned back.

"Then ask your impertinent question, Lady Tara, and I will decide if I will answer or not."

Tara nodded, and looked at Erian for support, before inhaling for speech.

"Are you really going to fight Lady Trerisia?" she asked, her words coming out in a rushed tumble.

"Fight Lady Trerisia?" Erian repeated in surprise. "But she's a woman!"

She noticed that several of the unoccupied Tyreans had looked across at them, and that many looked amused, though she was unsure whether she or Tam was the object of their grins.

She looked at Lord Tam, whose slightly narrowed eyes appeared to be reassessing Tara. Tara looked back firmly, though Erian had the strangest feeling that her friend was chagrined, as though she had revealed something she had not intended.

"I expected that Duke Rannis would know of that by now. He probably knew within an hour of our leaving firstmeal yesterday. I did not expect…" he broke off, and then smiled. "So you are his choice, Lady? I will remember that, and inform Lord Jareth."

Tara's mouth twisted ruefully.

"Perhaps not a good choice, if I can only keep the secret for such a short time."

Erian wondered if she had somehow missed a large piece of the conversation, as she had no idea what they were suddenly talking about.

"What secret?" she asked, puzzled.

Tara smiled at her, and looked around the room at the large number of people in it, many of them looking towards her with expressions of reappraisal similar to the one she had seen on Lord Tam's face a moment before.

"I'll tell you later, Ri. There are too many sharp ears in here."

Erian frowned and would have asked again, but her thoughts were pulled back to Tara's question as Lord Tam spoke.

"I will answer your impertinent question, Lady. Yes, I really am going to fight Trerisia."

Erian stared at him, missing the look of gratitude that Tara gave him.

"But she's a woman!" she repeated.

Lord Tam looked amused, but Erian realised that several of the female Tyreans present were now frowning at her.

"I have noticed that, Lady, and I am aware of Perrestian views about women fighting, but I think that several of your friends have already discovered that Trerisia is a formidable opponent."

Erian knew that he was correct: Lady Trerisia was strong enough to have severely injured several Group members. The fact remained that a large, powerful man stating that he was going to fight a woman, *any* woman, was simply *wrong*.

"But why are you fighting her?" Erian asked, puzzled,

"It's a challenge, Ri, a contest. He challenged her," Tara told her.

"But you can't fight a woman! It's not right! You're a man!" Erian protested, at the same moment that Tara asked him, "Won't you have to hold back your strength?"

Tam grinned.

"I have noticed that, too, Lady Erian, but it is not relevant," he replied to Erian, and then to Tara, he said, "We will both hold back a little; we have no wish to kill each other, but other than that, no, I will not hold back. To do so would be an excellent way to lose the fight and it would also annoy Trerisia. I would not dishonour her in that manner."

The women who had frowned a moment before were now nodding their approval of his reply.

"But it's not right!" Erian repeated. "You must be much stronger than she is. You're a *man*!"

Lord Tam shook his head.

"The difference in strength is not very great, Lady. She is faster than I am, and more flexible, and her reach is slightly longer. We are well matched and it should be an enjoyable fight. There's little point in a challenge to someone who is not of similar ability to myself."

He grinned, evidently enjoying the consternation on Erian's face. She glanced at Tara, and saw that her friend looked thoughtful.

"The strength difference is not very great?" Tara repeated his words. "How can that be? She is tall and fit, and I suppose she must be strong to be able to wield that huge sword, but Ri is correct: although you are slightly shorter, you are a man, and obviously very strong."

She looked at his well-muscled shoulders.

Lord Tam shook his head again.

"Lady, for over three thousand years every Tyrean has begun learning to fight at the age of five years. Even those with fewest Gifts train rigorously throughout their childhood, and must spend at least one month each year keeping their skills sharp. And this in a land permeated by transforming magic. Over the centuries, the constant focus on the need to be ready to fight the Shadowbringer, and his servants, has altered all of us. One of those changes is that the average Tyrean woman is only slightly less strong than an average Tyrean man, and all of us are much stronger and faster than any non-Tyrean Warrior, however skilled he may be."

He shrugged.

"In addition to that, she is a Ponfour, which reduces the difference further. Her skin is as tough as mine, her bones as dense, and her punch is as able to raise a bruise on my flesh as mine is on hers. Trerisia is at no disadvantage because she is female."

"It's true then? That the bonding changes a Ponfour physically? The stories say so," Tara asked.

Lord Tam nodded.

"It is true," he replied, in a tone that made it clear that he intended to say no more on the subject.

Tara nodded, and then looked at Erian, and grinned.

"Maybe your father was right to teach you to use a sword. It's almost like he guessed you might need to know how one day."

Erian found herself on the verge of a giggle that she was sure would sound hysterical, and pressed her hand over her mouth to stifle it as she looked around the room.

"You *will* be expected to practice swordwork if you come to Tyreen, Lady, but it is unlikely that you would ever see battle. There are many Tyreans who never leave our land. Not all can be fighters."

Erian realised that he had misunderstood her silence, and thought that she was afraid that she might be expected to fight in challenges. Then she realised what he had said, and remembered fragments from several old stories.

"Non-fighters do not leave Tyreen. If I go there I will have to stay permanently. I can never return!"

She stared at Lord Tam, and was surprised when he shook his head.

"You are Gifted but not Tyrean. If you come back with us, you can leave at any time, but if you do leave, you will not be granted a second entry," he told her, holding her eyes until she nodded her understanding.

She looked around the room again, and, for a moment, as she looked at the Tyreans gathered around the model, and those standing or sitting elsewhere in the room, she could almost see the millennia of dedicated service to the Light that supported each one.

She understood now that believing that any of them could stray from that service was ludicrous. They were all totally focussed and committed to the Path of Light and to the defence of the Protectorates and the people of Light.

"I think that I have a great deal to think about," she said. "I have learnt much, not only about you, but also about myself. I have choices to make, it seems, that I would never have dreamt could be in front of me."

Tam smiled at her, but then his face changed as, like Lord Karan earlier, he appeared to be listening to something inside himself.

"I must leave you, Ladies," he said. "Crystu is beginning to construct her illusion. Please feel free to remain and ask further questions if you wish."

He nodded politely to them, and then he and several others gathered beside the model as a new area sharpened into detailed focus.

Erian and Tara looked at each other, and then moved simultaneously towards the door. When they were out of the room and the door had closed behind them, both grinned, gathered their skirts, and began to run, laughing at the startled looks and exclamations from people in the corridors.

They dashed into Tara's rooms, slammed the door, and threw

themselves down to lie panting and laughing, Tara on her bed, and Erian on the long chair.

For a long time the only sound in the room was their gasping laughs, but eventually each regained control of her breathing.

"That would be a lot easier in trousers!" Tara declared. "You could use your arms to help run, instead of holding up skirts, and you could see where you are putting your feet."

Erian giggled.

"I'll let you know! I'll have to learn to wear trousers in public, if I'm going to be a G-Guardian," she gasped.

"Oh, Light! Did all that just happen, Tara? Or did I fall asleep and have a very odd dream."

Something hit her legs and she pushed herself up and looked down at the orange which now lay on her lap. She looked at Tara, who had thrown it to her, and then she picked it up. She looked at Tara again, swallowed and examined the fruit closely. Closing her eyes, she pictured it in her mind, and then imagined it green with red spots. She felt something shift within her, and opened her eyes to stare at the red spotted green orange in her hand.

"It was real, Ri. You are a magic user. You can go to Tyreen and live there if you choose," Tara said, soberly. "So what do you think about the Tyreans now that you almost are one yourself?"

Erian forced a laugh, but she knew that she must decide what she believed.

"I think that Kaliss is wrong; he must be," she said, realising as she said it, that she had no doubts left, but that she could not just leave the Group without a word. "I must tell him so, and the others. They believe a lie."

The thought of walking into the Group and saying that was daunting. She knew that many would simply reject her statement and might become angry with her for what they would see as a betrayal, even though she had never been a full member of them.

Tara must have seen her nervousness.

"You could ask Pendin to accompany you. No one would offer you insult in his presence," she suggested.

Erian shook her head.

"No, this problem is of my own making and I must face them by myself. They will probably think that I have been enspelled by the Tyreans, but they will not harm me."

She stood up.

"I'll go now, and then it will be over and I can concentrate on learning about this Gift that I have without worrying about them."

Tara stood too.

"No. You won't go alone, Ri, I'm coming too, and you know that I am not permitted to leave the palace without a protector in tow. You can blame his presence on me, but I will *not* let you go alone, even if I have to lock you in your room to prevent it."

Tara stared stubbornly at Erian until she nodded agreement.

"Good! That is decided. You stay here, or change, or whatever, while I go and make the arrangements."

Tara hurried out of the room and Erian looked again at the orange in her hand. After moment of concentration, the fruit was once again orange in colour. She placed it on the table and then picked an apple from the bowl. She studied the apple carefully, and then stared at the orange and attempted to change it into an apple. With a soft squishing noise, the orange dissolved into a sticky, moist, odd-smelling pile of something that was best described as indescribable.

She sighed and went into Tara's washroom in search of cleaning rags to clear away the mess. Perhaps it would be best to defer experimentation until Lady Vellte began to teach her.

When she had cleaned the table, she sat down to wait patiently for Tara's return. She did not have long to wait, and soon the two of them, along with five strong young members of the ducal guard, were sitting in a carriage and travelling along the city streets.

She leaned close to Tara and, glancing meaningfully at the two uniformed men sitting opposite while pointing above their heads towards the three that she knew to be on the roof, whispered, "A protector, you said, as in one. We seem to have acquired several others. Tammia will think we are intending to arrest someone."

Tara looked embarrassed, although Erian realised that she did not sound it as she replied in a normal volume.

"How was I to know that Captain Pendin had issued new orders after he had learned that the Tyreans suspect that we may have Zindons in Angate? I'm not going to complain though, Ri. If he thinks we need extra protectors then I am happy to have them with me."

Erian thought about some of the members of the Group, and of Tammia's likely reaction to her decision to leave, and decided that the extra company would make her feel less nervous.

About an hour later, the carriage arrived back at the Palace. Each woman had sat silently wrapped in her own thoughts for the return trip. Tara thanked the guards, then she and Erian walked up to her room.

"Well!" Tara exclaimed as she sank onto her bed. "That was...unexpected."

Erian sat and nodded absently, running over everything in her mind -the memory had a surreal quality that made it hard to believe it had happened. (She noted that that was true of most of that day, and wondered if she would wake up tomorrow and find that this whole day was in truth a dream.)

She had thought that Tammia would be scathing of her decision to sever ties with the Group of Light, and had expected insults, swearing, and possibly shouting, from the other woman. She had been afraid that Kaliss would be disappointed and would try to persuade her to take more time to consider her decision.

In the event, both had been friendly and supportive. Tara had been made welcome, the guards too had been treated as visitors and welcomed, and all had been offered refreshments.

Kaliss had told Erian that if she was certain that he was wrong, then of course she must leave. He had listened to her explain what she had seen and heard, and had expressed his joy that the Guardians had apparently returned to the Light.

He had then turned the conversation to lighter matters, and they had sat in his large comfortable office, drinking ice cold fruit juice, nibbling on small savoury snacks, and talking about a play currently on show at the theatre. Tammia had spoken little, but had smiled and nodded pleasantly.

Erian's mental replay of the events was interrupted when Tara said, "To be honest with you, Ri, that is not at all how I imagined Kaliss. You became involved with that group so quickly, and so deeply, that I assumed that he must be incredibly handsome! I couldn't think of anything else that might have overwhelmed your normal good sense but he is actually quite ordinary to look at."

Erian sat up abruptly and glared at Tara.

"I am not such a fool that I would let a handsome face sway my beliefs!" she declared.

Tara smiled.

"I know that you're not, Ri, but I could think of no other reason for the way that you have been acting recently. It really was not like you at all. You used to love the stories about the Guardians and had no doubts as to their integrity and then suddenly you were swept away from reason. What else could I think but a handsome man was at the root of it?"

Erian calmed down, and admitted to herself that her friend had had valid cause for her puzzlement.

"You're right, I suppose; it must have seemed odd, but his face was not what persuaded me; it was his *voice*. He can be so persuasive that disagreeing with him is impossible."

"I have heard that some people can sway people's beliefs by their words. Dap says that it is a useful gift for a ruler to have." Tara laughed. "He may want to try and recruit Kaliss; perhaps he could persuade the Kandarii to turn around and go home the next time they raid the east coast."

Erian laughed too, at the thought of Kaliss standing on the beach preaching to a crowd of Kandarii raiders, but shook her head.

"I think he is too committed to his Group. He would not abandon them to work for a duke, or even a king,"

"A dedicated man! It is a shame that he is dedicated to a false cause. Still, I am glad that you have realised that they are wrong, Ri. You can concentrate on learning to use your Gift without any doubts as to the integrity of your teachers. I wonder if you *do* have any other Gifts? Illusion perhaps, or healing, wouldn't that be wonderful?"

Tara spoke without a trace of envy in her voice, and Erian wondered if that was genuine, or simply excellent voice control.

Whatever her true feelings, she was soon deep in discussion with Tara about what methods the Tyreans might use to reveal whether or not she had any other Gifts, and how soon the Lady Vellte would appear to begin her training.

Part 4: The Mountain

"This will be interesting: I can find no record of ordinary citizens being invited to watch a challenge fight between Ponfourii. It could also cause problems. The idea of a man fighting a woman is not one that sits well with Perrestian mores. Jathte assures me that Tam and Trerisia are quite evenly matched, but still I find that I am struggling with the idea. It just seems very wrong. I know that Tyreans are not like us; I've had ample chance to see that now. Our rules do not apply to them, can't apply to them, but some of my people will find this spectacle offensive, especially if Trerisia is injured." Extract from the journal of King Perdon III of Perrest.

Challenge

"What are the rules?" Rannis asked Jathte as they sat down in the Duke's box at the Arena. The Arena was a large, wooden, semi-circular unroofed building. It had a sunken stage floor in front of the straight wall, with seats facing the floor in raised tiers up the walls, enough for one thousand people to have a clear view of the sport or play taking place. The lowest ranks were filled by Tyreans; all who were on their rest day had come to watch the match. In addition, there were hundreds of high-ranked Perrestians present, all eager to see a Tyrean challenge fight.

Jathte waited until Thianel, Tara, and Erian had settled themselves and then pointed to the small circular area that had been marked out on the wooden stage floor. A moment later a large image of it floated in front of the Duke's box.

"Zia opted for Lord Huryn's Game. Under those rules, each has to try and make the other leave that area, without using magic," he began. "There'll be six rounds, each of seven minutes length with a three minute break between each round. First round, they must not move their feet and cannot hit each other either. Second round they can step, but still no hitting or kicking. Third round, punching is permitted. Fourth round, kicking is permitted, fifth and sixth rounds both punching and kicking. Just to make it more challenging, the circle is made smaller each round. By round six, it will be about two paces across."

Rannis looked at the image that hovered in front of him and then used his distance viewer to look down at the real one. It didn't look large but, without anyone standing near it, he found the scale hard to judge..

"It's about five paces across at the moment," Jathte told him.

"And the object is just to push your opponent out of it?" Rannis asked. "That's … not what I expected."

Jathte snorted.

"You expected punching and kicking, magic and blood, until one of them is lying unconscious?" he asked, but continued without waiting for an answer, "If they were fighting under Ponfour rules, that *would* be what we would see."

"Aren't they?" Nell asked.

Jathte shook his head.

"Thankfully, no. Under Ponfour rules, the challenge can only end when one of them is unconscious or unable to continue. We are outside Tyreen, and Ponfour rules end with a Ponfour who cannot protect his or her Sorcerer until after healing." He shrugged. "They won't take that risk, not out here in the Protectorates, so they do it this way. There will still be punching and kicking and probably blood, but Lord Huryn's Game rules are more about skill and control. In fact, if one of them inflicts an injury that *does* incapacitate the other, they lose points for their lack of control."

Feeling confused, Rannis exchanged a puzzled look with Nell, Tara, and Ri, and shook his head.

"They *lose* points for incapacitating the other person? So how are the points awarded? What gains points?" he asked, trying to imagine any form of combat where injuring the opponent was a bad thing.

Jathte laughed.

"As I said, it's about skill, not about raw strength or brutality. The points are simple: one point if any part of your opponent touches the ground outside the circle, two points if you get them out completely. You can lose points if you step when you shouldn't or if you hit or kick when you shouldn't, or if you push your opponent out but you also touch outside the circle yourself. Once hitting and kicking are allowed, the aim is also to try and injure your opponent just enough to slow them down so it's easier to push them out, but not hurt them so much that they need healing. If you injure your opponent that badly, then you lose points."

Tara laughed.

"That sounds like the rule Lord Menias tried to introduce into lithrod!"

"Lithrod?" Jathte queried. "Oh…yes, it's a team game isn't it? With two balls, and three goals, if I remember rightly, although I don't know how you play it."

Rannis nodded.

"Yes, that's it." He grinned. "Menias thinks that there are too many injuries in the sport, so he came up with a similar rule to try and reduce them, but it had the opposite effect. He really should have known better! I had to over-rule him in the end."

"Why? What happened?" Jathte asked curiously.

"They all turned out to be first-grade actors!" Tara snorted. "The slightest touch and there'd be one of them on the ground, pretending to be badly hurt, in the hope that his opponent's team would lose points."

Rannis tried not to smile when Jathte blinked and visibly had to think about what Tara had said. Rannis wondered what it might be like to live in a land where the idea of someone cheating to win a game was something unexpected.

He wondered if everyone in Tyreen was as innately honest as all the Sorcerers and Ponfourii, Warriors and Soldiers, he had met in the last few days, or if they had their thieves, liars, and cheats as well but just didn't let them leave their kingdom. The Tyreans weren't naïve; they knew more about the evils of the world than any ordinary man, and yet all of them appeared to expect and assume honesty and integrity from everyone they encountered.

“Oh. I see. They lied just to win a game?” Jathte shook his head, apparently not comprehending why anyone might do that. “That can’t happen in a challenge. Even if someone did try it, the moment a healer touched them everyone would know the truth. The dishonour and disgrace would follow them lifelong! They would gain nothing.”

“Besides,” Lady Crystu added as she dropped into the seat next to Jathte, “These are Ponfourii; they cannot knowingly tell an outright lie.”

“Not ever?” Ri asked.

Rannis watched the young Rykatu carefully as she replied with a smile, "Not ever."

After just three days acquaintance he didn’t yet know her well, but he approved of what he had seen so far. He was close to becoming friends with Jathte and no longer thought of him as ‘Lord Jareth’ but the young Rykatu and her Ponfour were still ‘Lady’ and ‘Lord’ in his thoughts even though both seemed to attach as little importance to their rank as Jathte did to his.

"Isn't that sometimes inconvenient, my Lady?" Nell asked. "Sometimes a lie is necessary to avoid hurting someone's feelings. Bald truth can be very painful at the wrong moment."

Jathte shrugged.

"They manage. It's amazing how well they can sometimes make you think that they said the opposite of what they really said!"

“They could make you believe that black is bright yellow with fluffy green fur on it, but if you wrote down every word and examined it, you wouldn’t find a single falsehood,” Lady Crystu declared with a grin.

Jathte nodded agreement, but Rannis had a feeling that the Sorcerer thought that they should not discuss it so openly, although Lady Crystu obviously had no qualms. He decided to bring the subject back to the challenge.

“Are they almost ready, my Lady?” he asked.

Lady Crystu nodded.

“They’ll be out in a minute or two. Neither of them is completely happy about it being so public, but they’ll be here.”

“I’m sorry!” Tara said, guiltily. “It never occurred to me when I asked Lord Tam about it in the map room. I just assumed that everyone knew.”

Rannis grimaced at her tone. She had been upset when she had learned that the fight had been intended to be held privately and that none of the other Tyreans had known about the challenge until she asked about it.

"No, Tara, if there's blame then it's mine." He turned to look at Jathte and Lady Crystu, "I told Tara what Bredge had overheard, and I told her and Ri to ask as many questions as they could. I'm very sorry if it has upset your Ponfourii."

Jathte shrugged and was about to speak, but Lady Crystu interrupted him.

"I would have told everyone anyway, if it hadn't happened. I never wanted this to be a secret. Don't worry, neither of them is angry with either of you. They arranged it in an open hallway with other people present so it’s really their own fault, and they know that. Trerisia *could* still have insisted on a private match. It was her choice to decide to make it open in the end, and I for one, am glad that she did. Tam just doesn't like being the centre of attention. I don't know why Trerisia originally wanted it to be private." She glanced impishly at Jathte. "Maybe she doesn't want to be publicly defeated."

Jathte snorted.

"There's little chance of *that*!"

Lady Crystu grinned.

"We'll see."

A sudden roar from the crowd pulled everyone's attention to the arena floor and the two figures who had emerged from the doors at the rear, and were now walking across the floor to the circle. Both were barefoot and clad in light green sleeveless tunics and short trousers.

The image that Jathte had made focussed on them, and Rannis examined at them closely. On the face of it the contest looked unequal. Lady Trerisia was a foot taller than Lord Tam, but far less muscular and she was a woman. He knew what Lord Tam had told Tara: that Tyrean women were almost as strong as Tyrean men, and that the Ponfour Bond narrowed that gap further, but he still found it hard to believe that she had any chance against such a broad shouldered and clearly extremely strong man. He glanced at Jathte to find the Sorcerer looking back with a slight smile.

"You're still fretting about the fact that Zia is a woman, aren't you, Rannis?"

Rannis nodded.

"I know what Lord Tam told Tara, but," he looked at the floating image again, "he is very big! The idea of a man that size fighting a woman is almost…." He glanced worriedly at Nell and tried, unsuccessfully, to find a word that did not imply something extremely dishonourable. He shook his head. "I'm worried about how my subjects will view it. A man who uses his fists on a woman is viewed with…" he paused, "I'm sorry, Lady Crystu, but the best word is 'contempt'.

Jathte snorted.

"You don't need to worry about Tam's reputation. You'll see. Zia has a good chance of winning."

Lady Crystu grinned.

"He's right, Rannis, I may disagree that Trerisia is *that* much better than Tam," she mock-scowled at Jathte, "but she will certainly give him as many injuries as he gives her. She's at no disadvantage for being a woman. They are both Ponfourii and that is the important thing here."

"Lady Rykatu Crystu, Lord Jareth, Your Grace – Lord Duke, Your Grace – Lady Duchess, Lords and Ladies, and citizens of Angate, the challenge will begin shortly. Please take your seats."

Rannis looked back at the stage floor, as the illusion-carried voice from an unseen announcer stilled the babble of conversation around the building. He saw that the two Ponfourii were now standing in the circle facing each other.

"The Lord Ponfour Tam has challenged the Lady Ponfour Trerisia to combat. Lady Trerisia has accepted the challenge and they will fight Lord Huryn's Game."

As the announcer explained the rules of the match for the benefit of the Perrestians present, Rannis looked at his daughter and his ward, sitting together and both clearly admiring Lord Tam's physique and expecting to enjoy the game. He was relieved that Ri appeared to have no doubts remaining about the Tyreans, and had finally severed her ties with that peculiar Group of Light, especially in light of the revelation in the map room.

Rannis had been astonished when he had learned that Ri had magic Gifts and that the Tyreans proposed to take her back to Tyreen so that she could learn to use them. This was an incredible opportunity for her and also for him.

If she returned to Perrest, and he thought that she would, he would become the only king to have a full-fledged magic user in his court. That might cause him some problems with other monarchs in the long run and he would need to make plans.

"Lord Tam, Lady Trerisia, are you ready?" The announcer asked, and the duke brought his attention back to the image in front of him.

Both Ponfourii nodded and replied, "I am."

"Take your positions."

Lord Tam and Lady Trerisia stepped closer together. Each stood with left foot in front as they saluted each other and then lifted their hands to touch, palm against palm.

"Round one. Begin!"

Their feet did not move, but their arms began to circle slowly around each other as each tried to find and disrupt the other's balance. Rannis stared, barely blinking, as the two figures somehow twisted around each other without once moving their feet.

He watched as Lord Tam swept his right arm around under Lady Trerisia's left arm, while his left hand pulled on her right. Surely he was strong enough to pull her around, but somehow she twisted, while ducking down, and Lord Tam's arm went over her head. Her left hand then came up under his bicep while her right pushed at his left shoulder, then he too twisted and somehow moved his arms around and back. It didn't look as though they were using any strength at all, yet at the same time the movements looked powerful and graceful.

He heard Ri whisper, "Are their feet glued to the floor?" and it certainly looked like it. Some of the positions into which they twisted looked impossibly unbalanced, and yet even as they reached a point where they must surely fall over, they would twist back.

Ri continued, "How can they possibly push one of them out of the circle without steppin – oh!"

"YES!" Jathte's triumphant bellow, and a roar from the crowd, coincided with Rannis' realisation that suddenly, impossibly, only one figure stood in the circle. He switched his gaze from the floating image to the real stage floor in time to see Lord Tam landing nimbly on his feet, a good ten feet outside the circle.

"First points to Zia!" Jathte grinned as the unseen announcer confirmed, "Two points to Lady Trerisia."

"She tossed him into the air like a baby!" Nell gasped in disbelief. "I'm sorry, Lady Crystu, but I have to ask: did he *let* her do that?"

"No!" replied the two Sorcerers together, firmly.

"Nell," Rannis began, his own astonishment at what he had seen as great as his wife's, "if I stood here and let you try, how high could you throw me?"

She looked at him.

"I couldn't throw you at all," she admitted after a moment.

“Exactly.” Rannis looked back at the circle. The two Ponfourii were once again a blur of movement except for their motionless feet. “Anyone who can toss someone his size, that far, doesn’t need to be ‘let’.”

“SECOND POINTS TO TAM!”

Lady Crystu cheered and bounced in her seat as Lord Tam reversed the direction of his arms, caught Lady Trerisia’s wrists, and then pushed so that she fell backwards across the edge of the circle.

“Point, not points. She’s only half out,” Jathte pointed out.

"This time," the Rykatu retorted as Lady Trerisia flipped back onto her feet and returned to the circle. A second later, a push from Lady Trerisia made Lord Tam stagger backwards, but he stopped just before he would have stepped out. He returned to the centre of the circle and they began again.

Rannis realised that he was holding his breath waiting to see which of them would leave the circle next. A full minute passed and then he saw Lord Tam swoop low and circle his arm in a flowing motion. Now Lady Trerisia was the one flung through the air and well out of the circle. She landed as gracefully as Tam had done earlier, and ran back to resume the tournament.

As the gong sounded the end of the first round, the score was 6-5 to Lord Tam.

Lady Crystu grinned at Jathte, who shrugged.

"It's only round one," he pointed out. "There's five more to go."

As they waited for the next round, Rannis looked around at the spectators. He had had to restrict entry to those who had been first in the queue, but the Tyreans had insisted that there be no other restriction. A few nobles had been outraged to learn that they were expected to queue with lesser ranks and some others had simply not believed it until they had walked past those waiting patiently and been turned away from the door. He could see cobblers and bakers sitting together with lords and although, here and there, some members of the nobility appeared to be trying to pretend that they could not see anyone else, he could see several who were happily talking to their lesser ranked neighbours. Where Tyreans and Perrestians sat near each other, the Warriors and Soldiers were just as interested in the Perrestians, as the Perrestians were in them.

“This is going to last almost an hour!” Nell stated suddenly, sounded dismayed. “I just added it up.”

“Yes.” Jathte nodded.

Rannis hadn’t realised either, but now he thought about it, six, seven minute rounds, with a three minute break between each, was fifty seven minutes. “That’s a long time to be fighting on a hot day,” he commented.

Jathte shrugged.

“They’re Ponfourii,” he said, as though that explained everything; perhaps it did.

The floating image vanished.

"They won't be standing still now so it will be easier to see directly," Jathte explained.

Rannis nodded as the voice announced: “Round two – stepping now allowed.”

Lord Tam and Lady Trerisia stepped back into the circle, which was now smaller, and once again stood palm to palm.

“Begin.”

“They look like they’re dancing!” Ri said, and Rannis agreed. Dancing was *exactly* what it looked like: They stepped and circled around each other, first one way and then the other, now quickly, now slowly, forwards and then backwards, like a couple performing an intricate dance. The only difference was that, unlike a dancing couple, each was still trying to unbalance the other. Their hands pulled and pushed and twined around each other, and they ducked and whirled as each tried to gain leverage to make the other step from the ring.

"Tam's foot was out there." Jathte grinned

"Both of Trerisia's were out *that* time!" Lady Crystu replied a moment later.

Then a particularly rapid twirl sent both combatants out of the ring together.

Rannis looked a question at Jathte, who shrugged.

"Neither gets a point if they both go out fully."

Rannis nodded and looked back in time to see Lord Tam roll, and flip Lady Trerisia over his head. She landed out of the circle, but managed to pull on Lord Tam's right arm, so that one of his legs followed her out.

"That's two to Tam and one to Trerisia," Lady Crystu said. Rannis nodded. The seven minutes rushed past and the gong sounded again moments after Trerisia had flipped Tam over her head again and out of the ring.

"Lady Trerisia wins round two at 11 points to 8."

Jathte grinned at Lady Crystu, and Rannis was startled to see the most powerful woman in the whole world stick her tongue out in reply.

"Did you say that they start punching each other in the next round, Lord Jareth?" Tara asked.

Jathte nodded.

"Yes, that's right, and kicking in the round afterwards." He grimaced.

Rannis frowned, remembering a few things that he had noticed over the last few days. He wasn't completely certain, but he thought that Jathte wouldn't be offended so decided to ask.

"I have the feeling that you don't approve of this sort of contest. Don't you?"

Jathte grimaced again as Lady Crystu grinned at him.

"No, I don't. I've never seen the point of these challenges. What does it matter who exactly is the fastest or the strongest?"

"You were cheering as loudly as anyone a few minutes ago!" Lady Crystu reminded him.

Jathte shrugged.

"So? I can enjoy watching Zia win even if I don't approve. And besides, the first two rounds are different – no one bleeds."

"They'll heal," Lady Crystu pointed out, "As for the point: look at all those Warriors and Soldiers out there," she waved her hand to indicate the whole arena, "Every one of them, who wants to be a Ponfour, will go away and train harder after watching this. Challenges like this inspire others to work harder to become that fast themselves."

"I know the arguments, Crystu." Jathte sighed. "I just don't like seeing someone punching Zia in the face, which will happen very soon. At least, not someone I know can actually hurt her."

"She's a Ponfour, she'll cope," Crystu laughed, "and she'll heal within a few hours. Tam's not going to do anything serious to her."

Jathte shrugged.

"Accidents can happen, even to the best."

"Round Three – punching now allowed. Take position."

Lord Tam and Lady Trerisia, who had been sitting together amicably drinking water, stepped into the ring together and then turned to face each other about three paces apart in a ring which was now only about four paces across. They saluted and then each stood, apparently relaxed, with their arms hanging loosely. Rannis, used to seeing fighters stand with fists high in front of their faces, thought that it was an odd starting position for a fight.

"Aren't they going to pad their fists?" Tara asked.

"No. Zia said no padding," Jathte replied without taking his eyes off the circle.

"Begin."

The two Ponfourii stood motionless, looking at each other, for a full six seconds and then, simultaneously, leapt towards each other, collided savagely in the middle, and landed together with Lord Tam's legs wrapped around Lady Trerisia's waist. They rolled around the circle pummelling each other, sometimes Tam on the top and sometimes Trerisia. The entwined pair then somehow flipped up four feet into the air and crashed back to the ground with Tam coming down on top. Rannis winced as the man's fist smashed into Trerisia's face as he fell onto her, and then flinched when he saw where *her* fist had landed.

"Ow! That must have hurt!" Ri whispered, aghast.

Rannis wasn't sure which of them she meant, or perhaps she meant both. She was right, those punches must have hurt and yet neither Ponfour had shown any sign of it. He glanced at Lady Crystu and Jathte, both leaning forwards in their seats and watching intently. Lady Crystu was nibbling her lip, and Jathte had his fists clenched, as they watched their Ponfourii pound away at each other. As they fought, and rolled and flipped around the circle, first one and then the other ended up with part of them outside the boundary. Rannis wondered how the referee could possibly keep score and yet a glance at the scoreboard showed that the numbers were changing rapidly. Both Ponfourii were bleeding now from their noses and from split lips. Rannis had seen Lord Tam spit teeth out to the side, before punching Lady Trerisia in the stomach, and then spinning round to throw her over his shoulder and slam her into the ground, her legs out of the circle. He dropped down to punch her face, but she caught the punch in both hands, and then, somehow, used Lord Tam's arm as leverage to bring her feet back into the circle. In a split second she planted both feet on his stomach and pushed up firmly, while pulling on his arm, and threw him bodily through the air over her and out. He fell hands first, rolled to his feet and immediately span around and leapt back into the ring to continue the fight.

"She used her feet. Is that allowed?" Rannis asked Lady Crystu, who replied without taking her eyes off the match, "Yes. It was a throw, not a kick, so it's allowed."

The gong sounded, and the two Ponfourii rolled apart and got to their feet. Their tunics were smeared with blood and sweat now and Rannis was a little surprised that they weren't torn, but he reminded himself that maybe the fabric was transmuted to be strong.

"They aren't even breathing hard!" Tara exclaimed. "After all of that, you'd think even Ponfourii would be panting a *little*!"

"Not yet, but they still have three rounds to go. Even Ponfourii will tire in this game," Lady Crystu replied, leaning back in her chair and looking at the score. In that round Tam had gained 19 points and Trerisia 16. "That puts Tam ahead by one point." She smiled at Rannis. "I told you that they are well matched."

Rannis nodded. He could feel sweat trickling down his back and was glad that he had decided on informal dress. If he had been wearing his full Ducal regalia, he would have been sweltering.

"What a day to fight!" he muttered, glancing up at the morning sun. Despite being only mid-morning, the day was hot and just watching the two fighters made him feel thirsty. The Lord of Light only knew how they felt, fighting in this heat.

"Round four – kicking, but no punching"

Rannis watched Lord Tam and Lady Trerisia walk back into the circle and salute to each other.

"Begin."

Lady Trerisia leapt forwards and Lord Tam aimed a heel kick at her midriff. Somehow she slipped sideways, and knocked the leg away while simultaneously aiming a side kick at Lord Tam's face. He caught the foot, pivoted and swung her out of the circle.

"That's always the danger in this round," Lady Crystu murmured. "Because they have to slow the kicks to try to avoid serious injury, it's easier to catch the leg.

Lady Trerisia had run back into the circle, then rolled under Lord Tam's round kick, coming up to lift him from underneath and throw him bodily out of the circle.

Rannis watched, as they continued to pull, push, throw, and kick each other, marvelling at just how much punishment Ponfourii could endure. Jathte had said that they wouldn't be pummelling each other until one was unconscious or incapacitated, but this didn't appear to be stopping much short of that. Jathte and Lady Crystu had obviously been right about Lady Trerisia's strength and at the end of this round, the score was thirteen to Lord Tam and eleven to Lady Trerisia, which put him three points ahead overall.

"They are evenly matched, you were right, Lady Crystu," Nell commented. "I wish I had *half* of Lady Trerisia's strength."

"I'm fairly glad that you don't," Rannis murmured.

"The next two rounds will be more like what you expected, Rannis," Jathte said. "Almost everything is allowed so long as no-one is incapacitated."

"Round five: Kicking and punching allowed."

Lord Tam and Lady Trerisia now stood in a circle that was only about 3 paces across.

"Begin."

As in round three, they stood just looking at each other and then Lady Trerisia dropped low and threw out a circular kick aimed at Lord Tam's ankles which he avoided easily by jumping. He landed on top of Lady Trerisia, and now the two of them were locked together in a spinning, rolling embrace, first one and then the other on top. Rannis was astonished to note that they were both somehow managing to keep within the small circle. Had anyone described it to him, he would have called it impossible. Then Lord Tam managed to plant both feet on the ground and swung Trerisia out of the circle. She landed feet first and ran back in to ram him with her shoulder. He staggered backwards out of the circle and then returned with a punch that rocked Lady Trerisia onto her back with arms and head outside. He tried to catch her foot before she could recover but she kicked him squarely on the jaw, jumped to her feet and threw a punch to his nose followed by two kicks in quick succession, to his chest. The first knocked him backwards but he caught the second and then hooked his right leg behind her standing leg and sent her back to the ground. She twisted as she fell and wrapped her arms around one of Lord Tam's legs and now they were rolling on the ground pummelling each other again. The fight went on in that manner. Rannis flicked his eyes from the fight to the scoreboard. First one and then the other inched ahead, but neither was ever more than three points in the lead.

Then round five was over and the two combatants, both now breathing heavily, stepped out to rest as the circle shrank for the final round. Lady Trerisia was now ahead by one point.

Jathte relaxed back into his seat and wiped sweat off his face.

"I always find myself clenching my muscles and fists as if I can help her somehow," he explained a little sheepishly.

Lady Crystu grinned.

"Tam hasn't fought many challenges since we bonded, and all were from Soldiers so it was nothing like this. I'm enjoying this; it's fun!"

"Lady Crystu, the circle is only two paces across now and they are both taller than that. If they go to the ground, their feet and heads will be outside all the time. How will the referee keep score when both have bits on the outside?" Ri asked.

"The scoring is slightly different for the last round," Lady Crystu told her. "The points are only awarded if someone is sent out fully, both feet and both hands and whole body on the ground. A foot here or a head there doesn't count."

"I see. Thank you." Ri smiled and Rannis was delighted that she was much more at ease with the Tyreans now.

"Final round."

Lord Tam and Lady Trerisia stepped back into the ring and faced each other again. They saluted each other.

"Begin."

Both dropped low as they rammed into each other shoulder to shoulder. Their punching fists moved so quickly that their arms were a blur. They looked too close together to kick as well, but somehow Lord Tam managed a kick at Lady Trerisia's jaw, at an upwards angle that looked impossible to Rannis, and at the same time she hooked her foot around to kick with the underside at the knee of Lord Tam's standing leg. He twisted to take it on the front of his knee while punching her in the side of her ribs. They fell together for a while and first one and then the other was thrown out, each time jumping back into the ring so quickly that it looked as though they had bounced like a ball.

Most of the time Rannis could not make out exactly what each was doing, but then Lord Tam threw a high round kick at Lady Trerisia's head, she ducked under it and, with a twist, aimed a round kick at his standing leg. She must have caught him off balance and Rannis gasped as Lord Tam's leg bent sideways. Lady Trerisia's leg changed direction into a sidekick into his chest as he fell, and he rolled fully out of the ring.

"Light! That looked bad!" Tara exclaimed, as the whole audience fell silent. This time Lord Tam did not immediately jump back into the ring or even straight back to his feet. Instead he lay where he had fallen, breathing deeply.

"Pause!" The unseen announcer's voice called.

"Crystu? Was that as bad as it looked?" Jathte asked, sounding concerned. Lady Crystu had her eyes closed, presumably trying to judge the severity of the injury. Rannis knew that Sorcerers could feel their Ponfour's health, but had no idea how much detail was involved. He looked from Lady Crystu to her Ponfour and then to the scoreboard. Trerisia led by three points.

"It's hard to say," Lady Crystu replied. "It's painful, but I'm not sure how badly damaged it is."

"Lord Tam, can you continue?" The announcer asked. Lord Tam pushed himself to his hands and knees, still breathing deeply, and then, with visible effort, climbed back onto his feet.

"What happens if he can't continue?" Rannis asked. "Lady Trerisia is three points ahead but you said that points are deducted if someone is injured."

Jathte grimaced.

"If Tam can't continue then he wins. Trerisia would lose four points."

"He won't quit," Lady Crystu said, without opening her eyes. "You know that he won't. Not if he can still walk. He wouldn't want to win that way; no-one would."

Rannis heard Tara mutter, "Except lithrod players." He stifled a smile.

Lady Crystu opened her eyes.

"I can't tell. You know how it is if you are injured in a fight; it never feels all that bad at the time. It's only later, when it's swelled up and stiffening that you really feel it. Ponfourii heal quickly. It may not have been as bad as it looked. If he can take the pain now, it may heal before it can swell."

"You mean, if he stops now and rests it, it *may* heal before it stiffens and swells," Jathte corrected.

Lady Crystu nodded.

"But he's not going to stop."

She was right. Rannis watched Lord Tam take a few experimental steps. After a moment, he evidently decided that he could continue because he limped back into the circle. The crowd roared its approval as Lady Trerisia said something and Lord Tam nodded and saluted her.

"Two minutes and three seconds left. Continue."

"Maybe it *wasn't* as bad as it looked," Nell said after a few seconds had passed. Rannis nodded, but a glance at Lady Crystu's frown made him wonder.

Lord Tam appeared to be fighting as well as ever, and within the first minute had thrown Lady Trerisia from the circle and reduced her lead to one point, yet it seemed to Rannis that he was not kicking as much as he had been before – he had switched to using his fists almost exclusively.

The last minute went swiftly, with each managing to throw the other out once. Lady Trerisia was still leading by one point. Lady Trerisia threw a punch with her right fist which Lord Tam avoided. As he swung his head back, his right hand caught and pulled her towards him and he ducked and swung his other arm under her legs. With a heave, he threw her from the circle but the gong sounded while she was still in the air.

"Yes!" Jathte cheered. "Well done Zia!"

Lady Crystu pouted a little and sank back into her chair, but then grinned and also began to cheer.

"Well done Trerisia!"

"But he threw her out!" Tara protested.

"It doesn't count. She hadn't touched the ground before the gong," Lady Crystu explained. "Trerisia has won, but it was very close the whole time." She grinned at Jathte. "It was a good fight."

Down on the floor, Lord Tam limped across and held out his hand to Lady Trerisia. She pulled herself to her feet and the two of them saluted each other.

"Score for round six, eleven points each. Final score Lord Tam 66 points, Lady Trerisia 67 points," the unseen announcer said. "Lady Trerisia wins the challenge by one point."

After the challenge

Tam sat as still as he could manage, and poked his tongue into the fresh gap in his front teeth, feeling the hard tips of the new teeth that were already beginning to grow.

The cut on his lip from its impact against those teeth, at the moment that they were encouraged to leave his mouth, had almost closed, though was still swollen enough to make drinking difficult.

The swelling around his left eye was beginning to reduce and he could almost fully bend his right fingers again. The cracked ribs would take longer to knit, but even there he could already feel a slight easing of the soreness. The lesser bruises and lumps would be healed within another hour.

Beside him, at the table, Crystu was eyeing him from the corner of her eyes, and he could feel surprise, concern, and a growing exasperation emanating from her.

Across the table, Trerisia, whose appearance similarly betrayed graphic evidence of their recent challenge fight, was watching him with suspicion, while Jathte looked amused.

Tam continued to pretend not to notice the looks that the women were giving him, and concentrated on trying to drink without spilling it out of his misshapen lip.

They were all sitting at a small table, which, along with many others, had been brought outside into a large flat lawn. The chairs around the tables were filled with Tyreans and Perrestians, all happily eating their midday meal and discussing the recent fight.

Duke Rannis had arranged for the mid-day meal to be served here, and enough tables and chairs were provided for most to have a place to sit and eat.

Crystu, Tam, Jathte, and Trerisia, along with several other Sorcerers and Ponfourii, sat around tables that had been placed in the shade offered by a spectacularly large oak tree. Duke Rannis and his family, including the Lady Erian, had joined the group beneath its branches.

"How's the knee, Tam?" Jathte asked, grinning.

"It will be fine," Tam replied, ignoring Crystu's snort of disgust beside him.

"It has been more than an hour. If it needs healing say so," Trerisia said calmly.

"It…does...not!" Tam stated firmly. "It will heal on its own."

"I don't understand," Duchess Thianel said from the adjacent table, which had been pulled close to theirs. "Why does it matter?"

Crystu pressed her lips together and glared at Tam, as Jathte said, "As you already know, under the rules by which they fought, they must demonstrate total control over their strength. Therefore, if someone inflicts an injury that is severe enough to require healing, he or she is penalised by the deduction of points. This rule continues for a few hours after the contest. If Tam's knee hasn't healed by itself sufficiently within two hours then Zia can still lose the points."

He waited for the Duchess to nod that she understood so far, and then continued, "Ponfourii heal much more quickly than the rest of us do, and are generally better able to continue fighting with injuries that would incapacitate Sorcerers, which means..." He paused for breath, which gave Crystu a chance to interrupt.

"Which means that it can be extremely hard to get one to *admit* it, if he has sustained such a severe injury that he will need healing if he is to be able to walk anywhere tomorrow."

She glared at Tam as she spoke.

Duchess Thianel smiled.

"A common masculine trait, Lady Crystu," she said softly. "None of them like to admit it when they are hurt. Ran would suffer for days rather than admit pain, even if he broke an arm."

"I heard that," Duke Rannis said.

"You were meant to," his wife replied.

"There is another factor, I suspect, Lady Thianel," Jathte said, his grin broadening. "Tam and Trerisia's scores were so close that if his knee does in fact require healing..."

"It does not!" Tam interrupted.

Jathte ignored him.

"If it does require healing," he repeated, "then Trerisia will lose enough points that she will have lost the contest too. No fighter ever wants to win a challenge that way, no matter how well fought the match was."

Duke Rannis nodded.

"I can understand that," he commented,

"Conversely, I do not want to win a match that I should not. If I misjudged that kick, then I deserve the penalty."

Trerisia stared at Tam's leg as though trying to see through his trousers to his knee.

"My…knee…does…not…require…healing!" Tam said, enunciating each word clearly.

"Does it, Crystu?" Trerisia asked, ignoring him. Crystu glared at Tam again.

"I think so! It's certainly painful enough, but without looking properly, I can't be certain," she said honestly.

"I was able to stand, and continue the fight. The injury is not that bad," Tam insisted.

Crystu ignored him, and spoke to Duchess Thianel.

"In the heat of battle, an injury may not feel too painful. The fighter may well be able to ignore it and to persuade himself that it will soon heal by itself. But afterwards, when the fight is over and he has sat down for a while and cooled down, it may well stiffen until the joint is unusable. This can happen even to a Ponfour."

"She's right, Tam," Jathte agreed.

Duke Rannis, Tara, and Erian, listened with unhidden interest to the Tyreans.

"It is not that bad. I can walk on it. I walked here," Tam insisted.

"You limped here," Crystu retorted. "If we were attacked right now could you even stand, let alone fight? I don't think so."

"I could do both!" he told her.

He knew that as long as he could stand on it, he could bear the pain and fight if necessary.

"If I could not, I would say so, and have it healed, but it's just sore. I can use it."

He felt the sudden shift in Crystu's emotions from exasperation to decision and wondered what she was planning.

She smiled sweetly.

"In that case, you won't mind getting me another slice of cake." She pointed to a distant table laden with various sweet desserts.

Tam looked at the distant table and nodded. He could do it.

"Of course, my Lady," he said. "What flavour would you like?"

"Oh, I don't know. Why don't you surprise me?"

Her smile was sweet and her eyes wide with feigned innocence, but Tam knew that she believed that he would fail to take even three steps.

He would show her!

He pushed himself to his feet. Crystu had been correct about the stiffening: the pain was excruciating as he straightened the leg.

Once straightened, however, he could put weight on it without it buckling.

The knee was agony, but he could stand it. Each step felt as though he was squashing ground glass inside the joint but he forced himself to walk steadily. Crystu could feel it of course, and would doubtless over-react, but he knew that he could manage until it healed by itself. He was not going to let a little injury win him the challenge.

His last thought seemed illogical somehow, but, before he could consider what was wrong with it, something hit the back of his good knee, buckling the leg, at the same moment that something pulled hard on his braid. His injured knee, unable to take his full weight, collapsed and he fell backwards to the ground at Crystu's feet.

He had been concentrating so hard on trying to walk normally, that he had not realised until that moment that Crystu had come up behind him.

She wasn't alone. Before he could even try to rise, several people pounced and pinned him to the ground. He caught a glimpse of some familiar faces before someone's stomach pushed his head back to the ground, while someone else sat on his stomach. The hands and knees restraining his arms and feet had to be Ponfourii, judging by their strength.

The sound of good-natured laughter filled that area of the lawn and he could hear movement as, presumably, people came closer for a better look.

Try as he might, he could not move an inch, and he quickly gave up the attempt. He briefly considered using magic to free himself, but today he was supposed to refrain from magic use. He had been transmuting the model all day for the last two days and needed to replenish his strength. Besides which, they were all Tyreans too, and Crystu alone had stronger Gifts than his. He knew that he would fail if he made the attempt.

Tam would have protested this treatment aloud, but the stomach across his face made speech impossible, especially as that stomach was vibrating with someone's uncontrollable laughter.

All he could do was concentrate on pushing aggrieved indignation across the bond to Crystu, who responded with internal laughter at his predicament.

"Now then, my stubborn Ponfour, let's have a look at that knee," Crystu said with a great deal of satisfaction, and Tam felt her begin to pull the bottom of his trouser leg upwards, as a pair of hands held his foot still.

Sudden agony exploded in his knee as she attempted to pull the fabric over the swollen joint. It would not go.

"Sorry, Tam, I'll have to cut the trouser leg to get it over your knee. I'll cut along the seam so you can sew it back up easily later."

Tam supposed that he was lucky that she hadn't decided to just remove his trousers altogether!

He felt the tugging as she worked and then a cold draft hit his knee as the fabric fell away. Several people gasped, and the person on his face shifted position slightly, presumably for a better look, but her new position blocked his nose and mouth completely leaving him unable to breath.

"Ease off a bit, Astley," he heard Crystu say, "he can't breathe."

The stomach on his face lifted slightly and Tam gratefully pulled air into his lungs. He was a little surprised to learn that the person lying on his head was Astley, but she and Crystu had become friends very quickly and she had been sitting nearby.

"This knee is actually worse than it felt, Tam, and it felt bad. I'm sorry, Trerisia, but this really does need healing."

"You're right, Crystu," Trerisia's low musical voice was shaking with laughter. "I clearly need to better control my strength when kicking. Men are such delicate creatures."

A ripple of feminine laughter greeted that remark.

If even Trerisia was laughing, he must look hilarious indeed and finally the humour of his situation began to overwhelm him, and Tam started to chuckle, which was a little hard with the person lying across his face, and the person sitting on his stomach.

“Crystu, not without consent.”

Jathte’s voice said chidingly from somewhere above. So that was who was sitting on his gut.

“I suppose you’re right, Jathte, but I think he may be ready to see reason now. Get off him, you two, and I’ll ask.”

Astley pushed herself up off him and grinned.

“Sorry, Tam, but Crystu was right,”

Tam would have replied, but as Jathte got off his stomach, Crystu dropped down onto it, forcing the air from his lungs as she sat. She looked down at him with a cheerful smile.

He smiled ruefully back, and then glanced above his head to see who held his arms. As he had suspected, Karan grinned back at him while keeping a firm grip on his right arm, and Gann had the left in an equally strong hold with one knee across his elbow for extra security. Two other Ponfourii held his feet with solid grips.

“Now, Tam,” Crystu began,

“You were right!” he interrupted. “If you could take me down that easily, then this injury is clearly affecting my ability to protect you. It must be healed.”

He felt her probe at the bond to check that he truly meant what he said and then she grinned happily.

"I'm so glad that you've returned to your usual good sense," she told him. "I'll heal it now."

"No!" he said firmly, although he knew that he was not in the best position for asserting his authority, pinned to the ground as he was. She frowned at him and opened her mouth, but before she could speak, he continued, "Not you, Crystu, you need to rest today, remember? It must be someone who has not used much magic recently."

She nodded reluctantly, as Gann spoke up.

"I can do it, Tam, I needed little magic yesterday as we found no new ant-hills. So if you agree, I will heal your knee?"

Tam nodded, and then gasped as the wave of healing power swept down his arm, and across his torso, to focus on his leg. The intense reaction confirmed that the knee was badly injured, and that left untreated, it might not have fully healed even by the following day.

As the healing effect subsided, he realised that Gann had focussed the energy finely, and that only the knee was healed. The rest of his bruises, lumps, and cuts remained intact. That must be a punishment from the older Ponfour for being stubborn. Tam admitted to himself that he deserved the reprimand.

He had truly believed that he could manage until his knee healed, but he had been deceiving himself. His refusal to admit the serious injury, even to himself, could have endangered Crystu.

"Are you satisfied now, Crystu?" he asked. She nodded happily.

"Then would you ask your minions to let go, please? I am suddenly hungry."

"Hey!" she exclaimed indignantly, and bounced on his stomach, making him grunt. The painfully increased pressure of Gann's knee on his arm, and sharp tugs at legs and other arm showed that those holding him had also noticed his use of a word normally reserved for servants of the Shadowbringer, along with its implication that Crystu was behaving like their foe.

"Ask nicely," Crystu demanded, staring haughtily towards the sky.

"Does that mean that you wish me to return to the more formal address, my Lady," Tam enquired politely, although he could tell by the immediate flash of alarm across their bond, that she did not want that barrier back between them.

Neither did he.

"Light, no!" She grinned down at him. "But I would appreciate it if you don't compare me to the Shadowbringer again."

Tam looked at her, and then glanced meaningfully towards his, still restrained, arms. He raised an eyebrow.

Crystu laughed, gesturing at the Ponfourii holding him to let go. Immediately, Tam pushed himself to his feet, spilling the young Sorceress onto the ground. He helped her up.

"Go sit down, I'll fetch you something to eat," she told him, giving him a push toward the table. He glanced down at his flapping trouser leg and sighed; that would take some time to repair, but at least she had kept to the seam.

Around them, people resumed their interrupted conversations, though many still cast amused glances in his direction as they talked.

Tam shook his head. Yet again, he was causing merriment among other people. He remembered promising himself to stop doing that; perhaps he should try harder.

A Zindon strikes

As Tam sat down, he saw that Erian and Tara were both laughing so hard that tears were streaming down both faces. The duchess was more restrained, but her eyes were suspiciously bright. The duke was frowning.

Tam met the duke's eyes and smiled ruefully.

"You are a strange people," Rannis said, looking thoughtful. "An odd mixture of formality and informality. If Pendin's subordinates tried such a thing with him, they would be severely punished or else discipline would begin to break down."

"Even if they were his friends?" Tam asked.

Duke Rannis nodded.

"*Especially* if they were his friends. There can be no favouritism, and they should know how to behave when on duty. I understood that Ponfourii are always on duty outside Tyreen."

Tam heard the disapproval in the duke's voice and saw it on the man's face as he looked around at the other tables, particularly when his glance fell over those who had restrained him for Crystu.

Tam shook his head, wondering how to explain.

"As far as the Soldiers and Warriors who are present are concerned, what happened was between Ponfour and Sorceress and has no bearing on my ability to act as their commander. They are not on duty, so may laugh at me, if they wish to, until they are."

He grinned, still ruefully, as Jathte added, "A Ponfour knocked down by his own Sorceress, without her using magic to do it, is a rare sight, and one to be enjoyed."

Tam nodded agreement, privately promising to himself that it should be an even rarer sight in future. He would not again misjudge his own fitness that far.

"The Ponfourii and Sorcerers who helped Crystu are a different matter – they are not, in fact, my subordinates while we are out here having a meal. Except when engaged in a joint mission as now, travelling Sorcerers and Ponfourii are independent and they expect to make their own choices and decisions. Even though I am in command of our mission here, in matters unconnected with that, like now, command is irrelevant. I outrank everyone here, except for Crystu, but even so, if Sorcerers and Ponfourii think I am in the wrong they will usually say so, clearly and distinctly. A disagreement between Sorceress and Ponfour is, by long custom, their business and no one else has the right to comment, or interfere, but as Rykatu, Princess, and most important, my bonded Sorceress, Crystu had the right to demand to inspect my knee, and the rank to have others help her do so."

"Exactly!" Crystu grinned as she sat down beside him and passed him a plate of meat and salad.

"Of course, you could just have told me to roll up my trouser leg so that you could see the knee for yourself," he pointed out. "You know that I would not have refused a direct order from you."

"I could have done that but it would have been far less fun!" She laughed. "You should have seen your face when you hit the ground!"

Tam shrugged.

"I knew then that you were correct to think that I was injured more severely than I would admit even to myself. Of course, Astley didn't give me a chance to say it."

Crystu laughed again.

"I knew that you are too honest to fool yourself for long, and I did not want you to capitulate too quickly and spoil the fun, so I'm glad Astley thought to do that."

"I hope that I never deceive myself like that again, Crystu," Tam told her, suddenly serious. "My ability to protect you was impaired because I genuinely thought the injury was not so bad, and I was wrong. If that happened when you needed me..." he paused because the thought that he might fail in his duty was appalling. Crystu shook her head,

"You rarely make such a mistake, Tam, and never twice. It will not happen again."

He could feel her total confidence in him and was reassured.

"Eat," she urged. "You were just healed, remember?"

Tam needed no further urging.

Rannis still looked puzzled. Jathte suddenly barked a laugh.

"Light, Ran! Do you think anyone will think the less of Tam, when it took six of us to pin him down long enough for him to admit that he had sustained an injury that would have crippled me?"

Rannis nodded slowly.

"When you put it like that, it does look different," he agreed. "I saw how your knee bent sideways when she kicked it, Lord Tam. I once sustained a similar injury which left me unable to walk for weeks and it was still occasionally painful months later. No one had to sit on *me* to make me realise that I was hurt."

Crystu grimaced and Tam looked at her, surprised by the sudden guilty spike in her emotions.

"Maybe this will have reassured people that we are still friends after the other day. I have heard some comments."

Tam put down his fork, suddenly angry.

"Who has made comments? That was between us and is finished."

Crystu shrugged.

"It's only natural, Tam, if against custom. I *was* very loud and that amphitheatre carried my voice efficiently."

"I still don't know what happened," Jathte commented mildly, "and I would like to, even if it is none of my business." He grinned hopefully.

Tam noted that Duke Rannis had turned politely back to his own table companions, and had begun to talk to his daughter and Erian.

Trerisia patted Jathte's hand.

"Don't be silly, Jath, you know what it was."

He looked puzzled.

"Don't you remember Bein? And Tarrow? And Samvar and Loshen and Casht and that *delightful* nameless village near the desert?" As Trerisia spoke the list of names, Jathte's eyes widened in recognition.

"Of course I remember, but what has that to do with… Oh! It was that?" He grinned self-consciously, and laughed.

"I understand! So you experienced that, Crystu? Poor Tam!"

She stared at him in amazement, for a full minute before she could find her voice.

"You too?"

Jathte nodded ruefully and he and Trerisia shared a grin.

"Oh yes!"

He rubbed the back of his neck self-consciously and looked at Tam, who had just cleared his plate.

"Do you remember when I told you that you could try running away, but that it wouldn't work?"

Tam nodded.

"Well, that's how I knew: I tried it," Jathte admitted,

"He led me quite a chase! It is a good thing that I can translocate, and that the bond lets us sense our partner's direction and distance. Every morning when I awoke, he had gone and I had to find him," Trerisia said fondly,

"You ran away from your Ponfour?" Crystu squeaked as Tam stared at her in sudden horror at the thought of what might have been.

"I'm glad that you didn't think to try that, Crystu, I would have had to get assistance to follow you."

She snorted.

"It amounts to the same thing! Jathte translocated himself, I translocated you!"

"You did come after me," he pointed out.

"Eventually, yes, but only after a long sleep, and a chat with Mother, and some food."

"Where did she send you, Tam?" Jathte asked, and Tam smiled at the memory of the moment that the nimbus had cleared to reveal his location.

"Mount Bangruaig and I was wearing only thin summer clothes and sandals," he replied.

Jathte laughed.

"Oh, Crystu, that was cruel! You could at least have sent him some warm clothes!"

She snorted.

"I did send his bag of ceremonial armour, although that wouldn't have been very warm, I know."

"So what triggered it for you, Crystu?" Jathte asked. "For me, it was when Da and Mother celebrated their fifty-third bonding anniversary, and it suddenly occurred to me that fifty-three years is a long time to be attached to someone who can feel everything that you feel."

Crystu looked down at the remains of her cake.

"I learned about the term 'double-bonded' and what it meant," she replied quietly. "It was something of a shock, as was the discovery that Tam already knew about it."

Jathte smiled sympathetically and Trerisia nodded with understanding.

"We can understand that," she said. "Suddenly discovering that well-hidden secret was a shock to me, too. Jathte, of course, already knew about it, from growing up with double-bonded parents."

"I'm not sure that made it easier, Zia, just less of a shock when I realised that I had the same kind of bond. And then I had to decide whether to tell you."

"He *didn't* tell me," Trerisia told Crystu dryly.

Jathte grinned at her.

"You do have a reputation for fierceness, Zia, I was afraid of what you might do if you thought you were being compelled to do something."

The two of them stared at each other, smiling for a long moment, but then Jathte pulled his gaze away with a visible effort.

"I had a similar worry," Tam said, apparently speaking to his empty plate.

Crystu hit his arm with her fork and he grinned at her, and opened his mouth to speak, but then he felt it: the faint but unmistakable tingle of distant magic use emanating from somewhere in the nearby city.

He jumped to his feet, hand on his sword hilt, as did every Ponfour and most of the other Tyreans. The Perrestians gasped, and one or two screamed as some swords were drawn fully.

All the Tyreans looked around silently and alertly, their eyes searching the area looking for any threat.

"What is it," Duke Rannis asked, looking worried.

"Magic!" Erian gasped. "I felt it, Uncle Ran, over that way."

She pointed towards the old quarter of the town. That way lay the old market, the poorer housing areas, the ancient Cathedral of Light, and the building occupied by the newer Group of Light.

"Magic," Jathte agreed. "Not one of us, and it is far too strong for someone using it instinctively without knowledge."

Tam nodded.

"Captain Amil," he called. The captain jogged into sight. "Take four Septines and see if you can refine a location for that."

The captain nodded and began barking orders and within a few minutes, he and a group of Warriors and Soldiers had jogged off towards the nearby buildings. None of them had armour with them, not expecting anything except a meal, but all had brought their swords.

"You were right, Jathte, there is a magic user here. This cannot be a coincidence, Tam," Crystu said, still looking in the direction from which the fading emanation came.

Tam felt her strong impulse to join those looking for the source and had to fight down the same desire within himself. He wished that he could just run off into the city with those Warriors, but he was in command. He must remain here and Crystu must stay with him, or go alone, but he would be foresworn if she went out alone to face an unknown foe.

Crystu glanced at him, then sighed and looked at the duke and his retinue, who were sitting quietly, though their faces betrayed their inner tension. Some of the other Perrestians present were clearly on the verge of panic. She looked back at Tam questioningly.

"Should we send Duke Rannis back to the palace? It is warded and safe."

The Duke answered before Tam could open his mouth.

"We are surrounded by dozens of Tyreans including you, Lady Rykatu Crystu. I can think of no safer place if there is a magical threat."

He spoke loudly with confidence and Tam saw that his words visibly reassured the Perrestians around. Then Rannis beckoned him nearer and said in a quiet voice, "Besides, I cannot in honour take myself to a warded place of safety, when others of my people must stay here in the open."

Tam nodded. The decision was the right one for an honourable man.

"What if they don't find the magic user?" Tara asked. "News of this will spread quickly and there will be panic."

Tam saw that she looked frightened, but she was composed and her question was pertinent. The emanation had already faded beyond his ability to sense it, although he thought that Crystu could still feel it a little. Unless they had got close enough in time, the Warriors who he had sent would also have lost it by now.

Tam looked around. He would have to reassign some of his people to patrol the city looking for this magic user. That meant that the model would take a few more days to finish. He made the decision.

“If you are agreeable, Duke Rannis, we will patrol your city while we are here. If we do not find this magic user before we must leave, I will leave one Sept here with you to search until the creature is found, whatever it may turn out to be, and however long it takes.”

He, too, spoke loudly, and he also used a little illusion to carry his voice further, to reassure the townsfolk that they would not be abandoned.

"Thank you. That is a generous offer when I know that you may need those people elsewhere," Rannis replied.

Tam nodded absently and reached to catch Crystu's arm and press her down into a chair. She had begun to move slowly in the direction from which they had sensed the magical residue.

"Stay close by, my Lady," he told her. "If you go, my Oath to protect you will conflict with my present duty, and I would find that unpleasant."

Crystu sighed, nodded, and settled more fully into the chair.

"I will try to restrain myself."

"What would you do?" Erian asked suddenly, into the strained silence as everyone waited for the Warriors to return, Tam frowned slightly, not understanding.

"If you had to choose between the two duties, I mean," she explained. "What would you do?"

Tam took a deep breath and considered her question. He glanced at Crystu, who smiled back sadly, knowing the answer, and then he looked at Erian's curious face.

"It would depend on the circumstances," he said slowly. "The Ponfour Oath takes precedence, but the oath of service to Tyreen is almost as strong. If Crystu left here, I would appoint someone to take my place here and I would follow her. The only choice would be how much time I gave to the choice. If she ran off towards danger I would have to choose quickly."

"And he would consider that he had failed in his duty to Lord Jareth by abandoning his assigned post," Crystu added. "It would take me *days* to get you to forgive yourself," she told Tam.

He nodded agreement.

"You are correct; I would consider myself forsworn, but that is preferable to you being injured or worse because I was not present to protect you."

He spoke lightly, but the thought that she might be hurt when he was not present to help, was terrifying.

"Then I will certainly try hard not to put you into that situation," she promised solemnly, and took hold of his arm as if to prove that she meant to stay close by no matter what.

Tam managed to grin at her.

"I appreciate that, my Lady," he told her with total sincerity.

"Is that true as well, then?" Tara began. "That, I mean if...," she faltered, and sent a strange look towards her father, who appeared to not notice it.

Tam remembered what he had realised two days earlier: that Tara was being trained to take Pendin's place at the head of Rannis' information service. Doubtless she had instructions to ask that question if the chance arose, but did not like to touch on such a sensitive subject.

He decided to answer the question. Although he addressed his remark to Tara, he looked directly to the duke as he spoke, to emphasise the fact that he had seen through the deception.

"Yes, Lady Tara, the effect on a Ponfour if his Sorceress is killed is both painful and fatal. Few outlive their partners for more than a few weeks. None survive longer than two months."

She opened her mouth, looking thoughtful, as if she intended to ask another question this subject, but Rannis gave a small shake of his head and she glanced at him and nodded.

"I apologise," she said instead. "That is not something I had a right to ask."

"I understand, Lady Tara," Tam replied, but made no further comment.

Erian was looking thoughtful and Tam wondered if she was once again considering the nature of the bond and whether it constituted slavery.

Hearing running footsteps, Tam turned to see one of the

warriors who had left with Amil, running toward him. The man slid to a halt in front of him, chest heaving as he gasped out his message.

"Lord Tam, we did not find the magic-user, but we have found the use to which that magic was put. A market building has collapsed! Its foundations were transmuted into sand. There are casualties. Captain Amil requests assistance."

Tam nodded once and looked around quickly as Duke Rannis jumped to his feet.

"We will assist," Tam told the duke, as he beckoned several Sorcerers, including Vellte.

"You are to escort Duchess Thianel, and the Ladies Taranel and Erian back to the palace and inform those on watch and in the model room what has happened. Warn them to be extra vigilant because this may be a diversion intended to draw us away from the palace. Stay there and join the watchers. Make sure nothing happens to that model or we will have to begin again. Vellte, you have command there."

She nodded and they gathered around the ladies. A translocation nimbus immediately surrounded the group. Tara had seemed as though she wanted to protest, but a look from her father kept her silent.

All the other Tyreans quietened, awaiting instructions.

"I leave it to your own judgements whether you can safely use magic today, but remember that you will need it tomorrow and the next day," Tam told them. "The snow-ants are our primary mission here and all else comes second, but we will assist in this crisis even if we must use our bare hands to move bricks."

He turned to the Warrior who had brought the message.

"Take us to the place," he commanded.

The man nodded, turned immediately, and began to jog from the field. Tam followed, the duke on one side, and Crystu on the other.

Aftermath

"Get some rest, Pendin; you will need to be alert tomorrow."

The captain nodded and walked away down the corridor.

Duke Rannis closed the door to his private relaxing room; he doubted that Pendin would take the advice, but he hoped that the man would at least get a little sleep. Tomorrow would be almost as busy as this past afternoon and evening had been.

The duke turned to look at the other occupants of the room, who had arrived with him a moment earlier. All were now sinking into soft chairs, exhaustion showing on even the Ponfourii faces.

The last nine or so hours had been nightmarish and tiring for all. They had arrived at the old market to be met by a scene of unimaginable devastation. The huge and ancient multi-level building, which had housed hundreds of shops and restaurants, was now a mountain of rubble from which screams and moans issued, along with rumbles and creaks as areas of rubble continued to settle and shift.

Around the mound, and dwarfed by it, Rannis had seen Warriors, Soldiers, and townsfolk, trying to rescue those who were close to the surface of the pile.

Aghast, he had turned to the Rykatu and pleaded with her to transmute the rubble off the trapped or to translocate the survivors out. She had looked at him sadly and shaken her head, saying that she could not. Rannis had *demanded* that she do it. If she could transmute the much larger ice mountain, she must have the power to cope with this and her refusal was unacceptable. Lord Tam's hand on his chest had stopped him grabbing her shoulders to shake the help from her.

"She cannot do it, Rannis," her Ponfour had said gently, and then had proceeded to explain *why* she could not.

"How many people are likely to be in there?" he had asked, pointing. "I can sense many hundreds still alive, but I can't guess how many may be dead."

Rannis had looked at him, uncomprehending.

“At this time of day? There could be as many as two thousand!” he replied. Lord Tam nodded.

"And that is the problem. Crystu could turn that rubble into air, but if she did, all the people within it would fall to the ground, landing on top of each other – the living and the dead in a huge pile. Only those at the top of the pile would survive because the others would be crushed by the weight of flesh and bone above them. She could transmute the dead to air too, but the number alive is still great enough, and the distance to fall far enough, that few would survive. Translocating when we cannot see the people we need to move would be slow and dangerous. We can feel their lives but knowing exactly where they are in enough clarity for translocation is time consuming, and even then, again, translocating them from beneath rubble could destabilise an area and kill others!" He had shaken his head.

"We will do what we can, using magic where we can, but even transmuting or translocating small areas is dangerous and could destabilise the rubble around about, causing more injuries. We will have to do much of this by hand, Rannis, there is no other way."

During the following hours, Rannis had learnt a great deal about what magic could do and what it could not.

The Tyreans had worked side by side with his own people, and they had used magic where they could. Slowly, carefully, transmuting small areas at a time, while making sure that nothing became unstable as large pieces of rubble vanished into the air.

For the most part, though, they used their hands and physically lifted lumps of masonry and slabs of mortar from the pile, to carry away. As the day drew on and the sun began to set, they were joined by those who had been out that day working on the model building. They could not create an illusion once the land was too dark to see and, returning to learn of this disaster, had rushed to join the rescue.

Rannis learned that the healers could sense the pain felt by those trapped, and so they could target their efforts on places where they knew there were lives to be saved, leaving until later those areas where no sign of life existed.

The Tyreans were all considerably stronger than his own men and this was especially true of the Ponfourii.

He had watched in astonishment as Lord Tam and Lady Trerisia had, between them, lifted a slab that six of his men had been unable to move even an inch. He did not know if they were assisting the lift with magic, but once they had moved it up a foot with no sign of anything shifting from its loss, the slab had evaporated into nothing and they had moved on to something else.

He had seen many things that day, much of which he hoped would eventually fade from his memory. One of the things he had seen, that he believed would be with him until he died, had been a small hand stretched through a gap between pieces of wall, the fingers moving as if trying to reach something. The owner of the hand, a small child, was whimpering with pain and fear until Lady Crystu threw herself down and grasped the hand.

Rannis knew that she must be using her healing to block the child's pain, but he could see enough to know that it would be impossible to heal her fully until she was released from the rubble that had crushed her lower limbs and hips, and held them pinned. He did not understand how she had survived that long, but he, Lord Tam, and several others had worked frantically, desperately trying to remove enough of the encasing masonry to free the child, while below them, the Rykatu whispered comfort to her and held her pain at bay.

Despite their best efforts, the child had died before they could release her. He had set a team to work at a more relaxed pace to remove the body and they had moved to another spot where they knew that someone survived out of sight.

Lady Crystu's face had been like rock, with no sign of emotion, but the compassionate looks that Lord Tam gave her, suggested to Rannis that her lack of emotion was a mask to allow her to work. He understood that – he too could not allow himself to feel anything while lives depended on him staying strong.

As the sun set and darkness began to fall, the rubble and the surrounding buildings started to glow with a gentle but pervasive light, which allowed the rescuers to continue working, until they had found and removed every person still living from under that mound.

The injured were taken to the Palace of Healers until that building could cope with no more, and Rannis had to arrange for additional emergency shelters for the rest. He commandeered schools, the theatre, and part of the Cathedral to house those who would need nursing.

The Tyrean healers kept many people from death, but there were too many for them to be able to heal any individual fully without risk to themselves. They healed enough to keep the worst injured alive, but the rest of their wounds must heal naturally.

With the Tyrean help, the workers removed or destroyed the piled rubble, until only dust and tiled floors remained visible on the site. The death toll was surprisingly small compared to the number who had survived, but there were more than five hundred bodies carried into the Cathedral and laid out in the grounds behind it. Some of those bodies were distressingly small.

Rannis knew that without the Tyreans, it would have taken his people at least a week to remove the rubble and few if any would have been pulled alive from under it.

He sincerely hoped that none of them had heard some of the ungrateful comments that *he* had heard from among the gathered crowd of watchers. As he had done earlier, there were many who misunderstood what magic could do and thought that the Guardians should be able to save every life. Yet others thought that the presence of Guardians had attracted the Zindon that had caused these deaths.

His thoughts were pulled from the painful memory, by Tara, who appeared in front of him holding up a mug of steaming taret. Rannis took it gratefully, smiled at her, and sipped at the hot bittersweet liquid.

"Thank you, Tara." He glanced around the room, and then asked, "Where's Ri?"

"She's gone to bed, Dap, she was very tired," Tara answered, stifling a yawn.

"And you're not? Go to bed, Tara, before you fall asleep where you stand," he replied with a weary smile.

"I'm going now. I just wanted to be sure that you got a hot drink before I went. Goodni..." She stopped, aware that no one could have a 'good' night tonight. Turning, she slipped out of the room without another word, closing the door behind her.

Rannis walked to his favourite chair and sat with a sigh. Tara had already served their visitors mugs of their preferred hot spiced fruit drink, before she brought him his taret. One or two of the Tyreans had tried taret, but few had liked it; they preferred something less bitter. As he settled back in his chair, Rannis thought about Ri. She could drink taret morning, noon, and night, and he wondered how she would manage without it in Tyreen.

He recognised the thought as an attempt to avoid thinking about what had happened that day.

He looked around at his visitors. Crystu and Tam occupied one long chair, Jathte and Trerisia another, and Vellte and Gann had pulled two chairs across to form a group with the others. Without thinking about it, they had all dispensed with titles between them earlier in the day. After what they had experienced together, such formalities had become unimportant trivia.

The evidence of their earlier fight had almost vanished from the Ponfourii faces, but all bore scratches and bruises from their work in the rubble.

Crystu was leaning against Tam, who had put his arm around her, and Rannis realised with a start that tears were streaming down her face, although she made no sound.

He reminded himself that she was little older than Tara or Ri, and he was glad that *they* had been shielded from the worst sights.

He knew that the two of them had gone to give whatever assistance they could to the healers, and would have seen a great deal that he wished they had not. At least those people were alive, and largely in one piece. He pushed down the memory of a small foot lying by itself.

"Thank you for your assistance today," he said quietly. "Many more would have died had you not been present."

"And perhaps none would have died at all if we had not come here," Crystu whispered.

Rannis swore mentally! They *had* heard the muttered comments!

Vellte and Gann both shook their heads at Crystu, but Tam spoke first.

"Nonsense!" he said firmly. "If we had not come here, that mountain would have grown ever larger, and spread across this area, until everything living had been consumed by the ants. We did not do this or cause this, Crystu. Place the blame where it properly lies – at the feet of the Shadowbringer, and his servants here."

"I had hoped that you had not heard the comments of a few wrong-thinking ingrates," Rannis began.

"Ponfourii have sharp ears," Trerisia reminded him tonelessly. "We doubtless heard more than you."

"They were right in one thing: this is part of our long war with the Shadowbringer, and you are caught between us and his servants," Crystu insisted, wiping the tears from her face.

"*Your* war?" Rannis interjected. "The last time I checked, this country was still a part of the Church and Congregation of Light. The war is against all of us! We are *not* unconnected bystanders in someone else's conflict."

"We are supposed to protect people from things like this," she persisted, unpersuaded.

"We are not Gods, Crystu," Vellte told her. "We are neither all-knowing nor all powerful, thank the Light! Without a gleaning to warn us that this attack was imminent, we could not have prevented it, and God sends those warnings as *He* decides will best serve his will."

"Do you believe there is a purpose to His allowing such

carnage?" asked Crystu. "Because I find it hard to understand how that could work to any good."

"I do believe it," Vellte replied, "even though I will probably never know what His purpose is for not giving us warning enough to prevent it."

Crystu might have continued to argue, but Rannis decided to ask a more practical question.

"Regardless of what God may intend, the shadow minion that caused this presumably intends it to serve *his* lord's purpose in some way. What reason might he have to perform such a seemingly random act of destruction?"

"It will delay us," Tam replied after a moment. "We cannot ignore this, or just continue our work on the model as if nothing has happened. We have no choice now but to patrol this town, night and day, to search for this minion, and prevent any further acts on its part. That will mean fewer to work on illusion or transmutation, so it will take longer until we can destroy that mountain."

He glanced at Crystu, who looked close to sleep.

"In addition, many of us will require a long sleep to recover from the unexpected magic use that was necessary to prevent further loss of life. That too will cause a delay."

"The Shadowbringer wants you held here?" Rannis asked.

Tam nodded.

"Or prevented from going somewhere else," he replied.

Rannis saw that the others were nodding their agreement with Tam's assessment, and it matched his own reading of this attack.

"We have no choice," Tam continued. "Although I dislike doing what the Shadowbringer wants, now that we know for certain that one of his servants is still present, we must stay until the mountain is destroyed and the minion is killed."

"Thank you," Rannis said simply. "I appreciate that, even if some of my more ignorant subjects do not."

"They're frightened, Rannis." Jathte sounded almost ready to fall asleep in his chair. "Frightened people often look for something or someone close by to blame, and we are here and unusually visible, and the Zindon is killing them."

He saw the looks from the others and shrugged.

"Yes, it could be some other form of shadow creature, but with such a well targeted attack, I think we all know that it must have an intellect, and that means a Zindon."

He yawned.

Rannis closed his eyes.

"The last confirmed Zindon presence in Perrest was over forty five years ago. I had hoped never to see one here in my lifetime."

“The Shadowbringer is moving against us,” Trerisia said. “This is the second that one of us has encountered this year.”

“That we know of,” Tam added, he shrugged as Rannis looked at him. “We don’t know yet if any others have met up with Zindons as they investigate the various rumours of dark activity.”

Rannis suddenly realised that the three Sorcerers were now fast asleep, and their Ponfourii all wore similar looks of mild satisfaction.

“They’re going to be quite annoyed with us for this,” said Gann. Tam and Trerisia both shrugged fractionally.

“I can live with that,” Tam said. “I told her that I would do this if necessary and she was exhausted.”

Rannis stared.

“What did you do?” he asked, curiously, grateful for something that distracted him from the deaths, even if briefly.

"A sleep compulsion," explained Tam. “They will sleep so deeply that nothing will awaken them until we lift the compulsion, which will not be until late tomorrow morning."

"I could use a good night's sleep myself," Rannis commented, "but I cannot afford to be so deeply asleep that my people cannot awaken me at need. A king must sleep as lightly as a Ponfour when his people are threatened."

Tam nodded.

"We understand that, Rannis, but there is another form of the compulsion that we could use, if you wish."

Rannis suddenly remembered something that Pendin had told

him two days before.

"You can make me sleep until someone speaks my name? As you did to the men who followed you the day you arrived?"

Trerisia looked surprised.

"Some of your men tried to follow Tam and Crystu? After their lesson when I caught the ones following Jath? That was foolish."

Rannis shrugged.

"Their job is to gather information. They were merely doing their duty as they saw it."

He smiled at the outraged look on her face.

"I have told them not to follow any of you again, Trerisia, and they will obey."

"What did you do when you caught them?" Tam asked her.

She shrugged.

"I explained my disappointment at their rudeness," she replied.

"With her fists," Rannis added dryly. "The four of them are still walking with crutches."

"They will recover," she said unconcernedly. Then she looked at Tam and smiled faintly. "I suppose that you were gentler than I, and just made them sleep?"

"He didn't *just* make them sleep, Trerisia, they also needed some treatment from the healers, but at least they had no broken bones," Rannis told her.

Tam frowned.

"Really? I thought I broke one nose at least," he said, trying to remember the detail of the fight.

Rannis shook his head.

"Perhaps I should have said, no *important* broken bones. You are right: there was one broken nose."

"Good!" Gann said with satisfaction. "Tam, sometimes, is too gentle. I'm glad that this time he overcame that."

"However, the point I intended to make, was that you made them sleep until someone spoke my name to them." Rannis returned to his original question. "So could you do that for me? I need sleep if I am to be clear headed tomorrow, but after everything today, I suspect I will lie awake a long time."

"We can," Tam answered, "and if that is your request, we will."

"How? I mean, will you have to be there when I lie down in my bed?"

"No," Tam replied. "I can make a compulsion that will not take hold until you place your head on the pillow. When you do, you will sleep deeply until someone speaks your name. Your dreams will not be troubling either. Is that your wish?"

Rannis nodded.

"Yes. Thank you."

"It is easiest if I have skin contact," Tam said as he reached across and grasped Rannis' hand. Rannis felt a slight warm tingle run through his head, but nothing else. Tam removed his hand.

"Is it done?" Rannis asked.

Tam nodded.

"Be sure that you have dealt with everything before you lie down, because from the moment that your head touches your pillow, you will enter a deep sleep, and you will not awaken until someone says your name."

"Thank you," Rannis said, as the Ponfourii all stood up.

Rannis noticed that one of Tam's legs was bare from the thigh down. The fabric that had flapped about his leg after Crystu had sliced the seam, had been cut away at some point in the last few hours.

Tam lifted Crystu from the long chair, one arm under her legs and the other behind her back, and Gann lifted Vellte in a similar way.

To Rannis' bemusement, Trerisia threw Jathte over one shoulder, holding him in place by one arm across the back of his knees, so that his arms hung down behind her.

Gann looked at her in a disapproving way.

"That is not a very dignified way to carry him, Trerisia," he told her.

She was unconcerned.

"It is the easiest way to carry him, and the most practical. I have one hand free to open doors, or draw a sword." She waved her free hand.

Gann looked at Tam as though considering it.

"She has a point, Tam."

Tam shook his head.

"I will not carry Crystu like a sack of grain, whether she knows about it or not. It would be disrespectful."

"So what will you do if you are attacked and must fight?" Trerisia asked.

Tam grinned.

"Drop her, of course. I can always heal her afterwards if necessary."

Trerisia snorted.

"You have a strange idea of respectful, Tam," she told him.

He shrugged and then nodded to Rannis.

"Goodnight, Rannis, we will resume our work tomorrow, and complete it as quickly as we can."

Then he and the other Ponfourii carried their burdens out into the corridor, Trerisia closing the door behind them.

Rannis sighed. He knew that tomorrow would be long and difficult. He must arrange for the identification of those who had died, so that they could receive appropriate burial. That would be hard in some cases; not all would be recognisable even if their own mothers looked at them, because their injuries were too severe. The was a strong possibility that the names of some might never be known.

He yawned, picked up a lamp, and walked along the dark hall to his bedroom. He was not surprised to find Nell still awake.

"Was it bad?" she asked gently.

"Yes," he admitted. "I'm glad you and Tara did not insist on helping at the scene."

"Will you sleep? You need it," she said, mercifully not asking for details. Not that she would; she had clear ideas about appropriate roles for women and men.

Helping to nurse the injured was appropriate work for a lady, digging through rubble was not.

Rannis wondered what she thought about the Tyrean princess who had dug as untiringly as her Ponfour.

He realised that she was waiting for his reply, and shook his head sharply to clear it long enough for him to change from his dusty, ripped, and blood spattered clothes.

"I will sleep. Tam has seen to that. Once my head touches the pillow, I will sleep until I hear my name spoken," he told her. He knew from her satisfied expression that he had made a mistake.

"I will make sure that you sleep as long as possible then," she said. "I will not awaken you until you have slept at least twelve hours."

Rannis shook his head, wishing that he had said nothing.

"Nell, I can't be unconscious that long. There will be much work to do to do. The Duke cannot be seen to sleep late at such a time."

He breathed a sigh of relief as she nodded reluctantly.

"You're right, Ran, of course. I will wake you at eight, but no earlier," she told him.

He smiled back.

"That is acceptable, thank you, Nell, for understanding."

He climbed into the bed beside her and lay back. He fell into sleep like falling into a hole. The darkness closed over him and he began to dream relaxingly pleasant dreams of his childhood.

A pleasant morning

Erian's eyes snapped open and she almost bounced out of bed. The strange jumbled dreams about snow, and mountains, and people from the Group of Light, vanished from her memory instantly. The excitement that had been growing within her for the last week had reached a level that was almost uncontainable.

Tara had found Gerine a place in the Ducal household because the maid could not come to Tyreen with Erian. Erian had been happy for her to make the change immediately, so she hurriedly washed herself and dressed without assistance.

She checked her two bags again to be sure that she had packed absolutely everything that she could not bear to leave behind.

Duke Rannis had arranged for her home, and dependant relatives, to be well looked after while she was away. She had travelled back there for a day to fetch a few things that she would want, like the portrait of her parents, and a necklace that had been her mother's, and she was now almost ready to leave.

She had just one more thing more to buy: she could not possibly do without taret so would go into town this morning to acquire a supply to take with her.

Eleven days had passed since the collapse of the old market building, and yesterday Lord Tam had told Rannis that the model was finished. Today, most of the Tyreans would rest and recuperate their strength, and tomorrow they would destroy the mountain of ice and its unwelcome inhabitants. The day after that they would rest again, and the day after *that* most of them would leave for Tyreen, taking Erian with them.

Today, a few Tyreans would monitor the mountain to be sure that snow-ants made no major alterations to it that might affect the Rykatu's ability to transmute it, and a few continued to patrol the town, but the rest would relax.

Duke Rannis had greeted this news with an announcement of his own: that he intended to throw a feast throughout this entire afternoon, and all in Angate were welcome to attend. The Ducal grounds would be thrown open to citizens.

Captain Pendin had muttered with annoyance at the security nightmare that his liege-lord had just placed in his hands, and disappeared to organise his men.

Erian wondered if any members of the Group of Light would attend. Despite what she had told them, they had continued their protest outside the palace gate, and were as sure as ever that the Tyreans were enslaving their Ponfourii.

Erian shook her head, the whole idea now seemed absurd to her and she was glad that she had had the opportunity to learn the truth.

She pulled her comb through her hair one last time, threw it into her bag, and rushed across to Tara's room, almost running into her friend when the door opened as she reached for the handle.

"Ri!" Tara squeaked in surprise. "I didn't think you'd be up yet. The sun is only just above the horizon."

Erian grinned.

"How can I stay asleep. Tara? Two more days after today, just two, and then I go to Tyreen."

She was so taut with anticipation that she felt like jumping up and down and grabbing Tara's arms to pull her around in a dance. She managed to restrain the impulse, however, and instead just said,

"Libby said that he would have the taret jars ready for me today. I want to go and fetch them this morning. Will you come and help me carry them?"

Tara looked at her suspiciously.

"How many jars, and we are taking a carriage aren't we?"

Erian laughed. "Just eight jars, and yes, I know that Pendin gave orders that I'm not allowed out unaccompanied or on foot, while the group continue their activities by the gate, so we'll take a carriage."

"Just EIGHT! That's enough for the whole year! Why so many?" Tara asked astonished.

"Libby made me promise to try and convert the Tyreans to taret. I think he has ideas about setting up a trade link to Tyreen."

Tara laughed.

"I don't think that you will have any luck. The ones I saw try it all thought it is revolting, and you should have seen Lady Trerisia's face when she realised that her drink had milk in it. I almost thought she was going to spit it out!"

Erian grinned.

"I know, I told him that, but he said that taret is an acquired taste, and maybe I can persuade them to acquire it. He said that if I drink it and show how much I like it, maybe some of them will make the effort to acquire the taste for it, and then they will need a supplier. He is giving me all eight for nothing, if I will only make that effort."

"Well, I suppose that anything is possible, even Erian Tolene turning out to be a transmuter and an illusionist," Tara grinned, "but there's no point going this early because he won't be open yet."

Erian nodded.

"I know. I thought we could go midmorning. The house taret will be at its best then – hot and strong."

She bounced down onto Tara's bed.

"So, will you come?" she asked.

"Of course I will," Tara laughed. "I like Libby's taret too." Then she frowned slightly, remembering Erian's earlier words.

"You said that Pendin won't let you out without an escort, but you managed to elude them yesterday. Where did you disappear to?"

Erian frowned with puzzlement.

"What do you mean, Tara? I never left the grounds yesterday."

Tara gave her a strange look.

"You didn't? Pendin said that you had disappeared and could not be found anywhere. He was frantic! There were men rushing everywhere looking for you. He thought that you must have slipped out to go into town or something."

Erian shook her head blankly.

"When was this? I certainly did not go past the palace walls. I had no idea that they had mislaid me, or even," she frowned in sudden irritation, "that they were trying to keep such close watch on me! I don't like being spied on, Tara!" She stared accusingly at her friend.

"They must stop that. I will not be followed like I am suspected of some wrong-doing!" A flood of anger surged up through her chest. "I went for a walk in the woods yesterday, which is no one's business but my own. They may escort me outside the palace, but if I cannot have privacy within it, I will return home until it is time to leave for Tyreen!"

Tara looked shocked, and Erian realised that she had been shouting by the end of her sentence. She had a sudden incongruous image of Kaliss's face speaking to her urgently, but that was from her strange unsettling dream last night. She pushed the image from her mind and forced herself to calm down.

"I'm sorry, Tara, I know it's not your fault. I shouldn't shout at you for Pendin's overzealousness, but really, he has gone too far."

Tara smiled tentatively.

"Perhaps you're right. It's not as if anything dangerous can happen to you here in the palace. I'll speak to him, and ask him to pull back a little for the rest of the time that you are here."

Erian made herself smile back, although she still felt unusually and irrationally angry; Tara wasn't responsible for the insult.

"Thank you, Tara. I know he is just worried about possible attacks by certain members of the Group of Light, and I really don't know why I got so angry about it when it's for my safety, but I don't like being followed."

Tara nodded.

"I can understand that," she said, wryly. The security imposed on her own movements had quadrupled since the Zindon attack. "It's just that I don't think I ever saw you lose your temper like that before."

Erian sighed.

"You're right: I suppose that the anticipation of going to Tyreen is making me over-react. All those tests and lessons that Lady Vellte has inflicted on me don't help either. Magic is *tiring.*"

She sat on the chair beside the bed.

"I really am very sorry for shouting at you, Tara. Please forgive me."

"Oh, of course I forgive you, Ri, we won't talk about it again. How is your training progressing?"

Tara sat on the edge of the bed. She with avid interest as Erian held out her right hand and concentrated. A mist appeared suspended above her hand, and slowly coalesced until a perfect diamond lay on her palm. Tara gasped as the light caught it and its facets sparkled.

"It's just an illusion, unfortunately," Erian sighed. "I've tried to transmute a real one, but it is much harder to make a real thing than just the illusion."

"It's a very nice illusion," Tara said. Erian grinned at the hunger in her friend's voice.

"Can you sustain it for long?" Tara asked.

Erian sighed.

"Not yet, although Lady Vellte says that I should be able to learn how to fix an illusion so that it lasts for several hours. So far, the best that I've managed is about three minutes."

The diamond vanished from her palm. She grinned at Tara.

"If I ever do master that, I will never have to buy another piece of jewellery. I can just make what I want when I need it, and if someone has a larger stone, I can increase the size. Those Dallish sisters will hate me the next time we all arrive at the same party."

Tara nodded.

"They certainly will! They think that they should always outshine everyone else. I hope that I am there to see it when you walk in covered in real-looking illusory jewels. They will probably fall over in a dead faint!"

They both giggled at the thought, although privately Erian knew that the possibility existed that she would remain in Tyreen for the rest of her life.

"Will you ever come back, Ri?" Tara asked, suddenly serious. "Or will you stay there?"

Erian's smile disappeared.

"I don't know, Tara; I really don't know. I don't want to go away forever and never see you or Uncle Ran and Aunt Nell, again, but at the same time..." She paused.

"At the same time, this is the chance, and adventure, of a lifetime and you must grasp it and see where it leads," Tara finished for her.

Erian nodded.

"Plus which, they said once I enter Tyreen, that if I leave, I can never return there."

"Then let's hope that Tyreen is a horrible ugly land so that you are happy to leave once your training is finished," Tara said brightly, although Erian could tell that she was trying to hide her sadness that they were to part, possibly forever. "Now, can we go and eat? I can smell firstmeal and I'm hungry."

Tara jumped up and pulled Erian out of her chair, and they hurried out of the bedroom in search of food.

The carriage entered the great square that lay in front of the Cathedral of Light and pulled to a halt outside one of the buildings on the side opposite the great double-doored entrance into the ancient building.

On this side of the square were several large restaurants catering to the nobility and the wealthy, a few smaller that catered to the less well off, and Libby's taret house.

Compared to the restaurants on either side, the taret house was small. It was so small that a stranger could easily overlook its presence if not for the constant stream of customers entering and leaving. Anyone and everyone was welcome under Libby's ceiling, so long as they made no trouble for other customers.

A few tables were set up on the side pavement in front of the door, and most of the seats were occupied. Inside, the main dining area was crowded with people from all walks of life, all with one thing in common: a love of taret and a particular fondness for Libby's methods of preparing it. The wood-panelled, narrow but long room was welcoming, and the wooden tables with their high-backed bench seats were spacious and comfortable.

Followed by their assigned protectors, Erian and Ri entered and made their way to the large rear counter, behind which Libby, his wife, and their grown children, prepared simple but filling food, and their renowned special taret brews.

"Ladies! Wonderful to see you again!" Libby waved a spoon from the stove where he was cooking bacon, and smiled as though he had not seen them in a month, when they had been here several times this week already.

Tall, slim, and muscular, with a large black bushy moustache that sometimes appeared to have a life of its own, Libby would have stood out in a crowd even if his skin had been as dark as their own, but his pale skin, and slight accent, betrayed his exotic origins. He was a Kandarii by birth, from the mysterious land across the ocean to the east. Most Kandarii came to Perrestian shores as raiders, and Libby had been no different.

As a boy of fifteen years, he had joined his first raiding party and arrived on Perrestian soil armed and looking for wealth. When the raiders descended on a village near the coast, to find it defended by the king's own regiment, they had been beaten back to their ships. Libby had been badly wounded in the fight, and had been abandoned as dead by his people as they fled.

To the boy's considerable surprise, the people, who he had come to attack, had nursed him back to health without apparent rancour or ill-will.

By the time he was fully healed, he had converted to the Way of Light and, having no family to return to, had elected to stay in Perrest. He had travelled inland with the king's Soldiers, eventually joining their ranks to defend his adopted homeland and faith from all attackers, including his own former countrymen.

He had been happy to learn that Perrestians knew about taret – a favoured drink in Kandar – but appalled to learn how they prepared it; they simply boiled it and added honey.

He had set about educating his new friends, beginning with colleagues in the army, and acquired a reputation for having an almost magical Gift with the brew.

Kandarii had many methods of preparing, flavouring, and sweetening the brew. They had different recipes for different effects. One recipe was said to strengthen a man for battle, another to aid sleep, another to increase the likelihood that a woman would conceive a son, and yet another intended to help her have a daughter.

There were many such uses, and those which Libby had not learned, in his fifteen years in Kandar, he made up by experimenting continually with different flavours.

When he left the army after serving the usual ten years, he had found this small property tucked between two large and prosperous restaurants, opposite the great Cathedral, and knew immediately that this was where he should be.

Those who had tasted Libby's taret, while he was in the army, told their friends about it. Soon he had a large loyal clientele and had started a trend that spread across Angate. Similar taret shops appeared around the town and its surrounding villages, but everyone agreed that no one could match Libby's expert touch with the drink.

"Sit, sit, I'll bring your taret. Do you want anything with it? A cake or a biscuit?"

He smiled at them as he waved one hand at the display of baked sweet pastries and cakes, while the other hand reached beneath the counter for mugs. He expertly began to pour from a selection of containers to make Tara's favourite version of the drink. She noticed that he had not needed to ask what either of them wanted

"How many people's favourites have you memorised, Libby," Tara asked as she watched the fascinating process.

The escort had moved to stand in front of an alcove with seating enough for all of them, and were waiting patiently for the ladies to seat themselves.

Libby grinned, his moustache twitching slightly from side to side in a practiced movement.

"Only a few dozen have I completely memorised, Lady Tara," he replied, "but there are several hundred more that I can make a good guess at."

Tara grinned back.

"I'm sure it's more than that," she replied as Libby began to fill a second mug for Tara. He pulled three more mugs for their escort and quickly filled those.

"That one is for Jarl, that one for Elnar, and this last one for young Shol." he said as he poured them.

"Go and sit, ladies. I'll bring these over to you and then I will fetch the jars for you, Lady Ri. Telly!" He called through a door. "Come and take over the food for a few minutes."

His middle son appeared quickly and Libby put the mugs onto a tray, carrying it over to the alcove table that the escort had chosen. Then he disappeared down a flight of stairs into his cellar.

He reappeared a moment later carrying four large jars of prepared taret powder, which he placed on their table before running back down the stairs and returning with four more.

"There you are, Lady Ri," he said, smiling proudly. "A selection of flavours, including two of your favourite, and here," he trotted back to the counter and picked up a home preparation vessel, "is what you need to make it. I wrote instructions and they are inside."

"Libby!" Erian exclaimed, as she picked up the pottery vessel to examine it. "You must let me pay you for some of this; this is too much."

"No, no! Lady Ri, you are helping me. If even a few Tyreans start to drink taret I will be able to sell the ingredients to them." He winked at her. "And even if they do not, if it helps you to remember me when you are in Tyreen then that is a good thing."

She laughed at his nonsense.

"I don't think anyone could ever forget you, Libby, but I promise to close my eyes and imagine I am here every time I drink taret."

She inhaled the rich aroma and then sipped at the liquid. It almost scalded her mouth, which was just how she liked it.

"Perfect, Libby, as always," she told him.

Tara and their escorts all made appreciative sounds as they sipped their taret and Libby beamed.

"If you show the Guardians how delicious taret is, they'll be sure to want to try it."

"Try it maybe, Libby, but so far they have all detested it," Tara told him, shaking her head.

"It's new to them, that's all. It takes time to acquire the taste, time and the example of someone who enjoys it."

Libby beamed at Ri.

"Just drink it exactly as you are now, with that contented face, and some of them are sure to try it a second time, and then a third, and then discover that they like it too."

A large group of customers walked into the room and, throwing a parting smile, Libby went back behind the counter to take their orders.

"I'm going to miss him," sighed Erian, "and this." She waved her mug. "I don't suppose it will taste quite the same when I'm trying to make it myself."

She took another mouthful, savouring her last taste of Libby's fresh taret.

They finished their drinks and between them picked up all the jars, and headed for the door.

"Goodbye Lady Ri! You show those Guardians what an Angate lady can do!"

Libby waved at her and Erian smiled back, her hands too full to wave.

"I'll try, Libby, goodbye and thanks for all this."

He waved her thanks aside, and then turned back to the taret preparation for his latest customers.

Tara and Erian, with their escort, loaded the jars into the carriage and then climbed in to fit themselves around it as best they could.

Erian looked out of the window as the carriage moved away. She could feel herself beginning to disconnect from this town and these people. She felt sad that in a few days she would cease to be a citizen of Angate, and would instead become an inhabitant of the fabled hidden land.

She looked at Tara.

"I wish that you were coming with me, Tara," she said softly.

Tara nodded.

"So do I, Ri, I would dearly love to see Tyreen, but I don't suppose I ever shall. You have to write and tell me everything so that I can imagine that I am there too."

She had said just the right thing. Erian found that anticipation now replaced the faint regret at leaving, and she and Tara spent the rest of the trip back to the palace, wondering which of the many tales about Tyreen life would prove to be true.

The shock at the feast

Erian and Tara walked regally down the great stairs, across the ornate hall towards the great double door. One of the guards opened the door for them and bowed as they walked through, closing it behind them. Outside, another six stern-faced soldiers prevented any but family and household from coming too close to this part of the ducal palace. Duke Rannis had opened the rooms of one wing for the celebration, but all other areas of the building were carefully guarded against intrusion.

The two young women had dressed in their finest for this event, in rich satin skirts that billowed around their legs in such a fashion that anything other than slow, graceful gliding steps would result in their heels becoming caught in the folds and tipping them over.

Erian suspected that if she did fall, the skirts were so full that they could probably hold her up all by themselves while she regained her balance. She had no intention of putting it to the test, however.

The grounds of the palace were already beginning to fill with the citizens of Angate, all dressed in the best that they owned, who had come for this rare chance to see the Ducal grounds, eat at the duke's expense, and gaze, at close range, on the mythical Sorcerers who had come here to rid them of the threatening creatures of shadow.

The Tyreans themselves were easily spotted, not only because most were at least a head taller than the tallest Perrestian, but also because they had all donned full armour for the occasion; the gleaming brass and steel shone brightly in the early afternoon sunshine. They were also the only people, aside from the duke's own soldiers, permitted to carry weapons.

Erian still found it strange to see women wearing trousers, armour, and carrying swords, but she supposed that she would get used to it in time.

Almost all the Tyreans were present, except for a small number tasked with protecting the model from the curious, and those patrolling the town to safeguard it from any more attacks from the still undiscovered shadow minion.

In strategic places in the grounds, large tents housed eating areas well stocked with food and drink for the ordinary Angate people, while a large room in the wing, its huge window-doors thrown open, held the food and drink intended for the Tyreans and the Angate aristocracy.

"Look, Ri, there are Caffy and Allyn from that first day, do you remember?"

Tara nodded towards the two young Soldiers, who, like most of the Tyreans that they could see, were surrounded by a large group of wide-eyed questioning youngsters, who were in turn watched by their equally wide-eyed elders, many of whom, Erian suspected, wished that they dared ask some questions of their own.

Erian grinned.

"I hope that he doesn't drop anything on the children," she said remembering the previous incident.

"He has learned to be more careful! The lesson was taught very thoroughly."

A dry voice spoke from behind her, and Erian turned to see Lady Vellte and Lord Gann, both smiling faintly.

The Ponfour's smile showed a pronounced element of satisfaction as Allyn's eyes widened in alarm when he saw them looking at him. Erian wondered what other misdemeanour he might have committed and what his punishment could have been, but dismissed the thought as none of her business.

She smiled at her magic tutors when they looked back at her. Behind them, she could see Allyn taking his chance to disappear into the crowd.

"I hope that you are exercising some caution in your practice, Erian," said Vellte, her eyes narrowing slightly as she gazed searchingly at Erian's face.

"You look tired, child. You must remember to rest as well as to practice. The dangers of using too much magic are real and I would be disappointed in you if you burnt out before you have mastered your Gifts."

Erian hastened to reassure her that she had rested conscientiously.

"If I appear tired, Lady Vellte, it is only that I slept poorly last night. I had many strange dreams."

Vellte's gaze sharpened.

"What kind of dreams, girl? You must overcome that fear you have of the mind probe. It would tell us immediately if you have other Gifts, such as dreamwalking or gleaning."

Erian shrugged uncomfortably. Although she had never again reacted to the proximity of Tyreans as she had that first day, she still could not bring herself to allow one of them to probe her mind. The idea terrified her though she could not understand why.

"They were just dreams, Lady Vellte. Snow, and people I know, and places, all jumbled together. I have had many such dreams in my life."

Vellte nodded, looking thoughtful.

"Perhaps they are just dreams, child, and perhaps they are more." She shook her head. "Don't worry about it now, there is no rush. We will have lots of time to assess your abilities when we return to Tyreen."

"Vellte." Gann nodded towards the house, and Vellte turned to see what he had noticed.

"Oh, I must speak to her, thank you, Gann. I'll see you tonight for your lesson, Erian, as usual."

She nodded to Tara and Erian and then she and Gann hurried towards the house.

Erian spotted Lord Tam and Lady Crystu walking across the garden towards the open palace wing, and came to a decision.

"I have to ask Lord Tam something," she told Tara and, before her friend could reply, she walked as rapidly as she could after the Rykatu and her Ponfour.

Their boots were better suited to walking across the lawn than were her high heels and she quickly realised that she could not catch them.

"Lord Tam!" she called, trusting to his Ponfourii hearing to catch his name in this noisy crowd. He turned and saw her and said something to Crystu. While his Rykatu continued onwards, the large Ponfour waited for Erian to reach him. He then matched his steps to her much slower pace.

"Lady Erian, how may I serve you?" he asked courteously.

She took a deep breath and collected all her courage.

"Lord Tam, there is something that I have been wanting to know since that first morning at Firstmeal. What does it mean to ask someone what their full name is? You all found that funny, so what did I really ask?"

She spoke rapidly to get the words out before she changed her mind.

He grinned at her, and so did several other Ponfourii close-by who had obviously overheard her words.

Erian suddenly had an embarrassing thought, and stared at him, willing him not to say what she suspected he was about to say.

“Are you sure that you want to know?” he asked, still grinning.

She nodded resolutely.

“Alright then, I will tell you. Only our closest family know our full names, so if you ask someone to tell you their name,” he paused, took a breath, and then continued, “it means that you are asking to become close family. In other words, by our customs, you asked me to marry you.”

Erian stared at him and wondered if she could transmute a hole underneath her feet to swallow her.

"Oh!" she said, feeling stupid. "I, err, hope that, err I mean, I'm sorry…"

"There's no need to apologise." He laughed. "No man could take offence at a proposal from a beautiful young lady, even if she knew what she was asking, and to take offence when she did not, would be unpardonable."

Erian saw the good humour in his eyes and started to chuckle despite her embarrassment.

"No wonder you all looked so amused. I'm glad I learned this now. I will be very careful how I ask someone about their name when in Tyreen. Are there any other such customs waiting to trap an unwary visitor?"

"Very probably; we have many different customs," he replied, "but people will understand that you are an outsider, and they will not hold you to any unintended accidental promises of that kind."

"Thank you." She smiled back and then, greatly daring, said, "If you had held me to the proposal, I don't think that I would have complained very much, although I suspect that Lady Crystu might have had something to say about it."

Tam stared at her for a second and then chuckled.

"Oh yes, Lady, she would have a *great* deal to say about it."

He glanced towards the palace and, although Erian could not see her, she knew that he was looking directly towards Lady Crystu.

"Does *she* know your full name?" she asked suddenly, and was immediately furious at herself for her rudeness.

"I'm sorry, I had no right to ask that," she said quickly as he looked back at her, clearly startled at being asked so personal a question.

Tam smiled ruefully.

"I can hardly take insult when you are only asking what others are wondering."

He glanced at some of the interested faces, most of whom grinned back at him.

"The answer is no, she does not," he finished.

"Not yet!" An anonymous voice could just be heard above the noise of the crowd. Lord Tam directed an amused glance in that direction.

"Have you had a gleaning you have forgotten to tell me about, Jolen? If not, my answer stands as it is. The future remains unknown."

If Jolen replied, Erian could not hear it, although the way Tam paused before turning his head back towards her suggested that his sharp ears had caught something that her ordinary ears could not.

"I don't think I would want to know my future before it happened," she said. "It would spoil all the surprises that should be wonderful, and knowing exactly when something bad would happen," she shuddered, "would make the time before it very unpleasant. It would also leave you feeling that you had no choices about your life, but had to walk an assigned road. I prefer to experience things as they happen."

"I agree." Tam nodded. "Perhaps that is why those who can glean knowledge about an individual, are rarely able to see more than a few hours or days into their future, while those whose Gift reveals long range warnings usually have much vaguer images which require considerable experience to interpret and are often not fully understood until afterwards."

Their slow steps had finally brought them into the large hall. Lord Tam excused himself and left to rejoin his Sorceress. Erian smiled to herself. The affection between the two Tyreans was so obviously deep and growing that she doubted Lady Crystu would be ignorant of her Ponfour's full name for very much longer.

Erian smelled something appetising and peered through the crowd. The centre of the hall contained long tables laden with plates and bowls of delicious looking food.

Three massive crystal bowls stood on pedestals between the tables. Each was full to the brim with a spiced fruit punch that was an especial favourite of the Tyreans. The tables and pedestals were barely visible between the visiting Guardians and the local nobility. The people present spoke in much quieter, and more languid, tones than the crowds outside, as befit their higher social standing.

Erian could see Duke Rannis with Duchess Thianel talking with Lady Crystu, Lord Tam, and several other titled aristocrats, and she wondered where Thian and Serrel were. She couldn't remember seeing Rannis' son and his wife since that first morning when the Tyreans had arrived.

She shrugged mentally. Perhaps he had been sent to take care of his father's Royal duties while Rannis was living his ducal persona. It would not be the first time that Thian had covered for his father's absence from the Royal Court.

She looked again at the food and drink, and decided that she was both hungry and exceedingly thirsty. She liked that spiced punch too so would have some.

She picked up a plate and joined the crowd of people who were moving slowly past the food and filling their plates. As she chose from the plates, her mind drifted and she began to daydream about what mountains might look like, and what it would feel like to live somewhere that had no flat plains, or uninterrupted horizons, but land that went only up and down.

She regained awareness of her surroundings suddenly as she was stirring the fruit punch with the ladle and holding a mug ready to fill. Her plate was on the table beside the pedestal. She realised that what had disturbed her daydream was Tara's voice and she looked over her shoulder to find Tara looking at the ladle, that she had lifted to pour into her mug, with a puzzled frown.

"I'm sorry, Tara, my mind was many miles away from here. What did you say?" she asked, smiling.

Tara moved her gaze to Erian's face, still looking puzzled.

"I asked you what you just added to the punch, Ri," she said slowly.

Now Erian felt puzzled.

"Added to the punch? What do you mean, Tara? I haven't added anything. I'm pouring myself a drink, that's all."

She poured the contents of the ladle into her mug, dropped the ladle back into its holder, and turned to face her friend lifting the mug to show her.

Tara looked at her sharply.

"You poured something into the punch, Ri, from a small clear bottle. I saw you do it. You put the bottle into your pocket and then began to stir the drink."

Around them, conversation began to cease as people heard Tara's words and turned to stare. The quiet spread across the room rapidly.

Erian stared at her friend, confused and beginning to feel afraid. Why was Tara making this absurd accusation?

She tried to laugh.

"This is ridiculous, Tara; there is nothing in my pocket."

She thrust her free hand into her pocket, intending to pull it inside out to show that it was empty, but her fingers hit a cold hard surface, and she heard a clink as the object she had touched knocked against something else.

She pulled the objects out and stared at them in disbelief. Three small, clear glass bottles lay in her palm, two empty and one filled with a translucent, faintly orange liquid. She had never seen them before, and yet at the same time she saw an image in her mind of her hand holding one of those bottles, and pouring its contents into the punch.

The utter silence in the room was a sharp contrast to the unconcerned babble of sound audible from outside. People entering from outside quickly hushed as they sensed the tension that had built so suddenly.

Erian felt each eye that was staring at her as though it was a needle jabbing into her skin. In a daze, she looked up from the bottles in her hand at the surrounding faces. Those who knew her looked almost as bewildered as she, but others stared at her with the interested enjoyment that some feel when another is in trouble while they are safe.

Duke Rannis was pushing his way through the crowd toward her looking puzzled and concerned. Those who would normally have stood back to let their Duke past now were so held by the tableaux before them that they failed to notice his attempts to push through.

A hand took the bottles from her and she looked up to see Lord Karan removing the cap from the one that was full.

Holding her eyes with his own, he sniffed at the opening. His eyes widened fractionally and then he tipped a few drops from the bottle onto his other palm. He still looked at her, but she could see the concentration and feel the magical emanation as he used his

Gifts to identify the liquid.

His eyes widened further in shock and he stared down at his palm as though unable to believe what he held.

"What is it, Karan?" Lord Tam asked, stepping into the space that had opened around Erian, Tara and Karan. Duke Rannis joined him, followed by Lady Crystu.

"It's cherryth extract, Tam," Lord Karan answered, in a tone of complete bewilderment.

There were gasps from some of the nearer Tyreans, especially those holding mugs of punch, but the Perrestians looked at each other blankly.

"Are you sure?" Lord Tam asked. He sounded shocked.

Lord Karan nodded.

"Believe me Tam, I wish that I was not, and I hope that I have made a mistake, but it is cherryth. Here, test it for yourself, and please tell me that I am mistaken."

Erian watched as Karan handed the full bottle to Lord Tam, who repeated the test and then passed the bottle to Lady Crystu, who also placed a drop on her palm.

"You are correct, Karan: it is cherryth," Lord Tam said.

Karan stepped to the punch bowl and placed one finger into it and concentrated, other Tyreans did the same with the other two bowls.

"There is cherryth in this bowl," Karan pronounced,

"And in this one," said another.

"This bowl is clear," said the woman who had tested the last bowl.

"Three bottles, three bowls, two bottles empty, two bowls of drink contaminated."

Tam looked at Erian.

"Why, lady?" he asked.

“Lord T-Tam,” she stammered miserably, “I have no knowledge of any of this. I don’t understand what is happening.”

Lord Rannis had watched in silence while they tested the drink, but now spoke.

"What is cherryth, Lord Tam? Of what is she accused?"

"It is a poison," Lord Tam replied, "but one that affects only magic users, and it is not fatal."

He added the last part hurriedly, as Perrestians began dropping their mugs as though burned.

Erian found that the stares directed toward her had changed to open hostility and she looked at the mug in her hand to escape them. She could not comprehend what was happening; a few minutes earlier she had been as happy as she had ever been in her life, and now she stood accused of attempting to poison the Guardians of Reyth! And what was worse, now that she thought about it, she had a memory of her hand doing exactly what Tara had accused.

A tear slid down her cheek and fell into her mug, sending ripples out across the surface of the drink. The new ripples enhanced those already caused by the fear tremors that she could not control.

Poison? She would have drunk this cup if Tara had not spoken and she, too, was a magic user so the poison would have affected her as well.

Lord Tam was still speaking, describing the symptoms of cherryth poisoning.

"It is slow to act. None of us would have known anything until a few hours later. The symptoms at first are the same as for any food poisoning: severe stomach cramps, vomiting, diarrhoea. Everything that you would expect as the body attempts to rid itself of the toxin. The stronger the magic Gift, the more severe the illness. That lasts up to two days and then subsides, but is not the end of it. Cherryth blocks our Gifts and it would have been five weeks or more before any of us who drank it would have begun to regain our powers. Any Tyreans who have drunk from either of the poisoned bowls must be healed within the next hour if they are to escape loss of their Gifts."

His last sentence was said loudly, and a rustling sound swept across the room as Tyreans quickly formed into orderly groups just outside the open doors, so that the healers among them could begin to heal those who had drunk the poison.

"What about the rest of us?" An extremely elderly man demanded from amongst the crowd.

"He said only magic users are affected, Elnat, and I don't think that your continued success with the ladies, magical though that seems to some of us, is enough to place you at risk."

Lady Shorante's tone was dry and a ripple of laughter eased the tension .

"When the healers have cleansed all of my people who have drunk the poison, they will check and heal any of your folk who wish it, Lord Elnat."

Tam nodded to the elderly man.

"A small number of Perrestians do possess some magic Gifts. Few of them are aware of it, but they would be susceptible to cherryth, and should be healed."

The nobleman nodded, reassured by the courteous reply and offer.

"We must have the truth about this!" Lord Rannis said decisively. "I can't believe that Erian would deliberately try to poison your folk, Lord Tam, and yet..." He shook his head. Erian looked up at the man who had stood in place of her father for several years, and felt a small spurt of hope; perhaps he could solve this problem.

"Tell us again what you saw, Tara," Rannis ordered his daughter. She nodded.

"I saw Ri pour something into that bowl, and then she put the bottle into her pocket and began to stir the drink."

She sounded bewildered, as though she still could not believe what she had seen.

"I thought perhaps she was adding alcohol to the drink, like Terres did that time." Tara shook her head. "It would not be in character for her to play such a joke, but you know that she has not really seemed quite herself for several mo…"

Her eyes widened in horror and she span to face Erian as she finished the word.

"..nths. Light no! Lord of Light, please no!" she gasped.

Erian saw sudden comprehension blossom in her friend's eyes, and then she felt something wrench deep within her. A painful, inexorable, tearing, as she was ripped away from her mind. The voices around her faded.

"No! Not Ri! Crystu save her! You must!" Lord Rannis voice was anguished.

"It is already too late, Rannis," the Rykatu replied. "Look at her eyes."

Rixol, the newly created servant of shadow, who now inhabited the flesh that had once belonged to Erian Tolene, sneered at the look of revulsion combined with grief on Duke Rannis' face, and laughed at the anger growing in the Rykatu's features.

Beside her, Karan quickly moved to push Tara to a safer distance from her former friend, then drew his sword and held it ready.

Within her mind, the Xiantona, who no longer needing to hide his presence, laughed uncontrollably as he took control of her voice to speak through her.

"You should see your face," he told the Rykatu's protector. "Of all people here you should have been able to recognise the signs, though I am far more skilled and patient than was my oath-brother who caught you in his snare this year. How did you escape? Not without help. You have not the power to fight one of us, but if you had been more alert, you might have saved this ridiculous innocent."

Baiting the Ponfour brought little reward; only a slight tightening around his eyes betrayed that the gibe had struck, so the Xiantona moved his attention onto Crystu.

"And you, Rykatu, we take someone in front of your nose, *again*, first him and now this child. Perhaps you left Tyreen too young? You should return to your studies until you have mastered your Gifts, and not leave again until you are fully grown."

That was more satisfying; Crystu snarled and stepped forward, arm half raised as though intending to hurl a firebolt, but then she stopped, nostrils flaring, and flicked her eyes at her Ponfour.

To both Rixol and the Xiantona's disappointment, she visibly controlled her anger.

If she had hurled magic in this room, more innocents might have been injured. Rixol would love to see her anguish if she injured the people she was sworn to defend.

The Xiantona commanded her to turn her head towards the duke.

"And you, King Perdon," she smiled as he inhaled sharply at that title and name, "too busy playing Duke to notice what was happening in your own town. I have found many willing recruits for my lord amongst your people yet you noticed nothing. Of course, you have been moving some of your intelligence sifting responsibilities to your daughter. Perhaps you should reconsider your choice."

She turned to sneer at Taranel, who stood nearby with her hands pressed to her mouth.

"You think you can take over the role of intelligence gatherer? You couldn't see what had happened to your best friend. You knew her well, and, despite my weeks of preparation before I took her, you *had* noticed that she was not herself, and yet you failed to consider this possibility. If you had told the Tyreans, they could possibly have saved Erian's life. You failed her, and your father."

That was rewarding – those barbs sank deeply. The princess closed her eyes, tears streamed down her face, and her shoulders shuddered with her sobs. Rixol and the Xiantona enjoyed the sight.

Something grabbed Rixol's throat roughly, and she looked up to see Tam's eyes blazing in his determined face. His mind plunged into hers and attacked the Xiantona. For what felt like an hour, but was only seconds, the two minds fought furiously within her.

The Xiantona appeared to be surprised that the Ponfour possessed this ability and even more surprised by Tam's strength. To Rixol's astonishment, the Xiantona fled with the Ponfour's mind clinging hard to him. At last, her master broke free, and Tam's mind withdrew from hers.

"I saw where he is." The Ponfour's voice was cold with anger, "He is sitting in a chair, opposite the Cathedral, drinking taret."

"Not for long," Crystu snarled. "I'm sorry, Tam. Follow me when you can."

A mist formed around her, and she vanished while Tam was still opening his mouth to protest.

Rixol giggled, remembering what he had told them several days earlier.

"You'll be foresworn now! You must go after her and that means abandoning your sworn duty here. Or else stay here and break your Oath to her."

If she had hoped to have more success at baiting him than earlier, she was disappointed again; ignoring her completely, he began snapping out orders.

"Astley, Karan, go after her, now!" Not waiting to see them vanish, he span round, eyes searching the crowd.

"Captain Amil!"

"Here!" The captain pushed to the front.

"All Sorcerers, Warriors and Soldiers here, who can translocate, and who have not drunk the cherryth, go with Amil and support Crystu. Not you, Jathte, I'll need you to translocate me."

Around the room, Tyreans converged on Amil, who led them outside to form up to translocate.

"Rannis, can you send some of your own soldiers into the town as quickly as possible, to assist as necessary? It may reassure your townsfolk if some of the armed people running through their streets are wearing your uniform."

Rannis nodded and a glance at Pendin sent the Captain hurrying out to organise.

"Vellte, take care of *that*; you know her Gifts best. You're in command here until I return."

He stabbed a finger towards Rixol's face and she playfully snapped her teeth at it. He did not flinch, even though her teeth closed no more than an inch from his fingertip.

"Jathte, Trerisia, let's go."

A moment later, he and the other two had vanished into the air, and Rixol was left grinning at the depleted room.

She was still outnumbered, but all the strongest Tyreans had just left, and few of the Perrestians would have the same ability to ignore the fact that, when they looked at her, they still saw Erian Tolene as she had always looked.

That would slow their reactions, and might make them interfere with anything that the Tyreans tried. If she was careful, she could make them believe that they had a chance to get the old weak Erian back.

She was annoyed that she had been discovered now, when she had not yet mastered her developing Gifts, but if she kept alert, she might have an opportunity to use them and escape.

Again, her neck was grabbed unexpectedly – this time by Gann. Rixol felt an emanation of magic from him and then her senses were muffled; even sight and hearing were dulled.

He let go, looking simultaneously satisfied and sickened. She rubbed her neck where first Tam and now Gann had dug in their fingers.

The chain of her necklace felt slightly different to her fingers so she tried to use her transmutation Gift to probe into it to find out what he had done. To her shock, although she could sense her power, it felt as though a wall stood between it and her. She could not reach it.

"What did you do, you old lightleech?" she snarled.

"Turned your necklace into a ward against transmutation and illusion," he replied calmly. “Its reach is only a few feet, but that is far enough to contain you without affecting the rest of us greatly.”

Rixol pulled hard on the chain but, instead of breaking, it cut into her neck. She tried to lift it over her head, but it was too small, and when her fingers found the catch, she discovered that it refused to open.

"A ward would be of little use if the creature being contained could easily remove it," Vellte said dryly. "We will not allow you to use our teaching against others."

"You shrivelled excrescence! You cannot keep me warded indefinitely! You have not the right!" Rixol hissed.

"We can, we will, and we do," Vellte replied sadly. "You would not be the first. We will not allow a creature of shadow to walk free in the Protectorates. You will still come to Tyreen, Lady Erian or whatever your name is now, but you will not see as much of it as you were supposed to."

"Lady Vellte," Duke Rannis spoke urgently, "can anything be done? Is Ri lost?"

"What do you mean, Uncle Ran? I'm not lost, I'm here?"

She tried to make herself sound pathetic and scared.

"Please don't let her take me, I want to stay here."

Rannis shuddered and turned away from her.

"Tara? I'm sorry I was mean, I'm just upset, please don't let them do this, I'm still Erian."

Tara stepped backwards, still sobbing.

"Don't bother, girl. Whatever effect you are trying for, you sound manipulative and cunning and nothing like Erian," Gann told her.

"I'm sorry, Rannis," Vellte said, with a look of profound sorrow. "The Zindon has destroyed her personality completely, and replaced it with darkness and hatred. There is no cure. This creature has some of Erian's memories as well as her flesh, but is wholly a servant of the Shadowbringer. We could remove the new personality, but that would not bring back Erian, and what we would be left with would have little mind of any sort. The Lord of Light does not permit us to create another new personality in a living body, but if even if he did allow it, it would not be Erian. She is dead, Rannis."

"Vellte, are you saying that she is a Zindon now?" Lady Shorante asked. "Didn't you tell me that someone had found a way to heal a Zindon so it became human? Why can't you do that?"

Vellte shook her head.

"She is a shadow-servant, but not a Zindon. She is still human, Shorante. Her Seta remains intact but her personality has been destroyed and replaced. We cannot heal that. The Zindon that was healed still remained a servant of shadow, albeit a powerless one."

Duke Rannis nodded gravely.

"What will you do with her?" he asked.

"We have a secure place in Tyreen," Vellte answered. "She will be well looked after, and carefully warded, for the rest of her life."

"Uncle Ran, Please! She is lying, I am still Erian, I have not changed. I still belong to the Lord of Light. The Zindon has gone from my mind now. He fled from Lord Tam, and I am free of him. He did me no harm. How can you possibly believe this old woman's lies?"

"Is it possible, Ran? I would never suspect Lady Vellte of lying, but could she be wrong?" asked Duchess Thianel urgently.

The muttering that swept through the room, suggested that others were considering the same possibility. Rixol suppressed the urge to grin. If she was clever she could walk free and the Tyreans would be accused of making a false accusation.

"Nell, we've known Ri since she was born." Rannis shook his head sadly. "I wish I could believe that this is some terrible mistake, but..." He shook his head again, and regarded Rixol sadly.

"There is an easy way for you to be sure of it," Vellte said briskly. "Ask her to say the Shadowbringer's name. He does not tolerate his servants using the mispronunciation that we use."

Rixol glared at the old woman; she knew that the Sorceress was correct.

"An excellent idea, Lady Vellte," Rannis said. "Then there can be no doubt at all." He looked sternly at Rixol.

"Speak his name, Lady Erian Tolene. Prove to us that you are still a child of Light, as you claim."

Rixol sought frantically for a way to avoid the question.

"My Lord, the Shadowbringer's name has never passed my lips. To speak it is unpleasant and unnecessary. Surely you can see that I am no shadow minion."

Rannis scowled at her.

"This is a direct command, not just from your Duke, but as

everyone present now knows, it is also from your king. The Erian I know would have obeyed without hesitation and without fear. Speak the name of the Shadowbringer! Now! Here! In front of these witnesses! Speak!" he commanded.

Rixol narrowed her eyes, and abandoning her failed pretence of innocence, glared her hatred at him, and at Taranel who had moved to stand beside him, blotting her tears on a cloth supplied by her mother.

Rixol crossed her arms and, obscured behind her arm, the fingers of one hand began to tug at a seam in her bodice. One of the bones in the garment was not entirely what it seemed, something that the old Erian had been prevented from noticing. She slipped out the narrow, but strong and sharp, blade concealed within it and held it hidden within her hand.

She stepped closer, stopping when Captain Pendin stepped silently out of the crowd from behind Taranel and her father, and stood watching her intently, with his sword drawn. She did not need to turn her head to know that Vellte and Gann stood close by and that they too both held their weapons ready.

She raised her head proudly. Both of her missions had failed, thanks to the over-sharp eyes of Taranel, She could not do what she had been created to do, and she had no intention of spending the rest of her life in confinement in Tyreen, so she stared Rannis in the eye as she spoke.

"My lord's name is Xian." She paused to smile at the gasps of horror that swept around the assembled Perrestian nobility. "You should learn to pronounce it correctly, Uncle Ran, because he will be your lord too, if you survive the next few months."

Pendin's flicked his eyes toward his liege lord and, as his attention left her, Rixol moved. The blade ready in her hand, she lunged at Tara.

As fast as she was, Pendin was quicker.

The blade dropped from her fingers as she looked down at the sword protruding from her ribs.

Her legs buckled, but as her weight began to pull the blade

down, Pendin pulled sharply and withdrew it from her flesh. He looked appalled but resolute.

Rixol fell to the ground, smiling despite the pain. This was what she had expected, although she had hoped to take Tara with her. Rannis and Thianel looked horrified,

"Lady Vellte, will you heal her?" Thianel pleaded, as the elderly Sorceress knelt beside Erian and examined her.

"No," replied Vellte. "I will not. This is the best outcome we could hope for."

She looked at Rannis.

"The Erian we knew would rather die than spend her life as a shadow minion, and she will die from this wound, though it may take a few minutes."

He nodded slowly.

"*I* would rather die than spend my life imprisoned in Tyreen," Rixol gasped weakly.

"You shall have your wish, monster – a quick death instead of imprisonment. I hope that the Zindon that did this to you suffers before he dies, but for the sake of the person I loved as a daughter... your dagger, Pendin, please."

Rannis held out his hand towards the captain, who hesitated a moment, but then drew his short blade and handed it, hilt first, to his king.

"No, Ran! You can't!" gasped Thianel, grasping his arm to restrain him, as she realised what he intended.

"I can and I must. I cannot watch Ri bleed to death slowly on the floor, and I can neither order, nor ask, someone else to execute the creature that now inhabits her body. This is my realm, my duty, and my responsibility, Nell."

He held her eyes until she let go and stepped back.

"I understand, Ran."

Silence filled the room like a tangible presence as he stepped to Rixol's side and looked down at her.

"Have you the courage to kill me yourself, Uncle Ran?" Rixol taunted, staring defiantly up at him. "This will haunt you for all of your life. You will see my face whenever you return to Angate, and remember my blood on your blade. I will be with you forever."

"No." He shook his head. "I will remember Ri, but I will remember her as she was. And I will remember that she was killed by a Zindon and replaced by someone who looked a lot like her, and that I killed the imposter," he told her as he knelt down beside her.

His hand pressed across her face, obscuring her sight and holding her head still. The floor pressed painfully against the back of her head as he leaned forward.

She felt a brief, searing pain as the tip of the blade sank into her throat, and then nothing further.

Perdon Rannis Targin Alnett, King of Perrest, and Duke of Angate, climbed back to his feet and, just for a second, looked sadly down at the body on the floor.

Then he straightened his back, lifted his head and looked around the room at the silent watchers gathered around. His eyes met his daughter's tear-filled gaze, where she stood with her mother's arm around her, and he wondered if she could forgive him for what he had just done.

He wondered if he would ever forgive himself, because, despite what he had told the creature before he killed it, he knew that one part of his mind would always remember that he had held the knife that ended her life.

As if she had read his mind, Tara nodded slightly once, and attempted a smile. Reassured that she understood, he handed the dagger back to Captain Pendin, who took it without comment and pulled a cloth from a pocket with which to wipe it clean.

Rannis looked around again, searching for a particular face. He found it,

"House Bredge, please have Lady Erian's body taken to the chapel, and begin the necessary arrangements for her burial. I believe cremation is recommended in such cases, is it not, Lady Vellte?" He directed a questioning look towards the elderly

Sorceress, who nodded once.

"It is," she replied.

Rannis wondered for a second why cremation was necessary rather than burial, but then decided that he would rather not know. He looked back at Bredge.

"See to it, Bredge, but make sure she is treated with respect."

His servant bowed.

"Yes my L.. Your Majesty."

Rannis kept his sigh hidden; he had valued his anonymity here in Angate, and now that was lost. He glanced at Erian's body and reminded himself that some had lost far more than he.

"We will assist."

Two of the Tyreans stepped from the crowd – a Sorcerer and Ponfour whose names he did not know. The Sorcerer stared down at Erian, and Rannis saw the floor beneath her shimmer and reshape into a pallet with handles. The two men crouched, lifted the pallet and body, and then followed Bredge from the room. To Rannis' surprise, the floor appeared undamaged with no sign that part of it had been transmuted.

The pool of blood that had lain there had disappeared. Rannis thought it somehow indecent that all trace of Erian's death could be so quickly and thoroughly removed.

He looked out of the window at the crowds outside, and realised with surprise that the activity was undisturbed by the events within this room. Even if the people in the gardens had seen the Warriors and soldiers leave, they did not know the cause and so had continued enjoying the celebratory feast laid out for them. Outside, the sun still shone, and people talked, ate, and drank, oblivious to the destruction and death of an innocent young woman.

"My Lord, I must protest!"

A voice interrupted his thoughts and he looked around to see his palace Cleric, Father Michan, beside him.

The man looked scandalised.

"What is it, Father?" Rannis asked wearily.

"I know she was like a daughter to you my Lord, and I am sorry, but she died a creature of shadow and as such she cannot lie within the chapel or be buried within a Garden of Light."

Rannis stared at the man in disbelief. He knew that Michan could be too strict about some things, but he had not expected such an objection.

"Nonsense!" Lady Vellte strode up and glared at the Cleric.

"In the eyes of our God, she is as much an innocent victim of the Zindon as those who died in the collapsed market building. There is no bar to her being buried in any Garden of Light."

Rannis looked around the room and was relieved to see a general agreement with the Lady.

"Even if Father Tandril at the Cathedral told me that, I would not agree," Michan said stubbornly,

"And if you hear it from the Revered Father's own lips in Tyreen?" Vellte replied, her eyes flashing. "Will you accept it then? For I tell you that you are in serious error."

Father Michan drew himself up.

"If the Revered Father himself tells me that I am in error, I will believe it, but I will accept such a judgement from no one less."

He glared back at the Sorceress.

"Very well!" Vellte snapped out the words. "Ponfour! I must make of thee a request!" Vellte turned to look at Gann, who had straightened at her formal words.

"Name it, my Lady. I am yours to command!" he replied equally formally.

Vellte smiled slightly at Gann, and he shook his head with a resigned look. Rannis suspected that he was watching them have an argument that was so old that they no longer needed words for it.

Gann walked over the Father Michan, placed one hand on his shoulder, and then the two of them vanished.

Rannis raised an eyebrow questioningly at Vellte.

"Gann is taking him to speak to the Revered Father. I am sure that Teiron will correct his misunderstanding of Church ruling in such cases," Vellte told him. "They will return in an hour or so. Meanwhile, I suggest that we assume that his objections have already been withdrawn."

Rannis nodded.

"Thank you, Lady Vellte. Michan is a good man, and sometimes becomes too focussed on rules, but he respects the Revered Father."

He straightened and looked round the room once more.

"As you all now know," he began, "I am not only your Duke, but also your king. I wish that was still a secret, but it is out now. I will not order you all to silence, as that would be foolish and certainly unsuccessful, but I intend to be sure that you all truly understand what has happened here today. I want no false rumours about Lady Erian to circulate."

He stared at one or two faces in particular, who he knew would probably have misunderstood what they had seen.

"The Lady Erian was an innocent Child of Light. Unknown to any of her friends, the Zindon that recently attacked our town had taken control of her, but had hidden its presence with great skill. When, after seeing her friend pour poison into the drinks, Taranel recognised what must have happened and confronted her, the Zindon destroyed Erian's mind and replaced it with a new creature. Lady Erian was fully dead at that point. The creature that attacked Taranel, and that I killed, was a shadow-servant using Erian's body."

"She was an innocent victim, and died a Child of Light," he finished, and caught the eyes of several within the room holding them until they nodded their understanding.

He nodded, satisfied.

"Now I suggest that we all adjourn to the chapel, to pray for our Guardians who have gone in pursuit of this Zindon, and for all innocents who may yet find themselves caught up in the battle."

Rannis led the mixed group of Perrestians and Tyreans along the halls, across a courtyard and into the chapel. He knew that Erian's body would be there, laid on the table in the side room kept cold for that purpose, and that would serve to sharpen his prayers. He could sharpen his sword afterwards, to have it ready in case the

Zindon fell into his hands.

The wrath of a Rykatu

Tam, Jathte, and Trerisia appeared in the square opposite the Cathedral of Light and looked around for any sign of fighting. The square was quiet but several astonished-looking people were all staring in one direction – the direction from which Tam could sense Crystu.

"This way!"

Tam let his sense of Crystu's location direct his feet, and he ran at a steady pace, along the square and down a side road. Jathte and Trerisia followed close behind.

Tam was furious! He had rarely felt so angry.

He was angry at the Zindon for destroying that intelligent young woman, but also angry at himself for not realising that she was controlled. He knew that recognising when a person was controlled was almost impossible, especially so if you did not know them well enough to notice that they were behaving uncharacteristically, but even so, he felt that he should have noticed!

Seeing Erian transformed, in an instant, from child of Light to a shadow-servant had made him understand even more clearly exactly how close he had come to suffering the same fate himself.

If Crystu had not realised that he was controlled. If she had been unable to keep that realisation from him. If Lord Jareth or the king had decided not to attempt a rescue. Then he, Tam, would have changed as Erian had.

The fact that he had been rescued, but that Erian, who was simply an innocent woman in the wrong place at the wrong time, should suffer the worst of fates whilst Guardians looked on helplessly, was monstrously wrong.

Tam hoped that he would have a chance to fight this Zindon. He also hoped to reach it before Crystu. *His* anger was hot, but *her* rage was burning incandescently. Tam worried that she might strike too quickly without thought.

At first, as he ran through the streets, he saw little indication that anything unusual had occurred. Most of the population intended to attend the celebration at the Palace at some point during the afternoon, but many planned to attend later in the day. The streets were slightly emptier than usual but people were going about their business. Some were showing signs of astonishment at the crowd of Tyreans who had rushed past them moments earlier, but others had apparently noticed nothing.

Somewhere ahead of them, though, Tam could hear screaming, the sound of collapsing masonry, and the crackle of flames. He could also feel the emanations of magic use, some of it powerful.

He ran ahead of Jathte and Trerisia; Jathte could not sustain the same pace as a Ponfour and Trerisia slowed her steps to match his. Tam was intent on rejoining Crystu as quickly as possible, and so was soon several streets ahead of them.

He raced around a corner and had to leap sideways to avoid tripping over the rubble in his path. Buildings lay partially collapsed across the street with Soldiers and Warriors working to free and heal those who were trapped and injured.

Tam did not stop, but picked his way over the rubble and continued running. He ran past further evidence of the Zindon's attempts to evade capture: burning buildings and people with blackened, charred clothing, some of whom displayed the pinkness of recently healed flesh.

There were other figures too, lying motionless, for whom there could be no healing.

More Warriors and Soldiers were here, healing those they could and putting out the fires, but Tam raced past them.

Finally, he reached a grassed area, across which he could see a large building, surrounded by Tyreans, one of whom was Crystu.

Tam could feel that she was gathering her power, and could see worried looks on the faces beside her. Karan, Astley, and several other Sorcerers and Ponfourii, were trying to talk to her, but she was not listening; her fury held her focussed only on her target.

Tam glanced at the sign beside the door of the building and

threw himself at Crystu, spinning her round to face him.

"My Lady, you must stop. Control your power! This is not the moment."

Her eyes focused on him, and the anger in them was almost a physical heat that blasted his skin like a furnace.

"Why should I stop? The creature ran into that building and remains within. It is the Group of Light! They have been hiding a Zindon all along and I will pull these walls down on top of all of them, and on the Zindon!" she declared hotly.

Her fury roaring down the bond was so fierce that it extinguished his own anger, but some of it now was directed at him. Tam redoubled his efforts to use the bond to calm her.

"Read the sign, Crystu, the Group of Light is not the only group renting floors in this building. There may be children within."

He pulled her in front of the sign beside the door and swung her around to face it.

"Read it, before you do something for which you could never forgive yourself."

To his relief, he felt her anger vanish into shock, and she allowed her power to subside. He heard sighs of relief from around them, as she pulled back from an act which would have destroyed Tyrean reputation for ever.

"Oh, Light! If you hadn't stopped me!"

Tam felt her horror at what might have been, as she read the large sign beside the door. Only the upper three floors were used by the Group of Light; the basement and first two floors were utilised by other organisations, including a local healer, and a school.

Tam looked towards the nearest windows and saw children's faces peering back at him. Thanking God that he had been in time, he looked back at Crystu who was looking where he had.

"Thank you, Tam," she whispered.

"That's partly what I'm here for, Crystu," he replied. "Perhaps you will remember that the next time you feel like running off on your own!"

He allowed his exasperation to colour both his voice and his emotions.

"You *did* promise to try to control your temper!"

Crystu grasped the pendent lying at her throat and drew a deep, though shaky, breath.

“You are right, as usual. I allowed my anger to control me and nearly committed an atrocity every bit as great as anything that Zindon has done. I will be guided by you, as I should. What should we do now?"

Tam smiled his relief.

"Now? Now we do this the right way! Captain Amil?"

He looked around to see how many people he had. Jathte and Trerisia were now among the group as they had arrived while he was calming Crystu. Amil appeared at a jog from around the corner of the building.

"Captain, Is the building surrounded?" Tam asked.

"Yes, Lord Tam. The Zindon went in, but has not emerged. We will know if he tries. We would have felt it if he had translocated so possibly he does not have that Gift.”

Tam smiled with satisfaction.

"Good! We must clear the lower floors and work upwards, keeping the creature trapped. I wa.."

He broke off at a clatter of hooves, approaching rapidly, and looked round to see a large group of local soldiers galloping up the road towards him. They drew up and the leader dismounted, handing his reins to the man beside him, another group arrived to join the first as the Captain saluted Tam.

"Lord Tam, I am Captain Arlor. We have been sent to support you! How may we assist?"

Tam smiled.

"Captain Arlor, you have arrived at the perfect time," he replied, as a third group of soldiers trotted up.

"We have chased the Zindon into this building, and are about to start clearing the lower floors of people. We will make sure that none of them is actually the Zindon, but I will need you to arrange for transportation, and secure accommodation, until we can examine all of them to be certain that none are controlled or otherwise contaminated."

"If you think that I am going to allow a group of soldiers to take charge of these children and terrify them, Tyreans are not as wise as they are reputed to be," an indignant voice called loudly from the nearby window. Tam turned to see a woman standing within the room, arms folded. He and Crystu stepped closer.

"Lady," Tam began, "I make no claims to wisdom, but we have to remove all of you, including the children, to a place of safety. If you can help us to make it easier for the children, then please do so, but none of you can remain."

The woman studied him with narrowed eyes and then looked at Crystu. She glanced around at the room behind her which contained twenty or thirty children of varying ages, and then leaned towards them and lowered her voice.

"Did I hear you correctly? There is a Zindon in this building?" she asked.

Tam nodded.

"There is,"

"And you fear that he may have people under control?" she continued.

Crystu answered her.

"We know of one woman who was controlled, and there could be others. He seems to have some connection with the Group of Light, so all who use this building may have had contact with him."

The woman took a deep breath and then nodded.

"Very well. I understand, but the children must not be frightened if it can be avoided. Where do you want to take us?"

Tam looked questioningly at Arlor, who looked thoughtful.

"What about the Cathedral?" the captain suggested. "The Children's rooms there will be familiar and not frightening, yet we can easily guard the two doors into them."

Tam nodded at the sensible suggestion.

"A good idea, Captain, I will send a small number of Warriors and Sorcerers with you just in case you need to argue with the

Clerics. Is that acceptable to you, Lady?” he asked the woman, who nodded agreement.

“My staff and I will get the children ready and we will march them to the Cathedral. We will tell them that they are lucky and are being allowed to march with a group of soldiers and Tyreans who are also going there. Hopefully they will be excited instead of frightened. I will require about five minutes to explain it to them.”

Her last sentence was not a request. Tam smiled and nodded.

She closed the window and Tam could hear her telling the children of the marvellous treat in store for them. Shortly afterwards, the door opened, and the children marched smartly out in twos, the eldest first, accompanied by their teachers.

As they walked past, Tam knew that Crystu had expanded her senses to their most sensitive to be certain that all of them were human. She could not tell if any might be controlled, but he was sure that she would be able to sense if one of them was the Zindon in disguise.

The children stared with large eyes at the armoured Tyreans nearby, and the mounted soldiers, but, as their teacher had hoped, even the youngest was excited rather than frightened. A selected group of mounted local soldiers led the way, followed by the children and their teachers, who were in turn followed by a few Warriors and Sorcerers.

When they were out of sight, Tam turned to Amil,

"I want you and half of the Warriors and Soldiers to stay out here and prevent anyone leaving who is not accompanied by at least two our people. When you have a large enough group, send them with their escort to the palace. The duke has secure rooms where we can contain them for testing. Anyone leaving this building must be watched by at least one Sorcerer and Ponfour, and preferably several Warriors as well."

Amil nodded.

Tam looked around and, after selecting approximately half of those present, led the way into the building. Crystu followed him with Trerisia and Jathte close behind. Next came Karan and Astley, then the other Sorcerers and Ponfourii, and finally the Warriors and Soldiers.

The building had one set of stairs, leading upwards and downwards from this floor. Leaving a group of Soldiers and two Sorcerers to watch the upward flight, Tam led the others down into the basement rooms. Weapons and air shields ready, they searched cautiously until they were certain that all the rooms were empty.

Far above them, Tam could feel the residue of recent magic use, which confirmed that at least one magic user was on an upper floor, but as they had no idea if there might be more, he intended to take no chances.

They climbed back up to the ground floor which held the healer's rooms and a few small businesses.

Quickly, they went through the rooms gathering together the occupants. After Crystu had checked that none were disguised Zindons, Tam ordered several Soldiers and a Sorcerer to escort them out.

Next, they climbed up to the first floor and repeated the exercise.

When the occupants of the first floor had been removed, Tam looked up the stairs to the second floor.

"Be ready; if the Zindon has been hiding within the Group of Light, he may have controlled or influenced many of them. We may encounter resistance up there, but most are probably innocent, if misguided. Where possible, just make them sleep."

The others nodded, and followed him up the stairs.

At the top, a double door opened into a large room which contained perhaps fifty people all clutching makeshift weapons, such as table legs, broom handles. They looked scared and defiant as they blocked the path that led between rows of seats.

"Why are you doing this?" a woman asked shakily.

"We are chasing a Zindon and he came up here. We have no wish to hurt any of you and if you lay down your weapons you will be escorted to a place of safety while we capture or kill him."

Tam spoke firmly, and hoped that they would listen.

Some of them looked puzzled.

"No one has come up here except Kaliss, and he said that you were chasing him," one protested.

Tam exchanged a surprised glance with Crystu.

"Then Kaliss is the Zindon we hunt, and we will have him," she said grimly.

"He is our leader, not a Zindon! You just want to silence him and stop him revealing what *you* really are."

The first woman hefted her chair leg defiantly.

Tam sighed.

"Remember what I said: make them sleep, and try not to injure any of them more than necessary."

He sheathed his sword, and then he walked purposefully forward. Constructing an air shield around his head, and relying on his armour to protect the rest of him, he caught the woman's weapon with one hand and grabbed her head with the other. She collapsed asleep onto the floor.

"He's killed her," one of them shrieked, and chaos ensued as some began attacking the Tyreans while others dropped their makeshift weapons and attempted to flee.

Several minutes later, most of the Group members, except for a few who had surrendered, were asleep on the floor. A few had sustained broken bones and other injuries, largely from running into and over each other. Tam realised that he would have to leave most of those with him to deal with healing the worst injuries, as well as guarding the group.

Accompanied by Crystu, Jathte, Trerisia, Karan, Astley and five Warriors, he quickly checked that the rest of the rooms were empty.

As they began to climb the final flight of stairs, to the last floor, they heard a scream above them and felt an explosion of magical use. Not only was the emanation powerful, but the whole building shuddered beneath their feet. They dashed up the stairs and burst into the upper level.

The room was large and filled the entire floor. It contained stacks of folded chairs and tables neatly placed along the sides, and several bookshelves holding boxes filled with sheets of paper and books. On one side, a long shelf held several ornaments, including two sun globes. The wall opposite had a large irregular hole smashed through it. A thick fog swirled in the gap, licking at the loose bricks at the edges of the hole.

"Fire burn and sear him!" Crystu growled. "He will not escape me so easily,"

She shapechanged and threw herself into the air, wings beating strongly. Tam caught her leg, as he had done the day they arrived in Angate, and pulled her back.

"No, Crystu, wait. You are reacting without thinking, again. Something is wrong here."

To his surprise, she changed back immediately, and nodded.

"I said I will be guided by you, Tam. What have I missed?"

Tam looked up at the roof and ran his eye along the joists, and smiled. They were all evenly spaced, except for the last one, which was unaccountably closer to the next than it should have been. He saw that Trerisia had reached the same conclusion that he had, for she held her sword ready and moved to stand between Jathte and that part of the room, her attention focussed on the apparently blank wall.

Tam picked up one of the sun globes and handed it to Crystu.

"Would you turn that into a ward, please, my Lady. Make it one that blocks all seven magic Gifts," he asked quietly.

Her eyebrows lifted.

"A full ward?" she queried, following his lead and keeping her voice low. "That will block our powers completely; we will become vulnerable."

Tam grinned at her.

"Then I suggest that you make it a fragile ward. If I am wrong, we will smash it and you can leap out the window as you intended. If I am correct, you had best hold it carefully, because if we are warded then so is the Zindon, and I think that he is still in this room watching us right now and wondering what we are about to do."

Crystu nodded, and Tam watched as the globe shimmered in her hands.

"I'm activating it...now!"

As Crystu spoke the last word, Tam felt his senses alter; sounds were suddenly muffled and colours less vivid. Beside him, Crystu shook her head as if trying to throw off the unpleasant, enveloping sensation.

In front of them, the wall vanished, reappearing a few feet further back. This change revealed two people, one of whom gasped in surprise as the other jerked her close and placed a knife to her throat. To one side, lay a man's body, limbs and face contorted as though his final moments had been spent in agony.

Tam recognised the woman. She had been at the table, beside the gate, when the Tyreans had first arrived. He knew that her name was Tammia and that she had been involved with the Group of Light since the previous year. At this moment, she looked disbelieving and indignant as the Zindon held her tightly.

"What are you doing? We have an agreement! Let me go!" she demanded, struggling to free herself.

"Please don't struggle, Tammia, you may cut your own throat against my blade," the robed figure said, holding his blade steady against her throat.

A trickle of blood appeared as her exertions moved her neck against the edge of the blade and she froze at the unexpected pain.

"She's not entirely innocent but I will kill her if you come closer."

The Zindon spoke calmly. He wore the brightly-coloured robes of a Cleric with the hood pulled forward over his head.

The illusion of dark skin, behind which he had been hiding, had vanished with the wall; within the hood of his cloak, pink eyes glimmered within a milk-pale face, under short white hair. The hand holding the blade revealed pale translucent skin beneath which purple veins were starkly visible.

Crystu, Jathte, and Astley, readied their swords, but stepped back, leaving the fight to the Ponfourii and the Warriors, as was appropriate.

Crystu clutched the globe tightly. There could be no magic in this fight, unless the ward broke. It would be sword against sword, and the Zindon was outnumbered.

"If she has knowingly helped you here then her death would be justice," Tam replied, conversationally, and saw the woman's eyes widen in fear as she finally began to understand that her life was truly threatened.

"You have only two options," Tam continued. "You die here, or you surrender and you will travel to Tyreen with us, to remain there under guard for your entire life."

"My life would be a short one, and my death excruciating. I doubt that you will allow me to replenish my energy when it is spent. It does not replenish itself as yours does and even *we* die eventually if we cannot replenish. You offer me death or death as a choice," the Zindon sneered.

Tam smiled.

"We can heal you and remove that dark energy. You would have a human Seta again and live a normal life span."

The creature's eyes widened in horror.

"You would disconnect me from my Lord? Remove from me his Gifts? No! Never!"

Tam had expected the reply. Zindons were not cowards; they served their Shadowbringer as bravely as any Tyrean served the Lord of Light. He was also not surprised when the Zindon slashed Tammia's throat and pushed her away from him.

The Zindon stepped forward and pulled a sword from within his robe. Knife in one hand, sword in the other, he held himself ready to fight.

The three Ponfourii and the Warriors moved to circle it.

"Eight against one is hardly fair," the creature sneered.

Tam shrugged.

"What you did to Erian Tolene wasn't fair; neither was pulling down that building onto its occupants. I offered you a choice, a chance to live, but you have refused it. We will kill you quickly, which is fairer than you have a right to expect."

He caught Trerisia's eye, then Karan's. The Warriors would wait for the Ponfourii to strike first and enter the battle only if necessary. For now, they would stay back out of the way.

Trerisia and Karan moved together, swinging their swords at the creature's neck and body, forcing him to spin round to evade Karan's strike, and deflect Trerisia's. Tam had glided forward as soon as his attention was on Trerisia and brought his sword down onto the man's skull with all his strength. As he had suspected, the robe was strengthened by transmutation, and blocked his strike almost as efficiently as an armoured helmet would have, but enough of the impact went through that the blow to his head dazed the Zindon.

The shadow-servant staggered and Karan's next thrust slid into his neck, as Trerisia's sword found the opening at the front of his robes and sank into his gut. At the same moment, Tam stepped forward and pulled the hood from the creature's head.

He stepped back, swung his sword, and the Zindon's head fell to the ground, his body collapsing in a heap.

"You're getting good at that," Crystu remarked with a fierce grin, as the head rolled to a halt under a stack of chairs.

Tam grinned back briefly, then glanced at the woman's body. To his surprise, she was still moving. Crystu saw where he was looking and threw the sun globe against the wall.

As it shattered, everything around them sharpened and gained colour. The ward was broken and they could touch their Gifts again.

Crystu dashed forward and threw herself down beside Tammia.

"She's still alive." She looked up at Tam. "Should I heal her?"

He nodded.

"Yes. She may be able to answer some questions."

A few minutes later Tammia sat up, rubbed her throat and looked around wildly. When she saw the Zindon's headless body, she gasped, but then smiled with satisfaction.

"You killed Kaliss? Good! I hope he suffered first."

She rubbed her neck again, and then stood up shakily.

"You healed me? Why?"

"Was this Zindon alone or are there others?" Tam asked ignoring her question.

"Is that why you healed me? You expect me to talk? And if I do, how will it benefit me?"

She looked thoughtful; Tam realised with incredulity that she intended to try bargaining with them.

"I'll tell you how it will benefit you!" Crystu grabbed Tammia's wrist and pulling her round to face her as she spoke.

"If you answer every question truthfully, then we will give you what we promised that Zindon if he surrendered – you will return with us to Tyreen and spend your life under guard. If you will not answer..." She smiled coldly. "We will leave you in Rannis' custody. You helped destroy Erian Tolene and I am sure that your king would enjoy a chance to talk to you about that!"

Tam suppressed a smile as Tammia's eyes widened with fear. Rannis was unlikely to be merciful to anyone who had assisted Kaliss in destroying Erian.

"Those are your options," he told Tammia. "Will you answer my question?"

He held her eyes, and could see that she was considering her choice.

After a moment, she nodded.

"I will. He was alone. There was another but he left in early spring and did not return. Kaliss told me later that the other was dead."

Tam glanced at Crystu, who still held the woman's wrist. She nodded. She was using a healing probe to tell if Tammia was telling the truth.

"Thank you. That is all we need for now."

Tammia crumpled as Crystu placed a sleep compulsion on her. They could question her in more depth later.

Jathte crouched beside the stack of chairs and used his sword to knock the Zindon's severed head out from underneath it. He knocked it across the floor to lie beside the body, and then stood looking down at the corpse.

"Rannis will probably gain some satisfaction from cremating this publicly."

Tam agreed.

"We will leave it for him."

He strode to Tammia and picking her up, threw her over one shoulder.

"We must examine the people we have taken out of here, and find out how badly they have been contaminated by the Zindon. Rannis has a list of all Group members; we will have to deep test all of them, but she may not be the only one to assist the Zindon by choice."

Explanations

Tam took the mug that Rannis offered him and drained the contents gratefully without noticing what they were. He sat down beside Crystu and leaned back into the soft cushions, rubbing his face wearily.

The last few hours had been exhausting. They had examined all the people they had removed from the building, and those Group members who had been arrested afterwards. They had read the healer's records and all his patients had also been brought to the palace for testing. Similarly, the parents of the schoolchildren also had to be confined for testing.

Most had been cooperative, once they learned the reason for their confinement, and were eager to be tested and proved free of contamination, even when warned that the process was painful.

Deep test after deep test to look for signs of control, alteration, or more subtle contamination, had left Tam's Seta diminished. He knew that he would sleep for many hours once he allowed himself to close his eyes.

Until today, Tam had rarely had to apply a deep-testing probe, and he had found it difficult, knowing as he did just how painful it was for the one tested. He had stared at many screaming faces that day, knowing that he was causing the pain that they were experiencing, yet having no choice but to continue the probe. Doing so had been emotionally draining.

Crystu, Jathte, and Trerisia were similarly exhausted. The four of them had conducted all the examinations except for those of the children. Tam had judged that they would be less frightened by Vellte and Gann, elderly and unarmoured, and their teachers had agreed.

They could not, of course, apply deep testing to children, but they had examined them as thoroughly as possible short of that. The six of them had returned to Duke Rannis' private chambers to share with him their findings.

"What did you find?" Rannis asked.

Tam looked at Perrest's king and saw the new lines of grief, anger, and determination, which had become etched across the man's face.

"We found three who showed clear evidence of having been controlled, all recent patients at the healer clinic. The Zindon's death freed them, but one of them must have been controlled for months, and had already been altered far enough that he may never fully regain his previous character, although he had not been completely converted. He must return to Tyreen with us, and our healers will do what they can for him. I'm sorry, but it is possible that he may never return to Perrest. The other two are tainted but it's already fading and we can release them immediately."

Rannis nodded.

"And the other people? The children? The Group members?"

"Except for Tammia and Adral Rogan, we found signs of influence, but nothing severe or permanent. Kaliss had been making them all more receptive to his stories about us, but did not attempt to alter their beliefs directly. All, including the children, will recover naturally within a few weeks," Tam replied.

"Thank God!" Rannis breathed a sigh of relief,

"Indeed!" Jathte agreed.

"Tammia and her brother are a different matter. They were neither controlled nor altered. They served willingly, by choice."

Tam found it incomprehensible that any citizen raised in a Light-following country could choose to serve the Shadowbringer, but that was what he had found when he probed their minds.

"Will you change your mind and leave them in my custody?" Rannis growled. Anger and a wish for revenge shone in his eyes.

"No!" Tam replied. "We have a place for them in Tyreen. They will be securely held and put to useful work. Whether they like it or not, they will serve the Lord of Light, even if only by ploughing fields."

Rannis nodded, and Tam was surprised to see him attempt to smile.

"You are wise. I think I would do something that I would eventually regret if I had them in my hands. Right now, I would enjoy hearing them scream, and I do *not* like what that says about me."

"It says that you are human, Rannis," Jathte told him, "as are we, even if we are Gifted as you are not."

Tam nodded. He had deep tested Tammia himself, and knew that he had felt some satisfaction when she began to scream. The thought made him feel uncomfortable and somehow soiled.

The idea that he could enjoy inflicting pain, even on someone who had done what she had, was appalling. He felt Crystu reprove him through the bond, and told himself, once again, that he was foolish to worry over a natural emotion. If he had given in to the temptation to deliberately inflict greater pain, then there would be cause for concern, but he had not.

"You cannot control what you feel, Rannis, you can only control how you react to your feelings," Jathte continued, mirroring Tam's thought.

Crystu poked Tam's side; he looked back at her and returned her smile.

"Exactly! And I was not controlling my reaction even slightly when I burst in on your interrogation of Tammia. I apologise for that."

Tam snorted.

“There is no need. Your unexpected appearance, and your demand that I turn her over to you, helped to persuade her that she did not want to do anything that might make me agree to give her to you. She was eager to answer every question after that, and although she did not know all their plans, she knew enough to enable us to make a few good guesses about the rest.”

“I have two questions, if I may?” Taranel spoke from the corner where she had been sitting quietly, subdued by grief and the shock of the day’s events.

“Certainly, Lady Taranel. What do you want to ask?” Tam replied.

“I thought you had warded the Palace against translocation, yet you translocated from the Palace into Angate.”

Rannis nodded.

“I was wondering that myself,” he commented.

Tam shrugged.

“After the collapse of the market building, we altered the ward to allow translocation out of, but not into, the Palace. We did not mention the change because I did not want the Zindon to know how quickly we could react if it tried again.”

Tara nodded.

“I see, that makes sense, thank you for explaining.”

“What is your other question, Lady?” Tam asked,

She sighed.

"I just don't understand the purpose of it all! Why make Ri use a poison that is not fatal? And why the punch? If she had poured it into the Palace water supply, no one would have known a thing until you all became ill. Did Tammia explain?”

“The water supply is guarded, and Erian could not have approached it unseen. We would have known, almost immediately, who was responsible,” Rannis answered. “With such a crowd of people around the food tables, if you had not seen what she did, we would never have known who had done it.”

“Exactly,” Vellte nodded, “and she would have become ill too, so we would never have suspected her.”

Tam leaned forward to the nearby table and refilled his mug, he looked at Crystu and raised his eyebrows enquiringly.

“Yes please, Tam,” she replied, passing him her mug.

“So what did Tammia tell you, Tam?” Trerisia asked.

Tam sipped his drink, and took a deep breath.

“This plan had several layers,” he began. “For a start, Xaliss and the other Zindon, Erex, did not come here to begin a snow-ant infestation, and then just happen to find Erian and pull her into their plan. They came here, to Angate, because Erian was here. She was central to the whole plan, and they knew exactly what she was. They arrived last year, and started the snow-ant infestation which was intended to draw us here. Xaliss, calling himself Kaliss, began to spread his stories about us, while using magic to make people more receptive, and so formed the Group of Light."

He glanced in the general direction of the Palace chapel.

"Tammia knew that Erian was a frequent visitor to the taret shop opposite the Cathedral, and so, becoming a regular customer herself, she became known to Erian and eventually struck up a friendship. She told Erian about Kaliss' tales and took her to meet him."

Taranel muttered something and Tam saw the rage on her face.

"Yes, Lady Taranel. They intended from the start to first influence, and then control, her. Xaliss bragged about his skill and patience with justification; he held Erian’s mind lightly and skilfully to reduce the signs that usually accompany control. You knew that she was behaving a little unusually, but you put it down to the influence of her new friends. They knew that eventually we would arrive and that she would be able to be here in the Palace when we did. They knew that, when we learned that she was an untrained magic user of strength, we would want to take her back with us to Tyreen."

"So that was their goal – to get a controlled person into Tyreen. Their second attempt this year if I understood the Zindon's remarks to you correctly."

Tam looked up as Rannis spoke, and saw the king's eyes

looking at him speculatively.

Tam could see little point in denying it, so he nodded.

"You did. If the first attempt had been successful, I would no doubt have alleviated any suspicions about Erian, and they would have had two people under their control inside Tyreen."

He glanced at Crystu.

"The other Zindon left in early spring. Tammia overheard it mention a place called Tanjisford."

Crystu's eyes widened.

"He was the one that...?" She stopped.

Tam nodded.

"Almost certainly. That was all part of a much larger plan. Whatever the Shadowbringer intends, he began this long before your dream."

"But why use cherryth, Tam?" Crystu asked. "Why not something fatal?"

Tam smiled.

"I think that the Shadowbringer still hopes to persuade you to change your mind about his proposal. To do that you must be alive. Deadly poison aimed at the rest of us might kill you too, and it could have killed Erian as well. He wanted us unable to rejoin the army for a few weeks, but he wanted both Erian and you to live, so she was given cherryth."

Trerisia spoke up.

"We would have been stranded here for about five or six weeks, but Erian would have been poisoned by the cherryth too and we would never have suspected that she was controlled. We would have taken her back to Tyreen with us. Her obvious fear of having her mind probed was an effective way to prevent us realising anything was amiss. Of course, if one of us *had* probed her mind we would have sensed the taint of control immediately, even if it was very faint." She looked at Tam and continued, "Had this plan worked, there would have been two of you, controlled, and with access to the Royal Court. Between you, you could have done a great deal of harm."

Tam nodded.

"But there is more," he said, and took a deep breath before continuing, "She did not know any details, but she says that she had the impression, from something Xaliss said, that the Shadowbringer expected that the bulk of the Tyrean army would be destroyed while we were stranded here in Angate."

Seven pairs of shocked eyes stared at him, and he nodded confirmation.

"Whatever his plan, it will reach fruition sometime in the next five weeks, and he is confident that it will be devastating. Tammia heard the Zindons speculate that by the time we returned to Tyreen, Crystu would be the only living Rykatu and the only surviving member of the royal family. Few other fighters would be left alive in Tyreen, and, if they had succeeded in their plans, Erian and I would have destroyed the shield wards that protect Tyreen."

Crystu gasped.

"Even though *I* was freed, thanks to you, Crystu," Tam smiled at her, "with only a little more training, Erian would have been strong enough to be able to do it by herself if necessary. We would have been invaded by Zindons and, with most of our strongest fighters dead, we would have been defeated."

Taranel stared at Tam with shocked comprehension on her face.

"You were controlled, and freed?" she exclaimed. "Then was the Zindon right? If I had told you that Erian was not behaving normally, could you have saved her?"

Tam could see the guilt beginning to grow in her eyes, and sighed, wondering how to answer, but Crystu spoke before he could frame a reply.

"Tara, if we had known several days ago that Erian had been behaving out of character, there is a small possibility that we could have freed her," she began, "but that chance was tiny. After we had freed Tam, Lord Jareth told me that in the last thousand years, we have successfully freed only four people from active Zindon control. One of those was Tam, and the others were also Ponfourii."

Tam stared at her. He had known that few had ever been

rescued from Zindon control, but he had not known that the number was so small. He suddenly understood just how close he had come to suffering Erian's fate. The thought was terrifying, and he was extremely grateful that Crystu had noticed, and that she had kept it hidden from him long enough for Jareth to devise a way to free him.

Crystu felt his emotions and smiled at him briefly before continuing, "Tara, it is almost impossible to tell if someone is controlled without using a deep healing probe, and you can't do that without the Zindon noticing, and then it is too late. Even with our bond, it was three days before I realised that Tam was controlled. It was very difficult to hide my realisation from both the Zindon and Tam, while Jareth planned a way to help him. Keeping that secret was the hardest thing that I have ever done. This was not your fault. This Zindon was skilful and hid its presence cleverly."

"She's right, Tara, listen to her. There was nothing we could do," Rannis told her. "I noticed that she was not herself, but never suspected that she was controlled."

Tara nodded.

"I know, Dap, it's just..." she stopped talking and curled up in the chair, burying her face in her arms. Rannis knelt beside her chair and put his arms round her.

"We should leave, Tam," Vellte's illusion-carried voice whispered in his ear. He looked across to where she sat, nodded at her, then pushed himself to his feet.

"We'll leave you alone, Rannis, we all need to rest and replenish our Setas."

He held his hand out to Crystu and pulled her up, as the others also rose.

"You won't destroy the mountain tomorrow, will you?" Rannis asked, without moving from his position.

Tam shook his head.

"No. All of us need an extra day after spending all evening deep testing. I'm sorry."

"You have nothing to be sorry about, any of you. You did not bring this threat to us," Rannis stated firmly, looking up. "I am grateful that you came to our aid, and grateful that you killed that Zindon. I wish that the Shadowbringer had chosen somewhere else for his plan, but he did not, and Ri paid the price, but none of that is your fault."

Rannis held Tam's eyes until he nodded, reluctantly.

"He's right, Tam," Crystu said as she stifled a yawn. "Do you remember what you said to me in this very room after the Zindon collapsed that building? Place the blame where it truly lies, at the feet of the Shadowbringer."

Tam nodded.

"I know. I do. But it is difficult to accept that we could not save her."

"The four of you are exhausted," Vellte said. "Go to bed, now, all of you. Gann and I will keep watch while you sleep. Examining children is far less draining than deep testing adults, so we are still alert."

She pushed Tam towards the door.

"Bed, now! You too, young Jareth."

"Yes, Aunt Vellte," Tam said automatically, from years-old habit.

She smiled as she opened the door and pointed through it. Tam let go of Crystu's hand to step through the door and check the hall – it was empty, except for the guards on either side of the door.

Crystu followed him out and took his hand again.

Before she closed the door behind them, Vellte nodded to Rannis.

"Try and get some sleep, both of you," she advised. "I know that will be hard, but you should try. If you want help sleeping, you have only to ask; Gann and I will be available."

She closed the door and looked from Tam to Trerisia.

"I said bed!" Vellte made shooing motions with her hands.

Crystu sighed and pulled Tam along the corridor towards their rooms.

"Come on, Tam, Vellte is correct. I am exhausted and so are you."

A new gleaning

Tam pulled himself awake and rolled out of his bed, landing on his hands and knees. He pushed himself upright and ran to the door, shaking his head to try and dispel the muffled feeling in his mind from awakening so quickly from a deep Seta-replenishing sleep.

His dreams before he awoke had been dark, confused, and then suddenly filled with flame. He had been unable to take control of his dreaming and alter them to something more pleasant. Given that the Zindon was dead, he could think of only one possible cause, and so had clawed his way out of the dreams and into wakefulness.

Crystu's aura in his mind was distressed. Tam pushed open the door to her room and knelt by her bed. Crystu was tossing and rolling in the grip of a nightmare.

He knew that she should be able to dispel an ordinary dream with ease, so this had to be a gleaning dream. The images in her mind had affected his own dreams, which was why he had been unable to take control of them.

Still kneeling beside Crystu's bed, Tam settled himself to wait patiently for her to wake up. He knew that if he woke her too soon she might lose part of the gleaning, and therefore miss part of whatever warning their Lord wanted them to have.

He glanced towards the shuttered windows, wondering how long they had slept, but the shutters were efficient and not a glimmer of light shone through anywhere.

Off in the distance, his sharp ears heard bells playing a short, repeated sequence which told him that it must be late afternoon; it was the sequence that announced the beginning of the five o'clock service.

Crystu's eyes snapped open and she sat up with a jerk, tears immediately spilling down her cheeks.

"Tam?"

"I'm here," he said. "Tell me what you saw"

With a sob, Crystu flung her arms round him and he held her tightly until she had exhausted her tears. When she had gone to sleep, her mind touch had been coloured by sorrow for Erian's death, but now profound deep grief flooded down the bond.

"What did you see, Crystu?" Tam asked again, although he was almost afraid to hear the answer.

She pulled back and took a deep, calming breath.

"I saw Seldar die in fire," she answered simply, "and I received guidance that I don't understand. I must speak with Trerisia – perhaps she can make sense of it."

Shocked, Tam inhaled sharply. He had received regular messages from Lord Jareth and remembered that Seldar, with his Ponfour, Trerin – Trerisia's younger brother – had been sent to investigate the rumours of Zindons in Bein. Jareth had said that he was confident that the rumour was another false trail, but even Rykatuii could be wrong.

"You are sure? Seldar is dead?" he asked, although he had felt her certainty when she spoke.

Crystu nodded sadly.

"Oh, yes. I'm sure. I wish I was not."

"I doubt that either Trerisia or Jathte is awake yet," Tam replied, considering how long they had slept. "The gleaning has woken us slightly before we would have awoken naturally. I will probably have to wake her."

He rose, reluctant to leave Crystu alone while she was still upset. She felt his reluctance and made herself smile,

"I will be alright, Tam, but I must talk to Trerisia, the more of these images I can understand now, the longer I will remember them, and I suspect that some are important."

Tam nodded again.

"I will be as fast as I can."

Without further delay, he dashed out of her room and ran along the hall to Trerisia's room. The door was not locked. Trerisia's hearing, like that of all Ponfourii, was so acute that the slightest sound would instantly bring her to full wakefulness. Even from a deep Seta-replenishing sleep, the sound of the door opening had her reaching for a weapon.

"It's Tam," he announced quickly, not wanting a blade to come flying towards him.

"Tam? What has happened?"

Her voice sounded concerned. She knew that he would not have woken her without an important reason.

"Crystu has had another gleaning and she needs to talk to you. She said that you may be able to explain some of the imagery," Tam replied, wondering if he should tell her what Crystu had said about Seldar.

"Then the gleaning concerns me in some way? Or Jath? No, you woke me, but haven't asked me to wake him. What did she say?" She frowned when he hesitated.

"Tell me, Tam!" she demanded.

She was a grown woman and a strong Ponfour, Tam could not attempt to shield her from the news.

"She said that she saw Seldar die," he replied simply, and heard her inhale sharply.

"And Trerin?" she asked after a moment.

"She did not say, but you know, as well as I, what will happen if he lives."

"He's either dead or will die of bondshock." Trerisia closed her eyes for one long breath. When she reopened them, her gaze was steady as she spoke again.

“I will wake Jath, and we will join you as soon as we can."

Tam nodded, closed the door, and ran back to Crystu's room.

Crystu had dressed and opened the window shutters, letting the late afternoon sun pour into the room. She had pulled a chair over so that she sat in a warm puddle of sunlight.

"I did not want to sit in darkness – my dream had enough of that," she explained.

Tam hooked his foot under the nearest chair, pulled it close beside hers, and sat in it. Crystu leaned over the arm of her chair and wrapped her arm around his, hugging it tightly.

"Trerisia is waking Jathte, and they will be here soon," he said. "I have told her about Seldar,"

For several minutes, they sat in silence while Crystu gazed up through the open window towards the sky. It was a deep blue with just a few clouds visible, and birds flew lazily or purposefully from trees to rooftops and back again, their calls sounding pure and clear.

"It all looks so peaceful," she said softly. "Seldar is dead, Erian is dead, and the Shadowbringer is advancing his plan to destroy us all. The sky should be full of black angry clouds and rain and wind! But instead it looks as if nothing could possibly be wrong anywhere in the world."

Tam smiled.

"That is because we stand between the world and the Shadowbringer. We have foiled his second attempt to infiltrate Tyreen, and we will stop his plan, whatever it is. His touch may reach past us sometimes, but it never reaches far enough to scar the sky."

Crystu's head bowed and Tam felt her fresh burst of grief.

"It didn't reach the sky, but his touch reached too far yesterday. And now this knowledge about Seldar." She shook her head. "Tam, do you sometimes wish that someone else could stand against the Shadowbringer for a while?" she asked.

Tam laughed.

"Of course I do, we all do sometimes, but this is our task. Besides, could you really stand to one side and watch while someone else did the fighting? I know you, Crystu, even if you had no Gifts at all, you would throw stones and if necessary would use your teeth to bite the Shadowbringer's ankles."

Crystu chuckled at the image.

"I'm not sure that would accomplish much, but you're right, Tam: I hate to stand back and watch another fight in my place, as I'm sure you have noticed."

She peeked upwards at him, with a small smile.

Tam nodded.

"Yes, I *have* noticed that and I always appreciate it when you master the impulse."

Crystu's smile broadened, but vanished at a knock on her door.

"Enter," she called, and Trerisia walked in followed by Jathte.

Seeing Tam and Crystu on chairs in the centre of the room, they silently took either end of a long chair and carried it to join them in the sunlight.

Trerisia looked composed, with just a hint of the worry that she must be feeling visible in her eyes.

Jathte took hold of her hand after they had sat down, and then he spoke to Crystu.

"What did you see, Crystu? Are you certain that Seldar is dead?"

Crystu nodded.

"I'm sorry but, yes, I'm certain," she replied quietly. "I saw much that was the same as the last gleaning, and much that was indistinct, but I saw Seldar walking along the centre of a road. He was armoured and held his sword ready. I did not see Trerin, unless..." She paused and looked at Trerisia.

"Is Trerin a shapeshifter?"

"Yes, he is," Trerisia confirmed.

Crystu nodded.

"Of course! The rest makes sense now that I know that."

She sat for a moment replaying the dream in her memory.

"There was a large cat. It had mottled brown fur with a circular yellow patch on its forehead."

"That is Trerin's favourite form," Trerisia told her. "He often fights like that."

Crystu continued, "The cat circled Seldar, and its gaze was constantly moving as if it was trying to watch their entire surroundings at once, but behind the buildings there were shadows that moved and grew and merged. The darkness built up until I could see nothing but a shifting dark grey cloud, with deeper shadows within it. Then I saw Seldar again. He was injured, bleeding, and surrounded by moving shadows, and then the scene vanished into flame, and I knew that he had died."

"And Trerin?" asked Trerisia, her voice sounding unnaturally calm. Tam wondered which would be worse, Trerin dead doing his duty, or Trerin alive, suffering the pain of a broken bond and a failed duty.

"I saw the cat staggering along a track toward a village. He was injured, thin, and near death. I saw the village in detail, and we can translocate there. We *must* go there, three days from now and catch the cat or he will die. He *must* live if we are to win this war."

"It would be better if he had not survived," Trerisia said. "He will find a way to die soon whatever we do."

"Zia," Jathte began, and would have put his arm around her, but she stopped him.

"No, Jath, I'm alright. I know that we must follow the guidance. If our God still has a purpose for Trerin, he will be able to fulfil his final duty with honour."

Tam glanced at Crystu. He could feel that something else was bothering her, something that she did not want to tell Trerisia and Jathte. He hoped that she would not try to keep it from him, as she had tried when the Shadowbringer walked in her dreams.

"I don't think we should tell everyone about this," Crystu said slowly. "We need them to concentrate on the task at hand."

Tam nodded.

"I agree. We should keep it to ourselves for now. We deal with this mountain tomorrow, rest the day after, and as soon as you have returned everyone to the Cave of cleansing, we go immediately to that village and wait for Trerin."

"Tam, you can't ask Zia to pretend that nothing is wrong," Jathte protested.

"Yes, he can, Jath," Trerisia corrected. "Our duty has priority, and at the moment, nearly everyone is feeling pleased that we have caught and killed the Zindon. That will make them stronger and more confident tomorrow, when we attempt to use the new method to destroy that ice-mountain. If we reveal that a Sorcerer has been killed, it will shock them and may reduce their effectiveness tomorrow."

She smiled at Jathte, and Tam was impressed by how natural she made it look.

"You must behave naturally too, Jath," Trerisia told her

Sorcerer. “No solicitously asking how I am, or hovering close, or concerned looks. Those would make it much harder for me to continue the pretence. I will need your support, not just your sympathy.”

Jathte nodded slowly.

“You have it, Zia, always. I will behave as I usually do.”

He looked at Tam.

“I don’t like this, Tam. Secrecy is not our way, but I understand the need in this case.”

“Thank you, Jathte, Trerisia,” Tam said. He had known that they would understand and cooperate.

Jathte stood up.

“I can smell food,” he announced, “and several people saw us on the way here, so they know that we are awake. It would be unusual for any of us to miss a meal once awake, especially you, Tam.” He grinned almost normally. “So we should go down and eat as would be normal.”

Crystu snorted with amusement at the gibe about Tam’s healthy appetite.

“We will follow in a few minutes. Please save seats for us,” she said as Jathte and Trerisia walked to the door.

Trerisia stepped out first as usual and then beckoned Jathte through.

When the door had closed, Tam waited to find out if Crystu intended to tell him whatever it was that she had not already said.

When she had been silent for a full minute, He turned and gave her a pointed look, and a reproving pulse along the bond.

Crystu smiled wryly.

“Yes, Tam, there is something else, though I don’t understand it, and I certainly don’t like it.”

“You saw something else in your dream?” he asked her.

She nodded and looked down. Tam could sense her extreme reluctance to tell him. He placed a hand under her chin and tilted her head up until she was forced to meet his eyes.

“Crystu, you must not hide things from me. Tell me what you

saw."

She nodded, and without preamble said, "I saw the two of us, Tam. Together we tied a collar around the cat's neck, and together we held the leash that was attached to it. I don't know what it means, but the image was Guidance, I am sure of it."

Tam blinked, and let go of her chin.

"I don't understand it either, but perhaps when the right time comes, it will make sense. Our God would not waste his time giving guidance without making sure that we will have the means to understand it when we need to."

Crystu nodded and walked to the window.

"Less than five weeks. That's all."

"Yes." Tam joined her at the window, looking out over the palace grounds and the nearby buildings.

"I will be glad when the waiting is over, and now we know that it almost is."

A smell of roast meat wafted through the window and Tam's stomach rumbled.

Crystu grinned.

"You're always hungry, Tam. It's a good thing that you exercise so much or you would soon be as large as Sel.." She stopped mid-word, and a wave of grief swept over her again.

"Jathte is correct: we should go downstairs and eat," Tam said firmly, steering her towards the door. "We have a great deal to do in the next few days, and we will need to be strong."

He opened the door and looked out, then held his hand back towards her.

"Come on, Crystu, you will feel stronger when you are less hungry."

"You're right, as always, my wise Ponfour." Crystu smiled tiredly up at him as she took his hand. Together they walked down the corridor towards the rich smell of food.

Tam's technique

Crystu walked around the model, scowling at it as she studied it. The death of Erian, plus the strain of trying to hide the gleaned knowledge of Seldar's death, had put her into a foul mood!

She wanted to act, to translocate to the location that her dream had told her, to find Trerin and learn just what had happened in Bein, and then to go to Bein and find shadow-servants to kill. Preferably a lot of them!

Around her, in the map room, were many Sorcerers and Ponfourii, all waiting for her to indicate that she was ready to begin. Those who had the Gift of healing were finding comfortable positions on the many chairs that they had pulled in from other wings of the palace. In neighbouring rooms and on the floors above, others were similarly preparing for dreamwalking. When she gave the order, they would all enter induced sleep so that they could combine their healing and dreamwalk Gifts to send energy to Tam, who would send that power through the Ponfour Bond to Crystu, and she would use it to destroy the ice mountain and its enormous colony of snow-ants.

Crystu growled deep in her throat; she was going to enjoy destroying the creatures of shadow that lurked in that mountain of ice up on the plains above this town.

This would be the first time that this new method had been used on such a large scale, and she could feel the undercurrent of excitement that ran through the room, as those who were to participate knew that, if it worked, they were part of an event that would be written into the history books of Tyreen.

That too added to her bad mood!

Crystu knew that envying the others was unfair, but she wanted to feel excited too and couldn't. She had liked Erian, been impressed by her courage and honesty, and had totally failed to protect her.

Crystu knew that it wasn't her fault, and that she couldn't have known that Erian was controlled, but that knowledge did nothing to alter her feeling that somehow she should have seen it and prevented it. Instead, she had watched in horrified shock, as the girl's puzzled and fearful face had changed. Not a muscle had moved, but the eyes had suddenly radiated arrogant disdain.

The young woman's personality had been destroyed by a Zindon, in front of a crowd of watching Tyreans and a Rykatu, who were all powerless to prevent it.

"Stop that!" Tam spoke quietly in her ear.

Crystu jumped. She had been so lost in her thoughts that she had not even realised that he had left his seat and come up behind her.

She glared at him accusingly and he smiled, amused that he had startled her, but then he became serious again.

"You were thinking about Erian, not about that." He nodded to the model. "I understand, but you must concentrate on the mountain, Crystu, or you will not transmute it smoothly and that could be disastrous for this town and the land around."

Crystu bit her lip and nodded. He was right.

"Yes, Tam," she said meekly.

Tam chuckled.

"Meekness really doesn't suit you. A moment ago you were ready to attack that ice mountain with your bare teeth, which is much more like you."

He put his hands on her shoulders, turned her round, and pointed her head at the model.

"Focus!"

She tried, but once again her thoughts drifted.

She wondered where Trerin was, and how he was. When a Ponfour died, the bond snapped and the magical recoil slapped into the Sorcerer's mind, causing some slight, though painful, inflammation, and leaving what was effectively a magical scar. Despite that, Sorcerers usually recovered almost fully from their loss and most eventually rebonded so that they could continue travelling.

The effect on the Ponfour if the Sorcerer died was far greater. The first Oath bound both together, but the second Oath, taken only by the Ponfourii, fixed the bond much deeper within their minds and bodies. Together with the combined healing and transmutation at the bonding ceremony, that Oath triggered the physical changes that made Ponfourii so much faster and stronger than ordinary Tyreans. It also meant that they suffered more intensely if their Sorcerer died.

For them, the bond ripped out of their minds and setas and, as it tore from its anchors, it caused extensive inflammation in the brain, affecting their memories and their ability to think. It could be days before they even remembered their own names. Even healing magic could not repair the damaged Seta; its decay eventually led to an excruciatingly painful death, but few lived long enough for that to occur.

They called it the Last Duty.

Once physically healed enough to remember their names and Oaths, they would leave Tyreen forever to seek a better death. If their friends were lucky, they would eventually learn that the former Ponfour had died heroically facing terrible odds against a shadow creature.

"This is more than just Erian's death, isn't it? And it's not just," Tam paused for the merest fraction of a second, because the Ponfourii present would be able to hear his words, no matter how quietly he spoke, and they had agreed not to mention Seldar's death, "about your dream. You usually have more discipline than this, but I can feel that you have lost concentration again. So what is it? Tell me!"

Crystu sighed.

"You're right, as usual: there is something else worrying me."

She had been trying not to think about it, and her mind had gone in two different directions, neither where it was supposed to go, but she knew what the problem was.

"Tam, if we were going to try and transmute this mountain the usual way, every transmuter here would link his or her gift with mine and we would form a unit. My stronger Gift would form the framework into which everyone, including you, slotted their Gifts so that we could function as a single entity, but although I would direct the transmutation, all of you would remain in control of your own energy. We each would work on our own area of the mountain, but this is different."

She frowned, not sure how to put into words her concern.

"Yes, it is: we will pass our energy to you for you to use," Tam nodded. "I know that you are well able to contain and use that much power. All those tests Lady Aren put you and Lord Jareth through, certainly persuaded *her* that a Rykatu can safely hold almost any conceivable amount of Seta. If she is certain of that, then I am confident it is true, and I know that you are equally sure of it."

He looked at her appraisingly and she could feel that he was considering what he sensed from her.

He nodded suddenly.

"You are worried about not being able to control yourself when you are filled with so much power," he said.

"Yes, I am," Crystu admitted. "Tam, no one has ever done this before, and no one has ever had control over as much power as I will have when we do this."

She glanced around the room.

"I know that it won't be everyone at once, that you have arranged for people to take turns sending their energy to you, so that no one risks burn out, but I will still be receiving energy from about a hundred people at once. I could do almost anything I want to with that much power; suppose..." She paused.

"Crystu, if I feel you starting to believe that you should be ruling this planet, or that you are considering challenging the Lord of Light for the universe itself, be assured that I will simply wake myself from the dream and stop sending you the power. At which point you will return to your usual level of strength. You need have no fear that you might lose control of yourself – I will not allow it!" Tam smiled slightly.

Crystu stared and then smiled a little self-consciously; she should have known that he would understand! She threw her arms around his neck and hugged him tightly, and whispered, "Thank you," in his ear, before spinning back around to stare at the model.

She felt as though a weight had lifted, even though, until that moment, she had not been aware that she had been so afraid that something like that might occur. She should have known that Tam would be there to prevent it. Another thought occurred to her and she turned back to catch his arm before he had taken more than a pace back towards his chair.

"You will be careful when you stop the flow, won't you Tam?" she said earnestly, eyes wide with worry. "Not just if you have to cut me off, but when we are ready to finish. If you get the timing wrong..." She could not continue.

Tam covered her hand on his arm, with his free hand.

"Don't worry about that; I will be extremely careful. I know that if I stop sending the Seta to you, before I have disconnected from those sending theirs to me, I will quickly fill with far more Seta than I can hold. I'm no Rykatu! I have no desire to burn out, so I will take great care that I make no such mistake."

He gave her a push back toward the model.

"Now, let's get this mountain destroyed? Before lunch would be nice."

Crystu grinned.

"I'll try not to make you miss another meal, Tam. I promise."

She pointed back towards his seat.

"Now sit down! You are keeping everyone waiting!"

Tam snorted at that outrageous statement, but did as he was told, and Crystu went back to contemplating the intricately detailed model on the table.

This time her focus was undisturbed by distracting thoughts and she quickly built the image of the mountain in her mind.

"I'm ready!" she announced.

Immediately, a Ponfour who had been beside the door, left the room to pass on the instruction to begin to those who waited in nearby rooms. As they received the order, all those assigned to the first group slowed their breathing, slipped into induced sleep and prepared themselves to walk into Tam's dream and transfer healing energy to him.

The others held themselves ready in case of attack. Those sleeping would be vulnerable if another controlled person was in the Palace. Tam had taken every precaution to be certain that there were no more like Erian, but he had decided to take no chances at all.

The king had agreed readily to the restrictions that Tam had requested. No Perrestians at all, including the royal family, were allowed within this wing of the palace while the transmutation was taking place. Tyrean Warriors and Soldiers were on guard at all entrances and would detain anyone, even the king, who tried to bypass the restriction.

Tam knew that Rannis had been aware that the 'request' was in fact no such thing, but an order phrased as a request out of courtesy. Tam had already issued the orders and had no intention of changing them, but even though he had the rank to do it, he did not like giving orders to a king in the man's own palace.

Besides which, Rannis certainly was owed the courtesy after the hospitality that he had shown his Tyrean visitors. So Tam had asked politely, and Rannis had considered the request and agreed that the precaution was sensible, and issued orders to a scowling Pendin, who did not like it at all, to allow the Tyreans to secure that wing without Perrestian assistance.

Satisfied that he had done everything possible to ensure Crystu's safety while he slept, Tam quickly fell asleep, took control of his dream, and carefully built the image he would use for this energy transfer. The image needed to be accurately detailed and carefully controlled, to reduce the chance of any energy accidentally flowing in the wrong direction.

The lake took shape, with a dam at one end, and a stream flowing downhill to another distant lake. At first, the small mountain lake looked identical to the one he knew, but, as one by one, the Sorcerers and Ponfourii in the map-room and in the rest of the palace began to walk into his dream and send energy to him, he gradually altered his dream.

The lake lengthened and widened, as new streams began to drain into it from the upper slopes of the hill. At the same time, he widened the stream that was to take the power to Crystu, and began to open the dam gate.

The lake reached the largest that he dared make it. He must now make sure that the amount of power flowing out was identical to the amount flowing in, or his lake, which represented his own Seta, would overflow and he would burn out. He felt along the bond to be sure that Crystu was not in any discomfort from the torrent of Seta energy that was now roaring down a wide rapidly-flowing river, but she was already starting the transmutation process.

He felt her sudden astonishment, which was followed by deep sadness and then focused determination. He wondered what had caused that, but he could not waste concentration on the thought; he must keep control of his dream.

Tam could sense no indication that Crystu's sudden rise to near omnipotence had gone to her head in any way. Not that he had thought that a real danger, but she was wise to be concerned about the possibility; power certainly could make people change character.

He felt peculiar with that much seta flowing through him. His muscles felt as though they were vibrating but the feeling was not unpleasant. In fact, it was quite the reverse: the sensation was wonderfully soothing. Tam found that he had to concentrate to avoid falling fully asleep. He could get used to this feeling, and would miss it when it ended.

Tam found himself hoping that it would take a long time to destroy the snow-ants so that he could experience this pleasant thrum for longer. The sensation was like lying on warm grass with the hot sun beating on your face while a refreshing breeze kept you at a comfortable temperature and ruffled your hair, it was like relaxing into a hot bath on a cold day, it was like the feeling of contentment after a good meal, it was like...

He suddenly realised that Crystu, was not the person who was in danger of enjoying this experience too much. *He* was the one at risk! This feeling could be addictive! In fact, it almost certainly was! He had not expected that, but at least he knew that it would end, and he hoped that he would never have to do this again. No!

He hoped that he would get many chances to experience this wonderful, warm, pleasant, and soothingly sleepy sensation. He wished it would end quickly. No! He never wanted it to stop.

Light! This could be dangerous! If he fell fully asleep now he could lose the image which enabled the energy to go through him to Crystu. The power would build up within him until he burnt out, and it would kill him!

Worse, if he did not master his enjoyment of the sensation, and Crystu *did* begin to suffer a problem caused by the amount of energy that she was receiving and storing within herself, he might hesitate to cut off the flow to her.

He felt Crystu's surge of power as she attacked the ice mountain, and hoped that it would not take her too long to destroy it. He was battling himself as she battled the ants.

The group who were sending power to him began to leave his dream, and as they did the next group replaced them. Light! Had it already been fifteen minutes? Surely he had been here only a few seconds, and yet he also felt as if this battle had lasted an eternity.

He would master this; he *must* master this!

Crystu felt Tam slide into sleep as she walked slowly around the low table that held the model. She held her eyes firmly on the miniature mountain, adding more and more detail to the image she had built in her mind.

She felt the first thin stream of power begin to flow down the bond, and channelled the flow into her Seta. The thin stream increased, becoming broader and deeper, as more and more healers found the path into Tam's dream and began to send their power to him. As the energy poured into her Seta, she could feel her strength growing and her awareness began to expand. Keeping the image of the model in her mine, she pushed out her senses towards the reality on the downs above the town and began to trace its position and match it to the image.

She carefully started fitting the image, that she held in her mind's-eye, over the reality that was too large to fully imagine.

She felt the immense size of the mountain, its base covering many square miles and its tip rising into the clouds. The ice was packed so solidly that it resembled rock in all but colour. Even the texture was more like granite than ice, or perhaps more like limestone – the kind where you could easily see that it was made of thousands of tiny fossil shells packed tightly together. The ice was like that, resembling hailstones glued together rather than compressed snowflakes. The detail was incredible, she could see the rough, cracked edges of tiny cracks in the ice, and feel the life sparks of the deeply buried ants.

Crystu now realised that the detail that she was adding to the image in her mind came, not from the model, but from the reality outside. She could see the mountain, the real mountain. She stared at it, seeing it not only with her mind, but also with her eyes. The palace walls were transparent, and the shoulder of the downs that should hide the lowest reaches of the mountain, might as well not have been there.

She saw the mountain itself, from its lowest reaches to its highest point. She saw the side that faced her, but she could also see the further side and the detail of its summit with equal ease. She realised that somehow the unprecedented level of energy, that currently filled her Seta, had expanded her Gifts and her consciousness to such an extent that she could see the entire mountain and comprehend it fully.

The model had become unnecessary, so she ignored it to concentrate on the reality before her. Nothing like this had happened when they had practised the technique, but then they had not tried it with more than eight or nine people until today.

They need not have wasted all that time on the model! They could have done this within a few days of arriving! They would only have had to give everyone a chance to meet Tam to make it easier for them to find his dream. Had they known then what she knew now, they could have destroyed the mountain, and then gone to help Seldar and Trerin who would not then have been alone when they confronted whatever had killed the Sorcerer.

Seldar would still be alive, and Trerin would be undamaged.

But they had not known, and so had wasted all these many days on pointless activity. The revelation was heartbreaking!

The torrent of power flowing into her Seta stopped expanding, and Crystu knew that all those in the first group must now be actively sending Tam their power. She could tell that he was close to his limits, but he was not in any discomfort. In fact, he felt relaxed and was enjoying the sensation that the passage of so much power was creating.

She began to fill her mind with power from her Seta, and triggered her Gift of transmutation. The mountain hung clearly before her eyes, white, gleaming in the sunlight, and majestically beautiful. She could sense the strange life forms hidden deep within it. They swam through the ice, as easily as birds flew through the air, constantly searching for any rogue element of heat that might invade their domain.

Crystu reached out and surrounded the mountain with her Gift.

She knew she would have to act swiftly once she began, because the snow-ants would feel the attack on their home and they would swarm to defend themselves. They would attempt to reverse the transmutation with their own powers, and there were millions of them in that mountain.

She waited, filling her mind with more power than she had ever held in her life. It throbbed under her skin and behind her eyes, building to ever higher levels. She hoped that Aren was correct that a Rykatu's Seta could expand to accommodate any power level needed, because no one before her had ever held so much! She could not only see every ice grain within the mountain, but she could also see the land for miles in all directions, including, far away in the distant west, a smudge of darkness that hung over the land like smoke over a fire.

She knew instinctively that it was over Bein. Light! What had Seldar and Trerin walked into?

She pulled her mind from the question, she had work to do!

Gently, she sank her power into the outer surface of the ice, both above and below ground. She made sure that she held every square inch of it before she did anything further. Once satisfied that she was ready, she transmuted the mountain's surface into solid granite, to a depth all-around of about ten feet, and then, happy that this would contain any water if the ice melted, she began the plan that Tam had suggested, inspired by a geode on a mountain.

She concentrated and the ice crystals beneath the granite changed into pointed diamond crystals whose sharp tips stretched inwards as they grew, layer on layer reaching inwards towards the heart of the ice.

The snow-ants had felt her attack on their home, and swam outwards to meet the challenge with their own transmutation abilities – changing diamond back into ice. Crystu increased the rate at which she changed ice into diamond. She sent the sharp points flying inwards, cracking the carapaces of the creatures as they hit them, causing each one to disappear in a tiny blue explosion that melted the nearby ice and attracted other ants to repair the melt.

At first, the task seemed impossible. Surely the ants would easily force back her diamonds and change them again into snow and ice. There were so many of the insects boiling up from the depths of the mountain, but the energy flow from Tam continued to recharge and strengthen her and slowly Crystu's diamond teeth bit deeper into the ant colony.

She could feel Tam struggling with something, but she could not spare any of her mind to wonder what the problem was; she was committed to this attack and must see it through. The thing that was disturbing him did not affect the flow of energy that he sent along the bond, and she was confident that, whatever it was, he would solve it.

The ants began to retreat from the teeth that bit and chewed them, but they had no way to escape. The diamonds surrounded them and closed in on them, and then they were gone. Only the mountain remained.

Crystu was not quite finished yet. She could feel deep cracks running through the underlying chalk. The weight of the ice mountain, growing inexorably over the last few months, had caused these, and the newly transmuted mountain of diamond was much heavier. The landscape was unstable and she had to correct that, before the massive expanse of rock, now looming over the lower ground, triggered an earthquake.

She sank her mind into the ground and considered the best way to strengthen it. Lower down, far below the soft chalk, she found much harder limestone. That would do it.

She extended the limestone upwards, replacing the soft chalk above with its harder cousin. She fed this spur of limestone up into the granite and diamond mountain and merged them together, changing the granite, and much of the diamond, into limestone, and forming one solid and stable structure that had its roots deep underground. She left the central part of the diamond unchanged on a whim, not wanting to completely destroy something that was so beautiful.

She wondered if anyone would ever find it, and what they would think if they did. Although much smaller than at first, it was still larger than five cathedrals put together, and made of solid diamond!

Crystu grinned to herself wishing that she could see their faces when, and if, it ever came to light.

The energy flowing down the bond ceased. Tam had sensed that she had finished and had ejected the dreamwalking healers from his dream, ending the flow.

With a feeling that was both loss and relief, she felt her power reduce back to its previous level, and her sense of the new mountain and the downs around it faded, and the room around her once more claimed her eyes. She turned to look at Tam, who was pushing himself into a sitting position. Around them, people were waking up and stretching.

"Tam, that was amazing! I could see for miles and I felt so strong. We need not fear anything the Shadowbringer may do because we will be able to use this to foil it."

"No, Crystu, I don't believe we can ever use this again, except in direst need. Even then I will not dare to risk it a second time, not with so many people sending energy through me," he replied, sounding exhausted.

Crystu stared, as his appearance registered on her consciousness!

Sweat had plastered Tam's hair to his head and soaked his clothing. He felt as tired as though he had run hundreds of miles.

Crystu sent her awareness into the bond to judge his condition. Light, he was exhausted! Triumphant, but completely drained of strength.

"Tam?"

She wanted to ask what the problem had been, but he sensed her intention and gave the slightest shake of his head, as he interrupted.

"Were we successful, Crystu? Are the ants destroyed?"

Crystu nodded slowly. Of course! He probably wanted to wait until they were alone before they began to examine how well the technique had worked and what the problem was that he had apparently encountered.

"Yes, Tam, all the ants are killed. There is a new mountain of limestone, with its roots set firmly deep into the earth. They will not need to import building stone here ever again because now they can quarry it."

She decided to tell him about the diamond at its heart another time.

"Good!"

Tam smiled at her tiredly, and then looked over to where Captain Amil stood waiting.

"Captain, Please tell Rannis that the ants are gone, but that we will all need to rest now. I will speak to him later today, at his convenience."

He spoke briskly now, with scarcely a trace of his fatigue in his voice, as though he had already recovered, although Crystu knew that he had not.

"Yes, my Lord."

Amil nodded and left the room.

"Thank you, everyone, the new technique was successful and Lady Crystu has destroyed the snow-ant infestation."

Tam was using illusion so that everyone in the neighbouring rooms would hear what he said.

"I suggest that everyone gets plenty of rest. We will return to Tyreen the day after tomorrow."

Crystu nodded. Erian's funeral was tomorrow and all the Guardians would attend. Even those travelling Sorcerers, who were free to leave whenever they chose now that the ants were destroyed, had indicated that they would stay that long.

All those in the room who had been dreamwalking, stood up, began to stretch, move around, and talk to each other. The atmosphere in the room was noisily celebratory. Many from the other rooms came to offer congratulations to Crystu for destroying the ants, and to Tam for discovering this new and powerful technique.

Those who had heard what he had said about not being able to use this method again, were less openly triumphant and some were already speculating about what problem Tam might have encountered, but still they were obviously glad to have been a part of this historic achievement.

Tam stood up, and walked to stand beside Crystu, and looked at the model for a second before speaking.

"Let's go somewhere quieter," he suggested, his voice pitched for her ears alone.

Crystu knew that the other Ponfourii in the room would be able to hear him, but that, out of courtesy, would ignore anything obviously intended for her no matter how curious they might be. What was between Sorcerer and Ponfour was no one else's business by long tradition.

"You need to sleep, Tam, so we'll go up to our rooms and we can talk there, if you can stay awake that long."

She did not move yet, but frowned up at him, puzzled by his pronounced fatigue because he had had to use no magic at all when he acted as the nearly passive conduit for that energy. He would have had to keep his dream carefully controlled, but the other dreamwalkers had walked into *his* dreams, not he into theirs. Unless he had misjudged the flow, his Seta should be undiminished. It *was* undiminished! This close to him, Crystu could not possibly be mistaken about his condition – his Seta was undamaged and yet he was as tired as if he had fought a dozen challenges. She felt something else, as well, which she could not quite interpret without a healing probe. Her hand twitched at the thought, and Tam’s eyes flicked down to the movement. He smiled.

"The sooner we are alone, the sooner you can do that, my Lady."

His formality reminded her that he was waiting for her to move. Crystu bit her lip guiltily; she was keeping him from his rest and he was becoming more tired by the minute.

"Do you need an energy boost to climb the stairs, Tam?" she asked, and blinked with surprise at the sudden shudder of revulsion that shook him.

Revulsion?

"No! Thank you, my Lady," he said quickly, then sensing her confused hurt at the rejection, continued, “Crystu, I'll explain upstairs. Please can we just go?"

She bit back what she had been about to say, as she could feel that he desperately wanted to be out of this crowd of people, and to leave without any of them knowing that anything was seriously amiss. She nodded and led the way from the room.

As they reached the door to their rooms, Tam grimaced at the sound of quick footsteps from behind.

"I want to know why you're so tired, boy, and why you feel that we should never try this method of combining energy on such a large scale again!"

Crystu turned to find Lady Vellte advancing purposefully along the hall, with Gann a step behind her.

"Lady Vellte," she began, intending to do whatever necessary to persuade the older Sorceress to leave.

"Of course, Aunt Vellte." Tam's unexpected agreement stopped what she had been about to say.

"It would be a good idea if someone with more experience knows what occurred, and I may need you to heal me,' he continued.

"Her!" Crystu was hurt. "Tam! You wouldn't take energy from me, and now you want someone else to heal you?"

"My Lady, if I am correct, this is something that you have never encountered before, and I know that Aunt Vellte has, which is the only reason I am asking her. Please, Crystu, wait until you have heard everything."

She could feel his sincerity, and his genuine regret at upsetting her. Still, she felt hurt by what appeared to be a rejection, but she knew that he would never deliberately hurt her, so he must have a good reason and she would wait and learn what it was.

Tam smiled wearily and pushed open the door into their outer room, despite his tiredness, he still examined the room carefully for danger before gesturing to her to enter.

Gann and Vellte followed, closing the door behind them and Tam sank gratefully into a chair.

"Let me look at you, boy." Vellte strode across as she spoke and laid her hand gently on Tam's forehead.

Crystu firmly forced down the sudden feeling of jealousy, reminding herself that Vellte was his close relative after all, and they both lived in the same Homestead, even if Vellte would have often been absent travelling. She didn't like the older Sorceress, finding her acerbic and unfriendly, but she knew that Vellte was an accomplished and experienced healer, who was far more experienced than Crystu. If Tam thought that he needed that experience, then he had every right to ask for it and was sensible to do so.

"You have sense enough to ask when you need help, boy, that's a rare trait in a man!"

Vellte's side glance at Gann and his sniff suggested an old joke between them, and Crystu grinned at the similarity between Vellte's words and her own thought that preceded them.

"Over here, girl, and merge your Gift with mine. I doubt you will encounter this often, especially not in one of our own people."

Crystu frowned at being called 'girl' but obediently merged her healing with Vellte and, placing her hand over Vellte's on Tam's head. She sent her awareness into the healing probe that Vellte had slid into Tam's mind.

Crystu gasped.

"You'll have been taught about this, girl, but seeing it for yourself is the best teacher."

Crystu frowned, as she examined the alterations that had affected Tam's brain. The blood vessels appeared constricted and there were signs of dehydration; he had the beginning of what would be a severe headache without healing. There were other changes too, and she puzzled over what she could see. She recognised the pattern of damage, and she knew that Vellte was correct: she had been taught about this, but had certainly never expected to find it in her Ponfour.

"Do you recognise it, girl?" Vellte asked, and Crystu nodded.

"I know what it looks like," she answered. "Healers who lack our Gifts use medicines that can be effective, but some have a pleasant effect that makes people want to take more, and some are addictive. Some of them can cause damage like this, if taken regularly over many months. But that's ridiculous, Tam has not been taking medicines! He has no need, and I would know if he did."

"It was the energy transfer, Crystu," Tam said wearily. "All that power flowing through my mind acted like one of those medicines. It felt wonderfully pleasant and I wanted to drift away on the sensation. Staying awake and in control of my dream was one of the hardest things that I have ever done."

Crystu stared at him horrified.

"If you had lost control..."

Tam nodded.

"I know. I would certainly have died."

Crystu gulped.

"I'm glad that you kept control, Tam."

She imagined how she would have felt if their bond had snapped while she worked on the ice mountain. The surviving snow-ants would have escaped to begin anew, and there would have been severe flooding, because the ants she had killed had caused much of the ice to melt and that would have escaped when the others broke out of the rock shell that she had made. Worse than that though, was the idea of her feeling Tam's death and having to go on alone. Just the thought of it was unbearable and she felt her hand trembling violently against Vellte's on Tam's forehead.

"Calm yourself, girl, it didn't happen."

Vellte's voice sounded far away and unusually gentle, as Tam placed his own hand over hers and sent his understanding strength through their bond.

Crystu took a deep, steadying breath, and made herself smile.

"Let's heal him before his headache gets worse," she suggested. Tam rewarded her with a grateful smile.

"I would appreciate that, Crystu."

"Follow my lead, girl. I know that you were well taught, but I have done this before."

Vellte took control of their merged Gifts and showed Crystu where she wanted her to apply her healing touch. A short time later, they withdrew from his mind. Crystu was startled when Gann touched her shoulder and guided her onto the seat beside

Tam. He handed her a hot drink and then passed one to Vellte and gave another to Tam.

Tam looked much better as he sipped his drink, and he smiled at her, completely alert again.

"Thank you, Aunt Vellte, Crystu." he said, "I am glad that the energy transfer worked and the ants are destroyed, but you can see why I do not think we will be able to use it unless absolutely necessary. A small number seems safe, but not as many as we had today."

Crystu stared at him aghast.

"Tam, Lord Jareth said that we may need to use this technique to defeat the Shadowbringer's plan, whatever it may be."

He nodded.

"I know, but unless the numbers involved are much less than today, whoever transfers the power will experience the same thing that I did."

Crystu nodded.

"How many do you think would be safe, Tam?"

lyHe shrugged.

"I only began to notice the affect after about the thirtieth healer had started sending me their power, but it may have already been having an effect before I felt it. I think we must do a great deal more testing before we know how many or how few is safe."

He sipped at his drink again, and Crystu sensed that he had not finished. He looked up at her.

"Regardless of what we eventually learn, I'm sorry, Crystu, but I do not believe it will ever be safe for me to do that again. I would not risk it unless your life is at risk and there is no other choice. The sensation was extremely pleasant at the time, but now the memory of it makes me feel in need of a hot bath. At the moment, just the idea of accepting energy from someone else, even you, is profoundly disturbing and it both attracts and repels me in equal measure. I do not like feeling like this, and I hope it fades, but I do not think it ever will go completely."

"Tam is correct, girl: his mind has been sensitised to the effect. We have healed the damage, but if he tried it again, he would find it harder to resist the effect and would almost certainly suffer greater injury from fewer people."

Vellte's voice had returned to its usual acerbic nature, and Crystu wondered if she had imagined the softer tone of a moment before.

"Aunt Vellte!" Tam said, and Crystu was definitely not imagining the reproving note in his voice.

"Must I remind you, again, that 'girl' is not an appropriate way to address a Rykatu?"

To Crystu's surprise, Vellte laughed.

"Good! I was quite worried when you let me get away with that earlier, but now I know that you have recovered."

Tam snorted.

"Another of your tests, Aunt?"

"You know how she likes to play her games, boy," Gann commented.

"'Boy' is not an appropriate term for my Ponfour, either!" Crystu began indignantly, but then paused when Gann grinned at her, she stared at him for a second and then she chuckled.

"Vellte is not the only person who likes to play games, I see."

Gann's grin broadened and Crystu stuck her tongue out at him before twisting on the seat to turn her back on the older Ponfour. She looked carefully at Tam next to her, using her eyes and the bond to judge his health.

"You don't feel at all tired now. That's much better."

She looked across at Vellte who had sat down in another chair.

"Thank you, Vellte, I'm not sure that I would have recognised that, or remembered how to heal it, without your help."

"You, and Tam, are very welcome, Crystu." The elderly Sorceress inclined her head graciously.

"Crystu," Tam began, and she looked back at him, smiling, "when you began the transmutation, you were surprised by something and then you felt sad. What was it?"

The smile left her face as she remembered what she had realised as she began to concentrate on the ice mountain,

"We could have done it on the first day, Tam; we never needed the model. The power enhanced my Gift to such an extent that I could see the mountain clearly and in detail. If we had known, we could have destroyed the ants immediately and then we would have been free to join Seldar and Trerin, and maybe if we had..." she paused, remembering that Vellte and Gann knew nothing about her gleaning.

"If you had, maybe you could have prevented whatever it is that you two, and young Jareth and Trerisia, have been hiding for the last day or two? It is something to do with Seldar then? What trouble has that idiot landed himself in now?"

Crystu blinked in surprise, but Tam shrugged ruefully at her.

"Don't be surprised, gi.." Vellte's pause was brief, before she corrected herself, "Crystu, I've known Tam since he was a baby. I can tell when he is hiding something."

"My Lady, the reason we kept the news hidden no longer applies, and I strongly recommend that you tell Lady Vellte about it. We will need assistance and I would prefer that at least another two Ponfourii come with us."

Crystu blinked in surprise not only at Tam's formality, but also because he appeared to be expecting her to make the decision, and then she understood: she had become used to Tam being in command during the last few weeks, but he was in command of the mission to destroy the snow-ants, and once everyone had translocated back to Tyreen, that mission would be over. When they went searching for Trerin, Crystu would once again be in charge.

She wondered if he minded that, and then scolded herself for such a thought; she would know at once if he was unhappy about relinquishing command, and she could feel no trace of such a thing in his mind touch. He was waiting for her answer, with a slight fond smile that showed that he had guessed where her thoughts had strayed. She pulled her mind firmly into focus.

"You're right as ever, and I think we should also ask Astley. Will Karan and Gann be enough do you think?"

Tam considered and nodded.

"I think so. Trerin may be wearing a large cat form, but he will be weakened. The four of us should be able to hold him long enough for one of you Sorcerers to make him sleep."

Gann inhaled sharply, obviously drawing the correct conclusion.

Vellte glanced at her Ponfour's shocked face, and then looked at Crystu.

"I had heard that Seldar had rebounded. Is this Trerin his Ponfour?" she asked.

Crystu nodded, as Gann said, "Yes, that was the Warrior's name. I've seen him around – extremely tall, and yellow hair. He looks a lot like Trerisia. Are they family?"

Tam nodded.

"Trerin is Trerisia's younger brother."

"Younger?" Vellte asked in surprise. "Seldar bonded with a younger man? I *am* surprised! I would not have expected that of him. This Ponfour will need holding while we place sleep on him? What has happened to Seldar, that his Ponfour requires restraint and induced sleep?"

Tam glanced at Crystu, silently offering to tell them for her, and spare her the necessity. She shook her head. If she was in charge again, she must do her duty.

"Seldar is dead, Vellte," she said sadly. "I saw it in a gleaning the night after Erian died. Trerin survived and the Guidance said that we must find him. After I have helped translocate everyone back to the Cave, Tam and I, with Jathte and Trerisia, will translocate to a place I was shown in the gleaning and there we will find Trerin. Will you come with us and assist?"

Vellte glanced at Gann and nodded once.

"Of course we will. I never liked Seldar; he is," she paused and corrected herself, "*was*, an excellent illusionist, but he was unable to take anything seriously, and his love of practical jokes could be irritating! However, he was far braver than he realised, and of course we will assist his Ponfour. You said he may be in cat form?"

Tam nodded.

"A large cat I assume?"

Crystu shrugged.

"We won't know for certain until we see him, but Trerisia says that his favourite form is a large cat, and I saw a large cat in the gleaning."

"They went to investigate that wild story about ships full of Zindons invading Bein," Gann said.

Crystu remembered what she had seen out to the west, while she prepared her assault on the ice mountain.

"It may not be a wild story," she said. "I have told you that the extra power gave me the ability to see far more than I can usually. One of the things that I saw was a dark cloud hanging on the western horizon. It was in the right place to be over Bein."

She sighed.

"If we had only known that we didn't need the model, and that we could have destroyed the mountain on the first day, we could have gone with them."

Tam disagreed.

"Crystu, even if we had been free to help them, Lord Jareth would not have sent all of us to investigate such an unlikely tale. At most he might have sent the two of us, and whatever killed Seldar might have killed you too. Also..."

Crystu looked up and started to speak, but he spoke over her half-formed protest.

"*Also*, Erian would still be here, still controlled, and these people would still have a Zindon in their midst. We only learned of it because we stayed so long. Erian might still be alive, but she would have had no rescue. She would still eventually have been transformed, and she would have been here, close to this country's royal family. She could have wreaked havoc here."

Tam held Crystu's eyes until she reluctantly acknowledged the truth of his words.

"Perhaps our presence there would have saved Seldar and Trerin, or perhaps we too would have been caught in whatever trap they walked into. We cannot know, and it is pointless to speculate. We did not know that the model was unnecessary, and we could not know that until today. We can only base decisions on what we know at the time, Crystu; we can do no more than our best with what we know."

He was right, and Crystu knew it, but that did not change how she felt about it.

"He's right, Crystu. I know it's hard, but try not to waste too much effort regretting things over which you had no control. Everything is in the hands of the Lord of Light, and he knows what he is doing."

Vellte smiled, and Crystu felt herself beginning to warm to the old Sorceress. Perhaps she was not as unfriendly as she usually appeared.

"I agree that it will be advisable to have Karan with us," Gann said thoughtfully into the silence that had followed Vellte's words. "A Ponfour who has survived his Sorcerer's death is unable to think clearly. He may not recognise us, or understand that we are trying to help him. He may well fight us, and if he is indeed in the form of a large cat we will have difficulty in holding him. We do not want to injure him, but he may have no such qualms about us. Remember how many of us it took to hold down Tam, the other day? And he was not fighting us."

"I can shapeshift, and so can Astley; we can help," Crystu said, and then sniffed at Tam's instant stubborn refusal, which she felt clearly through their bond even as he said his firm, "No!"

"Tam! I can help," she protested.

His face and mind were stubborn.

“Yes, you can help, by making him sleep while we hold him, but you will stay clear while we catch him. No, Crystu!” He placed a finger on her upper lip as she drew breath to protest.

“Gann is correct. If Trerin does not recognise us, he will fight, and he is still a Ponfour, with a Ponfour’s speed and strength, even weakened as he may be, he could easily injure you.”

She could feel that he was immovably determined, but this time he was wrong.

“Tam,” she said firmly. “Trerin is a shapeshifter, and you are not. Neither is Trerisia, or Karan, or you, Gann. If he changes shape and flies away, only Astley and I can go after him. Unless we bring along even more people to help, there is no alternative.”

Tams mouth twisted in frustration, but he could not argue with her logic, but then Vellte spoke.

“You are wrong, Crystu,” The elder Sorceress said quietly. “Trerin will not be able to shapeshift.”

Crystu frowned in puzzlement. “Why not?” she asked.

Vellte sighed.

“You have never seen a Ponfour who has survived his Sorcerer’s death, Crystu, or you would know. I have, and I can tell you now that if you are harbouring any romantic notions about being prepared to sacrifice yourself for Tam, this will end them.”

She shook her head.

“Trerin will have little memory of anything, probably not even his name. He will be unable to even think. Healing may return that to him, but until then, he has no recollection of shapeshifting or any other magic. He will be operating on pure instinct, and unless some stronger duty has overridden it, his instinct will be to find who or whatever killed Seldar and attack it with teeth and claws. I have seen it, once, and I know that I could never deliberately do that to Gann. It is worse than dying, Crystu, far worse. Even when they have been healed and can think again, they have just one urge and that is to find a way to die in combat.”

Crystu stared at Vellte, her mouth suddenly dry. Her mother had said that Ponfourii paid a terrible price if they failed in their duty, but could it really be that bad?

Vellte looked as though she was remembering something that she would never forget until the day she died, and Tam agreed with every word she said.

“My Lady,” he told her firmly, “you will stay away from the fight until we call you.”

Crystu nodded dumbly, accepting the restriction.

"You’re tired, Vellte; it’s time you rested!" Gann announced.

Vellte nodded.

"Gann is correct. You have had a lot of my Seta one way or another, young Tam, and I need to recoup it so if you will excuse us, we will leave."

"Of course, Aunt Vellte, and thank you again."

Tam and Crystu both rose to accompany Vellte and Gann from their rooms.

Tam closed the door behind them as Crystu threw herself back onto the chair and sprawled across it, suddenly feeling restless. She was bursting with energy, but the task was complete and she had nothing to do for the rest of the day. The next two days promised to be unpleasant, with Erian's funeral tomorrow, and then finding Trerin the day after.

After that the Shadowbringer's unknown plan lay like a black cloud across the future. She wished that she could forget what lay ahead, and forget that she was a Rykatu, and just pretend for a while to be ordinary.

She sighed, and then realised that Tam was leaning against the door and looking at her with a speculative expression, eyes bright and a slight smile on his lips. She could feel his sense of anticipation and knew that he wanted to suggest something.

"What is it, Tam?" she asked, her curiosity piqued. His smile widened.

"You are full of energy, not at all tired. The transfer replenished your Seta as quickly as you used it and you are still at full strength," he began. "My Seta was untouched. I was only tired because of the damage that the transfer caused to my brain, but that is healed now, and I am as wide awake as you."

She pushed herself upright in the chair.

"Yes, that's true,"

She wondered what he was planning. He was too enthusiastic to be about to suggest that they went to talk to the king.

"I suppose we could go and see Rannis and tell him all about the transfer," she suggested, not at all serious, and was not surprised when Tam shook his head.

"I told Amil to tell Rannis that we all needed to rest, and I think we should take advantage of that, as neither of us is tired."

Tam grinned, deliberately holding back his idea for another few seconds to tantalise her.

"Tam," Crystu said firmly, "if you don't tell me what your idea is soon, I am going to turn all of your clothes pink, and order you to wear them!"

He laughed.

"I would be more worried if I didn't know that you detest that colour even more than I do."

Crystu concentrated and pointed at his, now bright pink, boots.

Tam stared down at his feet for a second, as the colour began to creep up his trouser legs, and then continued, "However, if you insist!"

He walked to the window and pointed outside.

"There is a completely new mountain out there," he said, deliberately speaking slowly.

"I know that, Tam, I made it!" Crystu tapped her fingers impatiently against her arm and the colour spread past his knees.

"No one has ever set foot on it," he said quietly.

Crystu gasped. Her eyes sparkled as she finally understood what he was suggesting.

“We could be the first people to walk on it. We could be the first to climb it. Tam! That’s a wonderful idea! I have never been the first person anywhere. I would like that!”

She turned his trousers and boots back to their previous green and brown colours, and he heaved a sigh of relief.

"It will take several hours to get to the top of it, if we climb it from its base. Should we be gone for so long?" Crystu said, suddenly uncertain whether they should do it.

"Why not?" Tam replied. "We have nothing else to do. You have killed the snow-ants, and I don’t believe there is another Zindon in this town, and even if there is, he will not be looking for us on the new mountain, when everybody knows that we are here, resting. You can translocate us to its foot and we will climb to the top. Not even the Warriors on guard duty will know that we have gone."

He really wanted to go, and she had to admit that the idea of taking a few hours for herself, with no distractions, and no one aware that she had gone, was attractive.

"We will need water and food," she said decisively. "Come on! We’ll go to the kitchens and get something to take. Then we can just translocate straight to the mountain. Let’s see if we *can* do it without anyone at all realising that we have left."

"I'll get a bag,” he said, running through into his room and returning with a long-strapped bag looped over his shoulder. Crystu kicked off her light shoes and quickly replaced them with boots. Tam opened the door and looked out.

"There's no one in sight."

Grinning, Crystu followed him along the hall, ready to create an illusion to hide them from any eyes if necessary.

A few minutes later, they arrived at the palace kitchens.

"Stay here," Tam told her, indicating a dark corner below a flight of stairs. He waited until she had pressed herself back into the shadow, before opening the kitchen door and strolling in. He left the door ajar, so she could hear him asking for a few bottles of water and juice, plus some bread rolls, cold meats, cheese and fruit, for his lady. Without ever actually lying, he implied that Crystu was tired and wished to have lunch in her room.

A woman's voice offered to bring things up to the Rykatu and serve her, but he replied that he would serve his lady himself, thank you, and just a few things to put in the bag would be enough.

Crystu grinned in astonishment at his duplicitousness. He had not told a single lie, but everyone in that room now knew that Crystu was resting in her room and would eat lunch there.

Tam emerged from the kitchen, the bag looped over his shoulder, and closed the door. Crystu scrambled out from her hiding place and hurriedly translocated them both to the foot of the new mountain.

"Tam! You are such an accomplished liar!" Crystu laughed, as the nimbus faded from around them to reveal the lowest outcrop of limestone of the new mountain.

Tam looked shocked, although the effect was somewhat spoiled by the fact that, although he *tried* to project appalled innocence along the bond, it was equally mixed with internal laughter as he replied,

"Crystu! I told no lies, not one. Every word was the truth!"

Crystu shook her head, grinning.

"The words were true, even the sentences were completely factual, yet put together they added to a lie. You lied! I have completely corrupted you, my stalwart, upright, pious Ponfour."

Tam grinned ruefully.

"Yes, I suppose that you have, but I don't intend to complain about it."

"Well, I hope not!" Crystu retorted, and taking hold of his arm tugged him along with her as she headed toward the bare rock ahead.

When she reached the edge of the grass, she paused, looking at the rocky surface in front of her, and then took a careful step onto it.

"There! I am officially the first person to step on this mountain," she declared with satisfaction. "Come on Tam, you are the second!" She pulled him onto the rock.

Tam smiled.

"We are the first people ever to walk on this land, and that is a rare privilege."

He looked upwards at the slop of the mountain. Its peak was hidden behind a shoulder of rock.

"There are no trails or paths to follow, not even a sheep track. We will have to be careful where we walk, and we will have to try and pick put the best route as we go."

"I think that I can remember enough detail to pick out a good route," Crystu replied. "This way!" She pointed upwards. "We want to go to the left of that spur. There is a deep crack just hidden around the other side that would block our path if we go to the right."

Tam nodded and they began to walk upward on the strangely shaped surface of the limestone.

"It looks odd," Tam commented after a while. "I have never seen such smooth limestone. Usually it has visible layers through it. This rock will probably be good for carving because it is so smooth that a sculptor can carve it easily without fear that natural layering will deflect his chisel into the wrong direction."

Crystu looked around.

"You're right," she said, surprised. "I didn't even think of that at all! I just turned the snow into rock exactly as it lay. If the snow had been deposited naturally, it would have had layers that might have appeared like rock strata, but it was created by the ants so was structureless and completely smooth."

"This bit is a bit too smooth!" Tam said a few moments later as he stared up a steep rise. "There is not even a crack for a toehold!"

Crystu looked at it, trying to remember an alternative way that they could go, and then sighed.

"I think that we will have to cheat here; there is no way around this that brings us to anywhere easier to climb."

She frowned at the mountainside.

"Next time I make a mountain, I must remember to add hand and foot holds."

Tam grinned, and leaned one hand against the smooth rock surface. Crystu felt him concentrate, and her scalp tingled with the emanation from his magic. Cracks and holes appeared across the slope.

"Thank you, Tam."

Crystu scrambled up the slope, with Tam following close behind.

An hour later, both were sweating and had removed their jackets and tied them around their waists by the sleeves. They were discussing whether to stop to eat or wait until they reached the peak, which was probably still a good two hours away. They walked over a shoulder of the mountain to find themselves on a broad plain where the land had flattened out before rising sharply again towards the peak. The plain was hollowed and in its centre a pool of water had begun to grow, fed by a tiny stream that descended from the higher slope.

"You put a stream on it!" Tam exclaimed with delight.

"Of course I did. I added several!" Crystu replied, laughing. "We can't have a mountain without streams and waterfalls."

Tam smiled.

"This looks a lot like the shape of the land around my lake, and that pool will eventually become a lake."

He turned to look out at the view. Below them, the chalk downs spread a short distance before plunging down to the plain where they could see the city of Angate.

“Let’s eat here,” Crystu suggested, looking around at this empty expanse of rock.

Tam was correct, she thought – one day this would look similar to the lake in the hills above his Homestead. She remembered the day that they had spent there. It felt like an eternity ago and yet had not been more than a couple of months, if that. She puzzled for a moment, trying to work out exactly how long ago it had been, but then shrugged mentally. It had been a wonderful day and one she would long remember, and that was all that mattered.

She glanced sideways at Tam; a wistful quality to his emotions made her think that he was remembering that day too, the sudden hint of amusement confirmed it.

"At least this pool is not deep enough for you to throw me into!" she commented with a smile.

Tam grinned.

"Not yet, but it is deepening as we watch. If we stay long enough, it will be easily deep enough."

"Then we will eat quickly," she informed him with a lift of her head, as she walked across to a convenient bump in the rock, spread her jacket across it, and sat.

"Come on, my Ponfour, I am hungry, serve me!" she commanded haughtily.

"Oh yes, my Lady, of course, my Lady," Tam replied earnestly, as he trotted across and, swinging the bag off his shoulder, he knelt and quickly began to remove its contents.

He handed her a bottle of water, which Crystu unstoppered and sipped at, as he pulled out wooden plates, and some ceramic containers which proved to contain bread, cold meat, and salad. He assembled a selection on a plate and handed it to her. Then he sat back on his heels and waited, eyes fixed attentively on her face.

"Is that satisfactory, my Lady?" he asked, still adopting a tone of anxious subservience although she knew that he was laughing inside.

"It will do," she replied with her nose in the air, and then paused for a second wondering whether to stretch the joke and make him wait before she gave permission to eat. He would wait if she did, without complaint, but she knew that it would stop feeling like a joke to her if she did that,

“Eat, Tam, and thank you,” she grinned, abandoning her game.

Tam smiled back and untied his jacket from his waist. Following her example, he placed it on the rock beside her and sat down with his food.

They ate in silence, watching the pool grow in the hollow in front of them.

The water crept slowly forward. Sometimes the front edge rushed ahead in one wide unstoppable wave as it found a slight downward slope, and sometimes a thin rivulet pushed forward more slowly along some invisible channel in the rock surface, until the leading edge stopped in place, as the thin stream behind it widened and deepened.

Crystu sighed as she stretched out to lie on the sun warmed rock.

“What is it?” Tam asked.

She twisted her head to look at him.

“I was just thinking that it will take a long time before all this solid rock begins to weather enough to allow any plants to take root.”

“Yes, it will,” Tam agreed, “and even when it does crumble, limestone does not make the most fertile soil so it will be a long time before plants grow here.”

Crystu sighed again.

"I wish I could speed things up. I would like to see things growing here, but even if I transmuted the top of this rock into the richest soil, it would be sterile. I can’t transmute the worms and insects needed to make the soil live and without them nothing will grow."

"You could translocate soil here," Tam suggested. "There is a massive mound of topsoil near the sheds at the back of the Palace gardens, intended to repair the damage caused by the large numbers of feet. I am sure that Rannis wouldn’t mind if you brought some up here."

Crystu sat up, considering the idea, but then shook her head, "No, Tam, it still would be futile. Most of it would blow away before anything could begin to grow."

"Not necessarily," he replied. His tone was unusually hesitant.

Crystu laughed.

"If you're thinking that I can speed plant growth with my healing Gift, I wish that I could, but I can't. I always wanted to develop that facet of healing, because being able to speed the growth of plants must be wonderful, but it doesn't matter how hard I try, I can't do it."

"You know what people say about plant healers?" Tam asked.

Crystu frowned, puzzled by the odd emotion that suddenly streaked his mind aura with jagged shades of purple.

"That they are usually among the weakest of our race? Yes, I know that is commonly believed, but several of my mother's family have had that ability and they were all perfectly strong."

She stared at him, trying to make sense of his strange feelings.

"Tam! Surely you don't believe that?"

He shook his head.

"I? No, I have never believed that, but so many do..." he paused, and Crystu could feel that he was uncertain whether to continue.

"Tam?" she prompted.

"I am being a fool!" he announced unexpectedly and chuckled at her bemused expression. "Crystu, I have that facet of the healing Gift, but I have always kept it a secret, even from Da."

Crystu stared and then laughed and clapped her hands together in delight.

"You can make plants grow? That's wonderful! I envy you, but why keep it a secret?"

Tam's eyebrows rose.

"Why? Because I wanted to be a Ponfour! I may possess arguably the three most powerful of the Gifts but if people had known I was a plant healer too, it would have made some certain that I was not strong enough. So I told no one. Only one teacher knew of it, and he said that if it was known it could spoil my chances of ever becoming a Ponfour."

"I never thought you too weak to be a Ponfour. I knew you were my choice within a few minutes of our first meeting," Crystu said softly. "You could have told me. I think it is marvellous that you can do that."

"Yes," Tam agreed. "Which is why I just called myself a fool. There was never any good reason to hide it from you, but secrecy can get to be a habit that you don't even question. Until just now, I had not even thought about it in weeks. I use the ability so rarely that I sometimes forget it is there."

Crystu pushed herself forward so that she was leaning on her hands, she grinned excitedly.

"If I transmute some of this rock into soil, and translocate some of the good soil, which must have all sorts of seeds mixed in it, from the palace, would you make the plants grow to hold it all in place? I would love to see this spot turn green. Will you do it for me? Please, Tam?"

He laughed at her eagerness.

"Alright, but just a small area, not the entire mountain. I have never practiced this enough to become truly skilful or strong."

"That is going to change," Crystu said firmly. "But for now..."

She concentrated and the sloping surface of the rock to their right crumbled into a poor chalky soil. Then she pictured the pile of soil as she had seen it in the gardens yesterday. Her Gift reached out and translocated a portion of it into the air above the slope, dropping it into the wind so that it scattered across the ground, mixing with the soil she had created first.

Both of them turned their faces away and started coughing as some of the wind blew the soil across their faces.

"That was not a good idea!" Tam hastily made an air shield to protect them from the chocking dust.

"No, it wasn't!" Crystu agreed, feeling a little foolish, as she blinked her watering eyes rapidly to try and wash out the soil grains that had blown into her eyes before Tam could raise his shield. After a few minutes the dust settled and they could look across the hollow to see the soil scattered evenly across the further side.

"The soil has to be much wetter, but too much water will wash it away," Tam murmured, and Crystu felt the magical emanation as he transmuted a small part of the air into a fine rain that was just enough to moisten the soil thoroughly, but not enough to wash it off the ground on which it lay.

Tam anticipated her question before she could speak it.

"It's the same as healing a person, Crystu, you speed up what would normally take days or weeks so that it happens in seconds or minutes, but the new tissues must be built from what is already in the body or what can be introduced into the body as you work. For a plant, that means speeding up the rate at which it absorbs moisture and nutrients from the ground around it. If there is not enough water, then the plant will die."

She nodded; that made sense. The normal rules of healing applied whether it was a person, animal or plant.

Tam walked into the centre of the soil and squatted, placing both hands onto the soil. Once again Crystu felt the surge of magic as he activated his Gift.

Nothing happened – the soil remained bare earth.

Crystu was disappointed.

"Perhaps there are no seeds in there?" she suggested.

Tam smiled.

"Crystu, there are always seeds in soil. You are too impatient! They must grow roots first." He had not abandoned his effort, but continued to send healing magic into the ground.

Crystu blinked, and blinked again; the soil was shivering!

The movement increased as green shoots appeared, pushing the earth sideways as they came up through its surface. Within a few seconds the gentle slope above the growing pond was transformed from bare earth to waving grass and wild flowers. The feeling of active magic use ceased and Tam stood up with a sigh and walked off the new green carpet to stand beside Crystu looking at his work.

"Some of those plants will probably not do well at this height, or on limestone, but enough of them should survive and set seed that will grow in its turn."

Crystu nodded, waited until his attention was away from her, and then slapped his shoulder hard.

Tam looked at her with surprise as she blew on her hand to try to ease the sting from hitting his solidity.

"Why did you do that?" he asked mildly. "I hope that your hand is not too badly injured on my shoulder."

"Light, Tam! Hitting the rock would have hurt less," Crystu grumbled, as he took her hand and healed it. The sting faded quickly.

"Next time hit the muscle, not the bone," he advised her gravely. "It is softer."

"I will remember that," she replied, "I seem to recall that your face is softer too."

He smiled.

"When you hit my face, I can move with the blow so that it hurts you less. I can't do that if you hit my shoulder unexpectedly from behind."

Crystu nodded.

"The face it will be next time, then," she decided.

"You still haven't said why you did it," Tam reminded her.

She nodded again.

"You are *not* a fool, and you are never to call yourself one again!" she said firmly. "I will hit you again and again if you ever suggest anything of the sort in my hearing."

She looked at his shoulder and laughed.

"Even if I have to break every bone in my hand doing it," she finished.

"My Lady, if the only way to stop you hurting yourself on me is to promise that, then I will promise."

"Good!" Crystu nodded with satisfaction and then looked across the transformed land again. She smiled a little ruefully.

"Mother always tells me that it is good for me that there is something that I can't do," she said. "I have tried many times to heal plants, but with no success."

"You have to be able to feel and recognise the life in the plant to be able to touch it with your Gift, but most people can't do that," Tam replied.

"What does it feel like?" Crystu asked curiously.

Tam laughed.

"Crystu, what does green look like? Or a strawberry taste like? I can't describe it without referencing the thing I describe. It feels like itself and there is nothing else like it."

Crystu picked up the food bag and pulled an apple out of it. She cut it in half with her belt knife and passed one half to Tam.

She looked closely at the creamy white flesh with the tiny brown seeds within it. Probing the fruit with her mind, she tried to find some spark or indeed anything that might be an indication of life energy within the seeds. She found nothing.

"The fruit dies within minutes of leaving the tree, and as proof..." she concentrated and the fruit in her hand changed colour – its flesh now a golden bronze. The seeds remained unchanged.

"The fruit is dead, but I know that the seeds contain the spark of life. I can't transmute them, try as I might, but I also can't sense any difference between the dead flesh and the living seed. There is nothing, except my inability to transmute it, to prove it lives."

She sighed, and then smiled at Tam.

"I like that you can do something I can't. It is a wonderful ability, and I wish that I had it."

A thought occurred to her and she grinned mischievously. Tam's eyes narrowed suspiciously.

"What are you thinking now?" he asked.

She laughed.

"Only that if I ever again want strawberries in the middle of winter, you will grow them for me, won't you Tam? I recall a lecture about patience last winter when I wanted some. If I had known then that you could do this..." She gestured at the new plants.

Tam smiled.

"If you had known, you would have wanted them every day! But, if you wish for strawberries this midwinter, I will grow some for you occasionally, if you are good."

"Of course you will because you can refuse me nothing, remember?" Crystu laughed.

Tam nodded.

"Nothing," he repeated seriously.

The smile left Crystu's face as she thought about next midwinter, and she walked back to where she could look down on Angate. Tomorrow, she would attend Erian's funeral, and the day after...

She raised her eyes to stare toward the far western horizon, remembering the dark smudge she had seen that morning. She could not see it now; it was too far without the extra power she had possessed then. Somewhere out there, she knew, Trerin was alone – more alone than he had ever been in his life. She knew that they would find him, but what would happen afterwards?

He would die soon, whatever they did, yet her gleaning had implied that they needed him. For what? What could he do? What did the collar in her vision mean? What had he and Seldar found in Bein? Would he be able to tell them? Was that why the Lord of Light's guidance had stressed that they must find him?

If he and Seldar had indeed encountered the Shadowbringer's threatened strike, presumably the army would start moving towards Bein.

The army was too large to translocate, so most would march and ride, but perhaps Jareth would send some on ahead. It would depend what they could learn from Trerin. Next midwinter was a long time away and a great deal would happen before then.

Crystu could feel Tam's growing dissatisfaction at her drift into worry, but then a surge of mischief from him pulled at her attention, and then she felt a small emanation of magical energy from him.

"You should have left some of the snow, Crystu. A mountain needs some here and there."

She began to turn, intending to say that snow would soon form on the mountain's peak.

She squealed as something icy hit her cheek, shattering and sending freezing lumps down the front of her clothes. She stared at Tam, and her eyes widened as he transferred a rock into his right hand, held it up for her to see, and transmuted it into snow.

He grinned and launched the snowball with deadly accuracy. Crystu spun round quickly so that it hit her back, then dived sideways rolling across the ground to reach the area with the new topsoil. She filled both hands with a mixture of soil and plants and squeezed them together. If he wanted a fight, she would give him one!

Her worries forgotten, she jumped back to her feet and threw her missile, now snow mixed with the plants that she could not transmute, with an accuracy that was only slightly less than his.

By long convention, a rule learned as children and seldom transgressed, magic was forbidden in a snowball fight, except to provide snow if there was none. Normally when Ponfourii took part in one, they held back their speed and strength to fight at the level of their opponents. Tam, however, was shamelessly taking full advantage of his greater speed to bombard Crystu with snowball after snowball, all perfectly aimed, while he dodged most of her throws.

She did her best but could land only one or two for every ten or so of his. She ducked, and ran, and rolled, but whenever she threw, he dodged easily and launched missiles from each hand that pelted her shoulders, stomach and back, making her shriek as the cold water seeped through her clothes.

Eventually she collapsed onto the ground, laughing and panting so hard that she scarcely had breath to speak.

“Enough! Tam, enough! I’m exhausted, I give up!” she gasped as she rolled onto her back and stared up at his upside-down silhouette against the bright blue sky. He grinned and held two snowballs threateningly above her as though to drop them on her face. She shook her head and waved her hand up at him.

“No, Tam, really, I’m finished!”

Tam smiled and tossed them aside and knelt beside her, looking down at her face.

He was scarcely even breathing hard, which was extremely unfair, and he radiated satisfaction at the success of his diversion of her earlier train of thought.

“You were cheating!” she accused, pointing up at his face.

He grinned.

“How can you accuse me of such a thing? I used no magic, except to make the snowballs,” he replied, trying to look innocent.

Crystu snorted.

“You know perfectly well that Ponfourii are supposed to hold back their greater speed in such a contest. It is the rule.”

Tam's eyes widened with mock outrage.

“A rule? I would never break a rule, if indeed such a rule exists. Where is it written down, Crystu?”

“You know perfectly well it is not written down anywhere, but it is a rule, and you know it, and you broke it shamelessly to batter me with snow, so I feel perfectly justified in doing *this*.”

Tam gasped as she solidified the air around his body, holding him firmly in place while she pushed herself to her knees and transmuted the ground before her into snow.

“Crystu, you wouldn’t!” he said warily.

Crystu grinned at him as she slowly gathered up a large double handful of snow, letting him see what she was doing, and then she went behind him. She waited a minute to give him a chance to properly appreciate his position and anticipate her next move, and then she pushed the snow down the back of his sleeveless shirt, packing it well down.

He yelled in a very satisfactory fashion.

"That's for throwing me in the lake that time," she told him.

Then she walked back in front and picked up another two hands full of snow.

"Admit that you cheated just now," she ordered.

"Never! You can torture me all you wish, heartless Sorceress!" he declared with a stoic lift of his chin, spoiled only by a tremor of suppressed laughter.

"If you insist," she murmured as she pulled his shirt neck forward and pushed the snow down it.

"Gaarrhhh!" he gasped as the cold snow touched him.

"There's still your trousers, Tam, I'm sure I could pack a lot of snow in there," Crystu said pleasantly. He blinked as she sent a strong feeling of determined intention down the bond.

"You are right, I admit it, I cheated," he said hurriedly as she picked up another ball of snow and looked meaningfully at the waistband of his trousers.

"Crystu!" he said worriedly, as she hesitated, but she nodded – it was enough.

She dropped the snow, released him, and grinned as he shook the snow out from under his shirt. He grinned back.

"Did you enjoy that, Crystu?" he asked, meaning the whole fight as well as its end.

She laughed.

"Yes, I did, I haven't laughed like that in far too long. Thank you, Tam."

She knew that he had started the snowball fight just to distract her from her dark thoughts earlier, and she was grateful.

"I am glad, even if I did end up with my shirt full of snow," he replied as he transmuted his wet clothes dry.

Crystu grinned.

"It serves you right for cheating and then lying about it. Even if every word was true, the whole was a lie. You should not lie to me."

"I will remember that, my Lady," he replied with a half bow and a laugh.

"See that you do!" she ordered haughtily.

Then she glanced up at the sun and sighed.

"We should start climbing again or we will not reach the peak before it is time for the next meal," she said regretfully, not wanting to leave this place where she had been able for a short time to forget her responsibilities. She looked around and gasped.

"Oh Tam, look at what we have done!"

She was horrified by what she could see!

Their fight had left much of the new plant growth in ruins. Plants lay squashed and trampled, and everywhere there were places where the soil had been scooped up for use as raw material to make the snowballs, revealing the bare rock underneath.

Tam squatted, placed one hand on the ground, and concentrated.

Crystu smiled with delight as the damaged plants healed before her eyes, and soon little evidence remained of the snowball fight, beyond the occasional patch of bare rock.

"Here, Crystu."

Tam held something out to her, and she took it and laughed when she saw what she held. She looked down and saw a small clump of strawberry plants growing at his feet.

"Thank you, Tam, you are very good to me," she said happily, and bit into the red, sweet, and perfectly ripe, fruit.

Rannis heard the door open and his daughter's light footsteps as she stepped into the room, but he did not look up; the view through the eyepiece of this large distance viewer was far too interesting.

He was in the highest room of his palace: a small room, atop a high tower, with large windows in each wall from which he could look out over the town and the country around him. His distance viewer was large and powerful. He often came up here at night to point it at the stars and gaze in awe at their beauty. He had pointed the viewer at the ice mountain that morning and watched it change, impossibly but incontrovertibly, from ice into rock and he had remained here staring at the mountain through the viewer and wondering what difference it would make to his land. He would not rescind his order banning people from going near it until he heard from Tam that it was safe.

"I should have known I would find you still in here, Dap. That mountain is fascinating, isn't it?"

Tara sounded amused. Rannis was impressed yet again by her resilience after losing her closest friend in such a way. She looked tired and was grieving, as were they all, but she had not let that interfere with her duties.

He could not comment about it, though. He must act as though her ability to keep going, despite everything, was simply what he had expected of her, and that he had never considered that she might need time to recover. Any comment could cause her to accuse him of thinking she was still a child, still unready for full responsibility, so he simply responded to her question as though no other thought had crossed his mind.

"Yes, the mountain is extremely interesting," he said, with a half-smile, still not moving from his position.

Tara was silent, probably waiting for him to explain his interest, but he said no more.

"Our guests have almost all reappeared from their rests," Tara reported. "Except for Crystu and Tam; they remain in their rooms."

Rannis chuckled and finally looked up.

"Come and look through this, Tara, and see what it is I find so interesting on the mountain."

He beckoned, and with one puzzled look at him, his daughter obediently put her eye to the viewer eyepiece, and adjusted the focus for her younger eyes.

"Is that...? Yes, it is! What in the Light are they doing?" she exclaimed.

"I believe they are having a snowball fight," Rannis replied with a smile.

"It looks like they're having fun," Tara said after a moment.

Her words sounded almost like an accusation.

"You think they should not be enjoying themselves at the same time that I have people building Erian's funeral pyre?" Rannis asked her.

When Tara looked up and nodded, he continued, "My initial reaction was similar, but I was wrong and so are you."

"Why?" Tara asked him. "Why is it wrong to think that anyone who met her should be in mourning for her, and that playing a child's game as though nothing has happened is disrespectful to her memory?"

Rannis smiled and gazed out the window toward the mountain.

"A few minutes ago, Crystu stood looking down toward us. She looked as though she felt that she had the weight of the world on her shoulders, and in many ways she does. When they find and confront the Shadowbringer's attack, she will be in the forefront of that battle. She is a Rykatu and that responsibility will fall to her, and that may happen very soon now."

He glanced at Tara, and she nodded, but still did not look as though she understood. Rannis sighed,

"Tara, the more responsibility a person has, the more important it is that they know how to relax. That is why I have always valued my anonymity here in Angate, because I could relax in a way that is impossible where everyone knows that I am their king."

He sighed again at that lost opportunity, and Tara nodded. Rannis was relieved to see the beginning of understanding in her eyes. She knew how important it had been to him to be able to escape the cloying security and heavy responsibility that surrounded and weighed upon him in his role as king, even if he could escape it only for short periods.

He gestured toward the mountain.

"Tam started the snowball fight, and I am sure that he did it to distract her and give her a chance to laugh and play. He is wise. A leader who cannot relax will may eventually fall into darkness, madness, and tyranny. But she is a Rykatu – one of the two most powerful people in this world. If *she* fell into madness and tyranny, the whole world would suffer."

He paused to let Tara think about it, and then asked,

"Do you understand?"

He was relieved when she nodded.

"Yes, I do," she replied. "I hadn't looked at it like that, but you're right: a chance to forget worries and just have fun is something to be grasped and cherished if it occurs."

"You must always remember that, Tara," Rannis told her. "The job of intelligence gatherer and interpreter, for which you are training, is often highly stressful. You must always make time to relax, even when there seems to be no time for anything but the work. It is *especially* important when there seems no time because if you *don't* rest then, you may miss something important or see something that is not there." He smiled.

"I wish we could have Ponfourii to remind us of that like the Sorcerers do. I am certain that that is as much one of their duties as is protecting the Sorcerer."

Tara smiled.

"Captain Pendin sometimes appears to see himself in that role, I have noticed."

Rannis chuckled.

"You're right, Tara. He has often been the one to suggest that it is time to take a holiday here in Angate. He is usually right too. I wonder if he will find an alternative for me, now that everyone here knows who I am? If nothing else, I would like your brother to have somewhere to go and hide when he is king."

Tara smiled.

"I hope he will not become king for a long time, Dap!"

"So do I," Rannis agreed. "I plan to remain alive for a long time but that is something none of us has much choice about."

Tara's face saddened, reminded that her friend's body was even now being prepared for cremation, and Rannis sighed.

"I'm sorry."

He wished he could say everything that he was sorry for. The Zindon had destroyed and replaced Erian's personality, but Rannis' own hand had held the blade that killed her.

"We've been through this, Dap. Erian's death was not your fault or responsibility. A Zindon killed Erian and also many others of our people. The Guardians killed the Zindon, and those who served him will be imprisoned in Tyreen. Pendin saved my life, and you killed the creature that the Zindon had created within Erian's body. You have nothing to apologise for."

Rannis made himself smile. Tara had spoken forcefully and he knew that she was correct.

In the silence that followed, he bent down to look once more through the viewer.

"They've gone. I suppose they are climbing the mountain to be sure it is safe," he said.

"Maybe they are climbing it for fun?" Tara suggested. "They will be the first to the top, and the view from so high must be spectacular. I would like to climb it myself sometime."

Rannis nodded. He had not considered that they might just enjoy the climb, but he suspected that being the first person to stand on the mountain might well appeal to Crystu, especially as she had made it.

"Dap," Tara began, sounding thoughtful. He looked up,

"You said that the responsibility might fall on Crystu soon now. Have you heard something new?"

Rannis suppressed a smile of pride. He had wondered if she would pick up that brief clue and she had done so.

"I persuaded Tam to explain the disturbance early yesterday morning," he replied.

Tara raised her eyebrows.

"When Tam woke Trerisia and Jathte and they all disappeared into Crystu and Tam's rooms? That disturbance?"

Rannis nodded.

Although his men had pulled back from actively following Sorcerers around the palace, they had continued to keep a more discrete watch on the visitors. Rannis was sure that the Ponfourii were aware of the surveillance because there had been a few more instances of his people disappearing and being found asleep in cupboards.

One observer had even managed to so annoy a Sorcerer that he had suddenly found himself lying face down in the muddiest, most noisome corner of a field of pigs! For the most part, though, the Tyreans had accepted the distant observation so long as it was not overt.

Rannis' people had reported Tam's early morning dash to Trerisia and Jathte's rooms, and that Jathte and Trerisia, both looking shocked, had followed him back to his and Crystu's rooms.

"Yes. That disturbance!" he confirmed. "I dislike people keeping secrets from me in my own palace, even if they do outrank me, so when it was clear that they were not going to volunteer the information, I asked Jathte what it had been about."

At that time he had not understood the quick look that Jathte had exchanged with Trerisia before refusing to answer.

"And?" Tara prompted, as his pause lengthened. Rannis pulled his mind back to the present.

"He told me that Tam was in command and that I would have to ask him directly. He would say nothing more on the subject. So I found Tam and asked him."

Rannis smiled.

"I think that he really did not want to tell me, because *he* said that it was not connected with their present mission, and that it was therefore Crystu's decision whether they would tell me. He looked surprised when she told him to tell me and then she left the room. Once he explained I could understand why she had not wanted to listen."

"And?" Tara repeated with a hint of impatience.

"You know that there have been many rumours of strange occurrences around all the Protectorates?"

Tara nodded with a look of exasperation on her face – of course she knew about that! Rannis grimaced an apology, and continued, "The Sorcerer, sent to investigate that unbelievable tale about hordes of Zindons in Bein, is dead. Crystu saw it in a gleaning dream."

Tara blinked.

"Dead? How?" she exclaimed.

Rannis shrugged.

"Tam did not give details, and I did not ask," he replied. "There is more: the Sorcerer's Ponfour has apparently survived, but is injured and requires assistance. As soon as they leave here, the day after tomorrow, Crystu, Tam, Jathte and Trerisia will go searching for him."

Tara frowned.

"Why wait? They could have gone immediately, or they could have gone as soon as they recovered from transmuting the mountain. Why stay here if one of their friends is in trouble?"

Rannis had asked the same question. The mountain could wait, and the Tyreans did not have to attend Erian's funeral. If a friend was in trouble, why stay here?

"Because they must, and he is not just a friend, Tara; he is Trerisia's younger brother."

Tara gasped.

"I spoke to her last night and she gave no indication that anything was wrong, but if it is her *brother* in trouble, then it is even more inexplicable that they have not gone to his aid."

She stared at her father, eyes wide in puzzled outrage.

Rannis sighed.

"Tara, they stay because they must. I did not fully understand, but Tam implied that the gleaning contained some sort of instructions from the Lord of Light, and that they must wait until the day after tomorrow to be in the right place at the right time if they are to aid Trerin. Trerisia has her duty, Tara, and if that includes pretending nothing is wrong, when her brother is alone, his bonded Sorcerer dead, then she will do just that, and do it well."

Tara inhaled, probably remembering what was said to be the fate of a Ponfour in that situation. 'Painful and fatal' Tam had confirmed.

She had walked away from the window as they talked, but now went back to it and looked up towards the new mountain. She appeared to be thinking hard. She turned and looked at him with a clear and determined gaze.

"Bein. We have some people there, do we not? Have we heard anything from them that could shed any light on this supposed invasion of Zindons?"

She said the word with understandable loathing, but otherwise spoke crisply. Rannis picked up a sheaf of papers from a nearby desk.

"One of the largest ports in the Kingdom of Light? Yes, we do. We receive a pigeon from them once a week with short reports, mostly unimportant trading news, but occasionally something of interest. I asked for the last few weeks' reports as soon as I returned to my office after speaking with Tam. I received them this morning. See for yourself."

He handed them to Tara.

"It's not really surprising that no one noticed," he continued as she started flicking through the pieces of thin paper, creased from being wrapped around a pigeon's leg.

"The reports were read by different people each time, which is a practice that I intend to change," he said grimly. "If the same person had read each report we might have noticed the problem there. Do you see it, Tara?" he asked, savagely. "Do you see what we missed? Once you see them all together it is obvious!"

"They are all the same!" she said in astonishment, flicking from one sheet to another. "For the last six weeks, each report is the same."

She stared at each sheet as if unable to believe her eyes.

"They are *exactly* the same! The same hand writing, the same words, Light! Even each line ends in the same place as the previous week!"

She looked at him in shock.

"You think this is the Shadowbringer's attack? The rumoured invasion of Zindons is real? Light! An invasion? But Zindons come in ones and twos, or three at most. They wreak carnage and then are killed or vanish back wherever they come from. They don't invade!"

"Where do Zindons come from Tara?" Rannis asked quietly.

She frowned and shook her head. She did not know and neither did he.

"They must come from somewhere," Rannis went on, "but where? We never think of that. They are just creatures of shadow who appear in our midst. We call them Zindons but that is not what they call themselves – it cannot be. They must have a name for themselves, and a people, and a land where they raise their children to serve the Shadowbringer. The rumours about Bein call the invaders 'Shantoo'," he said the word carefully. "Jathte told me several days ago that the word is similar to the name that they believe Zindons use for themselves. He said that his father was hoping that this was a coincidence, a deliberate similarity intended to draw attention to another false lead and away from the true strike."

Rannis shook his head.

"I think that hope was wrong. I think that an army of Zindons has invaded the Kingdom of Light, and that this Sorcerer and his Ponfour walked into a trap. If I am correct, it is astonishing that the Ponfour survived to escape."

"Have they seen these?" Tara gestured with the papers in her hand, and Rannis shook his head.

"They were delivered to me this morning after the Tyreans disappeared into the side wing to work on the mountain. I have not yet had an opportunity to tell them about this, but I suspect that it will just confirm what they already surmise from the gleaning."

Tara nodded, and looked out of the window again. This time she looked across the town and further away to the land beyond.

"There is nothing at all that we can do to help them, is there Dap?" she said after a moment.

"Nothing," Rannis agreed, "except pray that the Lord of Light stands with our Guardians when they place themselves between us and the servants of shadow."

He walked to stand beside his daughter, and as one they looked at the mountain, towards the unseen figures that they knew to be climbing it.

"It makes a difference, knowing some of them well enough to use their names, knowing something of their interests and personalities," Tara mused. "Some of them will die if they must fight an army of Zindons, and some of them are now my friends, not just distant powerful Sorcerers sworn to defend us. Tam is fascinated by our gadgets, and he and Crystu have both spent hours taking things to pieces with me and learning how they work. Crystu is little older than I am, and I would not want to face an army of any kind even if I had her power."

"I don't suppose that she does either, Tara, but she will do her duty, as you would if it were yours. Which reminds me..." Rannis walked back to the table and picked up a long object that had been leaning against it. "This is for you."

He held the sheathed sword across his palms and offered it to Tara. Her eyes widened in disbelief.

"A sword? You're giving me a sword? Women don't fight!"

Her hands hovered near it but she did not take it from him.

Rannis smiled sadly.

"*Perrestian* women do not fight, but that is going to have to change," he said. "If the Shadowbringer is beginning a strong offensive, the time may come when all of us need to know how to fight. Women should have the right to learn the skills they need to defend themselves if necessary. I intend to make certain that they can."

"But the Guardians will fight for us," Tara protested, and Rannis nodded, still holding out the sword.

"Yes, they will, and I will hope and pray that they will be victorious and that you will never need to use this, but I have no intention of just blithely hoping that everything will be all right. Take it, Tara, I want you to learn to use it, so that you at least have a chance to defend yourself if it is ever necessary. Pendin has agreed to tutor you."

Tara stared at him and then slowly took the sword from his hands.

"I will learn, Dap," she promised, staring down at the sheathed blade. "I will learn because you're right: I would not want to stand idle and watch others fight for me if I had a choice. I cannot assist our Guardians but if another Zindon ever steps foot in this land, I would dearly love to hold the sword that felled it."

Rannis hid his dismay. He had intended her to learn swordsmanship solely for self-defence, but he realised now that Tara would never stop at that. If she mastered it, and he knew that she would work hard to do so, then she would want to use her skills to defend the land.

It was too late to withdraw the offer, and the reasoning still held good – if the Guardians fell, then Perrestians would have to fight for themselves, and giving swords to those women who wanted to learn their use would increase his potential army. He would do it because he must. Even if the Guardians were successful in defeating the Zindons in Bein, the Shadowbringer would certainly try again one day. Rannis's decision would offend many, women as well as men, probably even his own queen, but many others would welcome it. His people would change; they would have to, and he wondered where it might lead.

Perrestians were patriarchal, with a solid belief that women belonged in the home. Deep down, he believed that as well, and yet, the Guardians clearly had no such concept. Their women fought beside their men, and he had seen Trerisia beat Tam in fair fight, even if her win had been discounted afterwards. Of course, they were magically altered, the women almost as strong as the men, and Perrestians were not, but he knew that in some kingdoms women fought. They were just human like his own folk.

He sighed again.

"What is it, Dap? Worrying that everything will change now that you have decided to allow this?" Tara grinned, and he could see a sparkle of anticipation in her eyes.

"Something like that," he admitted. "But change we must if we are to survive. We should not rely on the Guardians to protect us as though we were children. We should do what we can to protect ourselves."

"Zindons use magic, Dap, how can we defend against that?" Tara asked dubiously.

Rannis smiled.

"I have given much thought to that, Tara. Erian had cousins who are also descendants of that Tyrean ancestor; perhaps some of them have Gifts without knowing it."

Tara inhaled to reply, but Rannis spoke on before she could comment.

"Vellte has said that many of our healers have small Gifts too. I wonder how many others there may be. I intend to find out, somehow. If we have magic of our own, maybe one day our great grandchildren can aid the Guardians properly by fighting beside them to rid our world of this evil."

Tara grinned.

"I like that idea, Dap. I like it a lot!"

Rannis smiled and glanced out the window towards the mountain.

"I think you will also like my other idea," he said, pausing deliberately until she gestured at him to tell her what it was.

"I have named the mountain: it is Mount Tolene."

Tara inhaled sharply, and then walked to him and hugged him as tightly as she could with a sword clutched in one hand.

"It's a wonderful idea and Erian would have been proud to have a mountain named after her," she said as she let go.

"Yes, she would," Rannis agreed a little huskily, and put his eye to the viewer once more, pretending to look at the mountain although the sudden moistness in his eye made the view fuzzy.

Tara looked at the reports from Bein that she had put back on the table.

"Shall I take these and show them to Jathte?" she asked, picking them up again.

Rannis glanced over his shoulder, looked at what she held, and straightened.

"I will come with you, Tara. I think I would like to apologise to him for not noticing the evidence earlier."

She nodded.

"He was in the formal garden with Trerisia, before I came looking for you. Perhaps they are still there.

Rannis nodded, replaced the coverings on his viewer, and walked to the door. He wished that he had more to do that day, to keep his thoughts from the coming night when he would light the pyre for Erian.

Epilogue: Tenjian's gleaning

Tenjian looked around the stone-preparation workroom wondering why he felt uneasy.

Everything looked normal. The waterwheel against the far wall was turning slowly but steadily in its water channel. It was powered by river water, which poured onto it from the chute that projected down from high up on the wall.

Outside, a complex system of wooden chutes collected water from the waterfall at the top of this small canyon, channelling it into the different workshops to turn waterwheels for various crafts.

There were large iron-making bloomeries, forges, and the blacksmith, all safely on the other side of the river, where sparks and fire could not endanger the mill.

The water in the mill's wheel-channel flowed out of the room through a low arch, and eventually rejoined the river. Just outside, the youngest children would be using that water to wash the sand and gravel brought out of the gold mine looking for the smallest pieces of that useful metal.

The mill stood on the other side of that solid wooden wall. The water-wheel's axle went through the wall and turned a peg-toothed vertical wheel, which turned a similarly peg-toothed but horizontal wheel. That wheel rotated a massive vertical pole which reached up, through the ceiling to the upper floor, to turn the large millstones which ground grain from the Homestead and surrounding smaller farms into flour for the city of Tyre.

The whole building, including the floor, was made of wood to minimise the risk of an accidental spark. In the mill side of the building, the flour dust misted the air when the mill was very busy and a spark could be dangerous, but on this side of the wall, the air was clear and the wooden floor slightly damp from the splashing wheel.

Tenji could see nothing to explain his very slight unease, but then he heard a tinkle from behind him as something was spilled.

He closed his eyes, took a deep breath and turned to see what had happened *this* time.

Jori was staring with dismay at the stones that should have been sitting safely on a tray on one of the many shelves, but which were now, along with the tray, scattered across the floor.

Tenji sighed. He had guessed that it would be Jori. The boy appeared to have developed clumsiness until it was almost a Gift!

"What happened?" Tenji asked as he crouched beside the lad and began to pick up the gems.

"It slipped out of my hand, Craftsman Tenjian," the seven-year-old boy replied, close to tears. Chereya, an older apprentice, left the pedal-operated grindstone that she had been using, and came over to help.

Tenji shook his head, wondering if he had ever been as accident-prone when he'd been the same age.

"It's all right, Jori, they seem to have survived uncracked, so there's no harm done," Tenjian reassured the boy, as he quickly gathered the stones back onto the tray and carried them across to the nearest work-table. *Thank the Light that the floor isn't flag-stone*, he thought.

"Let's check them over together," he suggested, holding one, a beautiful blue translucent gem, up to the glowstone. Most of them had indeed survived, although a few were scratched and would need smoothing down. One had a large crack through the middle. Glancing at Jori, Tenjian saw that the boy was concentrating on the stone in his own hand, and wasn't looking, so he quickly slipped it into his pocket; there was no need for the boy to feel worse than he already did, and Tenjian thought that he might still be able to salvage something from the two halves of the stone with careful cutting.

Jori still had nine weeks of his three-month pre-apprenticeship to serve, and Tenjian hoped that his clumsiness was just a matter of nerves and would ease as he became more familiar with the work. If the accidents continued for much longer, he would have to talk with the boy's parents, but Tenji had known equally clumsy lads who had grown first into competence and then into skill.

Jori was artistic and his drawings showed a fine attention to detail that should mean he would be an excellent jeweller one day. If he became a full apprentice, he would learn the basics of all the crafts: wool preparation, spinning and weaving, as well as smithing, building, carpentry, and jewellery making. Once a senior apprentice, he could begin to choose the crafts that interested him most. Eventually he would become a full Craftsman in his chosen field, and then eventually rise to Craftmaster, as Tenji would do later this year.

Like his father, Tenji looked on the title as more of a formality than something essential to his life. He loved making beautiful things that made other people happy and having the official title was unimportant to him so long as people liked his work. Tenji was happy with his life; he had a beautiful wife and three children, and was content.

The only cloud was the fact that tomorrow he must leave them to join the mustering army, which was camped in the Tyre valley.

Tenji, his father, and many of their family would leave Tyreen for the first time in their lives when the army rode out in two days' time.

The room darkened, and Tenji glanced out of the window and realised that the sun was close to the horizon and would soon set.

"Jori, why don't you go next door and tell Miller Jeshia that we would like to stop the wheel soon. Come back as soon as she says that she's ready. I'll finish here."

"Yes, Craftsman Tenjian," the boy replied and trotted off on his task.

"Craftsman Tenjian?" Chereya had come to stand by him. "Are they really all undamaged? He tries so hard."

"I know he does, and yes, look, they are all fine." Tenji smiled. "Thank you for helping to pick them up."

He looked at the four barrels nearby, one marked with a strip of red cloth.

"Are those ready?"

Chereya nodded.

"I helped Jori do it. The stones are all packed neatly in their bags with the right amount of sand."

She reached for one small barrel, obviously expecting Tenjian to check it, but Chereya had been an apprentice for three years now and he trusted her skills.

"Leave it, Chereya, I know if you helped then they are right," Tenji told her. She smiled happily at the compliment.

"Craftsman Tenjian!" Jori came running back in. "We can stop the wheel now! Miller Jeshia says that she has finished for now and she will tell us when she needs it started again."

"Thank you, Jori."

Tenji strode to the upper lever, of the two on the wall, and pulled it. Outside he heard clanking and rattling chains, and the flow of water from the chute abruptly slowed to a trickle and the wheel slowed. The lower lever applied the brake that stopped the wheel completely. Tenji removed four of the barrels from their niches within the wheel and replaced them with the prepared four.

"Chereya, would you rinse and sort these stones please?" Tenji asked the older girl as he carried the barrels, one at a time, to the right-hand bench. He turned back to the waterwheel and saw that it was turning again. Confused, he looked at the chute and saw water cascading from it. The flow widened and grew and then he realised that he was standing outside, near the waterfall. He turned, expecting to see trees and the river with the workshops on either side of it, but they weren't there.

Instead, he was inside a room made of ice. Rykatu Crystu stood in front of him, wearing what looked like a bridal dress but the colours were wrong: black and deep blue, instead of yellow and gold. In her right hand, she held a strangely shaped sword with blood dripping from the blade. In her left, she held aloft a man's head and offered it to a shadowy figure whom Tenji could not see clearly, and did not want to try. On the ground lay a man's headless body.

Tenji looked at the head, held aloft by a thick braid of hair. It rotated slowly until he saw the face and recognised his younger brother, Tam.

Tenji staggered backwards gasping and retching.

"Craftsman Tenjian? What's wrong?" At the sound of Chereya's worried voice the vision shattered and Tenji was back in his craft room, his mouth working as he struggled to control himself.

"Is it a gleaning?" Jori asked with excited eyes.

The image of Tam's dead face swung in Tenji's memory, and without a word, he turned and ran from the room.

He reached the river just in time and held onto a tree branch for support as he vomited into the waters. Eventually the tremors eased. He wiped his mouth and lay back weakly against the tree trunk, taking deep breaths.

"Are you ill?" A voice asked. Tenji looked up to see a Sorcerer and Ponfour looking down at him with concern. Beyond them, Jorji and Chereya were watching wide-eyed, and behind the children, Tenji could see his father approaching at a run.

"A gleaning! I've rarely had such a powerful one!" he managed to reply despite his dry mouth and throat, which were sore and closed from vomiting. He pushed himself shakily to his feet and accepted, with a nod of thanks, the water bottle that the Ponfour held out to him.

"I had better write it down, although I don't think that image will *ever* fade!" He shuddered and then drank deeply from the bottle.

The Sorcerer nodded.

"I've had a few of those myself!" he said sympathetically. "Including one that sent me running for the nearest ditch, and usually my stomach is quite strong. Go write it down and then try to rest. Keep the bottle," he added when Tenji offered it back.

Tenji nodded.

"Thank you. I have a feeling that the gleaning is not finished yet."

He could feel the truth as he said the words; this had just been the opening scene of something that was waiting for him to find a quiet place to show him the rest.

"Tenji! Was it a gleaning?" Da asked as he arrived.

Tenji nodded. He knew that Da would want to know what he had seen. How could he possibly tell his father that he had seen Tam murdered by Crystu?

"Yes, Da," he replied, "but I think there's more to come."

Da looked understandably surprised, but nodded.

"Then you'd better go home, rest, and wait for the rest."

"We'll finish up here," Chereya offered. "Won't we, Jori?" The boy nodded vigorously.

Tenji smiled at them.

"Thank you, I know you will do everything just as I would," he replied, pretending a confidence that he almost felt.

He bowed to the Sorcerer and Ponfour, somehow managing not to sway when tipping his head forward made him feel dizzy.

"Thank you for your assistance, my lords. If you will excuse me, I will go home and find out what else the Lord of Light wants to show me."

The Sorcerer nodded and Tenjian walked slowly along the road towards the Homestead, leaving his father to finish the required courtesies towards the lords. He hoped that the rest of the gleaning would contain guidance that would enable Tam and Crystu to avoid what he had seen first.

To be continued

Maps

The known world of Reyth

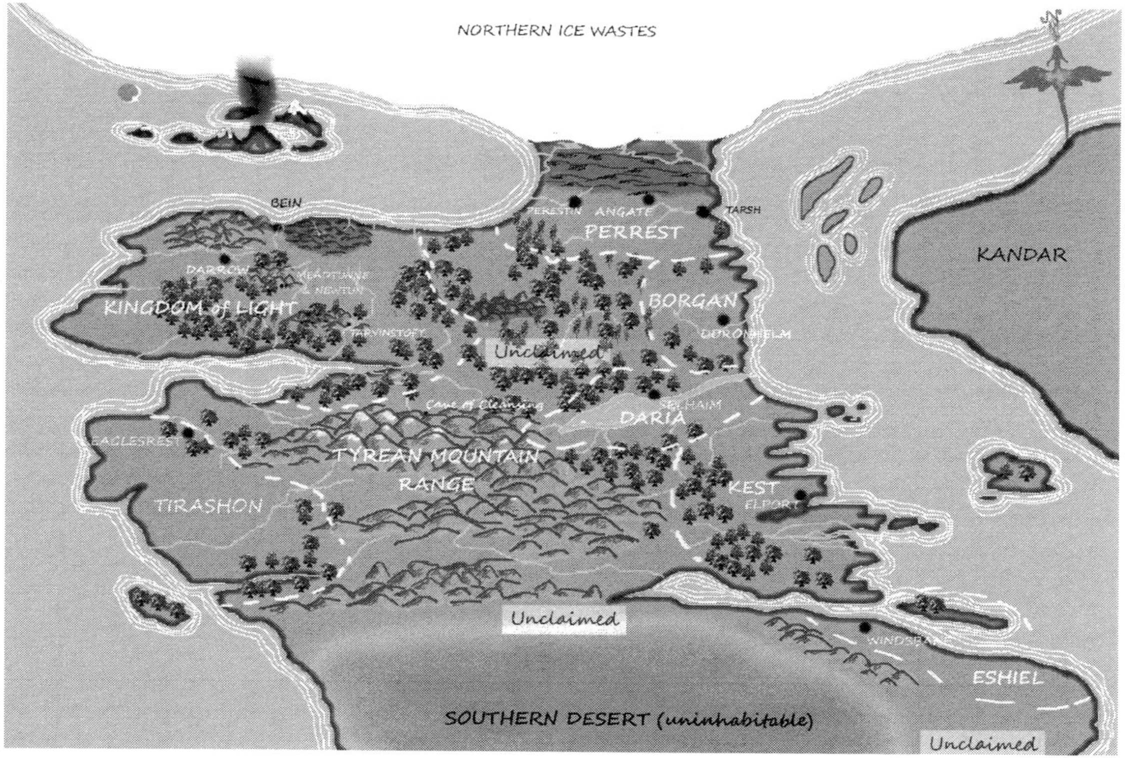

The Protectorate Kingdoms

Acknowledgements

There are so many people who contributed to this. First and foremost Tina Newsome, who provided the original inspiration in her medieval challenge writing contest, in an online writing group, and without whom none of this would ever have been written. She encouraged me to keep on going and try to create something worth publishing.

Damian Connolly for advice and much help with the cover design.

Janette Harrower and Sarah S. Miles for encouragement.

Helen Stevens for reading and commenting faithfully as I wrote and posted the first draft over several years.

Silvana Kelleher for proof reading and many helpful suggestions and advice. Mike Collins for patiently answering questions about colons and semi-colons.

Chris Broughton for proof reading the second draft and making many helpful suggestions. Also other beta readers, Judit Sogan, Rob Summerfield, and everyone who I've bored rigid about it over the years.

Lastly, grateful thanks are due to Kathleen M. Lance for copy-editing and encouragement.

If I have overlooked anyone, I apologise, but y'know the old memory is starting to go.

About the author

I'm a fifty-something Christian, archaeologist, martial arts practitioner, and amateur photographer. I was introduced to science fiction and fantasy at a young age by my best friend's dad, who had boxes and boxes of science fiction books dating to the 50s, 60s, and 70s.

In those boxes I met Isaac Asimov, Frank Herbert, Anne McCaffrey, Zenna Henderson, and many more, and I learned to love the smell of a printed volume.

This story was started as an entry for a contest and continued to find out if I could finish it. I wrote the sort of story I enjoy. I hope that you like it too.

The whole story is written and just awaits editing. This may take a while because it is …rather… long!

19164898R00255

Printed in Poland
by Amazon Fulfillment
Poland Sp. z o.o., Wrocław